# SOME
# DIFFERENCE

## Martin Harris

Printed in the United States of America

First Printing:  August 2009
ISBN 978-0-578-03592-5

# CHAPTER ONE

# A TYPICAL DAY

Everything started with the package.

Had to be four-thirty before I finally got back to the office, already out of sorts because of the meeting that morning and the farce over at the Holiday Inn taking up the whole rest of the day. Not to mention how godawful hot it was for late October. Long and rectangular and pointed right at me, like I was supposed to be appreciating the way it hung over the edge of the desk, almost lunging toward the spot in the office doorway where I stood looking at it. Which I suppose I did.

Didn't matter, though.

Same difference.

Point is I got it, and everything that happened happened because I did.

That was Wednesday and there was me closing the door with a heavy shove because it never did fit the frame quite right. Especially when it was hot one day and cold the next like it was that week. Thing locks automatic, but sometimes when it's super warm or humid it's like the door balloons up or something. Wedges hard against the base and along the sides and you end up having to lean hard against it to make sure it scrapes past the jamb and clicks shut.

Hung the dark gray topcoat I'd been carrying all day on the brass doorknob. Carrying and not wearing because of the goddamned heat. On the doorknob because the door, besides the piece being cut wrong, didn't have a hook or anything and the office itself didn't come with a rack.

I resumed my appraisal of the package and how it had been left for me, diagonal on the desk there. Flat, square face of the end nearest me lined up and centered with the office entrance. I hadn't expected anything in particular to be delivered to me on that day, but then there wasn't anything strange about that.

In fact, thanks to that little conversation that morning and the way my thoughts had been running all that day, I remember standing there looking at the box and thinking exactly that. How there was nothing especially remarkable about the unannounced appearance of such a package at such a time of day in an office such as mine.

Maybe I should explain what I mean. By such a this and such a that.

As it happened, it was earlier that same day when I'd first met up with this writer character. Involved in some fiction class or program down at the university. Actually hired me for an hour just to talk. We had spoken over the phone several times before we finally arranged to meet that morning at the Chock Full o' Nuts, the one across and up from the Holiday Inn where I'd end up wasting the rest of the day.

Weird little guy, but polite. To a fault, really. In fact, the first couple of times he'd called he was so overly gracious about the whole thing I completely misunderstood where he was coming from. Turned him down twice flat, forgetting all about him before the receiver ever made it back to the cradle.

What happened was he'd start out apologizing and going on about how he was from the university and wondered if he could talk to me for a story. Now I'm thinking the guy is some nosy reporter or something, where I'll admit I was and am more than a little gun-shy. Sounded to me like some sort of lifestyles-type deal for the student paper, something describing the day-to-day existence of one of the City's many self-employed detectives.

Which I don't have to tell you didn't interest me in the least.

Third time, though, we finally connected. That was the Monday before, the twenty-fifth. Finally he'd gotten together enough gumption to try me one more time. Explained who he was and what a help it would be for him to be able to sit down and talk with me.

"No bones about it, Mr. Owen," he had said to me, once he understood that I understood what the hell was going on. "Nothing takes the place of real-life testimony, the thoughts and feelings of someone who has actually experienced that which is being realistically represented, albeit in a fictional idiom."

I could appreciate the writer's convictions. And his willingness to do the leg work and research what it was he was doing. And I told him as much. How it all seemed first-rate in terms of effort and work ethic and all that. Real nose-to-the-grindstone, so to speak.

But I had a few albeits as well, the main one being, as I delicately put it to my new phone pal, that one of the real-life problems this particular detective had with sitting down with him had to do with my thoughts and feelings regarding the actual value of my time. That is to say, gumption was good, but could we have some bread with that?

Having broached what I knew to be a sensitive matter in most students' lives elicited what I thought to be an exceedingly realistic response.

"I'll get back to you."

Perhaps less realistically, he did get back to me, later on Monday afternoon. And so it was that same Wednesday, the day the package arrived, that we finally had our little session at the coffee joint.

Gangly little fellow with wire-rimmed glasses and uncombed jet black hair. And a honker like you wouldn't believe. From the other side of the booth firing off questions from a little typed-up sheet he'd brought with him. Designed to determine what constituted a typical day for me, the typical private detective.

"Well, first off, who's to say what's typical?" I had to ask.

"Sure, sure. But four years plus, right here in the City. What you do, your routine . . . it must be pretty well set, then? Wouldn't you say?"

"My routine," I repeated.

"Right, what you do each day. How you handle clients. Your policies regarding . . . "

"I get it," I interrupted. I sipped coffee and thought a moment. Had his blue felt-tip anxiously poised over the two inches of space he'd left himself to scribble my response.

"By routine, you're usually talking a prescribed course of action."

"Sure."

"Something mechanical, performed without thinking. Like a card trick."

"Well . . . "

"In no way would I advise describing what I do as being anything like that. Although it's true, you do come to expect certain things. Sequences of events or behaviors or whatever. And so these patterns do become familiar to you. In a way."

He nodded and began to write.

"What I'm saying is while there's nothing particularly routine about being a detective, there are routines. Things you come to know and which have something to do with how you conduct yourself and how you react to this or that situation."

"Sure, sure." Said without looking up, glasses starting to slide down that not-insignificant slope of a schnozz holding them up. Not exactly your everyday Roman, here. This something you wanted to tell your friends about.

"I mean, take today. Someone has asked me to try to find out if, as she suspects, her husband and her little sister are indeed having themselves a regular rendezvous at a certain hotel at a certain time every Wednesday afternoon."

"Okay!" Scribbling a little faster.

"Now, I guess you could say it was this woman finally recognizing several, very particular routines which inspired her to call me last week in the first place."

"Right. Good, good." Shaking the table now. A little brown liquid line escaped from the rim and down the side of my mug.

"The way she tells it, for the last five Wednesdays, this woman has had a brief though meaningful conversation with her husband's secretary from which she's learned that her husband, for whatever reason, needs once a week a little extra time to break for lunch. Say two-and-a-half hours instead of the usual one."

"Interesting."

"Along with that, Wednesday's the only day during the week her sister, who's enrolled over at City College, has no class. No classes, I mean. Not much class, either, I suppose . . . "

He turned the paper over and began scribbling on the blank back. I got the idea that it was the scenario that interested him, not the point I was trying to make by it.

"Interesting," he repeated.

"Well, yes. It could be interesting. What's really more interesting to my client, though, are these other, less plain routines. Such as what seems to be a gradual increase in the frequency and length of sisterly visits to the couple's apartment. Or, even harder to peg, what my client perceives as a certain, let's say *modulation* in the physical affection being expressed between her husband and her sister. You know, the shoulder pats and forehead kisses and whatnot suddenly seeming more . . . familiar than familial."

"Hmmm," he said, no longer writing. Glasses back to the top of the slide.

"Of course, the question is whether or not these other routines are really there or not. Whether the pattern is more in her mind than in what it is she's seeing."

Now he's looking up with his pen in his mouth and a dumb sort of who's-the-writer-here expression in his eyes.

"Anyway, to get back to your question, she's come to me with these routines, right? But it's *her* routines that dictate what it is I'm going to do. To go about confirming or dispelling her belief, I mean. So my routine or what I do each day is for the most part out of my hands . . . "

And so on like that. There's more. Lot of stuff about agencies and what it means to work for one. Which I don't. And licenses and what it means to carry one. Which I do.

We ended up leaving it open whether or not to meet again.

From my end, we're talking some of the easiest money I'd ever seen. And despite the unwanted after-effect of becoming a little overly self-reflective as the day wore on, I'll admit to having enjoyed it.

To a point, anyway.

Damned if I wasn't full of myself, especially once I got on that business about waiting it out at the Holiday Inn. And that a set-up, the whole thing a story which kept me out of the office and in the heat the whole freakin' day. Until four-thirty, at least.

But that's not really part of the story. The meeting, I mean. The only reason I even bring it up is to explain why it was my first reaction to seeing the package was to think to myself, well, that's not so strange. How it was the first thing about the whole damn day that seemed at all . . . typical.

So, sure. I'm standing there looking at this thing and I'm in a mood. Since despite all the talk about routines this really hadn't been what I'd call a typical day. First the face-to-face with the fictionalist. Second the stake-out, uncharacteristically unsuccessful. And third the thing waiting for me there at my return. All together introducing these strange rhythms into the day.

The whole idea of rhythms, really.

I took a look around before I did anything. Some of the offices on the upper floors had been hit in the past, so I tried never to keep anything of value in there. Art, who delivered mail and who oversaw the Wescott's sizable custodial unit, had the only other key. Which would explain how the box got in there.

I remember when I'd first signed the lease how the agent kept saying over and again how well the office suited my needs because it wasn't ostentatious. That was the word he had used. Which is true, the thing is pretty modest when it comes down to it. I only keep it to meet clients, take calls, and to have an address other than my apartment where I can get mail. You know, the odd package. Two-hundred-and-twenty feet square, one of several just like it in a row there on the Twenty-fifth-Street-facing, northeast side of the seventh floor. Very little clutter. None of the sort of paperwork and record-keeping one might expect to find.

In such an office, that is.

One might further deduce that after having endured the nightmare-without-end of ribbons, inkbands, carbons, dittos, white out, eraser tape, paperclips, staples, circulars, memoranda, seals, signatures, folders and other folderol during the four years and one month I had served as patrolman for the City's PD, my keeping the office so modest-looking might be some sort of immodest reaction to these former obligations.

Which assumption would be correct.

One way to reduce all the archival activity was to avoid taking on multiple cases at once, though it didn't always work out that way. And, as I'd described it that morning without actually showing it, I used to own a small, black leather notebook that I'd keep in my inside coat pocket in which to record clients' names, numbers, and needs. As well as expenses and earnings, which I had to have come tax time. So into the notebook went pretty much everything that presently, professionally mattered.

A modest office, then. Not ostentatious. A wooden desk and squeaky swivel chair; a second, cushioned chair for clients; a robin's-egg-colored rotary phone; a much-thumbed City directory; a single, low-wattage lamp; and a functional though unused metallic green file cabinet inherited from the previous tenant. Perhaps it's too modest to call it modest. The room was positively barren, with the yellowish-gray package its unquestioned highlight that strangely-warm, late October afternoon.

The piss-poor coffee at the Chock Full o' Nuts was all I'd had that day, and so as I'm walking around the desk my stomach was doing all of these noises like animals chasing each other around a cartoon. A low, mournful moan would somersault over into a kind of whiny whimper, all the voices reminding me that I'd spent the better part of the day watching other people eat rather than eating anything myself.

And for effect let's go ahead and add a little adrenaline there in my chest, just a touch of warmth as I got closer to the oblong box, some three-and-a-half feet long and a foot or so each high and wide. A mosquito had come in with me, and I swatted at it half-heartedly before I lifted the package by either end.

Blame all this little stuff on the interview, by the way. Like I said, it put me in a mood, like I was watching myself pretty good.

Of course, it wasn't just me doing the watching.

I picked up the box, a hand at each end, and stepped over toward the window. I shook it back and forth a little while looking down through the blinds and onto the street below. Nothing seemed to shift inside. I cradled it in one arm, holding one of the long corners in my palm sort of like you might cup the spine of a book you were reading.

With my free hand I tucked a finger over one of the curved blinds and tilted it downwards. There was a vendor I didn't recognize barking noiselessly at passers-by. His red, white, and blue canvas umbrella, another vestige of that summer's bicentennial, was angled over to the side, revealing a thin line of sweat evenly dividing his noticeably hunched-back.

I remember watching as pedestrians jockeyed to avoid this latest addition to the Twenty-fifth Street landscape. On the surface, it looks perfectly irrational, the way folks seem randomly to assign their allegiance to this or that purveyor of the street dog. Yet, as I knew full well from having started up my own business, the consumer's natural inclination is to distrust. Which it should be. Though you might say those days the economy was sliding fast enough to make distrust seem the only thing worth investing in.

But I'm just looking at the vendor and how nobody's stopping is all.

My stomach continued to ask wordless questions.

I removed my finger, allowing the blind to snap back into place. I remember thinking give him a week. You have to become familiar, non-threatening.

You can appreciate that.

"As a detective, then, am I right to assume that you are a person who distrusts first impressions?" The Nose had asked, felt-tip twirling.

I turned my body from the window and my attention back to the package. I rotated the box and set it down label-up across the arms of the swivel chair. The chair sat upright, audibly squeaking in response.

The typewritten address label yielded nothing: "TO: RICHARD OWEN, 708 WESCOTT BLDG." No return address.

Above, the postmark was smeared almost to the point of being illegible. It had originated from the City, I could read that much. The date was altogether rubbed out, though. I held it at arms' length, and gently shook it once more. Still no sound. The box looked old, like it'd been used before. The corners bore discolorations, there were superficial tears in the yellowy wrapping paper, and layers of transparent tape seemed to indicate a history of openings and closings.

I flipped the package over. Leaning against the desk with the backs of my legs, I pulled out a miniature Swiss army knife I used to have. Had had it forever, since before I'd even come to the City. Grandfather gave it to me. I used to use it all the time, too, though I know it probably looked a bit comical whenever I'd carefully edge the thin, tiny three-inch blade out of its plastic red casing.

That's because the man holding the tiny blade over the side of the package was six feet eight inches tall and weighed two hundred and sixty-eight pounds.

Mickey used to tell me it looked like I was still rising, even when I was already standing straight up. I'm fairly fit, though when I started walking beats in '67 that's when I began this crap diet. Which I'm still on. So sure, I've slowed down a little since juco, which is going on ten years ago now. Once-flat stomach now ringed with softer layers of self.

To give you an idea, I'm fair-skinned, probably some pink there in my cheeks and on my forehead while I'm bending over slicing through the packing tape. Face kind of meaty-looking. Not hard, not soft. Clean-shaven. And after a day full of head-scratching in the parking lot out in front of the restaurant at the Holiday Inn, the short-cropped, dark-brown hair was probably pretty well disheveled, interrupting the usual right-sided part.

No Romeo. But no Cyrano, either.

I had four dark gray suits and one black, so we're probably talking about yer standard dark gray with tie. Never blue or brown. You'd be surprised how formality of dress affects client confidence. Not to mention the size factor, which often seemed to work out as a positive selling point during first meetings. People generally warmed to the idea of having a giant on their side. Not every time, though.

So, yeah, you could say that, generally speaking, I distrust first impressions. Probably wouldn't be alive to be telling you all this if I didn't.

All right.

Have the mouth hanging open slightly as I'm ripping the long strip of tape away from the package along the incision. The size and shape were starting to add up to some kind of mail order gift. It had been a couple of months since my birthday. That'd be the last day of August. I'm trying to decide if perhaps this thing got misdirected, bounced from one PO to the next before finally reaching its destination. After all, the address was missing a few particulars.

Okay, it was unlikely. But I stopped for a moment anyway and thought about whether I knew anybody who might have reason to send me something.

I had no brothers or sisters.

We'll go ahead and get this out the way now, if you don't mind.

My father, having survived ten months in France and Belgium during the Second World War, as well as fourteen-plus years as a Chicago cop, died while mowing the lawn in the spring of 1960. I was thirteen.

Wasn't as pastoral as it sounds, though. Pop was felled by a single shot in the back of the neck, right in back of our house there in Downer's Grove. I was at practice when it happened. They never found the guy, although as I'd come to learn later, the search might have been pursued a little less vigorously than one might expect. In such a case.

Two things made it especially hard. First, it had happened off-duty, so Mom and I were denied whatever benefits we might have gotten otherwise. Which would have changed things, believe me.

Second, and most importantly, what I didn't find out until much later, there was talk that Pop was crooked, that the misfortune in the yard might have had something to do with the improper handling on his part of a certain transaction with a certain, well-known crime boss. Or, which didn't occur to me until fifteen years and hundreds of miles later, well after I'd done my own turn as a cop, it could have been there was some sort of in-house maintenance being performed by the department to which he had once belonged, and, allegedly, more than once betrayed.

Mom had taught voice lessons at home and might have been okay. Problem was she was already a budding alcoholic at the time of Pop's ignominious removal from the household. And so, she immediately embarked upon a kind of slow fade, a twenty-month dwindle during which young Richard found himself serving a necessarily accelerated apprenticeship to adulthood. It was almost anticlimactic when, just before the start of sophomore season at Southern, Mom took another one of those afternoon naps and forgot to wake up.

Guardianship went to my uncle, Emmett. Was at least ten years older than his dead sister, was outwardly critical of his dead brother-in-law, and was more than a little resentful at the pair's having bequeathed to him their fifteen-year-old man-child of a son. Was also a pretty mean drinker in his own right, and if my growth spurt had been later rather than earlier, I might have an even sorrier story to tell.

8

Had to change schools, which didn't please the coach at Southern too much. Ended up sitting out sophomore year altogether, which was probably a bad move, since by default the energies which might have been expended with ball were redirected toward returning some of Uncle Em's spite in kind. Started back a couple of games into junior year, and did all right. Having half a foot on everybody helped. Made all-conference. At the start of senior year I was offered a scholarship to play ball at Newton City Junior College over in Jersey, the acceptance of which was by then lay-up easy.

We're talking quite a while, then, since there'd been any family to speak of. Besides the unfeeling uncle, who as far as I knew still lived somewhere near Chicago but whose precise residence had been long-lost in a frankly uninspired maze of expired postal forwardings.

Besides, it looked like this thing had come from the City.

Rounding out the picture, as far as social circles went, mine had gotten considerably smaller since leaving the department. Not so many friends, really. More of what you might call acquaintances. Professional acquaintances, to be precise. I'm talking about contacts, those with whom you regularly exchange services. You can understand that. The sort of intercourse hopelessly compromised by interest and obligation.

There was still Mickey, of course, although thanks to an argument the last time we'd spoken it had been several months since I'd last seen him. And Russ and Phil and Moses and the other guys down at the Y, although I'm convinced half of them still think my name really is Lurch.

Okay, so we're probably not talking late birthday present.

The shadows in the office had by now fully enveloped the chair and desk. Still standing, I slowly began to unfurl the newspapers from the package, crumpling each piece of paper into a large, heavy ball and setting it on the side of the desk. I gradually became aware of a musty-flavored odor in and about the box and on my palms. The papers were old. Moldy, even. I noticed a couple of times tricky Dick's rubbery wince disappearing into another crumpled ball.

All right, I'm exhaling. Further dishevelling hair with scratching and making non-committal noises like "huh." Sitting back down. Stomach still growling. Whatever.

It's starting to look like that's all there is.

A box of nothing.

A typical end to such a day.

I'm wondering if there's anything else worth telling here before we get in too deep. Part of me wants to get the hell on with it. Part wants to keep on lingering here in the dark, enjoying the quiet of the moment before all hell started breaking loose.

This is where McGhee'd chime in with something smart. About how life was too short and the shadows too long to be wasting time this way.

9

Okay, one last thing. This'll be quick.

I do something like turn the chair around and face the window again, the box open and papers scattered everywhere on the desk behind me. Got a pensive look and doing something silly like rubbing the underside of my chin with my thumb. That'll be my thing. What's the difference, right? When the detective is thinking he rubs his chin.

And just now the detective is thinking about McGhee, his old captain. Who'd suspended me just before I quit, and about whom, even though we're talking almost five years down the road here, I'm still harboring some misgivings.

Like happens with clients, I'd say the majority of those with whom I worked either liked having a big guy around or had no opinion about it. Others though, especially those to whom I had to answer, would sometimes act like they saw some sort of challenge every time they saw me looking down at them. I'm talking about McGhee and Walton. Even Mickey, now and then. Looking like they thought my claim on the physical space available in the departmental offices, the streets, the City, was unfairly overextended. And so, here and there, guys like McGhee would get to acting like they wanted something back for these seventeen-double-E's having overstepped recognized boundaries.

"What world you come from?" McGhee had said to me that last morning, just before I'd handed in my badge. "Sure as hell ill-fit for this one."

Then had to come the McGhee shrug, actually more a tic caused by a pinched nerve under his collarbone. *That* was his thing. Every twenty seconds or so, Cap would involuntarily lean his neck forward and raise his shoulders, as if shaking off massive chips perpetually accumulating there. Sometimes, though, he'd induce the gesture to punctuate a point he had just made, or to lessen the impact of someone else's opinion.

"World's problem, Cap. Not mine," I had replied.

Something to that effect.

Not the most tactful response. Nor the most mature. I'd like to say that such self-indulgences were rare for me. Still, whenever they did occur, they were always memorable for the extent of the damage they wrought. As if the bull-in-a-china-shop business extended to social intercourse as well.

All right. Still digging that thumbnail into my chinbone. Just about done with the daydreams. Robinson, the coach over at Westbrook where things didn't quite work out, coming to mind.

"Don't be small," is about all I remember him ever saying to me. Looking up and hollering it over and again to his new center, the one with an inappropriate predilection for the outside shot.

"Big man like you can't afford it."

Entire office now in shadow, save two dozen thin rows of light snaking across the ceiling above me. Now-invisible mosquito whizzing past my ear.

With a backhanded wave I turned the chair around and stood up, forcibly sliding the chair back against the paneled wall where it lodged beneath the window frame. I started to switch on the lamp but didn't, choosing instead to plunge my hands back into the box one last time, smiling like some trick-or-treater who'd just been told go ahead, take all you want.

I stopped smiling when I realized my knuckles were buckling against something hard, then instinctively curling around a longish, tubular object buried underneath the newspapers. I pulled slowly, one end of it lodging stubbornly against the corner of the package. I shook it loose it and lifted it out from underneath its packing.

Adrenaline returning for real, suddenly causing my chest to burn.

I couldn't believe how light the bone was.

# CHAPTER TWO

# ET CETERA

**BONE OF CONTENTION.**

Or so a *Daily* writer had coined it, no doubt with a certain satisfied glee. Probably my favorite of the puns, which had spread like a brush fire, each further comment from this or that "official" containing the blaze at least as well as another can of gasoline. A headline writer's dream, to be sure.

**PETERS KILLER HAD A BONE TO PICK.**

The *Sunday News*, recapping known details. One girl apparently bludgeoned to death, another missing. A tall, mid-ranking patrolman, closing in on his forty-third hour without sleep, letting it slip to a fresh-faced cub the "distinct possibility" that the instrument employed to end the former girl's life had been rudely removed from the latter. As if staking out a shotgun shack solely occupied by the decaying remains of a state senator's daughter for the better part of two, subfreezing days weren't bad enough. Other, contradictory quotes from Officers Rowe and Harding, also on the scene, further established the solid foundation for the public relations imbroglio which had followed.

**DPT TO CONDUCT REVIEW FOLLOWING CAPT'S BONER.**

This from the *Times*, reporting fall-out two weeks after twice-decorated Captain William K. McGhee's much-reported gaff. From his White Plains residence at four a.m., some fifteen minutes after the discovery of the Peters girl's body, McGhee, "Cap" to colleagues and friends, had chimed in with inordinate optimism the unqualified assurance that indeed *both* girls would be found, "healthy and intact," within the week. The media debated over which was greater, the department's "obvious lack of communication" or McGhee's "alarming lack of sensitivity." The respected McGhee received a written reprimand. Which meant in the end that captain is where old McGhee would be topping out.

**WELL OF CLUES BONE DRY, SAYS NEW D.A.**

Forgotten all about this one. Probably because I'd never read it. A six-pager in the *Voice*, in which Solomon Severin, sworn in some eighteen months later after Mack McClellan surprisingly succumbed to a well-concealed case of heart disease, was featured "introducing some realism," or so he had phrased it, into the still-unsolved Henrietta Peters case. The *Voice* also briefly took up the cause of the missing girl, Barbara Rocca, the twenty-year old brunette late of little Italy, from whom the sensational discovery of Henry Peters's pretty daughter had diverted public attention from the very start. Severin refused to speculate about Rocca's well-being, although he did point out that the combination of her being seen with Henrietta during the weeks leading up to the murder, the prodigious amount of her blood being found at the crime scene, and the present scarcity of leads made the prospect of locating her safe and unharmed "remote at best."

So what had looked like packing material was more the makings of a scrapbook, something like the thing my mother had kept for the first few months after Pop was killed. Before money for the paper boy started to become an issue. There were several more pieces in there, too, all having something to say about the fiasco which put a big question mark at the end of my sentence working for the City.

You should know I didn't take the time to read these things in the office. In fact, it wasn't until later on that night I even bothered, and then only by accident, but I'll get to that. I didn't need all of the this-is-your-life business to know this was no birthday gift. Not even as a gag.

Officer Owen, trapped by the press, holding the ball and surrounded with no teammates in sight, resigned the force within a week of the incident. This occurrence went largely unnoticed, media-wise. In fact, by the time of that *Voice* piece in the summer of '73, the author of the so-called bone theory had seemingly evaporated from the pages of print still considering the event for which the theory had been invented. A year-and-half on and the headline writers still playing word games, apparently unaware or unconcerned with where or whom it had all started.

I guess that's not so strange. It only took two weeks for McGhee to get blindsided with that boner zinger. Once something like that is out there, no one is safe.

That definitely turned out to be a lesson for me. Namely, to try and be a little more wary of the newshound who is only talking to you during a break from sniffing his neighbor's backside.

There's more to it than that, though. Always be aware that when you tell your story, whatever it is, folks are going to make of it what they will. Doesn't matter how straight you shoot, somebody'll find a way to make it look crooked. And that ultimately, when it comes to the way you're story is going to get rearranged, there's no limit to the depths people will go. The uglier the better. Give 'em a fairy tale and they'll find a way to make it into the worst horror imaginable.

By the following summer, then, Officer Owen no longer fell under the heading of Human Interest. Besides, it wasn't long before they'd have another Richard to kick around. If you'd kept turning, though, back to the back of the paper, beyond the Automobile Exchange and Weekend Movie Clock, you'd have seen I hadn't disappeared from publication altogether. As a short, nondescript classified regularly appearing amidst other Offered Services quietly attested:

> PVT. DETECT., SURVEILLENCE, INFIDEL.,
> RECOV. STOLEN GOODS, WITNESS LOCATION,
> ETC. CALL R. OWEN, AL 3-7129 FOR APPT.

Not ostentatious? That's probably debatable. After all, look at the list. Not exactly ruling anything out there. Started it the last week of June, 1972. Took about four months for calls to start coming in. Then some referrals, people showing up unannounced. Of course, some folks ended up a little too far afield where that et cetera was concerned, if you catch my drift.

Still, I can't say I recall any stream of dark ladies showing up in silhouette and sporting enormous bodices hiring me to catch their husbands' enormous killers then ask I help them spend their enormous inheritances. Not off-hand, anyway. More likely we're talking about a spurned husband, starkly-lit, sulking through the office door after having been given the address by someone at the club. Uninsured victims of theft ringing up, somehow able to locate my number more easily than that of the nearest pawn shop. The occasional Wall Street employer wanting to know a little more about a prospective hire. Pretty soon your typical detective is keeping himself a typical little black notebook and so on and so forth.

Routine or not, the work was sure and steady, minus the administrative hassles and the more than occasional scrapes which came up walking, and eventually, for a short time anyway, driving beats on the upper east side. I'll admit it, I liked the control and the pace and being able to choose when and where risking my neck was worth it or not.

Although standing there at dusk, holding that thing over my desk, I sensed a not-so-tiny shift to all this happy tranquility occurring on the horizon.

The object was not a bone *per se* but a part of a bone. Technically, a fragment of what I guessed at the time to be one of those long bones you find in a human leg. Find in a book, I mean.

The piece was I'd say about sixteen or eighteen inches long and of surprisingly smallish diameter. The surface was super smooth, oddly so. There was a lengthy fracture running along one side, curling and fading a few inches before the relatively large, knotty end piece, which was itself about the size of a child's fist. The other side came to a sharp, slightly rounded point, like when you pull a tooth what the underside looks like, only a hell of a lot bigger.

I held the thing delicately, sort of rocking it back and forth there in the dark. Though light, it had a palpable solidity to it, especially at the knot-end, which even someone with normal-sized hands should've been able to palm.

I set it down, balancing the thing across the open box like an ivory bridge passing over the sea of newspapers below. I finally did switch on the lamp. Safe to say we're probably up to five o'clock now.

I pulled the chair back and sat down and still all charged up I grabbed up the phone with the idea of ringing up Mickey. I didn't, though. Instead I just sat there holding the receiver next to my ear while I flipped through the directory, awkwardly searching with one hand for the number to Lanford Williams's lab over at University Hospital.

Big cities usually have big directories. Bigger than you can manage with one hand. After repeatedly flipping past where I wanted to be I finally put the receiver down and before too long had the number for the University operator. As I dialed it I pulled a red Flair out from my pants pocket.

"University," the operator voiced impassively.

"I need the number of Lanford Williams, please." Oh, right. Kind of a sixteen-tons-and-what-d'ye-get baritone of a voice.

"Department?"

"Um . . . that'd be Pathology."

"One moment." While I waited I tapped the box flap with the pen, and up flew about a million of those fine little cardboard motes which stirred around in the narrow cylinder of light coming from the lamp's faint beam.

The operator returned. "I've got a general number for Pathology but no Lanford Williams."

"All right." I looked up at my topcoat hanging there on the doorknob. "Give it to me."

The operator relayed the number, which not having my notebook handy I jotted in the margin. Tucked the receiver between my ear and shoulder, pressed down once and getting a dial tone speedily dialed the number. It rang six times with no response. Hung up and dialed again. It rang three times before someone answered.

"Path," the voice chewed.

"Lanny?" The guy was always there.

"Speaking."

"Dick Owen calling."

"Hey, Dick, you caught me eating a sandwich here. How you been?"

"Fine, fine. Still up here on Twenty-fifth . . ."

"Yeah, yeah. Right. How are things going?"

"Good, good. Listen, Lanny, I have something here and wondered if you might be willing to take a look at it. You gonna be there a while?" Like I had to ask.

"Hang on a sec." Real loud swallow followed by throat-clearing.

"M-m-m-okay. What is it, Dick? "

Here's me doing something while I hesitate. Not pursing my lips. What, you want me kissing the phone? Lip-pursing, hand-wringing. When did you last see someone actually wring their hands?

"Well . . . ."

Well . . . all right. Rubbing my chin, then.

Lanny probably wasn't the guy to call. I know that now.

Still, that's how it happened.

And here I'm hesitating because I'm suddenly realizing how what I was about to say was going to sound.

"It's a bone, Lanny. Somebody just mailed me a bone."

"What?" A collective pause. "You're kidding."

"I know what it sounds like, Lan, but I'm sitting here looking at a bone the size of a claw hammer that was sitting on my desk in a cardboard box when I got back here a half-hour ago. Might be a joke. Might not. You gonna be around?"

Lanny whistled. "Human?"

I knew it was but didn't want to get into it over the phone.

"No clue."

"Yeah, yeah, sure come on 'n bring it down. I'll meet you in back. Nobody's here. Just wasting time anyway with these samples. Come on over. You remember . . . ?"

"Yes. Thanks, Lanny. Be there in about . . . ." That's when I checked my watch. Five-oh-five. Besides University traffic, I'd have to negotiate everybody escaping from the financial district zoo. "Thirty? No, let's say forty. Traffic."

"I'll look for you sometime before six, then. Damn. You think . . . ?"

"No idea, Lanny. See you in a bit."

There were three main reasons for my calling Lanny. One, he was the only person I knew personally who could look at a fossil like this and have anything meaningful to say about it. Two, he had been around the department that winter, the winter of the Peters girl, and so knew the story.

So, besides knowing bones, he also knew about *the* bone. Of contention.

Now that I think about it, first time I ever met Lanny it was McGhee who'd introduced us. For about a year or so, Lanny did all of the blood work for the department when its own lab had been down for renovations. This had to be all of '71, at least. Most efficient the department's lab work had ever been, as far as I was concerned. We still kept in touch through the Saturday morning game at the Y, which thanks to our respective work schedules we both only managed to attend sporadically. Our visits coincided often enough, though, for us to remain at least generally aware of each other's lives.

The third reason I called Lanny was a little more complicated, though boils down to my not wanting to call the department or anyone else before I had the thing checked out. If this was a prank, calling out the cops on it would have made for one hell of a reunion. And besides, even if I didn't consciously realize it at the time, it was just too good to be true. Having a bone literally dumped on my desk like that. Would have raised some eyebrows, for certain. So, in my mind, going to Lanny was the sensible thing to do.

The hallway commotion that usually comes right around the five o'clock whistle had pretty well died down and so the building had become relatively quiet. Pretty soon the custodial crew would be coming around, cleaning up the mess all the CPA's and lawyers had made of the place during the day.

I remember after hanging up with Lanny having this sudden urge to run out of there, to get the thing down to his lab as quickly as I could. It would be dishonest for me to say I felt at that moment I was in any specific danger. There I was, though, rapidly stuffing the bone back into the box and the papers in on top it, closing the flaps down and tucking it under my arm, switching the lamp off and stumbling in the dark around the desk and toward the door.

So basically I'm bolting out of there, but to tell you the truth I think it had as much to do with being hungrier than hell than anything else.

I yanked the coat from off the knob and threw it over my shoulder. Reached down and gave the knob a quick twist to the right. When it sticks like it does, you have to push first and then jerk it hard to pull it free. As I pushed I thought I detected a little shuffle on the other side of the door, but it didn't register fast enough. The brain had already sent the signal to pull.

"Christ!"

A shadowy figure was standing alone in the hallway at the entrance to my office, the back of his hand raised before him.

"Oh dear, sorry about that."

The middle-aged man stepped back and lowered his head with a tuck of a finger between his neck and the knot of his tie.

"Just about to knock. Am I too late?"

I must have stepped back-and made some sort of inviting gesture because next I knew this gentleman was walking past me into the office. He stopped and turned back, looking up at me and seeming to marvel for a moment at the difference in our heights.

"You're so tall," he said, or something like that. "Does being so tall make it hard for a private detective . . . to remain private?"

Smart question. All right, so I give a smart answer.

"You'd be surprised how few folks actually look up here," I said, sticking my neck out and pointing a long finger at my forehead. A six-foot, eight-inch lie, by the way. Who is this guy? I shoved the door closed.

"Grab a seat," I said.

17

I walked back over and switched back on the lamp and took a seat behind the desk while he sunk into the cushioned chair. He looked mid-forties, well-dressed and well-groomed. Neither balding nor graying. His complexion was pallid, almost clammy with the slight moisture that had formed on his upper lip and on what looked to be a largish forehead.

A light fog slowly evaporated from the lenses of his glasses, revealing tired-looking eyes. I remember having had the impression that he had climbed the seven floors rather than rode the elevator. I also remember confidently guessing all those lines under his eyes probably corresponded to the number of hours of sleep he'd lost contemplating his recent cuckolding.

"Somebody refer you, I take it?"

I rested the box cautiously on the corner of the desk, draping my coat over it with a disguised carelessness.

"Uh, yes. I was given your name. By a friend." He pronounced the words with care, as if he'd rehearsed them. He looked at the box. Probably nervous, I thought. Definitely nervous. Probably never thought it would come to this.

"And yours?"

"Harold Morgan," he said and reached forward and we shook hands. Bending toward him, I noticed the man's upper lip twitch a little. He was making me nervous, now, and so I tried to let my own face relax into a real accepting kind of smile. Which worked, as a visible relief started to spread over his face.

"What brings you to see me, Mr. Morgan?"

"Doctor, actually."

"Doctor. Where?"

"I've a private practice up on the west side."

"So we've got that in common. General practice?"

"No. Gastroenterology."

"Digestion, that sort of thing?"

"That's right." The doctor starting to tense up again.

"Very delicate muscle, that." Followed by a delicate grin. Again, some signs of relief.

"Indeed." The doctor swallowed and continued. "You'd be surprised how delicate. I'd say that for over half of the people I see it's all in their head. Stress."

"How is your digestion, doc?"

Morgan closed his eyes and showed his straight, white teeth as he forced himself to chuckle.

"Not great, actually."

The doctor leaned back in the chair, blinking slowly. I could sense what was coming next, how he was about to explain how he'd found out. A friend's suggestion. An anonymous note. A strange tie.

Not saying I wasn't listening to the man, but remember at this point I've got other things on my mind. This seemed to be a conversation I'd had before. One of those familiar patterns I was talking about, the kind which no matter how many times you see it, you still have to be wary not to close your eyes to it.

Thing was, it was the familiarity which made me even more anxious, made me want to cut Morgan off and get on down to Lanny's. So almost without thinking, I do just that and rise up behind the desk all of a sudden. The doctor looked up worriedly.

"Dr. Morgan . . . "

I slid a hand underneath the coat and across the grainy surface of the package.

"I want you to know I am here to help. I am willing to do all I can for you, whatever it was that brought you here. Thing is, you sort of caught me in a fix here . . . . I was just about to . . . ."

I found myself stopping and watching as the doctor nodded his head and stood up. Looking off into the corner of the room, he held out a before-you-say-anything-else hand and very deliberately retrieved a long, black leather wallet from his inside pocket. He pulled the zipper on the outside of it and slipped out a photograph. His hand shook a little when he handed the five by seven glossy to me over the desk.

"It's my daughter, Mr. Owen. Donna. She's . . . she's missing."

I took the photograph without looking at it, still staring at the doctor. Dumb expression, mouth hanging open. Okay, agape. Trying to mask surprise, but not doing such a good job at it. Morgan looking down, his head directed toward the picture in my hand, not seeming to notice my wonder.

"Really?" I said, genuine curiosity briefly turning me into a tenor.

The doctor's eyes looked up, his head still bowed. Clumsy silence. I'm avoiding looking at the picture, wondering to myself whether I should hear Morgan out or politely invite him to leave. I handed back the picture.

"Doctor . . . I'm not sure . . . "

"Please, Mr. Owen. I beg of you. Hear me out. You said you were willing to do . . . "

"Yes, but . . . ." Et cetera, et cetera.

Morgan's forehead glistened, his eyes nearing what was looking like panic-sized wideness. I took the coat off of the box and tucked it under one arm. I leaned forward, holding the flaps closed with both hands.

"Listen," I said. "There's a coffee shop next door. It'll be busy, but I think we can get a booth. It'll be private. You mind if we take it down there?"

"Um . . . no, not at all. That would be just fine. Thanks . . . ."

I saw his face was all washed out and instinctively I reached out and touched the doctor's shoulder.

"No problem."

# CHAPTER THREE

# SOME KIND OF PUT-ON

We left without saying another word. Walked side by side down the dim hallway toward the elevators on the opposite end of the building. I pressed the button and together we marked the cars' slow progress downward. The doctor continued to hold the picture against his chest.

"These take a while." I held the box gingerly with one hand while I put on my coat. Watch said five-fifteen.

"Nice offices."

"They're all right. Too bad they're all filled with lawyers. Your set-up similar?"

"No."

Morgan folded his arms as he spoke, the photograph pressed against the arm of his coat.

"We did at first. We shared a floor like this in a building for a number of years."

"Where's that?"

You should know this was a favorite conversational topic for me. Actually, I've got no huge problems with Wescott. Or maybe I should say I hadn't had any problems up to this point. In any case, whenever anybody starts talking renting or leasing space in the City, I can't help but start in with the twenty questions.

"Up on Minford," he responded.

"Where's that, High Bridge?"

"No, no . . . . Over."

"Morrisania?"

"East Tremont."

"Size? 'Bout the same?" Morgan seemed distracted. "Different . . . ?"

Morgan gave a cursory look down the hall. I also leaned back sympathetically and looked with him back in the direction from which we had just come. A short Hispanic man at the other end of the hallway pushed his cart toward us.

"About the same, I guess. The building was wider than this, though.

The floor had at least a dozen suites, plus lab space."

The right car had been stopped at sixteen for at least three questions. Left one wasn't lit up at all.

"Mind if I ask what it was you paid there?"

"Not at all. I think it was something like seven-fifty?"

I drew air through the sides of my mouth and blinked slowly, watching the words Out Of Your League flashing through.

"Pricey," I said. That would be what you call understatement.

"We had quite a large space, though. Also, all of the suites shared the labs, so there were some expenses added in."

"Like?"

"Oh, insurance, use of equipment, that sort of thing."

"So, you're out of there."

"Right. We were lucky and got to move into one of the row houses over in the old section when it came available. Little more space, little more privacy."

"Sounds nice. Several rooms, then?"

"Yes, yes. It once housed several apartments . . . "

I was about to ask what he was paying over on the west side when the right-side car finally arrived. We rode down without speaking, the Girl from Ipanema dancing over our heads.

At the third floor, a broad-shouldered maintenance man with dark, greasy hair got on, vaguely nodding at the back of the car before getting off on two. We stepped out into the lobby and I gave the desk jockey a nod, signalling him to sign me out. Those guys know every last person in the building, but I'll wager you a dime to a dollar not one in eighty knows them. I waited while Morgan signed the register. We walked through the glass double-doors and I quickly led Morgan next door and into Magdalena's.

Not to harp on this too overly, but by the time Morgan and I were sitting there in the coffee shop in one of the booths along the windows facing the street, it couldn't have been any later than five-twenty. Meaning the two of us weren't in the office together more than ten minutes tops.

As was usually the case around five-twenty on a weekday, Magdalena's was hopping. Those big window booths nevertheless gave us the privacy I had advertised to the doctor. I kept the package in the seat next to me, against the wall to my left. The doctor again handed me the photograph.

"So . . . . Donna, you said?" I still wasn't looking at the picture.

"It's been three weeks, now. Since just after her birthday."

"How old?"

"Nineteen."

The waitress's arrival interrupted us.

"Hiya, Dick." I tilted the photograph toward the window as I looked up at Carla's familiar face.

"Hey there, Carla.  Can you get them to fix me up a po'boy or something?"

"Roast beef?"

"Perfect."

"What on?"

"Everything."

"And you, sir?"  Carla and I both looked at the doctor who seemed to be fluttering his handkerchief surrender-like out over the table.

"Oh.  No, nothing for me thanks."

"And a Coke?" I added.

"Comin' up."

We watched silently as Carla walked over to the counter and hung the order.  I looked back to see Morgan neatly folding his hanky there on the table.  Carla reappeared and put the Coke with a straw in it down with one hand while she fished out a napkin-and-silver from her apron pocket with the other.

"Thanks."  I continued to hold the photo turned toward the window.  I leaned forward on my right elbow.

"Where does she live?" I asked, removing the straw.

Morgan held the folded handkerchief with both hands.  Blank look.

"She live at home?"

"Yes and no.  She did have a place near school, but she keeps most of her things at home.  With us.  With my wife and myself.  Central Park West."

"Nice neighborhood."

"Yes it is."  Morgan dabbed at his still moist brow.

"Who'd you say referred you again?"

"There you go."  Carla let the plate rattle down between us, causing us both to lean back.  "Anything else?"

"Nope.  Thank you, Carla."  I put the napkin in my lap and slid the plate closer.

"It was a friend, Mr. Owen, who gave me your name."  Morgan looked down into his pocket as he reinserted the handkerchief.  "A patient of mine."

"And this person said I'd help you find your daughter?"  Asked rudely through a mouthful of French bread.

"Yes, he did.  What do you mean?"

The question seemed sincere.

I washed down some sandwich with the Coke and looked sidelong at the box on the seat.  By then I'd say I had already basically persuaded myself to hear Morgan out.  A pretty easy sell, I must've seemed.  He made it easy, actually.  Something about his manner, perhaps to do with his being a physician, a person whose profession dictates he help others, that could inspire a person to reciprocate.

"Nothing . . . I understand," I said.

Referred by a patient, then.  Could have been the poor sap didn't bother to mention why it was he'd hired a private detective. Likely the guy's wife who had twisted his stomach into knots in the first place. Probably just a short, polite, usefully distracting conversation over a barium enema.

"So this . . . ." I kept eating as I waved the picture up and down. "Graduation?"

"What? Oh, yes. Graduation."

That's when I finally stopped and looked at the picture. Pretty girl, long dark hair, blue-green eyes. Seemed to share the doctor's flat forehead. Pale-looking, too. All right, ghost-like. Her mouth open slightly, showing her teeth. Little gap there in front. A capricious smile.

"Any ideas?"

"Well . . . yes, in fact." Dr. Morgan exhaled loudly. Again I'm thinking this all rehearsed. Which doesn't necessarily mean anything.

"We're thinking Donna might've run off with some people. We're afraid she might have gotten herself involved with the wrong sort of people."

"Some people."

"These people whom we think she might have gotten mixed up with, they're movie people."

"Movie people? What d'ye mean, imaginary? What?"

The doctor looked confused.

"No. Movie people. People who make movies, you know . . . "

"Blue?" I said.

Morgan's expression did not change. I tried again.

"Blue movies, you mean? Rated X?"

"Yes, right." He nodded a lot and cleared his throat. "That's what we think. We think that Donna might have gotten involved making these blue rated X movies."

"And what was it gave you that idea?" I'm done already, cramming the last of the bread and meat into my mouth.

"Because I have seen one of these movies. With her. In it, I mean."

I stopped mid-chew and stared at the doctor for a moment. I looked at the photograph again. A what's-on-your-mind look back. Smile suddenly looked like some kind of put-on. Like she's shaming you and shamming you all at once.

"You've seen one." Muffled a little. Big gulp of Coke.

"Yes, over on Forty-second on a machine in a building called the Show Place."

I wiped my mouth with the napkin. "I see, a short film. Put your quarter in and . . . "

"Yes, something like that. I was made aware of it, of the film, and went over this afternoon to see for myself . . . "

"Who was it made you aware of it?"

Short pause. "Does it matter?"

"Might."

The doctor peered over his glasses. I guessed this to be an effective gesture when attempting to draw out sensitive information from patients. My stomach purred.

"A colleague. I'd rather not give his name, if that's possible."

"Married man, I take it."

"Yes. That's right." The doctor seemed suitably impressed with my tactfulness.

"All right." I shook the ice free and tossed back the glass, crunching cubes as I watched the sidewalk outside busy with pedestrians. Again I saw the large canvas umbrella up ahead on the corner.

"There is one thing I do have to ask, though. You haven't been to the police about this, am I right?"

"Yes. I mean, no, we have not gone to the police."

"And can you tell me why you haven't?"

"To be frank, Mr. Owen, my wife and I would like to try and keep this private, if it's possible, for Donna's sake. For when we get her back. We think it would be easier for her later if we could keep the police out of it."

Just like the first time he'd said it. Before the wife, possibly.

I pushed the plate and glass over to the table's edge and leaned forward, for a moment towering over my new client.

"Yes, well, I understand. That is, I see your point. Of course, if what you say is true and that is your daughter starring in the film you saw this afternoon . . . "

"It is. It is true."

" . . . then it may be that she is going to make it difficult to keep things private for very long. I'll do what I can, though."

He closed his eyes and nodded. I leaned back in the seat.

"But tell me, doctor. Is there anything else I should know?"

"No. I think that's about everything."

"This would be her what . . . her second year at City?"

"That's right. Second year."

"Roommates?"

"No, no. As I've said, we've emptied out the apartment."

"No, I don't think you mentioned that."

"I didn't? Well, we have." As he spoke he gestured toward the picture in my hand and circled his finger around. I turned the photograph over.

"Those are my numbers there on the back. That's the office number first. You can reach me either at home or the office. The office is probably going to be the quicker of the two."

"Got an address?"

"Here let me . . . "

The doctor took the photograph back as he dug a hand around in his jacket pocket, pulling out one of those nice fake-wood looking pens. Carla stopped and took up the plate and glass and left the ticket while Morgan wrote something quickly beneath the phone numbers. He handed the picture back, recapping the pen.

"That's for the office, there."

As he spoke, I pulled out my Flair and noted "office" beside the street address.

"We can always meet there. We should meet there. My wife . . . "

"Can you think of any particular reason why Donna might have taken off?" I started to reach for the check, but the doctor beat me to it. Hey, I'd just eaten. Slow on the uptake.

"Let me . . . . To be honest, Mr. Owen, I haven't the foggiest. We haven't seen so much of her lately. I wish I could give you more to go on, but we're kind of in the dark ourselves. That's why we thought we'd come to you."

"Well, I sincerely hope I can help you, Dr. Morgan."

"Yes, fine. So do I." He had the long, black wallet out again. "Should I pay you now, or . . . ? How does it work?"

I paused. Runaways weren't exactly part of my usual trade.

To find a witness, we'd usually be talking twenty-five flat, then ten an hour, then expenses. This was different. Unlike your average hard-to-find witness, missing persons were usually missing on purpose. Little more leg work involved. Typically, I'd have taken the doctor back upstairs and at least had him fill out and sign a generic contract. Might have taken fifty off him as well, if I hadn't been in such a hurry to get downtown. My instinct was the doc was good for it, and even if he wasn't, a family wanting to keep their daughter's naughty ways hushed would serve as leverage, should collecting ever become an issue.

"Don't worry about it just now," I said. "We'll work it out."

"Well, anything is fine. You let me know." We shook on it. Our deal to make a deal.

"I'll walk you out."

Morgan left the bills on the table while I pocketed the photograph and carefully lifted the package up out of the seat. The flaps continued to behave, staying down. Sent a nod and a wave to Carla across the shop as we exited. Held open the door for Morgan, and followed him as the doctor moved out onto the crowded sidewalk.

We turned and shook hands for the third time.

The two of us stood there a moment facing one another, the doctor seemingly distracted by the crowd which had suddenly surrounded us. The doctor faced east, vaguely staring over my right shoulder, apparently preoccupied with his missing daughter. He blinkingly shook his head, snapping himself back to the present.

"Okay, then," he breathed. "Thanks in advance, Mr. Owen," he said, gesturing with his thumb westward toward the parking deck just down Second

Avenue.

"I will call you when I find out something," I said.

We departed in opposite directions.

I looked at my watch and started into a half-jog, weaving my way to the corner where I had to wait for the light to cross. The vendor was still there, his throaty, accented bark catching my attention. I read the cursive lettering on the banner that hung down over the edge of the cart.

King Weiner.

I was still hungry. I turned and took two long steps away from the corner and toward the red, white, and blue umbrella, thinking about whether the po'boy was going to do for the next couple of hours. The street lights had come on, and I could see the old guy bent over. A little guy, the shadow of his hunched-back just visible above his lowered head as he stood there vigorously stirring a container of relish.

I looked at my watch again and wheeled back around, rejoining the early evening throng traversing First.

# CHAPTER FOUR

# ONE INVITATION ACCEPTED, ONE DECLINED

"What happened?"

Lanford Williams, chief lab assistant at the University's pathology lab and inveterate night owl, used the weight of his short, stocky body to hold open the heavy door.

"Sorry, Lan. Client. Caught me as I was leaving. How are you doing?"

Lanny grasped my hand and let go, raising a finger.

"Smoke?"

I shook my head no.

"Never mind, then. Can't in the lab, and I was gonna have one before we went down. Let's go on, though. I can wait."

"Thanks."

We entered the building together. Stepping inside, Lanny let the door fall behind us, the long, slow whine of its heavy hinges echoing from behind as we walked side by side down the flight of concrete stairs which emptied into a long, ill-lit corridor.

"Never been this way, have you?"

I shook my head.

"Follow me." The whine of the door continued as we silently walked another hundred yards or so before turning right down another dim hallway.

"That it?" asked Lanny.

"This is it."

I stopped short, causing Lanny to turn around.

"I mean this is what was in my office this afternoon. I don't know . . . "

"Right, right. Come on."

Lanny's wrinkled, dirty white coat flared about him as he turned back down the hall. I continued a half-step behind him, looking down at the small patch of gray hairs protruding from his otherwise dark scalp.

"Working hard?"

"It's a living," he tossed back over his shoulder. "A reasonable facsimile, anyway. This way."

Thus began a sequence of quick turns through the labyrinthine network of basement corridors. After the fourth turn or so, the halls became narrower, and we had to walk single file. I started hearing faint little percussive-like sounds as we walked. A hi-hat shimmering, cut off by the snap of a snare. Echoing all around us. Seemed like there was a tom-tom or something thumping along irregularly behind us. The turns came more quickly. After an abrupt left, Lanny wheeled around and slapped a hand on my chest.

"Watch yer head, big man. Still hoopin'?"

"Been a while."

"Me neither. A month at least since I last went. They've been going out during the week some, here lately. So I've heard. I can't do it then either, though."

"Tough to squeeze it in sometimes."

"I've barely got time to smoke a cigarette," he laughed.

I kept following, ducking every twenty feet or so to avoid a crossing piece of water pipe. Now and again scraping the box against the wall as we turned. The noises became louder. I started feeling more than a little claustrophobic.

"Right around the corner, here."

"Good."

"Front way's quicker, but they had a break-in at the start of the semester and they say they're in the middle of changing the locks. In the meantime they've bolted it so no one can get in. Brilliant."

Me making some sort of sympathetic noise. We turned to the right. Lanny unlocked a large lavender door and opened it, letting escape a torrent of arrhythmic pounding and pummelling, accompanied by what could only be the contrapuntal yelping of baby seals. A second or two and I recognized the song, though I can't tell you what it was. You know it, though. The stuff is like the air. Let's-dance-tonight-'cause-it-feels-all-right-though-my-pants-are-too-tight or whatever.

Lanny seemed unconcerned by the noise.

"Take your coat?" he must have said, pointing at a closet full of labcoats.

Of course with the racket going on all I saw was Lanny moving his mouth and pointing at the coats. I looked up at the closet and saw all the coats and figured he was offering me a labcoat to wear.

"No, thanks," I yell. Afterwards I get it.

With a wave Lanny directed me through the front room and toward the laboratory in back. I passed through first, still clutching the box, and as Lanny followed he slapped the wall beside the door. The noise abruptly ceased.

"Neat, eh? Got it all wired up last week."

I make another sympathetic noise while Lanny points with both hands up at the small, toaster-sized speakers located in each corner of the lab. I set the box down on the white table in the center of the room.

"You got some plastic or something for this?"

"Right." Lanny slapped his hands and rubbed them together. He disappeared into the front room and reemerged with a black plastic tray about the size of a shoe box lid and a big old grin.

"Ain't gonna do it."

I slowly lifted the bone up through the papers and out of the box with one hand and held it aloft while I closed the flaps shut with the other. Lanny's face whitened.

"That's one hell of a claw hammer, Dick."

Lanny took two steps forward before turning back into the front room, this time returning with a much larger tray. He skipped ahead and slid it across the the table. I lowered the bone onto it gently, the pointy end lodged in one corner while the knot-end hung over the tray's edge.

Lanny stood there massaging his unshaven cheeks, his eyes dead set upon the bone. He leaned forward and placed both hands on the table.

"Looks like it could be old enough. Hard to tell, though, it looks like it's been treated with something. You know I'm not sure if I have what it takes to find out . . . . For sure, I mean. Whether or not . . . "

"I figured as much."

I also put my hands on the table. Lanny bent down closer to the tray.

"What can you do, though?"

"Well, it's definitely human. Looks like part of the tibia. This here's the joint down . . . down here. The tibia, part of the lower leg. See, look."

He lifted his labcoat and rubbed down alongside the bottom part of his own right leg in a vague demonstration. He let his coat fall and again held his face in his hand.

"This looks finished, though. Wicked." Lanny was pointing at the sharp end, which now that he mentioned it did look as though it had been filed down.

"There are a few things we could do."

He withdrew a pencil from one of his jacket's several pockets.

"What's this?" He touched a discoloration of the bone with the eraserhead.

"What's what?"

"Probably some kind of decay here. Well, anyway, as I was saying we can do some things, depending on what kind of samples we can get, if any. If there's any marrow at all left in here . . . ." He again pointed with the eraserhead. "We'd be able to tell more. Male or female. Approximate age, although this is obviously an adult specimen, which might make that more difficult. There are places where they could tell you more. DNA stuff. You know, typing. Race. Ethnicity, even. Whether the departed was diabetic."

"Yeah?"

"Well, maybe. It all depends on the quality of the samples. This obviously hasn't been preserved at all. Not the way you'd like for it to be, at least. Through the mail, huh? What'd they pack it in, bird feathers?"

"Newspapers."

"In that box there? Lemme see that." I opened the flaps and slid the package over to Lanny. He dipped his head down.

"Ugh." Collective grimace.

"Fragrant, ain't it?"

"Who sent you this thing . . . ?" Lanny turned the flap down to read the label.

"Your guess is as good as mine. See."

"Through the mail." He shook his head unbelievingly as he moved back over to the tray.

"Might have been through the mail."

"What do you mean?"

"Could've been dropped off, I guess. Some joke, huh?"

"This is no joke, Dick." Lanny slid the pencil behind his left ear. "Pieces of leg don't just turn up outside of autopsy rooms and crematoriums."

"I know."

We stood there silently for a couple of minutes while Lanny leaned over the bone. I thought I heard sniffing. Finally, Lanny looked up.

"You wanna wait or leave this here?"

"How long you think?" We started to walk back toward the front room.

"Well, I'm not going anywhere. I have to redo all of this anyway because this thing here was calibrated all wrong." He was pointing to some sort of measuring device on the counter along the front wall when he suddenly stopped, his shoe squeaking on the lab floor.

"Anybody else know about this?"

"You're it."

"Don't you think . . . I mean this isn't from a model or anything, this is the real thing here. Had to come from somewhere. We'll have to take it down to HQ, right?"

Right.

But suddenly I'm Dr. Morgan standing there explaining how maybe we could keep the police out of it. For now, anyway. Pretty convincingly, too. And Lanny a good audience, knowing as he did the source of my reluctance to scamper back there like some sort of runaway dog returning home years later just to show everybody what he'd dug up.

"Cap'd love this, you know."

"Ha."

"He's still there. I see him now and then."

"Can't say I run into Cap much these days."

"Lucky man. McGhee's okay, I guess. Until you get to know him . . . "

We both laughed.

"Okay, I'll see what I can get out of this and give you a call. You be at home?" Lanny had his pencil back down off of his ear and was holding it out to me.

"Yeah, sure. I might be going out later but I'll wait for your call." I took the notebook from my jacket pocket and tore out a sheet of paper. "Call as late as you like." I handed him the sheet with my number.

"I'll show you out."

"You'd better."

I went back and grabbed the now somewhat-lighter box and followed Lanny through the doorway to the front room. We walked back out through the lavender door and into the hallway.

Again I began the work of dodging the low-hanging pipes.

"Yeah, I see McGhee," he said as we walked. "You know they're still calling me up every couple of weeks or so. How long has it been? Paperwork stuff, just to sign off on this or that. I've forgotten about all of it by now. Every last one I'd signed off before, but it seems like anytime somebody pulls out a folder to look at it they need me to sign again before they can put it back."

"Quite a web they're spinning down there."

We walked the rest of the way in silence until we reached the bottom of the concrete stairs. I could see Lanny fishing a lighter from his jacket pocket.

"I'll walk out with you."

He opened the door and stood against it. We shook hands.

"Thanks a bunch, Lanny. Call me."

"Will do."

It was totally dark. I had to hold my watch up to the orangish lamp illuminating the parking lot behind the building in order to read it. Six-fifty-five.

I got into my car, a blue-and-white Plymouth Valiant, slid the box onto the passenger seat. Waved at Lanny standing there having his cigarette as I pulled away.

The Valiant's above-average reliable, I'd say. Gets nearly twenty in town. Came with a busted eight-track and AM whose reception is poor but intelligible. If not intelligent. Though chances are I'm probably not listening to people complaining about gas prices or the Giants much tonight, the hyper buzz of my own thoughts making enough static to keep me occupied.

Okay, say twenty minutes to go from the lab through the Village and back over to First, past Stuyvesant, past the hospitals and the U.N., before getting off and over to my place, a one-bedroom in this brownstone over on Fifty-first. Ten more minutes to find a spot, this time all the way the hell down toward St. Patrick's. Plus the walk back. I get to tell all this later is how come I remember it.

Can't be before seven-thirty when at last I'm climbing up the wooden staircase and into the living room of my third-floor apartment. I put the box down on the burgundy coffee table and remove my coat. Drop keys, notebook, and the photograph on the table there next to the box.

What else? Loosen my tie. Over to the kitchen to open a large can of pork-and-beans. That, three slices of white bread, and a can of Pabst and my stomach stops its grumbling. Open a second can of beer and over to the stereo. Real careful now as I let the record-player's needle fall somewhere amidst those rattles there at the start of *Sketches of Spain.* Have to step lightly back over to the leather chair in the middle of the room if I don't want the thing to skip. Sit down and pull the coffee table over. Set the can on last Saturday's *Times* laying there folded on the table beside the box.

Just as I took up the photograph, the phone rang.

"Yep."

"Luh-herch!"

"Russ, what's up?"

Russ, of the Saturday morning crowd. Russ only called for one reason. In fact, prior to then, I couldn't have told you the first thing about the man calling me other than he had some sort of job with the City. I remember talking benefits with him once and him telling me how he manned a desk down at City and Regional Planning. No shot whatsoever, but could jump a mile. Absolute maniac on the boards.

Anyway, the what's-up. Strictly rhetorical.

"Just wanted to let you know, we got a group headin' over for a little mid-week session. Eight-thirty. We got at least fours. You in?"

"Thanks, Russ. Can't do it tonight, though." I looked at my watch. Eight o'clock, straight up.

"No prob. 'Bout time you came out, though. Saturday?"

"You might see me."

"D-o-o-o-o it. Later, dude."

"Later."

I put down the receiver and looked at the picture again. Definite craftiness there. As if it were the photographer and not herself who had been captured. I turned it over and skimmed the back. Carefully-penned numbers in blue ink above; the doctor's hurriedly-styled office address underneath in black; my one-word contribution to the side in red. I thought about how the Show Place never closes, but I had to wait for Lanny's call. I'd go later. I slid the photo inside the front pocket of the black notebook.

Some moisture had collected on the outside of the can, and as I scooted forward to grab it the damn thing slides through my fingers and spills, missing the folded newspaper completely and foaming up all over the table. I whisk the box away quickly and set it on the floor by the chair, a couple of pieces of newspaper escaping up through the opening between the flaps as I did. I uncrumple one and am starting to sop suds with it when I notice McGhee's contorted mug, his fat face all screwed up like he's got a mouthful of chaw and no place to spit.

That's when I finally took a gander at those papers.

Next couple of hours I'm reading through them all, doing the Memory Lane business as I supposed whomever it was delivering the stuff had been inviting me to do. That is after I got a sponge and cleaned up properly.

What a mess that was.

# CHAPTER FIVE

# THE LONG AND THE SHORT OF IT

And here we were a couple of months away from the fifth anniversary with the case still in the open file.

Which actually isn't such a deal. Anything that far gone is usually out of reach.

The real mystery, as far as I was concerned, had always been why Mickey and I had been there in the first place.

Truth be told, it never should have been our business. See, Mick and I were beat cops. Upper east side. Both of us still at least a year or two away from making plainclothes. From becoming detectives, I mean, where one normally gets assigned to that sort of investigative duty. If that's where we wanted to go. Which later on Mickey did, as a matter of fact.

Stake-out stuff, then, was normally reserved for the upper graders. Not us uniforms. Like most precincts, ours began patrolmen walking eight-hour tours in uniform, rotating shifts every week.

Rotating shifts? Just what it sounds like. Work first shift five times, get seventy-two hours off, come back and do third, get your seventy-two again, then its second and seventy-two and then you're back where you started.

To be explaining that. That's some real edge-of-your-seat stuff, there.

By the way, the L-thing on the record-player's set on auto, so that's side one playing, over and over. Miles broods. Exhales, expands. Inhales, retracts. That through all this reminiscing business we're doing.

Anyway, like the record repeating, that's about how it was for me those first three years. Had my regular beat which I walked alone. A little after I'd started, Mickey came in and he too walked a separate though now and then overlapping beat. Summer of '70 we get paired up and start going out together every other week, driving what was essentially an extended loop including what we both walked. Call it a buddy system or whatever you like. What happens is every uniform gets to know a certain area, establishing something of a presence there, then shares what he knows with a beat partner.

Of course, well after I'd gone, the City started going overboard with this idea of establishing presence. A few months before, there had begun a push for one-man patrol cars. Which to me had a panicky sort of odor to it. And which I don't have to tell you didn't sit too well with the PBA, as I had been reading about in the previous Saturday's *Times*.

So while it's true, then, that Mickey and I weren't partners in the same way that upper grade detectives were, it was also true we'd worked with each other more than with anyone else. We had each of us been used singly as small-time plants here and there. And we had several collars between us. So when McGhee came to us it wasn't like we're talking completely out-of-nowhere.

Still it was pretty damn out of the ordinary for a captain, no matter how paranoid he might have been, to take two men out of uniform and put them in an unmarked car outside of a shack like that and keep them there the way he did.

The guys in our Homicide Zone had been working the Peters disappearance pretty much since the beginning, and they had managed through a series of interviews to connect Henrietta to the Rocca girl. Apparently, even before her vanishing in mid-October, two months before, the nineteen-year-old, yellow-haired Henrietta Peters had done a pretty fair job developing a reputation in certain circles as a girl who liked to party.

Better than the state senator knew, one would've imagined.

With Barbara Rocca, however, we're talking more than just reputation. Besides a couple of wrist-slaps for solicitation, there had been a coke possession rap the previous winter, though she'd either beaten it or had gotten it suspended. Whatever it was, the incident didn't exactly inspire her to throttle down, if you follow. This all courtesy of some mishandling of evidence somewhere along the line. That is to say, it's not because of the girl's innocence she gets off. She'd also been linked to several others who in their cases hadn't shared Miss Rocca's good fortune when it came to judicial lottery. And who had some things to say.

Somewhere in there Homicide had gotten ahold of a pretty-faced delinquent named Christina Salvadori, a friend of Rocca's, who had news about this meeting, that Rocca was set to hook up with some unspecified person or persons at the east Harlem shack sometime after ten o'clock that Thursday night. This is middle of December. 1971. Meeting to happen on the sixteenth, I think it was.

This was something of a breakthrough, because even though they had started to put Peters with Rocca, the Italian girl had managed to keep herself pretty scarce during the preceding weeks. Chrissie even passed along the make and model of a van they'd last been seen in. Or at least Miss Rocca had been seen in. The theory was, or so it was told to us, that this meeting was with suppliers. And the hunch to go along with the theory was that Peters would be there, too.

Shaky, but solid enough to check out. McGhee's second hunch, though, the one that put me and Mickey there, I never quite got that one.

Again, we get a story. What was true and what was just to get us to go along, well that was what we had all those hours in the car to think over. Fact was, at the time anyway, the idea of us going out on this held a lot of appeal for both Mickey and myself. Break from the routine, right? So maybe we weren't questioning it like we ought to've and instead just took it as it came.

There was some genuine pressure on Cap to get moving. Pictures of Henrietta in the paper every other day. Radio, TV, the whole bit. Official statements tacked up all over the place, not just from the state senator's office but from other government officials', as well. I'm thinking McGhee's thinking it's time to get creative, and so when he tells us how he didn't want to use Homicide for the plant, I'm nodding right along like I'm following. Said he thought chances were better for Mickey and myself not to be recognized, which should've seemed odd given that the Homicide dicks hadn't gotten close enough to see anything or anybody anyhow.

But there we were. Mid-afternoon Thursday we pull into position about a block-and-a-half from the shack and start waiting. And waiting.

From the city pound they'd secured us this scraped-up, butterscotch-yellow Mustang convertible with wide black stripes running up the sides. Seats slid back okay but didn't recline really, which didn't bother Mickey but was just this side of torture for yours truly. Arctic out, as well. Single digits, I think it was. Anyhow, once we'd settled in, it wasn't dinnertime before we started speculating about Cap's intentions. Probably onwards about eight or nine when Mick started playing out the idea that Cap suspected a fix.

Neither of us knew it then, but it had happened that several times during the previous six weeks Cap had found himself closing in on Peters's whereabouts only to discover too late that he had been a step behind. And I guess in retrospect you could tell something was up, even if Cap kept it private. Mickey thought Cap felt more than just snakebit, that maybe he had an idea somebody was making things hard for him. So when news of this East Harlem rendezvous came back, rather than following it up through the expected channels, Cap calls an audible, sending us out to the shack. Homicide he sends out after the van.

This is what we're talking about while we're waiting. And waiting.

Beat cops bring meals, refill thermoses, and spell us occasionally to visit the Port-a-Let a couple of blocks north. Meeting time comes and goes. Cap radios to wait, hold your positions, men. The thing might still be brought off. Night turns to morning. We don't talk for hours at a time, but neither of us gets any real sleep. Morning to afternoon. My legs not quite cramping yet, but my neck one big crick. Now we're hearing the meeting might have been pushed back twenty-four hours. The ten o'clock hour again passes uneventfully. As do the next four. Cap is all we talk about.

Finally word comes that the van had been found abandoned along the L.I.E. We waited something like forty more minutes for Harding, the uniform

supposed to be walking that section of the east Harlem beat. He finally showed
and we got set to go in. This about three-thirty, early Saturday morning.

Harding remained out in front, perched cat-like on the hood of his
vehicle, radio in hand, while the two of us sidled up to the dilapidated structure,
all four knees and ankles going snap-crackle-pop as we went. Mickey took the
front entrance, while I hoofed it through the jungle of weeds and ivy around to
the back.

As I tried to work the lock through clouds of my own breath, I
remember looking up and seeing through the back door window Mickey doing
the same thing in front and for a moment thinking I was looking in a mirror. I
think I even held up a hand just to make sure.

Come to find out Mickey wasn't jimmying his way in at all. He had a
key from the mailbox and was standing there in the living room when I had
finally crashed my way into the back foyer, slapping my head against this already-
broken overhead light fixture as I entered. My needless handiwork, incidentally,
would not go unnoticed by McGhee and the Internal Affairs guys he'd managed
to round up to review our conduct later on.

The small house was dark and cold and seemingly uninhabited.
Unsurprisingly, there was no electricity. There was nothing particularly eerie
about the place upon entering, other than the extreme cold. Just an old,
apparently-vacated junkie shack. Later, others would find in one of the
furnitureless back rooms several hillocks of metallic ash, the detritus of smoking
heroin heated on tin foil. Some other paraphernalia strewn about as well. A few
plastic straws, pieces of spoons and so on. I remember standing there in the
foyer looking at the ripped wallpaper, gaping swaths connecting small holes in
the walls. Not a place for living. Rather, a place where people came to kill
themselves.

Looking up at Mickey looking back at me, I stepped forward and felt
my foot sliding across the linoleum floor. I looked down at the several, winding
coils under my feet and remembered first thinking it mud from around the steps
in back. As if I were following the trail of an escaped wheelbarrow presently
hiding inside the house. But I figured it out.

"Hey Mick," I began.

"No, no . . . ."

Mickey's all animated, and I can hear moving around and him cursing in
the front room. Now he's disappeared. I can't see him.

Like that my heart's pounding. Chest, ears, all over. I remember
unfastening the snap of my holster. When I pressed the base of my hand against
the handle, I notice my hand's tingling and getting cold like its numbing up.

Little by little, the sound of Mickey's verbal convulsions begin filtering
through. I tiptoed through the kitchen and minding my once-bruised forehead
ducked into the front room.

Well, while I'm all worried about hitting my head again my big feet get caught on this unfastened shag carpeting and I stumble hard and loud into the room, catching myself just in time to keep from crashing into Mickey standing there with his back to me and facing the couch along the front wall. That's when, still frozen in this awkward-looking position like I'm reaching down to pick up something, I finally see why it is Mickey's cursing.

Henrietta Peters's unclothed body lay heavily on the couch, her face unnaturally buried between the cushions, her hair swept forward off of her neck. Her arms were bent back behind her, hands resting on her back, and one leg pointed out, oddly suspended over the floor. Her skin was bluish-gray, almost translucent.

"Fucking Cap I can't fucking . . . ."

Mickey suddenly stopped and sort of half-pivoted toward me like he was going to say something, his head still pointed downwards. Without looking up he started muttering. I couldn't hear, so I sort of leaned toward him, still eyeing the cold-stiffened body. A voice loudly responded over Mickey's radio, startling me, which in turn startled Mickey, who quickly moved away from in front of the couch to answer Harding. I took a step forward and bent down into a crouch.

There were a number of these strange little contusions on her shoulders and back. Like little stars. Or diamonds. Weird-looking, like the body'd been repeatedly poked with something blunt. Could've been brass-knuckles, the kind with the metal points.

Mickey walked back over.

"There's some blood back there," I indicated with a thumb.

"Where? What?"

"In the . . . in the back there. All around." As Mickey started back to investigate, Harding banged through the front door, causing us both to jump.

"Just called it in," he piped. "Not good, fellas."

"No shinola, fella," Mickey called back.

Harding looked over at the couch.

"Jesus," he mouthed quietly. He started to cough.

Mickey was saying something in the back. After looking at the body for a moment, Harding followed in the voice's direction. I stood up and surveyed the entire body once again.

*She* had looked like a bone. One big, broken bone.

Despite the unusual bruises, the Office of Chief Medical Examiner would report death as having been by asphyxiation. The coroner's autopsy report would corroborate the M.E.'s findings. Days later, toxicology would determine that Peters indeed had had traces of cocaine in her system, confirming the state senator's suspicion that her disappearance and death had been drug-related.

Which, when you look at the long and the short of it, did produce something positive, I suppose. Meaning all of these anti-drug programs and parent support groups and the Henrietta Peters Foundation and all that.

Yet, of all the post-mortem consequences and discoveries, the only one that really mattered was what the coroner finally decided to put down under "Time of Death." If he was to be believed, and I still don't see any reason why he shouldn't, Mickey and I had arrived at the shack at the most four hours, and at the least one, after the moment Henrietta Peters had stopped breathing.

Exhale.

Player clunks and clicks. Its arm waves back over the spinning disc. Stops over the outer groove. Poises. Lowers. Again, the rattles.

Inhale. Now, blow.

Other week somebody told me he lives right over on the west side, near Riverside. Never leaves his apartment. Still brooding, I guess.

The long one, the "Concierto," I could hum you that beginning to end, do all the voices, all the different characters swimming in and out of one another, joining together and pulling apart. The short one, though, that "Will O' The Wisp," the one that ends the side, that one always escapes me somehow. Wiggles away.

I walked over to the kitchen sink, poured a glass of water, and drained it. The stove-clock read ten-ten. Night still young, as it happens.

I grabbed another beer and returned to the chair beside the coffee table.

I picked up the phone to call Lanny, but again I realize after I've wedged the thing up under my ear that I didn't have the lab number. I rang the general operator, got connected to the university operator, who maybe was bored and unlike happened in the afternoon tried unsuccessfully to connect me before she gave me the number to try myself.

The number seemed different than the one I had dialed before, but I tried it anyway. Twice. No answer.

I thought about Lanny's new speaker system and decided I'd drive on down. Maybe stop at Show Place on the way back.

Again use the Saturday *Times* as a coaster, leaving the half-empty can on top of it. Stand up, big yawn. Stretch my arms up above my head and touch the ceiling.

All right.

I folded up the papers and crammed them back into the box and reclosed the lids. Put on my topcoat, tightened my tie. Put the notebook in my inside pocket, took up the box. Turned off the record-player and lights and left the apartment.

Walking west on Fifty-first toward where I was parked, I watched out of the corner of my eye a trio of men having a spirited discussion up and across the street. The group seemed to pause as I passed, though they didn't seem too interested in acknowledging my presence. Nor I them, for that matter.

They resumed. A high-pitched voice seemed to communicate incredulity with the proceedings. A husky-voice offered unaffected sympathy in response. Two cars passed. A third car approached, a squad car, scattering the conference in a cloud of profanity. I recognized the driver to be Fred Huffington. He came in a year or so before I left, and I knew he'd had St. Patty's on down to Bryant Park for some time now. One grade-A goldbricker, Huff. At least he was when I'd known him.

The trio had reassembled by the time I reached the car, and were now speaking in calmer tones. I opened the trunk and set the box inside. I figured I'd keep it with me, since somewhere down the road, maybe even that night, I'd be taking everything downtown.

I got in and pulled away from the curb, circled around and got headed southward, toward the lab.

Once I got out onto Second it wasn't long before I notice I got a little squarish pair of lights that seem to be changing lanes right along with me. Still there when I turn onto Thirty-fourth. Waiting a couple of cars back at the light to go left with me down Fifth.

Soon my mind's more on the rear-view than the road, and I'm calculating whether I want to lose this creep or invite him somewhere where we can dance. I take a left without signaling and he's gone. Then he's back, though now he's timid, keeping a little further back like maybe he's hoping I'm still ignorant. I know I don't want to take him to Lanny's, so we do a little unscheduled sightseeing, first taking it down to Chelsea then circling around and back up the Avenue of the Americas to see what the Empire State Building looks like all lit up.

As we weaved back by MSG and then headed west, toward the river, I'm starting to sweat a little thinking about the package and the old newspapers and everything. Not to mention how uncanny the whole ride was feeling. To be the mouse and not the cat, I mean. Hundreds of times it had been me doing the following. Whether before with Mick or here lately where more often than not I'd be tracking the comings and goings of unfaithful spouses from afar. The former would usually end in a garish display of lights and sound. The latter, a phoned report to the client, soberly dictated.

Neither helping me predict with any confidence how this was going to turn out.

Now whether it's because I'm nervy or impatient or some combination of the two, I'm getting a strong urge to meet my new friend. I gun the Valiant and make a hard right without braking, then wait. The lights come bucking after me. Now he's gotta know I'm aware. I take it slow as let him see me turn back east onto Forty-second, then floor it once more before skidding to a stop and getting out of the car there just up from the Port Authority.

I stood under a streetlight as I watched the lights approach from the left. It was still warm out and adding to the heat were a ton of folks milling all around where I stood waiting. He looked like he was slowing down, like maybe he was thinking about taking the bait.

About three hundred yards or so away he floors it, recklessly dodging a slow-moving sedan and right past the spot where I was standing. White Trans Am. Red pinstripes, black bird draped over the hood, and so on. As it passed, I saw the back of a sandy-haired head in the passenger's side turning away from me. Local tags, though it swerved back over in front of the sedan before I could catch any of the number.

I pulled out my notebook as I moved over to the sidewalk. I wrote as I walked, the many pedestrians pouring from the theaters parting to admit my passage upstream.

# CHAPTER SIX

# ONE LUCKY DOG

Time to cool off. Get off the road awhile. Let someone else play tag if they wanted to. Like I said, the night was warm. Mid-fifties maybe, and as I walked toward the theaters the moisture in the air was rubbing a blurry haze on all the neon up ahead.

It was probably quarter to eleven or so when I walked into Fun Sandwich. Heads intermittently rose and fell, trying to catch a glimpse of this oversized, dark-suited man walking through the glass-doorway, his arrival incongruously announced by the faint ring of a tiny, copper bell above the door frame. A second ring said the door had closed behind me.

I walked on in and tapped a stool with the notebook, exchanging nods with the man behind the counter on my way to the public telephones along the back wall by the cigarette machine.

"Coffee, Sal?" I gestured with my head back toward the stool as I walked.

"You got it."

Took some effort to wedge myself up into one of the booths and finger out two nickels from my pants pocket. I dialed the operator, this time asking not to be put through but taking down the university number myself. Hung up, retrieved the coins and redeposited them, and for the third time that day dialed the university's operator.

"University."

"Put me through to Pathology, please?"

"Hold one moment."

Long wait. I'm tracing along the gilt-edged frame of the booth's outer window with the Flair. The voice returned.

"I'm not getting an answer, sir. Would you like that number?"

"Please."

I write it down. Definitely not the number I'd dialed before leaving the apartment. I pressed down the lever and released it, dug out a dime and inserted it, then dialed the new number. Nothing. I pocketed the coin and dislodged myself from the booth. Walked back to the counter without incident. Either they've gotten their rubber-necking out of their system or I'm already old news.

Actually what's really happened is some joker's chosen the "Fun Sandwich Theme" selection on the jukebox, like you didn't hear it twenty times a day anyway, and as I shuffled over to the counter the loud, mostly drunk group in front started bopping along, laughing and singing and from all appearances really and truly enjoying their sandwiches.

Doo-doodle-doo-doo . . . Fun Sandwich.

Aaaaaaaaahhhhhhhhhhh . . . It's FUN!

Doo-doodle-doo-doo . . . Fun Sandwich!

Sticks in your craw right there By Mennen. Every time I hear it I feel like I'm in the middle of some sort of psych job, getting tested on how well I'm able to function when this thing whose imprint has already permanently altered usual brain fluctuations starts a-throbbin' like its picking at an old wound. Aaaaaaaaaahhhhhhhhhhh . . . .

Sal wards off a full-on conniption by sliding a steaming mug in front of me as I sit down heavily on one of the red stools.

"Black?"

"Yep."

"Doing okay tonight?" Little paper hat cocked to one side.

"Pretty good, pretty good."

Sal nodded and walked away.

I slid the notebook into my jacket pocket and lifted the cup. Blew over the liquid's surface, the reflected light coiling in response. Crowd up in front finally chooses to settle down, become a little more constructive with their lives, all getting jobs down at the car wash, working at the car wash, yeah.

I rubbed my forehead and my hand came back all moist and it's only then I realize how much I'd been sweating. I undid the knot in my tie and pulled it through, rolling it up and cramming it down into my pants pocket. I unfolded a paper napkin and started wiping dry my forehead and the back of my neck.

"Work . . . Work . . . Work my fingers to the bone . . . "

My head's already turned toward the door when the little copper bell rang again, the height of its pitch enabling it to sail over the noise below. Again all the diners at Fun Sandwich took turns popping up out of their booths to see who had arrived, and so for a moment I'm kind of lost in the crowd there, unnoticed while I stare at Fred Huffington's short, spiky orange hair.

Walked in with his square head turned to the side, talking to another uniform, whom I did not know. About five feet away Huff suddenly looked up with his mouth kind of half-open and seeing me there at the counter awkwardly twisted it into a half-smile, half-grimace.

"E-e-evening, Dick."

He stepped over to where I was sitting and we had us a nice, perfunctory handshake.

"Late night, eh?"

"You could say that." I'm sort of half-turned on the stool there with the coffee cup in my left hand.

"Anything cooking?" Before I could respond, he held up a hand. "You don't know Larry, do you? Dick Owen, Larry Bowers."

As the two of us shook hands and nodded, Huff began informing his beat partner of both my former and current professions, his account probably more tactful than detailed.

"Got out on your own, huh?" Bowers offered amiably, letting go of my hand. I sort of nodded in the general direction of his frosty-looking crew cut and tried my best to keep smiling.

"Why don't you join us, Dick? We're just grabbing a bite here."

"Sure, for a minute."

I carried my still full mug over to a booth with Huff while Bowers stayed behind to order for the two of them.

"Big man. What's the word?"

"Not much. Keeping busy."

"Almost too warm for coffee, wouldn't you say?"

"This weather's crazy. How you been?"

"Okay, I guess. Kind of feeling a little bit screwed over by this agreement they're talking about handing down. You follow any of this?"

"I think I read something about it. You're PBA, Fred?" Shaking my head as I ask.

"Naw. Was gonna at first but now I'm glad I didn't. Multitudinous hassle, know what I mean?"

"I hear you, man." I heard him okay even if I was only half-listening.

"Between you and me and the, uh . . . and the ketchup bottle here, we'd be in a hell of lot better shape if it won't for those Gracie Mansion guys. The City's using that stuff, now. Tell me why I have to work six-day weeks just to make up for these guys?"

Huff's boxy face gets this real choice-looking shade of sirloin when he gets hot, which he was there describing the union woes I think I might have alluded to earlier.

I'm not saying I knew the whole deal, but I can flesh it out a little. The union, the Patrolmen's Benevolent Association, had just come to this tentative agreement with the City over a whole mess of things. The skinny being the cops were finally going to see some back pay they'd been owed as well as start enjoying what was being called an improved work schedule. Along the way were some demonstrations and whatnot, including a bunch of off-duty officers creating a major league ruckus and getting themselves arrested back in September out in front of Mayor Beame's.

Anyway, this agreement they had worked out included the officers who had been charged with misconduct at the mayor's getting some sort of deal or at least a fair shake when it came time to face the music. Meanwhile, as part of the compromise, everybody was getting ten or so extra shifts a year.

Bowers returned with a tray bearing sandwiches and drinks. Young guy, no more than twenty-two, I'd guess. Smiling like a kid out late with big bro as he efficiently unloaded the tray. It's fun! Sat down and started wolfing it while Huff kept right on talking.

"They talk about turning it down and letting it go out to an impasse . . . "

"Arbitrator?"

"Yeah, what they call an impasse panel, but I don't think they will. Weaving and the bigwigs are afraid we'll get shafted worse than we already are. They're telling us that this is a deal."

"Tired of weaving on it? Weaving back and forth . . . ?"

"What? Oh, yeah. Right."

Huff finally looked down and acknowledged the little plastic basket they give you your sandwich in and slid it closer toward himself. Bowers, wide-eyed but obviously only half-interested in the conversation, continued chowing down.

"What's the story on the one-man cars?"

"Oh, Christ. Don't get me started. They might go through with it, you know. I wouldn't put it past 'em. You know Woolley?"

"No."

"Talking about the spreading us out like that, one to a car. The thinner blue line, he calls it."

We both chuckled. Bowers reacted by looking up from his crumbs, still smiling through a private reverie of bread and thousand island.

"That's what it boils down to, Fred."

"Don't I know it. Hell, already working a skeleton crew as it is. Hey, Larry. You think you might round us up some napkins?"

Bowers put down his drink and nodded. Huff leaned over his still untouched sandwich.

"I didn't want the kid to hear me saying this. He's heard me complain enough already to write a book about it. Things are getting bad, Dick. Guys packing it in, getting the hell out. You, my friend, are one lucky dog." Hairy-knuckled finger pointed at my chest.

"What are you talking about?"

"I'm talking about being your own boss. I envy the hell out of you, man. Setting your hours, working when you want to . . . "

"Yeah, well . . . "

"No, I mean it. You're in charge, man. You *are* the man."

I looked up from my coffee and scrutinized Huff's hot-red, well-fed, satisfied-looking face as he leaned back in the booth. Bowers returned, setting about forty napkins in the middle of the table. Huff took one and nodded at his partner.

"Not schleppin' around like Larry and me, chasing punks at all hours."

"I do my share of schleppin', Fred."

I set the cup back down in its saucer with a soft clink. I was starting to get weary of the impromptu reunion and especially with listening to Huff's troubles.

"So you didn't say before. What's cooking? You ain't in here just to listen to the choir, are you?" Huff lowered and pointed his head toward the front of the diner. "I do hope you're charging enough to be out at this hour."

"Hell, no. Hey, I saw you guys a little while ago. Out my way, midtown."

"Oh yeah? When was that?"

"Just now. 'Bout forty-five minutes ago, I'd say."

"Huh."

Huff turned and scratched behind his ear. He finally took up his sub and bit into it.

"So what're you following a hot lead?" Grinned facetiously through a mouthful of bread. What a question. Bringing to mind my morning pow-pow with Pinocchio.

"You might say that."

Difference is Huff couldn't pay me enough to answer him. No way I'm getting into it here. Only reason he's even asking is so he might find himself another reason to sit on his canister a little longer, anyway, I'm betting.

"What about you guys?" I looked over at Bowers, hands folded on the table. "Get to run the siren any?" I'm terrible. Bowers perked up.

"Naw, nothing special," said Huff with a sleepy look.

"Sounds like they had something at the university," Bowers eagerly interjected, darting his eyes toward his partner.

"Yeah, Dick, that reminds me. Where you been tonight? You didn't happen to be down at the university earlier, did you?"

"As a matter of fact, I was. At the hospital, anyway. What's going on?"

"When was that?"

"Dinnertime. Between six and seven."

The policeman kept chewing.

"Sounds like they had a break-in and now they've got a stiff at one of the labs. Glass on the steps. Body inside."

"Which one of the labs?"

"Why, you know something?"

"Which one?"

"I don't know. Just heard it before we came in." Painful swallow.

"Gotta go, fellas."

I stood up quickly and dropped a dollar on the table, both of the policemen looking up at me with identical expressions of concern.

"Dick . . . wait a minute, keep that . . . we don't need . . . "

"Later, Fred. Need to make a call." Said backing away. It'd been so long since I'd enjoyed the policeman's discount I'd forgotten there wouldn't be a bill for Huff and Bowers to settle.

"Dick, what's going on?" Huff leaned forward and loosely held my jacket sleeve between a thumb and forefinger.

"Nothing, Fred. Have to make a call is all. Good meeting you, Larry."

I moved quickly away from the table, unceremoniously lifting my sleeve up and out of Huff's grasp.

As I tripped the little copper bell, I could hear Huff's voice back over my shoulder as he finished informing his beat partner of both my former and current professions, his account probably more detailed than tactful.

I walked back toward my car. A light mist had begun to fall, though it had hardly diminished the sidewalk crowd still bustling about. A couple of girls had chosen the Valiant's hood from which to advertise their wares.

"Big fella," started the one with the red frightwig and brown-leather bikini top. The warmer weather had seemingly invited the freedom to be a little more direct as far as marketing goes.

"How 'bout a fun sandwich? Innersted?"

"Move it, ladies." I had out my keys.

"C'mon," said the other, whose long blond hair parted in the middle and tight yellow sweater was subtle by comparison. "It's fun."

I hustled into the car. They slid their hustle off my hood and back down toward the Port Authority.

The streets were busy, but traffic moved quickly. No one seemed to be following me.

My first impulse was to rush down to the lab, but sitting at a light near Chelsea I decided I'd try to call once more. And since I was close to the office anyway, I thought I'd call from there.

What am I thinking as I pull in front of the Wescott, as I walk through the large, glass front entrance and am waved through by the overnight guy manning the desk, as I pass through the moderately-lit lobby toward the elevators? Am I thinking about Lanny? About the white Trans Am? About Barbara Rocca?

Well, yes and no. Sure, these are the reasons why there's a little skip to my step, why that little fireball in my chest is starting to glow again, why I'm standing there bouncing up and down on the balls of my feet waiting for the car to come down.

But damned if I'm not catching myself half-humming, half-singing there in the empty lobby.

"Doo-doodle-doo-doo . . . "

The elevator doors finally sprung open. I stepped in and rode up in an unfortunate silence, none of the usual Musak there to save me from myself.

My floor was similarly deserted. I hurried over to the office door, unlocked it and pushed my way inside. I closed the door behind me but didn't lean on it, meaning it just rested there against the jamb. I walked over and sat on the desk and pulled the phone next to me, not bothering to switch on the lamp. I took out the lab's number and dialed it once more. It rang five times before someone, not Lanny, answered.

"This is the Pathology lab, who's calling?" Drawling voice tired, impatient.

"I need to speak with Lanny Williams."

"Who is calling, please?" The voice had changed considerably, becoming more articulate.

"Dick Owen. Listen, is Lanny . . . ?"

"Is Mr. Williams expecting you?"

"Yes, Mr. Williams is goddamned expecting . . . "

"Hold on."

I sat there uncomfortably in the darkness. Thought I might be hearing something moving in the hallway. Or maybe it was my pantleg swishing against the side of the desk. Like an idiot I start to wiggle my leg back and forth to see.

"Dick?" I immediately recognize the police chief's voice. "Marty Walton, here."

"Walton? What the hell's going on?"

"Dick, tell me something. You been around here tonight?"

"What's happening, Marty? Where's Lanny?"

"Dick, tell me, have you been here at the labs tonight? Piece a paper here with your name on it and . . . "

"Yes, Marty. Yes, I have. I just ran into Fred Huffington and he tells me there was a break-in down there. Is Lanny there?"

"Maybe you can come down here? Where are you now?"

"I'm at my office, Marty. Listen . . . "

"Maybe you should come on down here. Maybe you can help us out." If it was Walton's intention to piss me off, he was succeeding royally.

"All right, goddamn it. All right, Marty. I'm coming down there."

"Pathology lab. Meet you out in front, okay?"

"Yeah, okay, right. In front."

I listened until the line went dead before hanging up the phone.

I remember cursing as I slid off of the desk and moved quickly toward the door. I stopped and stood there with my hand gripping the brass doorknob and listened through the door to what sounded like footsteps in the hall.

Very slowly, now.

I pulled the door toward me, opening it just wide enough for light to start coming through the crack, a long slit of light shining on my face there, forehead to chin.

Feet shuffling behind me.

A sharp, hollow ringing sound.

# CHAPTER SEVEN

# THE SAP

First thing was I was wet. Damp seeping up and down the left side of my body, causing me to shiver and shake like one of those wind-up dinosaurs pushed over onto its side.

Next I have this idea like I'm rising up. And up. More like I'm climbing, really, up and off of the floor. I stand there with my chin against my chest and my teeth rattling inside of my head. A breeze blows through me, deepening the bone-chill. Which doesn't make sense indoors, but there it is.

Now I'm stepping backwards, falteringly, away from the body. Away from my body.

Then I see it for what it is.

The Peters girl. What looks like smallish, dark little dots crawling out of the little holes in her back, crawling down her arm, crawling in and out of her open palm and down the side of the couch and toward where I am standing.

I start to stumble backwards, feet all tangled, and I see these dots seeping toward me, surrounding the place where I stand. I open my mouth but nothing comes out but little clouds. I wildly shake my head and arms, trying to make whatever they are scatter, but they're frozen, not reacting at all to my flailing.

First one foot. Up, over. Then the other. Feet numbing up. Hands, too.

I step out of the circle and see where it is they're marching, back to the foyer, back over to where two men stand bobbing their heads and exchanging pleasantries.

"Yes, well you know that's the way it has to be."

"Yes, that's that."

"That's that, all right, and that's the way it has to be."

Mickey. In civs. A uniform stands next to him there on the torn-up linoleum imperfectly covering the area in front of the back door. The back door is open just a crack, admitting a slit of moonlight dividing the two men standing on either side. I step into the path of the light and they look up for a second before resuming their conversation.

"Aye, Captain say it passed that a-way."

"Cap. Aye, yea."

"Aye, Cap, the sap, and Captain say it passed a-way."

I'm still shivering, only now it's this scary kind of out-of-control shivering like I'm going under. I look down and see the dots getting bigger and more frequent on the floor around the pantry there to my left.

When I turn and open the pantry, the slit of light slides off of my body and falls inside, hitting the floor inside with a little pop and then all of sudden exploding, flooding the shack with blinding flash.

The three of us look at each other with wide, staring eyes.

The circuit breaker has been switched on, returning power to the house. Seconds later, a voice comes over Harding's radio, letting us know that the circuit breaker has been switched on, returning power to the house.

I start to get the feeling back in my hands and I let them hang there throbbingly from my wrists. My eyes adjusting to the glare, I squint and see that Mickey and Harding are looking down and pointing at my feet. I look down and there are my big black shoes, sloshing around in the middle of a shiny, four-foot wide pool of blood. The reflected light coiling in response.

I turned over, groaning. My back suddenly felt wet. Still groaning I tried without success to lift my head.

Rested a moment, trying to regather the strength in my neck muscles. My head felt like it was sitting on top of something, like I was wearing a helmet.

I blinked rapidly and found I was staring up into the night sky, small needles of rain pricking my face and hands. I rocked my helmet-head back and forth and licked my lips. Eventually I hoisted up onto my elbows, carefully balancing the weight I seemed to be carrying on top of my neck.

Eyelids still flapping, I managed to lean forward and with some effort look about the area where I lay. Pretty soon I recognized the shape of the block letters painted onto the dumpsters and figured how I'd been laid out there in the alleyway, beside the Wescott. I lifted myself up off of the pavement and pulled my body over to the brick wall and leaned up against it. I looked over onto the street, about forty yards away.

With a grunt I pushed myself up onto my feet and away from the wall and stumbled out of the alley, scaring the hell out of the young couple who happened to be walking by. I stood there a moment on the sidewalk looking around. The couple was it. I saw the Valiant and sort of threw my body toward it.

Falling forward, I landed propped up against the side of the car and waited a moment or two, still convinced that if I don't balance it just right my already-fat-and-getting-fatter head's gonna start toppling down off of my shoulders here any second. Instinctively I started feeling around for my keys. Nothing. I mean nothing. Pockets turned out all over. No keys, no wallet, no change. No Swiss army knife, no little black notebook with the picture tucked inside, nothing. I leaned forward and put my hands on my knees, and that's when I saw that the trunk lid looked like it had been raised up a few inches.

I walked around to the back of the car, keeping a hand out to steady myself. Lifted the trunk lid. There's the jack, the spare. An empty oil container. A basketball pump, no needle.

And no box.

I shut the lid and sat on it, the rain loudly drumming on either side of me. I held up my wrist and saw my watch was gone.

And yes, the goddamned Fun Sandwich song is gone, too. Though I'll thank you not to mention it while I'm in such a state.

I walked up to the front doors of the Wescott and standing under the canopy peered inside. The desk jockey, an old guy I knew by sight only, sat attentively at his post. I started to walk inside, but stopped when the building started to disappear. When it came back I leaned up against the doors and wiping my face tried to think.

A few cars pass. There's a siren, or at least I think there's a siren. I'm sure this is the sound of my head splitting open. Still sounds far off but I'm already seeing lights off to the right.

A second siren, the long curve of its wail chasing the first. I tentatively probe the back of my head and bring back blood.

I see the black-and-white rushing through my raised fingers. Siren's off now, but the lights are still flashing. I close a bloody fist.

I watched as the first squad car squealed to a halt before the Wescott, fishtailing just a tad there on the wet pavement. Driver jumped out, leaving the car parked catty-cornered behind the Valiant, and strode toward the entrance. The other uniform also got out and sauntered around the front of the car, a toothpick dangling from his lower lip.

Just as the driver reached the sidewalk, the second car appeared and skidded in behind the first, its siren off as well.

I stayed leaned up against the entrance, bent forward over folded arms, the reds and blues reflecting every which way off the building's glass doors. Clusters of gawkers, in groups of two or three, began materializing out of nowhere and began to wander over. No matter where you are, it seems, the flashing always brings out the moths.

"You Owen?"

Said the driver, a middle-sized, wide-shouldered man with attentive eyes and a dark, thick black mustache. Finger pointed accusingly toward the large, huddled figure nodding his head without unfolding his arms.

"That's right," I coughed. The cop started to shake his pointed finger up and down, his mouth open.

"Hang on, Louis!"

Marty Walton, chief of detectives, jogged onto the sidewalk holding one hand over his head while keeping closed his black and yellow raincoat with the other. He murmured something to Louis, who turned back toward his car, and stepped under the canopy, needlessly wiping his feet on the long, plastic doormat.

"Dick, what's going on?"

"You tell me. Here, take a look."

I made a quarter-turn and bent my head slightly, showing the bulbous, leaking gash to Walton.

"What the hell?"

"I got jumped, Marty. Right after we hung up. Someone in the office with me."

"Jeez, Dick."

"Might have been two guys." I swallowed, still feeling a little weak.

"Get a look?"

"Nah," I winced. "I think there was one in the hall. I woke up in the alley there. They took . . . ."

I began to rub the right side of my head, now and then exploring the round, warm lump on the top of my skull.

"Fucker sapped me pretty good. They took my keys, my wallet. Hell, I'm soaked, Marty."

Walton stepped forward and touched my left elbow, a gesture I immediately recognized as more professional than personal. I'm sympathetic, he's saying, and I know this is not the best time but, at the risk of sounding impolite, I have to ask . . .

"Dick, you know why we're here, right?"

I looked at Walton woodenly.

"You found Lanny?"

"You know about Lanny, then?"

"Dead?"

"That's right." Dropping his hand down as he said it.

"Christ."

I looked up from Walton's dangling hand and noticed Louis and his partner leaning side by side against the car door watching us. Again I look at my wrist before remembering my watch is gone.

"Dick, tell me. Is there anything you particularly . . . ?"

"When . . . . When did we hang up, Marty? What time?"

"It was . . . " Walton hiked up the sleeve of his raincoat. "Right about forty minutes ago, I'd say."

"Christ," I repeated.

"Dick, I have to ask you if there's anything else you want to tell me here. Or do you want to just wait?"

I knew what Walton meant. I closed my eyes and blew out, filling my cheeks.

"Not gonna tell me what happened, are you?"

"Tell you what?"

Now, if I was what you call the cynical type, I could see how I might be justified if I were to become a little less agreeable with the direction Walton's heading here.

Never mind what he's implying, which I don't have to tell you ain't at all flattering. I'm talking about his tone, his whole manner. Handling me like a suspect, sure, but also acting as though we'd never worked together before. Even like he might be enjoying this, just a little bit. If I'm more of a hardass maybe I'm cracking back, giving Marty some of the sarcasm his precocious interrogation seems to be warranting.

But you'd be surprised how getting your bell rung like I just had softens you up. What I mean is, at this point anyway, I haven't got the energy to feel sorry for myself, let alone get upset with Walton, who, after all, is doing just what he's supposed to be doing. No, I'll be honest, I'm just happy to be putting sentences together, here. I'm awake and talking and if you're talking back well then we're friends.

Besides. I ain't the cynical type, anyway.

"You're not gonna tell what happened at lab, I mean. To Lanny."

"No, not just this minute, Dick."

"All right. I understand."

Walton shook his head and looked off to the right, pretending to be interested in a vehicle slowing to survey the scene.

When I say Walton and I had worked together, I mean we were assigned to the same precinct and ran into each other in the halls and occasionally had cause to discuss a particular collar or case. More often than not, Walton would be sort of acting as the messenger between myself and another patrolman, passing on info. Like if you see a red Chevy Impala with the left tail light out in the area today, check the trunk. They might be starting a hubcap collection there. Or there was a break-in over at Gene's Guns on Eighty-third last night and there's some scope-rifles floating around, so keep an eye out. Or if you happen upon the Cubans hanging around the museum hawking what they're calling genuine Guggenheim replica plastic collapsable drinking cups, go ahead and confiscate their stuff since they've been warned.

But standing there under the canopy watching the chief sort of stare off at nothing in particular, I began to realize I never did know Marty Walton so well. In fact, this is about how it always was as far as our working together went. Him telling me the way it is, all the while looking forward to getting on to something else. Me nodding and listening and saying all right, I understand.

No, the sap hasn't gotten me nostalgic. I guess you could say I'm just looking for distractions, here. Trying not to think about Lanny.

Walton cleared his throat.

"Dick, we probably ought to . . . "

"Ask the old guy," I said, turning slowly.

"We'll take care of that, Dick. Don't worry. Right now, though, we probably should get somebody to take a look at that head. Is that your car here?"

I nodded over toward the Valiant.

"That there? The blue? I tell you what. We'll leave it here for the time being. We can take you by and get that looked at on our way down."

He kept on talking. I guess I could make up more stuff. Or you could. But I wasn't really listening.

# CHAPTER EIGHT

# OLD & NEW WOUNDS

By the time the sun finally rose early Thursday morning, all that unusual warmth which had characterized the first part of the week was gone. In fact, if I'm remembering right, it would turn out we'd seen the last of the warm days for quite a while. The overnight rain had ushered in a wicked cold front, with the accompanying cold temps settling in for the long haul.

Nothing like the chill, of course, which I anticipated when Captain William Kenneth McGhee finally came in to see me sitting there in his office waiting for him.

It was getting on toward five-thirty that morning when Walton finally invited me to leave the station, suggesting I go home and get some rest before coming back in to talk to Cap sometime during the day. I needed it. Unless you counted the forty-odd minutes in the alley, I was going on twenty-four hours without sleep.

I said no, though. Rather get it over with.

We hadn't made it down from the hospital until close to three a.m., by which time a suspect in the murder of Lanford Williams had already been plucked from a Washington Square bench and deposited in the station's holding pen.

The way Marty's boys were telling it, the journey from metal bench to concrete floor had apparently only briefly disturbed the intoxicated gentleman's slumber, the only real evidence of irritation at having his rest interrupted being the murmurs of disapproval he had uttered when a much-wrinkled lab coat with the words "Path" and "Williams" stencilled over the front right pocket was forcibly removed from his person just prior to his being dumped shirtless in the cell below.

While I was being seen in the emergency room, Walton had gotten the news about how they'd brought in the drunk. He didn't say anything to me about it as we rode in together, but I definitely noticed a slight shift in the chief's attitude. I remember us making some small talk about the Giants. The hapless Giants. Who were like oh-and-seven or something and had just that week finally broken down and canned Arnsparger.

But it really wasn't until after he had spoken with a certain Russell Davenport, who, much as I had suggested he would, had been able to confirm to the chief my whereabouts earlier in the evening, that I'd say Walton had finally let go of the idea of me as suspect. I guess all that agreeableness, however involuntarily bestowed, had had its effect. I was allowed to converse freely with Walton and the other officers concerning the evening's events.

As it happens, there was a hell of a lot to converse about.

It had been about ten-forty when a campus cop finally noticed a lower pane in one of the glass doors along the laboratories' front entrance had been smashed out. Creating a hole just about four feet to a side. The discovery of the body would come a few minutes later.

When Lanny was found, he still had on the lab coat I'd seen him wearing earlier in the evening. The investigating officers showed me the lab coat they'd taken off the drunk, which I confirmed as resembling Lanny's and as likely having been taken from the closetful of coats I had seen during my earlier visit.

Patrolmen were on the scene within fifteen minutes, and they had the M.E. from Bellevue there by eleven-fifteen. Apparently, Lanny had been doing some sort of testing for which he was keeping a close ledger that listed levels and the times at which he had taken them, significantly aiding the examiner in his estimation of time of death. His times had gone up to 6:06, stopped during the period of my visit to him, then picked back up at 7:22. There was a 7:29 and a 7:36. Then they stopped for good.

The corpse had already begun to cool by the time the M.E. got to it. That, along with the progress of the blood's clotting, caused the examiner to state that if it weren't for the ledger he might've been persuaded to estimate time of death as occurring even earlier, say between six and seven p.m. The entries' handwriting all matched up, though, and so he was encouraged to submit the victim had expired soon after completing the last entry, sometime between 7:45 and 8:15 p.m.

Other than the lab coat, nothing else had been removed from the lab. A small metal trashcan from the building's lobby had been found behind a bush outside the front of the building.

I reported to the investigating officers that I had indeed delivered the bone to Williams that evening, that it had been either brought to my office or mailed to me earlier in the day, and that the box in which it had been delivered had also contained old newspapers with articles pertaining to myself and to the Henrietta Peters case.

I explained how I had neither spoken to nor seen Williams since I had left him at his lab just before seven o'clock, despite several unsuccessful attempts to reach him by phone.

I also provided details about the car which had tailed me later in the evening, about the brief meeting I'd had with Officers Huffington and Bowers, and about the attack which had occurred at my office.

The Wescott's desk register was able to show who was in the building at the time I had been attacked. The Wescott is a big building, but around eleven-thirty that night it had been nearly vacant. Other than myself and my attacker or attackers, there were only four others on the premises. Two accountants, a lawyer, and his assistant. Closest one ten floors away. And all still around when Marty sent Louis in to check it out. No one had entered the building after I had. Nor had anyone left. Meaning I had to have been dragged out the back way, through the service entrance.

I explained how, along with the other items taken from my person, the box in which the bone had been delivered also had been taken from the trunk of my vehicle.

Finally, I expressed my understanding regarding the difficulty of the situation faced by investigating officers.

Especially considering that it was I who had unwittingly introduced the murder weapon onto the crime scene.

The door swung open and there was McGhee waddling through.

"Morning, Dick." Said amiably while closing the door. "Damn if it hasn't been a while. Good to see you, again."

McGhee removed his scarf and hat and advanced toward me, visibly tentative as he smiled and leaned forward with his hand outstretched, like maybe he was thinking I might not take it.

"Good to see you, Captain."

After sitting there waiting for nearly two hours, I'd forgotten all about the now-bandaged load I was carrying atop my skull, and so sort of lost my balance a little when I stood up to greet McGhee. The effect being a kind of overly-energetic pumping of the captain's hand while I tried to right myself. McGhee tensed up as I lunged forward, and I could see the distress in his eyes as we let go and he stepped past me toward his desk.

"Lookit, thanks for sticking around like this. You didn't have to, you know."

"Not at all. I wanted to."

"Quite a night last night?"

"Yes, it was. It was quite a night."

"How's that head?" McGhee removed his coat as he spoke.

"Okay. Stings a little."

"Hell of thing with Lanny. Good kid."

"Yes."

"You guys played ball together, right?"

"Off and on."

"Coffee?"

"That'd be great."

McGhee got up again and walked over and stuck his head out the door. He started to step back inside the room, then lingered there at the doorway to wait on the coffees. Between shrugs he swayed back and forth self-consciously, most of the weight of his short, wide frame being placed on the front part of his feet.

I remember thinking how it looked like the four years since I'd seen McGhee had been hard ones for the captain. His thin, combed hair seemed a little lighter, his jowls hung a little lower, and the wrinkles around his eyes and mouth looked a little deeper. What had once been the portrait of the classic curmudgeon having somehow become becalmed. Sort of an Ernest Borgnine quality, if you must have something to go by. Agitated impotence.

McGhee was fifty-five or so, getting on toward the time a person starts thinking about greener pastures. I knew there had been a time when he'd never have thought he'd be retiring still a captain, when he'd had ambitions otherwise. But they'd sunk along with the eyes in his sockets, and even though I knew that was his own doing, I couldn't help feeling a little bit responsible for having contributed to the weight that always seemed to be bearing down on the man's collarbone.

He was finally relieved from this awkward dance by two hands handing him a couple of styrofoam cups. He stepped back inside, the door closing on its own.

"You take anything?"

"No, black."

McGhee handed me the warm cup and set his down on the desk before closing the door. He walked back around the desk and sat down, appearing to adjust his chair as he resumed speaking.

"So, Dick, as we were saying, it was quite a night last night."

"Yes it was. As we were saying."

McGhee shrugged, and as his head bobbed forward and shoulders lifted up I was unsure whether the gesture had been induced or not. Time was I always knew. There'd be a difference in McGhee's expression when the shrug was forced, a certain detail which I couldn't presently recall. I knew I'd remember it soon, though, once I'd seen him do it a couple more times. The difference, I remembered having once explained to Mickey, was always the same.

"How you getting on, Dick. How's business?"

"Business is okay. How have you been?"

"Can't complain."

"That D.A. as good a guy as the papers make him out to be?" I began noisily sipping my coffee.

"I got no complaints with Sol Severin. He's a go-getter. He's a stand-up guy, though." He paused as if reassuring himself. "Yeah, I've got no complaints. Severin's no Mack McClellan, of course. Mack was a gem."

I nodded obediently, like I knew a ruby from a rube.

I guess I'd known McClellan about as well as any beat officer knows a district attorney. A couple of handshakes was all. Once at a funeral. The other at a Founder's Day parade where I was working and he was riding. Basically I knew him more by reputation than by any direct experience, and Mack's reputation had been as good as they come.

Town officials had loved him for his willingness to grease the wheels when the situation called for it. A master of compromise, and although some editorialists suggested him to be without convictions of his own, he always managed to give the impression that his decisions were heartfelt. The officers, meanwhile, also appreciated what seemed to be an unflagging loyalty to them, regardless of circumstance. McClellan had this well-rehearsed speech, practiced before many a luncheon, about how the shield had two sides, how the interests of those who serve and protect should in turn be served and protected. From a cop's perspective, McClellan practiced what he preached, often finessing even the most questionable overuses of force in order to bring about "a return to optimal efficiency" in the department, as he was often quoted as saying. And, of course, the people loved his "Call me Mack" approach to local concerns, condemned as lip-service by some, but praised as sincere by most.

"Severin's all right, though, you say?"

"Oh, yeah."

McGhee blew on his coffee and set it on the desk.

"He's all about getting it done. Stepped on a few toes, I guess. Seems to be pretty good at the PR side. The papers like him 'cause he uses big words. A real talker."

"Mack was a talker."

"Sure, yeah. Mack was a talker, too, but it was different with him."

We both sat and nodded as if waiting for the subject to evaporate along with the steam rising from our cups. Neither Cap nor I really wanted to discuss the art of talking to the papers.

McGhee raised the cup to his lips.

"You know, I had this crazy idea when they first told me, Dick. When they told me about the bone and all . . . "

"What was that, Cap?" Calling him Cap a signal, like no matter how forlorn a face you got on there, I'm willing to get up under your skin, if that's where you're inviting me.

"Well . . . how do I put this?" McGhee signaling back, you're coming through, loud and clear. "Lookit. When they called me up and told me about this bone, see, and how you'd said somebody had sent it to you and everything. Well, I gotta be honest with you. I had this idea come into my head like maybe nobody sent you the thing at all."

"Oh? Really?"

The cup shook a little and coffee dribbled down my fingers. Otherwise, we're talking extraordinary calm here.

McGhee continued talking down into his coffee.

"Yeah, you know, like maybe nobody had actually sent you that bone but that you'd gotten it some other way or something. Crazy, huh?"

McGhee turned up the cup. Sipping his coffee and watching for my reaction, both performed with care.

"How do you mean, some other way?"

"Oh, I dunno, I . . . "

"That I made it myself?"

"No, I mean . . . "

"That I mail-ordered it? Looked it up in a catalog and had it sent special delivery?"

"No, nothing like . . . "

"What then? What are you saying, Cap?"

McGhee swallowed hard and set the cup down.

"It's just too good, Dick. You have to admit that."

I sat back in the chair and wiped my hand on a pantleg. McGhee continued to watch me, his gaze now and again interrupted by a shrug. I relaxed a bit and looked up over McGhee's shoulder at the sky getting lighter and started cautiously touching the area around the bandage. I exhaled.

"You're right, Cap. It is too good."

I nudged a finger up under the gauze packing.

"There. You see where I'm coming from, here? I'm not saying that's what happened, I'm just telling you what was running through my mind."

"No, that's not what I'm talking about. Sure, a bone landing on my desk like that, that's something all right. What I'm talking about being too good is what happened to Lanny."

"I'm not following you, Dick."

"The story. From before. About the bone being used as a weapon. What's too good is somebody wanting to play it out, to make it happen. To show it could be done, and to make sure I knew about it. Even make it look like I was the one who . . . ."

I felt a little pricking sensation and quickly brought my hand down from behind my head while the two of us stared at one another for a few seconds. McGhee's shrugged his way out of it and looked back down, shaking his head back and forth. I waved a hand and set my cup on the corner of McGhee's desk.

"Don't make a lot of sense, does it?" he said.

"Safe to say. Hell, Cap, I don't know what it's about, either. All I know is somebody sent me the thing. I took it over to Lanny and then somebody used it to open his skull."

"Our friend downstairs."

I shook my head.

"Nope.  Not our friend."

"Right, not our friend, but . . . "

"No, I'm saying the guy downstairs had nothing to do with it."

"No?"

"No."

I leaned back.  McGhee sipped and spat.

"You'll see.  Wait until he sobers up 'n he'll tell you all about it.  How he woke up and the heavens had sent both the rain and a coat to keep him dry."

"Hell of a story.  Almost as good as yours."

I squinted at McGhee.

"Here's the way it went.  Not a break-in.  A break-out."

"What?"

"The front entrance was impassable.  They'd changed the locks and hadn't yet distributed keys.  When I went down, Lanny had to meet me at the back entry and walk me through to his lab.  A hell of a walk, I'd say at least a dozen turns.  Ten minutes, at least.  Maybe fifteen.  That's if you don't get lost."

"Okay."

"Now, when I get there Lanny's waiting for me at the door.  We go in and before the door closes someone follows us inside, through all of those turns, all the way down to the lab.  Where he waits.  Or they.  Outside."

"You don't hear this person?"

"Lanny's got his music up.  Covers everything.  We spend some time there in his lab, looking the thing over, then leave.  Lanny walks me out and sees me off.  Then goes back and the guy or guys are there, waiting for him."

"Go on."

"Now, my guess is there's no way in hell whoever it is goes out the way they came in.  The drunk'd probably still be wandering around down there, and besides, the hasty way whoever it was handled that bone seems to indicate a certain lack of patience.  Huff said glass on the steps, outside the front entrance.  The investigating officers said the same thing.  The pane's been knocked outward.  The can from the lobby outside . . . ."

"Why not the drunk, Dick?  Busting out sounds to me like the thing to do, given the situation."

"Check the coat.  All kinds of pockets on that thing.  Not a shard in one of them.  No chance.  The drunk didn't have a shirt, right?  If he's wearing the coat when he goes through that door, it's probably gonna have some glass on it.  If not, he'd have scratched himself to ribbons.  My guess is that coat left the building folded up under somebody's clothes, not on somebody's back."

I downed the last of the now-cold coffee while McGhee weighed what I'd said.  Starting to get riled, a little line forming there between his eyes.

"Hell, Walton knows it.  The guy didn't have any blood on him, anyway.  Not even his own."

A shrug, faked.  The line.  You see the line he's handing you a line.

"You sure did. When Marty got to you."

"What do you mean?"

"Nothing, I'm just saying."

"Saying WHAT?"

I slammed the empty cup on the desk. It bounced once before landing right in front of McGhee, rolling back and forth in a half-circle.

"Lookit, Dick. I have to say I'm glad you got that out of your system."

He reached forward and stopped the cup and turned it right-side-up.

"I mean the junior detective stuff, not the cup-tossing. That's why I wanted to talk to you in the first place. Seeing you're involved, you can't be snooping around this investigation, got it? You're a witness, Dick."

Shrug.

"At least."

I thought I sensed the wrinkles around McGhee's mouth working their way into a sneer.

"Just keep out of it."

"I don't believe this."

"I'm serious, Dick. Keep out of it."

"Keep out of it?"

"That's what I said."

I stood up to leave.

"Fine, fine. That's just fine, Cap. You're the boss, right?" I flashed a tired grin.

"Lookit!"

McGhee stood up glaringly.

"Right. I'm not your goddamned boss. But I can sure as hell relieve you of that license of yours, if I need to!"

He paused.

"If it's necessary, that is," he added. Unnecessarily.

"Might be a good thing, too, seeing how it seems to have gotten you that swell-head . . . !"

I kept grinning.

"No need for that, Cap. Someone beat you to it. Relieved me of all those annoying cards and keys and notes and everything else as well."

I quickly stepped over toward the door and opened it. Turned around and saw McGhee standing there looking at me with those same worry-eyes from before.

"Listen, Cap." I pushed the door to and moved back over in front of the desk. "I'll keep out of it. Okay? Let me know what's going on, though. You gotta know I feel awful about what happened to Lanny."

"Why'd you take the thing down there, Dick? What were you thinking?"

"I already told Marty."

"You tell me, Dick. Why didn't you . . . ?"

"Jesus, Bill."

"Why?" The disappointed Dad. Which Cap could pull off now and again.

I waited a moment before answering, further scrutinizing the look in McGhee's eyes as he turned them up toward my own. I could see the sincerity of his disappointment. In what happened to Lanny, sure. And in my decision not to have brought the thing down right away. But maybe also a little in himself regarding the way he and I had left things. Which, as he undoubtedly saw, had made my decision all the more understandable.

"I just wanted to make sure about it first, you know? Before I came back here with it like it was some damned trophy or something."

A slight nod.

"Well, you should-a brung it down here, first thing."

"Where is it now?"

"We've got it. Don't worry, we'll take care of it."

"Well, listen, you let me know. All right? You know where I am."

I stuck out my hand and McGhee grabbed it.

"Okay, okay . . . ."

Letting go, waving me out.

# CHAPTER NINE

# THE ORDER OF THINGS

One other thing McGhee said before I'd left, something in there when I said he was the boss and he said I ain't your goddamned boss.

"Let me clue you in to the order of things," he said. "You ain't the one in charge. In fact, if you'd wake up and take a look around, you'd see how you're the one being played in this one. Somebody's trying to pull your strings, trip you up. If you know what's good for you, you'll keep your big carcass out of the way and let us handle it and maybe you won't end up hanging yourself."

Something like that. I know he said something about my big carcass. And hanging myself. With my own rope, maybe.

I closed the door behind me. I could feel the blood rushing toward my crown, the spot throbbing in little waves as I walked. I resisted messing with it, though, and sidestepped through the several outer offices and out into the hallway.

If the City never sleeps, then it only makes sense that the City's PD doesn't either. All that stuff about twenty-four-and-seven is for real. Which it should be. Though standing there watching all of the stenopool ladies and the other first shifters shuffling their way in to take up their positions for the day, if you didn't know otherwise, you might guess this was any other office building, readying for another day of business.

The precinct is housed in one of those old, stately buildings that have the stairs in front and the offices extending back toward the inner part of the block. I maneuvered through the hallway and stepped out onto another, perpendicular hallway which is in effect the third floor landing.

Out over the staircase, against the front wall, are these enormous, majestic-looking wooden-framed windows, basically a row of narrow panes around twenty feet tall and every one of them topped off with little triangles. If the panes were colored, you'd think you were in church. Standing out front with all the strips of sunlight filling up the huge space there over the stairs and against the wall, damned if it doesn't look like the building's waking up, despite what I was saying about knowing better.

Now there's a couple of reasons why I'm taking the time to notice all of this. One, I hadn't been inside the precinct for years, and so the whole time I was there I was taking everything in right alongside my former recollection of it. So maybe I'm appreciating the way that east façade gets all brilliant-looking a little more than your average visitor might do. But that's only natural, right?

The other reason, though, is because once I'd left McGhee and gotten out onto the landing and leaned up against the wooden railing, I was sort of half-remembering that I had meant to do something else before I left the station.

That's about when a short woman dressed up in a mint-green pastel business suit crossed in front of me, nodding hello before disappearing through the door and into the hallway from which I had just come.

I remembered what it was. I eased myself down one flight in search of Mickey Rowe.

Once I'd gotten down to the second floor, I went into the hallway and sort of weaved on back toward the back part of the precinct, toward the large open room they called the Officers' Area. The trip back was relatively generic, but when I ducked into the large room there I was again, turning back onto Memory Lane.

More than anything it was that acrid smell. That sharp, cringe-causing blend of cigarette smoke, stale coffee, and human sweat which permeated most of my recollections of precinct life causing me to stop a second and stand there with my hands on my hips to look around.

The Officers' Area had definitely changed. The main thing was they'd brought in all of these movable partitions, each about six feet high, covered over with this pencil-lead colored fabric and irregularly placed all over the room. Completely altered the whole feel of the place. It used to be all open. You could curse somebody from clear across the space, fifty, sixty feet away, if you wanted to. Now they had it all blocked off and divided.

The whole set-up reminds me of these special units they keep coming up with, things like the Senior Citizens Robbery Unit and whatnot. No, the senior citizens are the ones getting robbed, not doing the robbing.

Although maybe by now they got one for that, too. See what happens is you got precincts right next to each other who don't ever know what the other's doing. They end up having to create these units to bridge the divide. So if there's some pattern of crimes going on in one precinct and the same thing's going on next door, they got some way to get together on it.

I stand there a little while, taking in the new decor. Wondering if they've gotten around to establishing some kind of special messenger unit here in the Officers' Area. Making sure these guys know what the hell's happening on the other side of the partition.

Thanks to the little gray walls, I couldn't tell if the arrangement of the room was the same or if they'd scattered it somehow.

My memory of it went something like this:

The front right corner was reserved for high volume turnover, with a small coterie of desks being shared by beatwalkers, traffic ticketers, and the like. The middle aisles they filled with persons engaged in lengthier forms of record-keeping and report-writing. Including clerical staff. Strategically placed here and there to facilitate the completion of such tasks. Then, over on the far left wall, you had the lower grade detectives. Along with what you might call the station house's provisional aristocracy, meaning the several divisional heads who intermittently got rotated in while on their long journey through all of the department's many precincts.

Standing up on my tiptoes I could see down into the little cubicles but I couldn't tell who was what. I guess it didn't matter anymore if it made sense to me.

But I did kind of wonder about this cantankerous-looking figure to my right. In uniform and seemingly without any papers or anything to engage his attention. Sitting all solemn-like at the desk there along the front wall. The sentry-looking one.

Why am I wondering? Because as far as I was concerned, the Officers' Area's greatest asset had always been the fact that it was just for officers. I'm talking about the conspicuous absence here of those who served as the precinct's real aristocracy, from whose offices I had just come. The higher-ups, so to speak. Meaning the captain, the division chiefs and sergeants, the detective sergeants and so forth. Those more directly responsible for the precinct's day-to-day operation and who themselves answered directly to Mayor Beame and all the other beams shining down from above.

Someone had decided somewhere along the line that it would be best for all if these guys did their governing from afar. That someone being a friend of mine, whoever it was. Of course, everybody had an opinion about it, but none could really argue with the fact that physically separating the managers from their minions increased the efficiency and morale of both.

You might say, then, given my already lukewarm review of the new order, I wasn't all that surprised when, having started to step over to the side of the maze where I thought Mickey might be hiding, I heard a voice calling me back.

"Looking for something?"

I lowered my head and turned around to go talk to the gatekeeper, sitting there with his arms folded and looking up at me like I've got two heads.

"Yeah, maybe you can help me out. I was hoping to talk to Mickey Rowe?"

"Rowe, you say?" He leaned forward and curled his arm around the base of his phone on his desk, pulling it toward him.

"Yes, Rowe. Detective Rowe."

"And you're . . . ?" Doughy-face turned up on one side, this look like maybe he's left his hearing aid at home.

"Name's Owen."

"Owen?"

"Owen," louder.

"And what is this about, Mr. Owen?"

I exhaled, too tired to mask it, and he read my impatience. I tried to relax. I put on an empty little smile and held out my hand.

"Don't think I know you, do I? Name's Richard Owen . . . I used to work here. In this room, in fact."

He took my hand and quickly released it, pushing his cap back onto his forehead.

"Oh, did you now?" Impassive. "Name's Kendall. Nice to meet you, Mr. Owen. You know Detective Rowe, then?"

"That's right. We had a beat together for awhile. I thought I'd try and catch him, if he's around."

"Well, I tell you what. Rowe, he ain't here anymore."

"What do you mean?"

Kendall looked up at the brim of his cap.

"Upstairs. You could try up . . . "

"Mickey's upstairs? At a desk?"

"That's right. You go up and talk to the lady there on the right as you go in, she'll tell you where he is."

Kendall sort of vaguely pointed as he spoke. Then quickly brought back his hand down, scooting his cap back down like he was anxious to get back to whatever it was he did in there.

"I thank you, sir."

No need for a second handshake. I turned and left, went back down the long hallway to the landing, back up to the third floor, back through the door and over to the wraparound counter-type desk behind which sat the lady in the mint-green suit from before.

"Good morning," she said.

"Hi, there. Tell me, is there a Maggie Seddon who works here?"

You see, earlier, when I saw this woman in the hall, it was Maggie she'd brought to mind. Maggie of the Officers' Area, with whom Mickey and I had often worked and who was a permanently shiny spot there burning through my shadowy remembrances of the precinct.

"She sure is, she's next door. To the right."

"She's up here, too?"

"Excuse me?"

"Nothing. Thanks." I pivoted back and forth. "Oh, also . . . "

"Yes?"

"Is Detective Rowe in? Mickey Rowe?"

"I can check for you. Do you have an appointment with Detective

Rowe?"

"No, I . . . "

"Actually, you should probably talk to Margaret. She should have his schedule."

"I'll do that. Thanks."

I followed to where I had been directed and pushed wide the already-open door with Maggie's name on it. There was no one inside, so I stepped in to wait. After a moment I walked over to look at the pegboard attached to the file cabinet next to Maggie's cluttered desk, every inch of which was covered with pictures and children's drawings.

Full of fatigue, I leaned forward and with hands on knees studied a small picture of Maggie with her face upturned, smiling and sitting on brick porch steps. Little Ali MacGraw in there, possibly. Same eyebrows. In the foreground, a boy and girl had their mouths open, each with a fistful of the other's hair. Her own hair, curly and black with a few, silvery flairs visible in the sunlight, surrounded one of those genuinely pleasant, rosy faces which make the rest of our mugs look even more bleak and suspect.

I must've stood there a pretty good while, looking down into Maggie's piercing brown eyes, remembering how Mickey and I used to say they should've had Maggie interrogate suspects, since those eyes made lying impossible.

I realized I hadn't even thought about Maggie for four years.

I reached over and lifted up the bottom corner of the photo, revealing a little Reds pennant underneath. Thought I detected a nice, lilac smell coming from somewhere. Suddenly something was touching my side.

"Reach, fella."

I stood up quickly and turned around.

"Maggie!"

We exchanged a cordial hug.

"Great to see you, Maggie."

"Judy said there was a giant after me. I had a feeling."

"You trying to make friends?" I lifted up the photo and pointed at the pennant.

"Oh, you better know they've been letting me have it," she laughed.

"You're from Ohio, right?"

"You betcha."

"The Big Red Machine . . . "

"That they are. How have you been, Dick?" Maggie pointed toward a plastic chair against the wall and I moved to slide it over.

"Good, good. You look great, Maggie."

"Please." Maggie held up a hand as she sat down. A concerned look flashed. "Hey are you okay, Dick? Look at that head."

"I'm fine. Need some sleep is all."

"Do you know about Lanny Williams?" One hand over her heart, the other flat on the desk.

"Yeah, actually, that's what I was here about."

"I can't believe it." Maggie looked down and then back up. "Don't tell me that bandage there, that's not . . . that doesn't have something to do with Lanny? Does it?"

This is why they've got Maggie working upstairs.

"To tell you the truth, Maggie, that's one of the things I wanted to knock around with Mickey."

Maggie shook her head.

"Mick's graduated, I hear?"

"Moved up about six months ago. The little guy belongs in an office, you know?"

"That what he wanted?"

"I think so, yes."

"When did you move up here?"

"About a year . . . when was it? A year and a few months."

"I was downstairs earlier. Hardly recognized it. Hey are these yours?" I pointed at the hair-pullers.

"Heavens, no. My nephew and niece. Uncontrollable."

"Cute."

We both looked at the picture in what grew into a melancholy-like silence. I'm thinking what's-his-name? Hank? Has his own business, electrical contractor or something. Hal.

"Still with Hal, I hope?"

"Oh, yes."

"He's doing okay?"

"He's doing great. Talks about retiring a lot these days. The golf has gotten out of control. Now he's talking about going out for the senior tour."

"He that good?"

"He's good, but I don't know."

"Well, it sounds like he's having fun."

"That he is."

Another pause. I was starting to fade.

"Mick's not in yet, but I know he's got a meeting first thing . . . you want to leave a note for him?"

"That'd be great. You think Mr. Big Stuff might be able to make time for me?"

"Don't be silly."

"I know, I know." Maggie handed me one of those pink 'While You Were Out' pads and a pen, and I left Mick a short note asking him to call me at home when he got in. I handed the pad and pen back over the desk.

"I'll take care of this," she said.

"You take care, Maggie." We both stood and I bent forward and kissed her cheek.

"Will do. Go get some rest, now."

I thanked Mags and left. Nodded to Judy on my way out.

Moving down the stairs, a step at a time, I finally gave in and did what I'd been thinking about doing ever since I'd left McGhee's office. I reached up and nuzzled my finger up underneath the bandage and started scratching real hard the area around the broken skin. Already scabbing up. Felt a little like bark under there.

On the ground floor I hiked up my topcoat sleeve and again looked at my empty wrist. Spotted a hallway clock on my way out which said eight-oh-five.

Walton had said something about a ride back to my office, but by the time I'd gotten out with McGhee he was long gone. Besides, I had to go home first to get the spare key, anyway, which was only a dozen blocks or so. So I hoofed it.

All right.

So now I'm walking along like this with all those sights and smells from the precinct still running around there in my bumpy noggin'.

Cap had his moments. In his prime was probably as mean a cuss as there ever was. Drove to distraction some of the more stable personalities I've had the chance to know.

What few of the other patrolmen were aware of, though, was the man could be right human, despite all the effort he put into dissuading folks of it. McGhee was something of a family man. Flew model planes or something. Would talk Knicks with you sometimes. A reader, too. Paperbacks. Detective stuff, actually. In fact, now that I think about it, that was part of what Mickey built his theory on in the car that night, this idea that Cap's suspicion of a fix came from his reading too many mysteries.

Yes, the captain could be a right amiable guy, if you caught him just right.

As it happened, whether there be some reason for it or it was just dumb luck, I had been one of a very few working under McGhee who hadn't endured first-hand the brunt of Cap's hair-trigger temper. And I sort of knew there in the back of my mind somewhere these relatively good graces between Cap and myself might have had something to do with him choosing Mickey and me for the Peters plant.

So Cap and I'd had our run-ins, sure. Nothing along the lines of the blow-up that would precipitate my surprise leave-taking, though.

I could tell right away things had changed when I went in the Monday following, Monday before Christmas it was. The good morning without looking up. Every sentence choked up inside of all these perhaps and even thoughs and nevertheless. Not to mention enough shrugs to at least place down at

Club Paradise's Friday night dance-off.

Even if assigning us had been unusual, which it had been, the post-op, that was procedure. Any special assignment warranted this sort of formal follow-up. But Cap's unhappy misfire over the phone early Saturday morning, along with my own non sequiturs at the scene, basically ensured our meeting would be anything but routine.

This ain't something I've wasted much time replaying in my mind, by the way. Like I mentioned before, I'm none too proud of it, and so I suppose you could describe this little trauma as one of those scenes the subject has consciously repressed, even to the point of having lost some of the particulars along the way.

Doesn't matter. Basically we're talking about a failed deal, here. Sort of thing you take to an impasse panel. He wanted something from me, I wanted something from him. Neither party in the mood to bargain. Probably because of all the bargaining each party had been forced to do separately for the three days prior. Smoothing over the foot-in-mouth business from before.

Once McGhee finishes all his preamblin', the thing finally starts for real when I ask him for an explanation of why officer Rowe and myself had been assigned in the first place, a request which McGhee refuses flat. Didn't want to talk about it, past history, water under the bridge, what have you. My motives not the issue, here, he says, stubbornly steering things away from his own bone-headedness and toward what everybody was hollering over, the so-called "theory."

Cap, speaking for the department he says, has to insist I publicly retract statements made regarding the strange markings upon the Peters girl's body. By then a few other things had come out. Such as how there had been at least one other person's blood found at the scene, blood which in fact matched Barbara Rocca's type. Along with some strange, hard little fragments on the pantry floor and in the kitchen. Little blood-stained chips or something. I'd even found a couple on the sides of my shoes later.

And while it was true, continues Cap, that Henrietta Peters's body did appear to have been beaten with some sort of pronged instrument, perhaps a cane or even some sort of metal object, such as a retractable pointer, the girl had choked to death and there's no two ways about that. And it would be best for everyone involved if Officer Owen would go ahead and issue some sort of public statement owning this was indeed the case.

Thing was, the theory wasn't mine to deny. What the reporter wrote was not what I had said. Besides, I explained, what benefit was there to be had from me coming out and taking back something no one believed anyway?

I had said something about the "distinct possibility" that the Rocca girl had been there. In fact, I had said a lot of things. Too much really. Nothing, though, that wasn't true. Responding to questions put to me, I did naively let slip that there was a lot of blood inside of the shack and that it looked like whatever it was that happened in there had taken some time to perform.

But this guy, this Moloch or whatever his name whose by-line it was, he wanted a story to tell. Once I'd given him the basics, he starts in about cults and sacrifices and so forth and its obvious the guy wants to hear me sing Helter Skelter to him. Hyped up by the state senator angle, this character thinks he's Ernie Pyle or something. Witness to war, and its atrocities.

So, in your opinion as an investigating officer, are you saying there was a "ritualistic" quality to what you found in there? Was this an example of what you fellows call a "professional hit"? Is it your impression, then, that dismemberment was a possibility? Did the markings on Miss Peters's body look as though they held any symbolic significance? How might the killing and/or killings function as a response to the state senator's recent statements regarding attacks on his character? To his position on defense spending? Inflation? The deficit?

All right. Maybe I'm exaggerating it a little bit. Like I said, my memory of it ain't exactly crystal. But you get the drift. It was a lot like those taste-tests they're always doing on TV and at the A&P. Basically asking you to answer a question about something you've never thought twice about before. To form an opinion where you never had one to start with.

Or that card trick, the only one I know, really. Pick two suits. Diamonds and clubs? Leaves hearts and spades. Pick one of those. Okay, you picked spades. Now pick seven spades. You took 2, 3, 4, 6, 8, jack, and king. That leaves the ace, 5, 9, 10, and queen. Pick three of those. Chose the ace, the 10, and the queen. Pick two. All right, ace and queen. Pick one. Queen? That leaves the ace.

You think you're picking it, but it's been picked for you.

Okay, voices are starting to rise, fists are clenching. I'm not budging, though the deeper we get the more I realize that by default I'm standing there arguing for this craziness, this thing that never even occurred to me before I'd read it along with everyone else in the Saturday afternoon edition.

I'm not saying I bought it, but the more I refuse to take it back the more it's mine.

Circumstances dictated several possibilities, I argue. No other ideas had been brought forward to explain the bruises or the extra blood or the fragments. Why rule out one interpretation before measuring its probability against others?

McGhee's response was to suggest impolitely that I had already had my chance to play detective and that now was the time to let it go. Not at all unlike the way he sent me off an hour ago, actually.

So I propose a trade.

If McGhee would explain to Rowe and myself why he'd assigned us, I'd make the statement. Cap, though, still speaking for the department, said he couldn't do that. Kept right on speaking for the department, before long suspending me right then and there. And so . . .

Things were said.

Things were thrown.

And Richard Owen was on his own.

A bitter breeze beat against my cheeks. About halfway home I felt the bandage start to flap up and down against the back of my head. Two-thirds of the way home I tore it off and carried it crumpled in my hand. Three-fourths of the way home I did my part to Keep Our City Clean, banking the sticky ball of gauze and tape off of a pole and into a trashcan.

In the little brick alleyway that runs underneath the brownstone I stopped at my mailbox and took out a dirty key ring containing spares for both my apartment and the Valiant. I walked up and after wrestling with the key in the spring lock for a few seconds let myself in.

The place appeared undisturbed. The half-can of beer still sat there on the Saturday *Times*. I threw the keys on the coffee table and sat down hard in the chair.

In my mind I was trying to piece together the story I had told McGhee, my explanation of what had happened to Lanny. Only this time without his interrupting. I'm trying to make the connections clearer, to make more plain each turn from one sentence to the next. Trying to pick out of the noise that tom-tom I think I hear thumping along behind me and Lanny.

Pretty soon I was asleep there in the chair, dreaming of pipes.

# CHAPTER TEN

# RESEMBLING A ROUTINE

I ducked, snapping awake at the sound of the phone ringing beside the chair. I carelessly lifted the receiver, bumping it against the side of my head.

"Yep," I croaked.

"O-wen! Good morning, sunshine."

"Mick! You bastard . . ."

"Going in late today, Mr. Lazybones?"

"Fuck you," I grinned. Scooted forward in the chair and damned if my knee doesn't bump the table hard enough to make the beer can tip. Turning slapstick, here.

"I heard about last night. You probably need the rest."

"Moving up in the world, I hear?" Mopping foam with the paper.

"You could say that. I bought a second tie the other day. Dick, I can't talk now. You free this afternoon for a bite?"

"Yeah, great. Mickey, I got some things to run past you."

"How about we try this place, the Giant Egg Roll? Right near here, on Lexington."

"Sounds fine."

"Four-thirty?"

"See you then."

I stretched and yawned and up from my lungs escaped this deep, gutteral noise ending in a just-about comical fit of wet hacking. What comes from snoozing in the rain.

Got up and walked over to the kitchen sink and spat. Filled a small, green pot with water and set it on the stove to boil. The clock over the stove read a few minutes after eleven. Head still heavy, but I'd live.

I rubbed my sandpaper chin while the water boiled, my thoughts going back and forth between last night's shenanigans and what I thought I might try to get done before hooking up with Mickey. Whenever I tried to think about something from the night before, such as whether or not what Lanny had got might've been meant for me, my head would throb a little. Rather the road than the rearview. Much easier to fix upon what lay ahead, such as locating a clean mug or a dimple on the countertop in which to balance an egg. Or walking to the office after eating, looking up Dr. Morgan's office number, and ringing him about getting ahold of another picture to replace the one I'd lost.

I scooped a heaping tablespoon of instant into a medium-sized mug and plugged in the toaster.

Was debating with myself just how much I'd need tell Morgan. Whether, for instance, it was necessary that he know exactly how it was the picture and I had parted company. Or, more importantly, I know, whether to own up and let him know how maybe I ain't exactly the one you call to round up runaways.

I filled the cup with steaming water and set it back on the stove. Several droplets landed near the burner, evaporating instantly.

Recalling Morgan's elusiveness regarding how he'd been put in touch, I wondered if maybe I had some leeway, here. A creative license of sorts. I scratched my head. Nice little baby-tortoise-shell going back there.

Selective communication with a client was bad policy, I knew.

I slowly lowered the egg into the boiling water with the spoon. It cracked instantly, a soft, delicate trail of white solidifying and circling the oval as it bobbed and spun just underneath the water's surface.

I ate standing over the sink. Undid my shirt and lumbered back into the bathroom.

In there's a small, foot-square mirror unreasonably bolted to the wall, either by the super or a previous tenant, right about neck-high for yours truly. The inconvenience of this thing never crosses my mind but for the five minutes a day I need to use it. Gives me two choices, either dip my head down and peer up at a foreshortened version of my face, or awkwardly squat, a hand on the water heater for balance, to get a straight-on look.

Neither way do I look any better, so I decide to shave. Plugged the sink with the black, rubber stopper and opened the hot faucet.

I decided to tell Morgan the truth. About the sap, I mean. Not the rest of it. Maybe I'm being stubborn, here, but I don't want to do it. I don't want to be referring the doc out to a specialist.

What? Hey, this stuff is starting to interfere with the story, I'd say. If you must know, the detective shaves like anybody else. Up and down, sides and cheeks. Continue by swiping blade over familiar contours of chin and neck. Squat. Squint into now-steamy glass. Reapply foam to chin, neck, and under each jawbone.

Rinse. If necessary, repeat.

Which reminds me. Could be getting interrupted so rudely the night before is what's invigorating me here, making me more desirous to get on with it. Or Cap, that junior detective jibe, getting my dander all up. Or that smirk from the photograph, looking up at me like it's a dare. Or even the doctor's fretful puss, saying to me here's another shot at the Peters girl, another chance to save a kid from herself, only this time without having to negotiate with a bunch of peers talking at you in code as you go.

There were a lot of reasons why I should keep on it.

I pulled the plug. Wiped my cheeks and ears with a washcloth. Ran cold water and waved a hand under the tap, clearing the sink of those thousands of little, peppery hairs stuck to the sides of the sink.

I felt much better.

I quickly put on a new shirt and tie, set the dishes in the sink, and grabbing my coat made to leave. Hesitated a moment over the damp newspaper and overturned can, admiring my work. Nice little makeshift castle with shallow moat there in the center of the burgundy table. I slung my topcoat over the chair and hurriedly grabbed up the fortress in my hands, depositing the drippy mess in the trash under the sink. Quickly ran a sponge over the table and tossed it backhandedly from the living room and into the sink where it landed with a loud clatter. Lifted up the coat with a finger and hurried out the door, locking it behind me.

We're only talking a mile and a quarter or something down to the office. So there I was, back on the street, walking a beat. Dodging the doo-doodle-doo-doo that inevitably occurs every thirty feet or so of sidewalk. Cringing at the cold. Felt like the wind was whipping right down into that hole in my head.

On the way down, I stopped into a Manhattan One branch office where, after some less than friendly conversation with the manager there, who, as he explained, was regretfully bound by a policy requiring photo identification for all transactions, a teller who remembered the tall guy was a share holder thankfully stepped forward and facilitated my withdrawal of one-hundred and fifty dollars in small bills.

The Valiant was still parked where I had left it, right in front. Had to smirk a little when I noticed a small yellow piece of paper flapping underneath a wiper blade. Ignoring it presently, I walked past the car and ducked into Magdalena's where I grabbed a *Times* and a coffee in one of those large styrofoam Spirit of '76 cups. They're still trying to get rid of those, I think.

The Wescott buzzed along like nothing special had been dragged out of there the night before. As I moved past the desk and through the lobby toward the elevators, several suits criss-crossed in front of me. I tried to disregard the familiar feeling of being surrounded, all these scurrying shysters winding their way from office to office, seeking legalistic loopholes through which to provide escape for their clients.

The system needs to be tested, was my understanding of their understanding. Its strength can only be discovered in its subversion. I joined the group crowding into the elevator.

The sound-system was back on, a duly-chastened House of the Rising Sun softly humming its cautionary tale to no one in particular.

"Have you been in an accident?"

At first, I thought maybe there'd been a commercial interruption of the elevator's usual programming.

"What?"

"You've got some blood, there."

A small man in a blue business suit pointed upwards, behind my ear.

"Oh? Thanks. Had a bump before."

The man looked down and straightened his suit.

"Probably dangerous up there," he said.

I acknowledged the man's comment with a half-smile as I passed from the car and onto the seventh floor landing.

The floor was busy. As I approached my office, I realized I didn't have a key. Looked around a moment, sort of smiling and nodding pleasantly to passers-by as I reached down and slowly tried the knob. It was unlocked.

I nudged open the door about a foot wide and looked around for any uninvited guests before stepping through. I pushed it to, then leaned against it hard with my shoulder to close it, feeling a little jolt on top of my head as I did.

In my head, too.

There'd been no scratches on the jamb or beside the knob. If there were air between the door and the frame, they might've loided the lock without leaving any marks. But there wasn't. That door fit more snug than a Times Square hooker did her halter. It was like they'd had a key of their own.

Quick once-over. No indication that anything unusual had occurred in the room. The desk had been slid slightly back from its usual position. Could have been I hit it on the way down, or it was moved when they transported me from the office. In daylight I could plainly see where someone might have hidden, where someone must have hidden, there in the corner beside the file cabinet. There was a slight trickle on the back of my neck.

I dabbed at it with my right hand and brought back a colorful mess. With my head tilted forward, I walked over and set down the coffee and the paper, lifted the desk by the edge and carefully pulled it forward, walked around and took a seat.

Foraged through the desk for a while before finally finding an old tissue. I did what I could to stem the tide while I paged through the *Times*. Looking for though not expecting to find mention of the attack at the lab. I sipped at the coffee.

There's Carter, big smile as he Pledges Aid at Garment Center. Garment center? Hey, why not? Having secured the all-important nude vote, the candidate now wishes to ensure the clothes-wearing public he's there for them. Who said he was the tooth fairy? Still shame-faced about the *Playboy* interview, "in which he discussed lust in earthy language." Right. If we must discuss lust, our terms really should conform to standards of propriety.

Ford, meanwhile, is Seeking to Cut Links to Watergate. Surely the headline he wanted. Adding to the fun, while Carter's sorry about appearing in a men's magazine, it looks like Ford's sorry he didn't. So say the magazine's editors, anyway. Apparently only the President's schedule and publisher's deadlines stood in the way of a lusty Republican rebuttal.

The Yugoslavs say they don't like being a debate subject. Complain they were brought up in the debate "in a typical American way, completely sudden and very superficially." I'd read on, but time is money. Moynihan Enjoys Slight Edge Over Buckley. Not a good time for incumbents. Being Unopposed Doesn't Lessen Task Ahead, Says Peters. For most incumbents, I should say. His reelection already in hand, Peters'll be putting in appearances in the City all of the way up to next Tuesday. Speechifying, doing what he can for the party.

Suit Over Pothole Pays $408,000. Victim's right knee joint had fused, leaving her leg permanently stiff. Mental note to dive headfirst into first available pothole. Severin Announces Support of Tentative Accord. This regarding the City-versus-PBA situation. No surprise there, I'd say. I'm sure the D.A. wants to get back to something at least resembling a routine. Elderly Bronx Residents No Longer Feel Safe Along Pelham Parkway. Daylight Savings Time Ends at 2 a.m. on Sunday.

Checking the blotter. Grim stuff. Forty-two-year-old man with long record of arrests for various crimes stabbed to death in hallway of his upper east side apartment. Two elderly men dead on apartment living room floor in Washington Heights; one woman, semi-conscious, in back bedroom. Had probably been several days. A caseworker trying visit last Friday was refused admittance by the woman. Teenaged boy found hanged in the Trinity Cemetery. Thought suicide, but no note. Car accident at the Thirty-fifth street overpass of the Brooklyn-Queens Expressway in Jackson Heights. Brooklyn narcotics dealer found shot fatally in his Milford Street apartment by an unknown gunman who fired four bullets through the door.

Nothing on Lanny. Not surprising, given the hour the campus cop finally came by. Might show up in the afternoon edition.

The Knicks are 3-0, their Best Start Since 1969. Ailing Namath Unlikely to Play Against Bills. Maybe he could sue the City as well for what it's done to his knees. McVay Takes Over As New Giants Coach. Listen to Kotar going on about Arnsparger's firing. "Maybe if I had caught that pass," speculates the halfback, "that five-yarder on our first series Sunday, we'd have made a first down and wouldn't have had to punt and maybe we'd have had a long march and scored." And maybe the Cowboys would start losing and maybe we'd get a streak going and maybe land a wildcard and maybe win the Super Bowl and maybe elderly Bronx residents could feel safe again on the benches at Pelham and maybe we'd get some decent candidates for once and maybe . . . .

Wait, though.  Forget all that.  The City is Having its Own Election!
Linda Lovelace for President.  See her razzle the elephant.  See her dazzle the
donkey.  Or how about *UP!*, a Robust American FUN Movie!  If you don't see
*UP!*, you'll feel down . . . .  There is hope, however.  See You at Check-In for
*Naughty Nurses II*.  Twice as Naughty, Twice as Nice.  Or, if you want the Best
Acting Ever Seen in a Porno Film, try *Sex Wish* . . . .

I'm reminded I need to get over to the Show Place, and so I set the
paper aside and pulled the directory over.

I finished the now-tepid coffee as I flipped through.  No gastro.  Tried
Physicians, then subheading Private, then Special.  Bingo.  Harold D. Morgan,
M.D.  Morningside Drive.  I dialed the number.

"Dr. Morgan's office."  The chipper voice sounded glad I had called.

"Hello, my name is Dick Owen.  I need to speak with Dr. Morgan."

"I'm sorry, Dr. Morgan is with a patient right now, Mr. Owen."

"Oh . . . I see."

"Can I take a message, Mr. Owen?"  Chipperness becoming homey
becoming downright familiar-sounding.  It must be Maggie I'm thinking of, I
thought.

Figuring discretion would be appreciated, I simply asked that she let the
doctor know I had called and hung up.

I scooted back and again opened up the desk's wide middle drawer.
Amidst broken rubber bands and one uncapped Bic was a small, medium-sized
red notebook with the plastic peeling off the spine, exposing the metal binding.
There were a few dozen sheets of filler paper inside.  I pried open the rusted
rings of the notebook and closed it back, pinching my pointer as I did.  The Bic
still bled, and so I managed to scratch Dr. Morgan's address and phone on the
first sheet.  Dropped the pen inside my coat and closed the notebook.

Thing wouldn't fit in my coat pocket so I stood up and slid it as far as it
would go down into my back pants pocket.  I turned toward the window and
again tucked a finger under a blind to look at the street below.

A light rain had begun, and several umbrellas were out.  Not the
vendor's, though.  He'd moved on, probably gotten impatient and decided to try
it up a block or two.  Shouldn't move around so much, I thought.  Stick it out,
let them get used to the sight of you.

Otherwise they won't notice you.

# CHAPTER ELEVEN

# PULLING BACK THE CURTAIN

Time to check out the doctor's story.

Obviously, I'd rather be snooping around down at the University, but I figured it best to wait until after I'd had the chance to talk to Mickey. See what the day turned up. For the time being, then, I'd be abiding by Cap's restriction to leave it alone, to let the department handle it, to go back to my own job. Which at this particular moment late Friday morning meant riding on up to the Show Place and finding out what I could regarding the girl with the gap-toothed smile and her budding movie career.

Now, if you want to be simple about it, this is what I do. Check out stories. No real formula, of course, since everybody's story is different. But yeah, there's definitely something similar in how I'll approach the thing.

Just about always, the story is missing something. Sometimes the teller knows it. Says listen, I know something's wrong here with the way my wife's been acting, go find out what's causing it. Sometimes they'll leave something out intentionally, either because they think it unimportant or because they want to be covering up something they know will make them look bad. Like oh, by the way, maybe I do smack her around now and then, but that's not what I'm hiring you for. Other times they've got no idea anything is missing, they think they've got it all figured out and are hiring me because their lawyer or somebody suggested it was a good idea. A business transaction, something along the lines of I'll pay for your report now so I don't pay alimony later.

So I check it out, and the way it ends is with me telling the story back. Sometimes it is the same damn thing only with some notes added here and there, fleshing out what the client already knew to be the case. Yep, you had it right, buddy, she's out there right now fitting you for a pair of horns, good luck in court. Sometimes it's a complete turnaround, a total rewrite of what we started with. Like surprise, she's ain't trysting the night away, she's got her a lawyer, too, and it looks as though you're about to get smacked around yourself.

That might be little more satisfying for me. You know, being able to dig in and find something that wasn't necessarily on the surface.

I get paid the same either way, though.

I left the office and went down to the ground floor to get another key from Art and to talk to him about what kind of timetable we'd be looking at as far as changing the lock goes. Instead of answering, Art tells me about the trouble he's having keeping staff. None of them stay long enough to learn anything, he says. Gotta do it all himself. All of which is to say he can't make me any promises. All the turnover also makes it hard for him to recall with any certainty if he or one of his people delivered the box to my office or not. I showed Art my sympathy by not showing him the hole in the back of my head.

I rode back up and locked it, then took off for the Show Place.

Walking back through the lobby and onto the sidewalk, I was trying my best to picture the face in the now-lost photo, but other faces kept getting in the way. Mostly of the dark-haired-girls-from-City-College-who-liked-to-party variety. A regular type there in my mind.

Kind of remarkable how often I'd encountered these faces, tripping over on 124th and getting themselves into trouble on the other side of the island. The College was outside of both my and Mickey's beats, so even when we were in the prowl car we'd usually never have specific occasion to make it over there. Still, there were numerous instances where we'd end up encountering something that had gotten its start over on Covent and 133rd in the Finley-Student Center. Which everyone knew was a safe place for dealers. And not just pot and hash, either, despite what college officials might've said to calm parents. Even if the detectives over at the West 126th Street house had a bead on it, there's always some interference when dealing with college campuses. Especially those that think they can police themselves.

Henrietta Peters had been at City. Barbara Rocca hadn't, but it was her face which kept getting in the way. I walked over to the Valiant.

I lifted the wiper blade and pulled free the yellow piece of paper, not a ticket at all but a crudely-printed flyer for the Giant Egg Roll. I pocketed it quickly, barely registering the coincidence. The spare key worked and I pulled away from the curb.

Fifteen minutes later I was idling on Forty-second, blocking traffic while I waited for one of our City's senior citizens to pilot his big, ponderous Cadillac Fleetwood out of a spot a block-and-a-half up from Show Place. Finally swung the Valiant in and jumped out.

The sun, almost directly overhead, was tentatively edging through a slight crevice in the bank of clouds covering the sky. All light, though, no warmth. I walked quickly with my hands in my pockets, looking out over the tops of the many hats appearing on the city's sidewalks for the first time in several days. Soon I was standing before the gaudy front entrance of my destination.

Other than the neon flood through which one must wade in order to enter the Show Place, the four-story building, unceremoniously sandwiched between a cigar shop-newsstand and a just-opened jewelry store, did little to distinguish itself outwardly. I leaned back on my heels and took note of the tall, necessarily blacked-out windows which solemnly looked down upon the tens of thousands of pedestrians who passed beneath every day.

Nearly inscrutable, this thing. And it is this quality which no doubt helps further fuel the imaginations of those for whom entrance is sometimes fantasized about, though for whatever reason, is ultimately forbidden.

I'd venture that if you stood outside the building for the length of an entire day, you'd be witness at least two dozen times to the slackened footsteps of a schoolboy, helplessly locked in a kind of troubled reverie obviously brought on by the sight of the towering structure. His pace involuntarily slowed, he tentatively edges over toward the curb, hypnotized by the thought of what those long, slender concrete pillars which repel down the building's façade might house within. Usually, this starry-eyed gaze is interrupted by the untimely arm-jerking of an adult companion. Sometimes the well-meaning guardian can be seen seizing the opportunity to deliver a mini-life lesson there on the sidewalk, the rapid, barely-listened-to proselytizing only serving to enhance further the child's horrible fascination with the building, still in plain view over the speaker's shoulder.

Adults, too, every now and then can be seen slowing before the entrance without daring to proceed, though usually the length of their tarrying is shorter and minus the drama. They're a little more practiced at self-deception, at disciplining their faces to freeze into acceptably ambiguous expressions.

I had been inside the Show Place a few times before. Usually seeking out a patron. Usually finding him. Like the lotus to some of these guys. You'd get the word somebody was in there, and no matter how many hours later you followed up on it there they'd be.

Most memorable visit for me, though, wasn't like that at all. It was way back, when I was on foot patrol. Late afternoon, the summer. I'd just gotten off and on my way home I'd stopped over at Nick's for a sandwich and a beer. I'm sitting there on one of the stools along the window, still in uniform, of course, when damned if this punk teen doesn't flash by, knocking a woman's stroller over onto its side. I reflexively jump up, and seeing that the toppled stroller had spilled only groceries I go racing after the guy, hollering to what seemed like the whole of the City to get the hell off the sidewalk as I did. I think he turned out to be fourteen. Had a purse tucked under his arm as he ran. Of all the places to go, the kid chooses the Show Place, and next thing he knows he's a foot off the ground, pinned by his neck against the stairwell door underneath the forearm of a heavy-breathing, hard-swearing cop more than a little upset at having his dinner interrupted.

So while I'd been before it had usually been the customers and not the merchandise that'd brought me. This time, I realize, I'm there to sample the godforsaken lotus. How do I distinguish myself? Should I?

I'll admit it, I'm walking through the long, narrow floor with my shoulders high, trying to look purposeful. Ridiculous, I know, to be self-conscious in this situation. It's hard not to be, though, especially when you start to sense that rigidity overtaking your own facial muscles, and suddenly you're wearing the furrowed brow and clenched teeth you've seen locking up others' mugs. The all-business, hyper-serious look that says no thank you, I am not here for that. Just gathering information is all. I'm just here to complete a task required of me by my work.

Of course no one bought it. No one cared.

The floor was surprisingly well-lit and at a glance looked more like one of those retail bookstores than a smut shack. Kind of a sour, metallic smell, though. Like the inside of an empty beer can. I started to look around awkwardly for someone who worked there.

The right wall nearest to me was lined from floor to ceiling with rows of brightly-colored magazines and paperbacks, before which stood at equal intervals a handful of men very quietly perusing. There were a few displays, the most prominent being for what was being touted as "Special Collectors Issues" of that fine publication, *Screw*. Featuring Governor George C. Wallace of Alabama? I walk over to read the article from the *Times*, photocopied, laminated, and posted alongside the display. Wallace is suing the publication for $5 million for using a photo of him, wheelchair-bound, with the caption: "If I Could, I'd Run For *Screw* Magazine." According to the ad, the Governor is himself a subscriber and via the magazine had "picked up a few pointers on sex tricks."

I successfully kept up the stern front. Appears Wallace isn't the only one looking to make a buck out of this. Now it'd take a cool hundred to take home all four of the issues featuring the ad. I continued walking toward the back.

The left side was even less populated. Three people stood in a group at the front end of the wall which was covered with cellophane-wrapped packages of various shapes and sizes. At first, the packages seemed to contain masks and costumes and other Halloween gear, but soon I recognized the items to be the sort of paraphernalia sometimes judiciously described as "marital aids."

I continued to scan the length of the wall, finally reaching its centerpiece. A six-foot inflated penis. It waved back and forth, magically without toppling. I was done for, helpless to stop the smile from spreading across my face.

Meanwhile, the balloon appeared to be the only thing in the room welcoming my arrival, no other ambassadors of Show Place having rushed forward to greet me. I decided to tap the shoulder of a man standing to my right.

"Hey, buddy. Anybody work here?"

The man flinched at my touch. He looked up from his selection, a slightly dog-eared copy of the October issue of *Big Butt*, and stared squarely into my tie.

"Who're you?" asked the man of my tie, promptly folding the magazine closed and tucking it under his arm.

"Who works here?"

"'Round back." The man reached with his forearm, the gesture considerably hampered by the magazine. I nodded and continued toward the back of the first floor, the muscles of my face having considerably relaxed.

In the back, a middle-aged man with horn-rimmed glasses smoked and manned a cash register while appearing to read with care the day's *Wall Street Journal*, which was open and spread out over the counter in front of him. He did not look up as I approached the register and loudly cleared my throat.

"Excuse me."

"Uh-huh." The man still didn't look up. Again the throat-clearing.

"I was wondering if you could help me out, here."

He finally glanced up and up and when he at last reached my face he let out a short, high-pitched noise from the back of his throat. He coughed and swallowed, and recovering took a long drag from his cigarette.

"What you need, big guy?" he said, exhaled smoke accompanying his words.

"Hard to say. What I'm looking for is a short film, a . . . "

"Up one. Second floor, pal." He tipped ash in a plastic cup and resumed reading his paper.

"Second?"

"Right. Up the stairs." Pointing without looking up.

"I thank you."

I went over past the counter to the door that led to the stairwell and recalled the face of an underaged kid I had once held against it. Kicking at my shins, he was. Connecting, too. I stepped through the door.

Inside the stairwell they've got a small, professionally-lettered sign offering shorthand descriptors and floor plans for each of Show Place's four stages. Intentionally or not, the place had been designed so that as one ascended physically, one descended morally, the level of degradation seeming to increase with each succeeding flight. The further up you go, the further down you go.

The second floor, besides carrying some more of the "literature" and whatnot I'd seen coming in, was reserved for the pornoloop booths and quarter-viewers. Of the sort frequented by Dr. Morgan's unnamed friend. The diagram of the third floor they had segmented into three dozen or so private booths wherein were shown the nude displays. Here was where customers rented booths, set up like tiny hotel rooms only without furniture, and conversed with the models as they ogled them. Or, if preferred, sat in silence behind the two-way mirrored glass. The description for the top floor was the least detailed, only three words long: "Live Sex Shows." The plan seemed to indicate three separate stages. To learn more, one had to make the climb. Or descent.

I stepped through the second floor door to find an elderly, glasses-wearing gentleman occupying pretty much the same position as Mr. Wall Street had below, only he was reading *The Sporting News* and was smoking a thin cigar. I could see the booths stationed at the far side of the floor, along the front part of the building. There were a few heads bent over the viewers positioned along each wall and down the center aisle. The old man saw me come in, and seemed to wave me over to the counter.

"Need something, son?" he said hoarsely.

"Yes, I do. In fact, you might be able to help me." I started to reach into my coat pocket, stopped, and continued. "My name is Richard Owen. I'm here basically to try to confirm something. Apparently you've got on one of these machines here a reel featuring my client's daughter."

The old man seemed suspicious, but at least he appeared observant.

"Unfortunately, I haven't got a picture of the girl, or this might be a lot easier. What I need is to do is to find the reel and see if anyone around here might be able to help me figure out how it got here. Who it was that shot it, I mean."

"You're serious?"

"Yes, sir." I leaned forward, placing a hand on the counter.

"What'd you say you were working for this fella? What do you mean, he employs you then?" The old man screwed up an eyeball at me.

"That's right, sir. I am a detective. I'm trying to help a client track down his daughter, whom he understands appears . . . "

"Yeah, yeah, I get you." He set his cigar carefully on the edge of a metal tray. "You want to look, go right ahead. Have a ball. You gotta pay, though. It doesn't really matter what kind of badge you got."

He pointed a back-handed thumb toward my empty coat pocket.

"Look Boxes are a quarter for three minutes. The booths you get ten minutes and it's two-fifty a piece. You gotta get the tokens here for those."

I stepped back from the counter as the old man spoke, putting my hands in my pockets. I'd tensed for a moment when he had mentioned my now-missing credentials. Not many folks realize private detectives are licensed, and so few think to ask to see any proof of who you are. Generally I show it unasked, since it usually greases the wheels a bit. Hence the slip.

I fingered the bills in my pants pocket.

"The viewers . . . Look Boxes?"

"That's right."

"Three minutes . . . is that all that's on 'em? I mean is there more?"

"What do you . . . ? Oh I see what your saying. No, they're regular one-reelers like the booths. Ten minutes. You gotta keep feeding it. Change machine up and to the right there."

I looked out over the floor. I counted twenty-nine Look Boxes and what looked like a dozen booths, although from where I was standing there could have been another row behind the ones that were visible. I decided to start with the booths.

"Okay. Lemme get some tokens, then. I'll take twelve."

"Okay, sir . . . that's thirty dollars."

I counted out the bills and the old man put them in his register. He opened a metal box and made a big show of dropping the tokens on the counter, three at a time.

"There you go, sir." I pocketed the large, round discs.

"You got the time?"

"It is . . . almost half-past twelve."

"I appreciate it."

I walked quickly across the floor and toward the booths. On the way I passed a couple of men on stools, heads bent and engaged in close study. I slowed my pace slightly as I passed behind one of the men and tried to catch a glimpse of the reel playing inside the Look Box. Slivers of gray and white were all that escaped around either side of the man's large, stubble-haired head which otherwise entirely eclipsed the screen within.

I dug out a handful of tokens as I got closer to the booths. I saw the second row up against the front wall. Making twenty-four.

I stood and thought for a moment. There were several ways to go. I could postpone all of this until I had another copy of the photograph, perhaps cutting down the time I'd be wasting here. I felt like I'd recognize her if I saw her face again, although maybe the old guy or someone else could, too. There were other things I could check out as well, such as the former residence at City College. I could track down some classmates and see if anybody knew where she might have gone. Or who she'd fallen in with.

My gut feeling, though, was that would be an even bigger waste of time.

So there I was. Walking over to the far left to where the first booth was. Thinking about these other things. Pulling back the curtain . . . .

# CHAPTER TWELVE

# FOLLOW THE LEADER

"Close the fucking curtain."

Spoken by a squatting figure. In a loose-fitting overcoat. And, most distressingly, no arms. Without moving his greasy-haired, flaky-scalped head.

I did as ordered.

I started to try the second booth but decided to put some space between myself and booth number one's angry occupant. I moved down the row, finally finding a half-open curtain in one of the middle booths, the seventh one from the left. Ducked inside and closed the curtain behind me.

I couldn't quite stand up inside the booth, and so in kind of a semi-crouch I twisted myself around to inspect the area within. There was a long rectangular cushion on the bench to the right, covered over with heavily-cracked, bright-orange imitation vinyl. A small, two foot-wide area separated the bench and the window to the left. The seat looked reasonably clean. I rotated around and sat, my knees banging up against the wooden paneling beneath the glass.

Sitting down in one of these things for the first time, you can't help feeling like you've just gotten on a ride or something. Like the metal bar is about to come down over your head to lock you in. I remember at Downer's once they had a carnival come through with this ride called the Brain Teezer which had similarly-shaped, tallish booths. You sat straight up in it and the thing rocked you forward as it whipped you around. Just as you were certain to be tipped right out the bottom of the apparatus dropped away and you had this feeling like you were floating upwards, like your car and your car only was being slowly disengaged from the ride to tour the park from above. Plenty enough to stick with an impressionable adolescent. Or an impressionable adult.

Thoughts like these quickly evaporate, though, once you glimpse through your own reflection the faint outline of the screen on the other side of the glass. Not quite confession-booth somber, though it'd be a lie to say that the idea of sin doesn't cross your mind. I grabbed the curtain and closed myself in, the metal rings singing out up above.

I slid one of the tokens between my fingers and let it fall into the slot on the right. I could hear the large coin noisily clanging through a metallic chute and drop into a box underneath, releasing a small buzzing sound from somewhere below.

I waited, staring up at the glass. My long, tired face looked back.

I leaned to the side back toward the slot and read the small instructions printed in dull, red capitals along the side: "ONE TOKEN TEN MINUTES. FEED EXTRA TOKENS FOR CONTINUOUS VIEWING."

I have crawled into a dryer, I thought. The buzzing continued. Finally got a clue and jabbed with my thumb the button protruding underneath the slot, and the booth suddenly filled with light.

Face muscles again tightened. Just a little.

The leader spooled through. Then, light.

The footage seemed old and grainy. And, as if to underscore its purposeful lack of subtlety, was overexposed. Black-and-white, though the window was tinted slightly, toward a kind of steely-blue.

Scene opened onto a empty bedroom. Within seconds a platinum-haired maid appeared with a hugely-plumed feather-duster and in stereotypical dress. Not who I was looking for. Back to the camera, she appeared busily engaged with removing the dust from a lampshade, although this was necessarily conjecture. Her positioning upstaged the lamp, hiding her work from the viewer.

A crude splice and the maid had magically turned to face the camera, the shock of cleavage tempered somewhat by the too-bright light surrounding her. The figure of a man came into the frame, her employer, one assumes, the maid's amateurish mime show communicating some combination of surprise and delight. A hasty fade to black. Again, the viewer recognizes his reflection. Expression still taut.

Act two. Same setting. Same cast, only now completely undressed and on the bed. The man on one knee, awkwardly closing the space between himself and the maid, who somewhat prematurely delivers ecstatic expressions of her satisfaction at how the relationship has progressed. Uninterrupted footage followed. It was about a minute or two before my analytical side fully took over. Or maybe you could say it was that long before my non-analytical side got bored. In any case, it seemed safe to shuffle from the booth before the reel had completed its course.

I stood outside of the booth for a moment, jingling the tokens in my pocket. Noticed the old man kind of casually sidling toward me, his cigar held tightly between his lips.

"Find what you're looking for?" Again, the screwed-up eye.

I unsuccessfully tried a fraternal look on him, forcing a sort of conspiratorial swagger which only caused the old man to screw up his eye even tighter. Before it popped out of his head altogether, I managed to cough loudly and step back.

"Nope, no. Not the one."

"Enjoy the hunt." The old man closed his eyes victoriously. I rolled mine and ducked into booth number eight.

Over the next two hours or so, I ended up covering most of the floor, peering into over twenty Look Boxes and sitting through parts of twenty-three of the twenty-four loops playing in the booths.

In none of the reels did I see a woman who resembled my memory of the face in the photograph given to me by Morgan. As I worked my way through, the repetitiveness of the reels necessarily made me more clinical, less self-conscious. I even nodded once or twice to the old man, who had become visibly less interested in my behavior. At one point, when purchasing a dozen more tokens, I decided it prudent to pick up a copy of the special, marked-down, all fold-outs bicentennial issue of *Young Sophisticate*, successively tearing out the large posters and using them as protective mats when the orange cushion in a given booth seemed a little too unsavory to sit on directly.

I became pretty familiar with traits seemingly inherent to the loop's form. Even to the point where I could appreciate the occasional divergence from the expected, whether or not such divergences were intended.

For the most part, though, we're talking mind-numbing routine here. Routines, I guess you'd call them.

Bodies emerged from shadow into spangled, spackled light. Some danced, some walked about as if unobserved, some engaged in a plainly-defined household task. Soon afterwards, couples, triples, and other multiples attempted to consummate all possible permutations within the desperately abbreviated time allotted to them. All positions exhausted, the splice would filter through, signaling by clicks and sputters the contours of the mechanism through which it fed. The darkness, though, was always only temporary. A pause before the return of the familiar. Bodies emerged from shadow into spangled, spackled light. Some danced, some walked about as if unobserved.

I was on the verge of leaving when I heard a shuffling from booth number one.

"Fuggin' Christ," came a phlegm-filled voice. The curtain flared out.

The man in the overcoat sleepily exited the booth, rubbing his eyes. Walking past me, I noted without much surprise that yes, indeed, the man had arms after all. I watched as he left the floor, apparently nodding toward the counter as he left, even though the old man had momentarily left his post.

I cautiously approached the first booth, tearing free the large image of Miss Bunker Hill as I did.

Sat down quickly, feeding the last of my tokens into the machine and punching at the button underneath with the impatience of a regular. The image annoyingly flickered, the film apparently catching somewhere, such as underneath the feeder spool. I wondered if the overcoat-wearing man had broken it through overuse.

At last, the scene abruptly fell within the rectangular frame. Two women kneeling on a carpet before a fireplace, each holding the hand of a man who, back to the camera, knelt down between them.

As the three began to arrange themselves, the girl on the right made a quarter-turn toward the camera. Her hair swept back from her face, suddenly revealing the stunning, smiling face I'd been looking for.

She was in profile for the next two or three minutes. I kept watching.

Finally, I looked away and down and began patting my topcoat for the red notebook. Remembering where it was, I reached back hastily to retrieve it. Felt a sharp, slicing pain and quickly withdrew my hand. There was a thin, bloody scar on the back of the middle finger of my right hand where I had scraped it on the metal binding.

I was still examining my finger when a rattle from somewhere behind the glass presaged another bit of raucous flickering. I looked up to see the image suddenly freezing before me, the rhythm of the trio coming to an abrupt and physically improbable halt.

Next thing I know the now-still light from the fireplace leapt up, engulfing the performers in a sudden and frightening yellow and brown sunburst. The screen went white, accompanied by a uniform slapping sound being emitted from behind the glass.

I stepped out and squintingly waved at the old man who had already started over. I held up my left hand to him and the old man stopped several feet away.

"Owner around?"

"Don't worry, son. I can handle this . . . "

"No. I need to talk to the owner or whoever it was who got ahold of the film in this booth here."

"This the one, then?"

"Yes, sir. This is the one."

I was too tired, physically and mentally, to hide my impatience, and for the first time the old man seemed convinced of the truth of my story. He stepped around to the front of the booth, unplugged it, and straightening waved a hand at me.

"Follow me," he said.

I followed him back toward the counter where he turned and motioned me around behind it and through an unmarked door. Down a short hallway was a service elevator reserved for employees and together we rode it down to the basement.

On the way, I explained as curtly as I could that I might be needing the copy of the film which had broken in booth one. My leader answered with a wordless nod. The further we got from his regular post, the less inclined he seemed toward the chit-chat.

The doors opened onto the basement floor. He removed his cigar.

"Straight ahead, then right. He's in, I think. Door'll be open."

"Who's in?"

"Cheerwine."

"Got it, thanks."

I stepped through the closing doors and followed the instructions. Found a half-open wooden door with a plastic-gold nameplate "CHARLES CHEERWINE" glued half-way down, off-center. Still nursing my cut, I rapped with the back of my left hand.

"Yello," came a voice from inside.

I stepped through to find a thin, angular man leaned back in a puffy, leather recliner behind a cluttered desk. Feet lazily propped on one corner of the desk, hands comfortably tucked behind his head. He looked about two-thirds my age, about half my weight. Seemed neither pleased nor bothered by my visit, and although I couldn't help feeling as though I had interrupted something, there was no apparent evidence of anything going on that could have been interrupted.

"Mr. Cheerwine?" I looked around unsuccessfully for a chair.

"Come on in." The man's face continued to look non-committal, even drowsy.

"Name's Owen. I need to ask you about where the Show Place obtained one of the reels up on the second floor."

With a grunt he pulled his feet down and slowly looked up, painfully deliberate in his movements. Had no suggestions as far as seating options went.

"What was that, mister . . . ?" he blinked.

"Owen. I need to know from where the Show Place got one of the reels . . . "

"The reels."

"Right, the films upstairs. On two."

"So you're saying you need to know . . . ." Looking like he was trying not to smile.

"Where it came from. The reel in booth number one. Where you got it."

That's when the odor finally made its way over to the other side of the room. The man, suddenly looking half my age, continued with his blank stare. I started over toward the desk and he began hacking loudly into a closed fist.

"Oh, okay fine. Hang on there a sec."

He brought down his legs and bent down behind the desk, momentarily disappearing from view, then reappeared, seemingly refreshed.

"Now . . . ." He rubbed his hands together and leaned onto the desk. "You were saying?"

I bend forward and find a clear spot on Cheerwine's desk, readying to lay into this character. As I speak I see the thin wisps of smoke curling up beside Cheerwine's chair.

"Mr. Cheerwine, let me explain. My name is Richard Owen. I am a private detective investigating your establishment."

The man slowly eased back in the chair, his right foot obviously busy crushing the joint below.

"I am interested in learning how it was that Show Place came into possession of a certain reel of film, currently residing inside the projector of booth number one upstairs." I pointed a finger up through the ceiling.

"Where it came from, you mean?"

"Yes, yes. That's very good." The smirk on my face firmly in place.

"You're bleeding."

"Yes, thanks." I brought down my hand. Smirk starting to fade.

"Well, mister . . . what was that name again?"

"Owen."

"Mr. Owen, I'm sorry, but you'll probably want to speak with Mr. Cheerwine about that."

Smirk completely dissolved.

"Mr. Cheerwine?"

"Oh, shee . . . shoot! Sorry, man. Mr. Cheerwine'll be back soon, though, don't worry."

"Cheerwine the owner?"

"Yes he is. I mean no, he's not the owner. Technically. He's the one you want, though, he manages everything. I mean he runs it for the owners."

"I see."

I looked over the clutter on Cheerwine's desk. Newspapers, invoices, W-2s, a few magazines. An ancient coffee spill. I was about to ask my vegetable friend if he could remember his name when the door opened.

A burst of laughter erupted from behind the desk.

"Mister Cheerwine," said my host theatrically. He held out an open palm toward the man in the beige-colored sweater vest and starched white shirt standing to my left.

"Man to see . . . you . . . ." Just managed to eke out the words before another coughing spell silenced him.

Charles Cheerwine was a nervous-looking, stockily-built man of about forty. Looked as though all of the hair on his head had rushed forward to collect into the two massively bushy eyebrows shading his face. He shot a quick glance up toward the area of my chin and stuck out a hand.

"Hello sir, I apologize."

I took his damp hand and dropped it quickly.

"James will you just get out of here please," he said without raising his voice.

James grinningly scampered out, closing the door loudly behind him.

Cheerwine swiftly took his place behind the desk, showing more agility than one might expect from such a figure.

Cheerwine rested his hands flat on the table.

"Again I am sorry about Jimmy there what can I do for you mister?"

"Owen. Richard Owen."

"Mr. Owen right then again very sorry for not being in before."

"Not at all."

"Right and sorry we don't have a chair for you there."

"Not at all."

"Right then what is it you need?"

I chose the most carefully-worded version of the request I'd rehearsed several times with James. Cheerwine folded his hands up under his chin as he responded.

"Right I see what you mean. The reel in the first booth you say which was that?"

"Man and two girls. In front of a fireplace."

"Fireplace fireplace. Right. That is I think one of the ones we got from Tettleton let me see. Of course Tettleton we had a call just this morning about that one. And you say it's broken apart on us then? Right we have a deposit coming to us then believe it or not Mr. Owen this is a business and we have insurance and so forth it broke right apart then. In the booth?"

Cheerwine's words all ran together, like they were racing each other down a hill. All in a moderately high-pitched monotone. Kept his round head perfectly still, his gaze just above my right shoulder. As though he were watching a locomotive advance steadily toward us as he spoke.

"Yes, yes. Tettleton?" I very carefully fished out the red notebook and the pen.

"Right. That's Joe Tettleton. Joseph Tettleton. Joe-y."

"And he is a distributor or something?"

"You could say that I suppose although to be perfectly honest with you Mr. Owen I have no idea personally by what title Mr. Tettleton goes."

"But he made it? The film."

"That he did yes."

"Do you know anything about the actors?"

"No that I do not know."

"These films you show, are they made locally?"

"That is hard to know really I'd say some are yes some are made here in the City I think."

"Tettleton local?"

"Yes that he is."

"Any idea when this particular film, the one with my client's daughter, might have been made?"

"Right when that would be hard to say Mr. Owen."

"Well, when did it come in?"

"When did we receive it?"

"Yes. When?"

"Right well then I could look I suppose but it would have to be . . . "

"Could you? Check on that, I mean?" Damned if I wasn't going to get something out of this character. Something other than the head-throb his syntax was causing to my still-susceptible skull.

Cheerwine leaned forward in his chair with his hands on the armrests and turned his head to the side. He bowed his head like he was going to stand and then sat back once again.

"Right then. The film you are interested in that one had to have come sometime in March or April I would say. That was the last time we dealt with Joey Tettleton."

"Are you sure about that?"

"Pah . . . pah . . . Positive. Excuse me . . . !"

Cheerwine sneezed horrifically into his hands. We waited in collective appreciation. Finally, his watery eyes peeked out over his fingertips and under his eyebrows as he asked in a muffled voice, "Is there anything else, Mr. Owen?"

"Yes, in fact. I'd like to take the reel, if I could. My client would surely appreciate it."

Cheerwine wiped his nose and refolded his hands.

"And who did you say you are who?"

"Come again?"

"A detective right then have you got some sort of proof of that then? Mr. Owen?"

"My license, you mean?"

"Right that would do it then, I think." Big sniff. A satisfied-looking pout.

"Right," I answered, echoing Cheerwine's verbal tic. Had to be pushing three-thirty by now. I moved a step closer to the desk.

"Mr. Cheerwine. I'm sorry to say I haven't any credentials to show you today. I assure you, however, that I am a licensed private detective. I also assure you that I will have my law-enforcing associates down finding out what brand it is young Jimmy prefers to smoke at your desk if I am forced to endure any more bullshit here."

"Your associates?" Questioning emphasis on "your."

"That's right, Mr. Cheerwine. Or is there some other means by which you might be motivated?" I stepped forward as I spoke, punctuating the sentence by letting a fist drop heavily on the clear spot on the desk before him.

"Right then. I see," he swallowed.

"So, as I said. I'll need that film. And if you could consult your records I'd like to know for certain when it was you received it from Tettleton." I straightened up, stepping back.

Cheerwine thought a moment, then sprang forward.

"Right well even so I'm afraid we won't be able to do that. For the insurance of course the deposit and all we'll have to return the film for that . . . "

"You don't need the film for that."

"No I'm afraid we do I'm afraid . . . "

"No. You'll work it out."

Cheerwine sank back into the recliner.

"Right then. I see." The eyebrows did a little hop. "How about this then . . . how about when you go back up just tell Mr. Baugh there . . . "

"Old guy? On two?"

"Right tell Mr. Baugh what you need there but have him cut the leader. We can get our deposit with just the leader I think then."

"Fine, fine."

Again the satisfied look. Like we were friends again.

Cheerwine slid the chair back and began to rifle through some folders in the bottom drawer of his desk. The smooth crown of his hairless head bobbed up and down like a boiling egg. He sat back up clutching the invoice.

"Here we are then."

"Could I see that?"

Cheerwine handed the pink sheet of paper up to me. Show Place Incorporated. Receipt of items from Tettleton and Associates. V.B.E. Prods. One (1) reel. Four hundred (400) feet. Times four (4). 1. Mudwrestle. 2. Airport. 3. Fireplace. 4. Bathtub. Received 3 February 1976. Eight-hundred and forty (840) dollars.

"February? That right?"

"Right, right."

"V.B.E.?"

"Right then that is the production company for whom Mr. Tettleton works."

"Sent you four reels?"

"Right."

"These titles?" I held the page down and pointed.

"Yes right just for reference right."

"You know, I think I've seen just about everything you have up there. I don't recall any mudwrestling or airport scenes."

"Yes right well that's because those films they aren't quite right for what we show here I'm afraid."

Cheerwine stopped a moment and began to squint. I thought he was readying to sneeze again. He continued.

"To be honest with you Mr. Owen I don't think we'll be dealing with Mr. Tettleton anytime right in the near future."

"Is that so? Why is that?"

"Right well it's like you were saying and you can appreciate this we would just rather not have to deal with the bullshit right?"

"Tettleton's bullshit?"

"Right."

"Whadd'ye mean, the way he deals?"

"No. I mean the what he deals."

"'Mudwrestle?'"

"Right."

Once I'd copied everything I handed the sheet back.

"This one, this one that broke. Where would you return it? Back to Tettleton?"

"No not Mr. Tettleton directly but well it's kind of complicated the way we have to send it back through the company and . . . . Actually something occurs to me, Mr. Owen. Your client he should be aware that this wouldn't necessarily be the only print of the film in which his daughter appears right? He should be made aware of that I would think?"

"Yes. You're right, he should know that. How many prints might there be?"

"No idea I'm afraid. Mr. Tettleton he might know particulars there."

"Tell me, where might I find this Mr. Tettleton?"

"I have an address here somewhere but it's no good of course . . . ."

Cheerwine made a show of fiddling through the papers on his desk.

"You should go by Constantine's a restaurant downtown it's underneath Chinatown. A Greek . . . ."

"Constantine's?"

"Right then Constantine's that is the Marathon downtown is where to look."

"The Marathon. That's the name of the place, then?"

"Right you should go and you might just try and ask somebody who works there because Constantine's is a place that Mr. Tettleton indeed frequents."

"Is Constantine's a place you frequent?"

"No sir I do not."

Cheerwine again distractedly rubbed at his nose with his palm.

"All right, then. One last thing. Could you give me an idea what Mr. Tettleton looks like?"

Cheerwine again leaned forward. Suddenly his eyebrows drew together as he shifted his gaze down from over my shoulder and right between my eyes.

"Fat fucker," he said, his voice dropping a full octave.

I looked up from the notebook, held open on my palm.

"Sweats like you've never seen. Big ponytail." Cheerwine seemed to be regaining his composure. "You won't miss him I assure you Mr. Owen."

He leaned to the side and pulled a handkerchief from his pants pocket.

"Anything else?"

"No, I think that's all for now.  I just tell Mr. Baugh . . . ?"

"Right I'll ring up there so he'll know."

"I appreciate your taking the time, sir."  I tucked away the notebook.

"Sorry again about Jimmy."

"Not a problem."

"My brother's son he's not usually . . . "

"Forget about it."

Cheerwine titled his head back, emerging from the shadow cast by those eyebrows, and nodded.  He fumbled with his hands as he attempted to reposition the handkerchief under his nose, anticipating another eruption.

I found safety in the hall, the closed door shielding me from the blast.

# CHAPTER THIRTEEN

# PIECEMEAL

Cheerwine must have survived the attack in good enough condition to place the call upstairs, because by the time I had retraced my steps back to the service elevator and up to the second floor, the elderly Baugh was already waiting for me by the doors. He held the reel toward me.

"Best of luck to you, son."

I took the small metal wheel and held it sideways. A rubber band held the broken film secure inside of the reel. I looked back up to see the old man holding up the yellow leader, as he had been instructed by phone. I handed the reel back to him.

"Keep it."

"Keep it?"

I nodded, back-pedaling. The elevator's doors shut between us.

Young James, Cheerwine's pot-smoking nephew, had replaced Mr. Wall Street at the first floor counter, and was speaking animatedly with a customer about George Wallace when I stepped from the elevator. He seemed not to notice the tall man edging his way out from behind the counter and out onto the floor.

Which was busier than before. I noticed two college-aged men laughing as they batted the balloon back and forth. I moved toward the brightly-lit doorways and out of the building.

I wanted to talk to Morgan. He'd still be at his office, I thought. I ducked into the cigar-newsstand to pick up the afternoon edition and scanned it quickly there in the store. Still nothing. Asked the gold-toothed proprietor for the time. It was ten past four. I was going to be late.

I jogged over to a kiosk and again tried Morgan.

"Dr. Morgan's office." The voice sounded slightly less chipper than it had that morning.

"Hello, this is Dick Owen calling again. I was wondering . . . "

"Mr. Owen, hello. I'm glad you called back. I haven't been able to locate your folder."

"What was that?"

"When was the last time you were seen by Dr. Morgan?"

"No, no. I'm not a patient. I'm a friend of Dr. Morgan's. Is he around?"

"Oh . . . of course. Hold please."

I stood motionless as Mozart's clarinet quintet purred along in my ear. The first thing I thought about was that woman's voice. The second thing I wondered was if Morgan had even gotten the earlier message. Finally I was left trying to decide whether Mozart improved digestion. The speculating halted with an abrupt clicking noise.

"Mr. Owen?" Pronounced cautiously.

"Dr. Morgan."

"I received the message that you called. Obviously, I haven't told my secretary anything about this. Have you any news?" I recognized the doctor's soothing intonation from before. I slouched up against the side of the booth.

"Not a lot. I have seen the film."

"You have?"

"It's Donna, all right."

"Yes?"

"Dr. Morgan, I have a favor to ask of you. I'm going to need to get another copy of the picture you gave me. I have the name of the person who supplied the print to Show Place and am going to try and track him down. I want to see if he might have an idea about where Donna's gotten to."

"Sure, sure. What's going on? Did you have to give the picture to someone?"

"So to speak." All that fretting over telling Morgan the truth suddenly didn't make a damn.

"Sure, no problem. Let's see . . . tomorrow's a half-day for us here. But you need it right away, I assume?"

"Yes, it would help."

"You're planning to meet this fellow tonight?"

"I could try, yes."

"Hmm . . . . We'll be finishing here soon . . . will you be in your office later?"

"I could later, by six?"

"You won't be there until six?"

"Right?"

"I'll need to run home first. Is there any way I might just leave it at your office? I could maybe slide it under the door . . . ?"

"Fine. I'm going out for a while and then I'll stop back by the office before I go out again to talk to the person who might know something about the film. The print of the film. So, yes, just stick it in an envelope and I'll get it later tonight. You remember . . . ?"

"Seven-oh-eight. Thanks again, Mr. Owen. My wife already feels better. At least we're trying to do something. You know where to reach me."

"Yep. Talk to you soon." I pulled the receiver away from my ear.

"Goodbye, Mr. Owen. Wait, wait . . . "

"Uh-huh?"

"You said it was a print? The film . . . ?"

"That's right. Thing is that print they had over at Show Place might not be the only copy floating around. I'm hoping to find out more about that tonight, actually."

Morgan paused.

"Well, I guess that makes sense. To be expected, right?"

"Yes, I suppose so."

"Six of one, half-dozen of the other."

"What's that?"

"As long as we find Donna."

"I guess you're right. I'll call you, Dr. Morgan."

"Call me Harry." I heard a small, forced laugh. "Thanks."

"Yep."

I was probably fifteen minutes late by the time I'd made it down to Lexington and found the Giant Egg Roll. I pulled into the restaurant's parking lot and hopped out. As I trotted toward the corner of the building, I thought about the last time I'd seen Mickey. Had a real boiler of an argument then. About something stupid.

Oh, right. About McGhee.

I turned the corner and there was Mickey, waiting for me outside.

"O-wen!" Mickey dragged out the word as he usually did. Sounded like "oh when."

We shook hands and patted shoulders. As we'd soon establish, it'd been about five months since we'd last spoke, though it seemed longer. Mickey looked to be in good shape, as always. Charcoal-gray suit, pinstriped vest and tie. Square-toed black oxfords, recently shined. Could only be a cop.

"Place open?"

"I dunno what the deal is. Should be. What do you want to do?"

"Damn, I'm hungry. Let's just walk a bit."

"I follow you." Mickey held out a hand and we began moving slowly up Lexington Avenue.

"Looking great, fella."

I tapped the back of Mickey's head. Still kept his light brown hair cut extremely short, almost crew-cut length. Which meant that instead of coming away remembering the broken pug nose, or that tease of a grin he often wore, all anybody ever noticed were those big, flaring ears. From which came the nickname. Real name Michael. Michael Andrew Rowe.

Mick stood about ten inches shorter than myself, so we'd heard plenty of the Lenny-and-George business during our time together. We'd helped each other through a few scrapes. More than a few, really. Nothing I'd describe as headline-heroics, though. None of that Sunday Night Mystery Movie gunplay that seems to punctuate every collar.

Not that that stuff didn't happen. Things were bad for City cops, sure. In fact, this was probably a time when it was as bad as it'd ever been. Huff was a first-class whiner, but he had his reasons. With guys coming and going the way they were, responsibilities tended to get divided with a little less care than they ought to've. Making it hard sometimes for guys like Huff to know whom they could trust. Definitely less than ideal when you have cops too busy watching their own backs to look out for each other.

But it still took a special breed of miscreant to decide to take a potshot at a uniform.

There had been two occasions where I'd been somebody's target. That is to say, two occasions before that week. Both happened when I was on the force, and both early in my career, before I'd hooked up with Mick. Before I'd learned about taking risks.

And both times I'd been lucky. Mickey'd been even luckier, until about a year before. Got his shoulder clipped stumbling on a deal one night in the Park. The way Mick told it, the kid who shot him was more surprised than anything. Popped off without knowing what he was doing. I remember thinking at the time how this was the same, non-reassuring story he had probably come up with to reassure his wife. Nothing reassuring about an uptight teen with a .44, though.

Still, I'd probably do the same thing, if I felt it was necessary. In the way I'd tell it, I mean.

"Life easier behind the desk?" I asked.

"It's good. It's good." A little tentative.

"Still at Third?" Detective Third. Which Mick'd been for a year and half or so.

"Yep."

"This how you wanted it? Upstairs, I mean."

"I did want it, Dick. I asked and they gave. Doris sure appreciated it."

"How is Doris?"

"Great. She's with her mother this week over in Hoboken, which is why I'm eating with you."

"You guys still trying?"

"Still trying."

Married two-and-a-half years, and basically from the get-go trying to have a kid. Was probably time to see a specialist, though I didn't have to tell Mick that.

We stopped at a corner.

"How about you? When're you settling down and raising a family?"

"I'll pass, thank you."

The light changed, and we crossed.

"Saw pictures of Williams today. Rough stuff. You knew him pretty well?"

"Not that well. Good guy, though. We hooped. Hell of a passer, saw everything."

"Couldn't have seen this."

"Pictures pretty bad, I'm guessing?"

"They did a job, that's for . . . "

"They?"

"Not sure, as yet. How 'bout here?"

We were standing before some Indian place. American, that is. The Pemmican something or other. I pulled my hands from my pockets and drew out the yellow flyer from before.

"Wait, I got this today. Weird. Okay, Giant Egg Roll, two for one special. According to this they don't start serving 'til six."

"Lemme see that."

I handed Mickey the sheet of paper.

"I got this same thing this morning. Should've read it more closely, I guess."

"You know, I'd really rather just grab a steak somewhere."

Mickey handed the sheet back to me and I crumpled it in my fist as we continued walking. Thing ended up back in my pocket.

"Sounds good."

"They still holding the drunk?"

"Let him go before lunch. Cap came in with this great story about glass in the coat pockets or something. Whatever it was, it convinced them they'd picked up the wrong guy."

I smiled.

"The drunk say anything? Did he see anyone?"

"Nada."

We ended up about three blocks up at the Grill & Griddle, a twenty-four hour joint the two of us had frequented many times in the past. After a few minutes of waiting around up front, we walked to the back and sat ourselves in one of the empty booths.

We both turned over our coffee cups. Mickey resumed.

"I did hear a couple of things. They're looking at the bone now."

When Mickey said the word "bone" his volume lowered perceptibly.

"What Lanny was going to do. Anything yet?"

"No, it'll be a while on that. McGhee's pretty hot over it, though, so they might speed it through."

"I saw him this morning."

"I know. Sweet as ever, eh?"

"Lotta hollering. Both of us. He actually ordered me to lay off. Big old grandstand, saying how I'm not to snoop around the investigation."

"Is that what he said? Not to snoop?"

"That's what he said. Said I'm a witness and because of that couldn't be snooping around this investigation."

"Sounds like him. It's those stories, I'm telling you."

"What?"

"Those detective stories. Mysteries, *Maltese Falcon*-type stuff." Mickey began looking around impatiently.

"Right."

"Other day I walk in and he's in the middle of this harangue with Marty Walton over *The Postman Always Rings Twice*. You ever read . . . ?"

"No."

"Me neither. They're going on, though, something about lawyers being crooks or whatever, when I pipe up. Never having read the book, there's really only one question I can ask about it . . . "

"Does the postman always ring twice?"

"Yeah. Sends McGhee into a fit about how that's beside the point, it's a dumb question, the title is symbolic and so on. Turns out there is no postman."

"Ha. I could see how that'd get under his skin."

"Come to think of it, there's no Maltese falcon either. In the end, I mean."

"Oh yeah?"

"You know his wife died."

"No, I didn't hear that."

"During the summer. June."

"I hate to hear that. He's past pension, ain't he?"

"Well past. Keeps hangin' on, though."

The waiter finally arrived delivering glasses of water and filling our cups with regular. We ordered without looking at menus. Mick gets the Grand Slam, the all-day breakfast special. Me, a T-bone, cooked medium rare, with fries. Mickey took a large swallow of his water, draining half the glass, and continued.

"This whole thing . . . ." He wiped his mouth, and his voice again lowered. "However this all fits in . . . with what you said. This is crazy."

"Pretty crazy from the start, Mick."

We sat in silence for a moment. Probably both thinking the same thing, that moment when the reporter, Moloch, found Mickey and asked him to offer his view on the "bone theory" proposed by his partner minutes before. I remember Mickey's face. Crestfallen, like he'd been sucker-punched. He'd been as diplomatic as he could about it. Said it was premature to endorse any theory about what had been discovered in the house. Might have staggered him a bit, but he landed on his feet okay.

Mickey tore open two packets of sugar at once and stirred them into his coffee.

"So. Tell me about what happened at the office."

"Two guys, I think. They were waiting for me. Might have been tailing me earlier in a white Trans Am. I walked in, phoned Marty, then on the way out one clubs me from behind with a pipe or something."

"Two?"

"There was one in the hall as well, I'm pretty sure of it. Woke up in the alley and a few minutes later got the greeting from Marty."

"And they robbed you."

"Everything. Wallet, watch, notebook, keys."

The food arrived. Some of it, anyway. The waiter hastily set the steak in front of Mick and a small bowl of hash browns before me. We silently exchanged the dishes as the waiter darted to another table.

"Did you have much money on you?"

"'Bout fifty."

"Anything special in the notebook?"

"No. Addresses, numbers. Client stuff. Replaceable. And the box, of course. They took the box, as well. With the articles, the stuff about the bone, Peters, Rocca . . . "

"So taking the other stuff, that's just for show."

"Yeah, I'd say so. Taking the box sort of seals that."

"They toss the office?"

"Didn't touch it."

"Those clippings, somebody held onto those for a while."

"That they did."

Mickey shook his head, eyebrows raised. We began our meals.

"Well, the scene at the lab," Mickey swallowed. "Some possibilities, there, though not a lot. They've got several sets of prints, though there's no telling how many folks frequented that lab."

"Some mine, I'm sure. Anything on the . . . on the weapon . . . ?"

"Nada, probably meaning gloves which probably means forget about those prints . . . "

The waiter again appeared with my fries and eggs and toast for Mick.

"Nothing about the bone yet?"

"Not until morning, at least. Don't I get some meat with this?"

"Best of luck to you, brother."

We ate for some time without talking. Steak a little overcooked, but I tore through it nevertheless.

"Any jobs?" he asked.

"Yeah, actually. Had a guy come in late yesterday looking for his lost little girl. Sort of like another Peters, in a way. This bird has flown."

"Runaway?"

"Yep.  The daughter cut loose.  Fell in with some movie . . . "

"I thought you were sticking with the small stuff.  Husbands and wives."

"This one just landed in my lap.  Fell out of the sky."

"This was when?  Yesterday?  Before you went down to the lab?"

"Yeah.  Right before."

"Isn't that a little odd, this guy showing up now?"

"It's out of the ordinary, sure."

"Maybe you should lay low.  Let somebody else help this guy with his daughter."

"Starting to sound like McGhee there, Mick."

"You know what I mean."

"I know, I know."

"Tell me something . . . ."

The place was starting to fill up.  Mickey interrupted sopping the last of his egg with a piece of toast and leaned over the table.

"You carry a piece?"

"What?  No.  I don't."

"You have anything?"

I shook my head.

Mickey exhaled.

"Damn it, Dick.  Somebody . . . "

We both sat back as a dish of sausage links clattered haltingly in front of him.

"Somebody's watching you, Dick.  Watching you close.  Time you watched yourself a little more closely."

I nodded.

"I'll get you something.  That was some hardball with Lanny.  You can't just be walking around . . . "

"You're right."

"You're right I'm right."

Mickey scarfed down the sausage, washing it down with the last of his coffee.  Started looking around impatiently for the disappearing waiter.

"That was a regular three-course affair," he grinned.

"Looks like a hash house but really it's French."

"The girl," he said, still searching for the waiter.  "What's the story?"

"Just started trying to put it together.  I was up at the Show Place today.  Took the whole afternoon.  That's one happy place during the day."

"Man oh man.  Love those loopies.  I staked it out once, the Show Place.  About a year ago . . . "

"Yeah?"

"Oh yes.  What's the guy . . . Cheerwine?  Still running?"

"Yep."

"There's a piece of work for you. He stools, you know."

"He does?"

"Yep. Been working with Vice for like six or seven years now. Only this one time he thought there was some dealing going on, a guy selling right there on the property. He said when to come and they sent me over. Put on my best plaid jacket and spent an afternoon waiting for the man."

"Cheerwine's a stoolie. Explains a couple of things."

Mickey held his cup up, raising an eyebrow over my shoulder.

"Guy never showed," he said.

"Huh."

"Apparently Cheerwine's like that. Alarmist type."

"He seemed tense, all right," I offered.

"Well there's no such thing as the perfect stool. Wasted a whole day there. Felt like I was in a loop myself by the end."

"I know the feeling. That's where the girl ran. Into one of the loops."

"She's a star, then?"

"In some circles. I ended up getting the name of a guy who's supposed to be the filmmaker or something. Joey Tettleton's the name. Know him?"

"Not off-hand."

The waiter came over and Mickey stopped him with a raised finger before he could refill his mug with decaf.

"Leaded, son." The wait looked unfazed.

"That's reg-u-lar." Mickey broke the word up into pieces, successfully reg-is-tering his impatience with our server, who promptly vanished in a cloud of shame. I silently remarked on what appeared a new character trait in Mick. What comes from moving upstairs.

"Come out to the car with me when we're done," he winked.

I nodded and finished the last of my coffee and set it down near the table's edge for a refill. The busboy arrived soon after, clearing all of the dishes, including my mug, at which both Mick and I chuckled. I rose and walked over to the waiter's station, withdrew myself a mug and, coffee pot in hand, skipped back over to the table.

"More, monsieur?"

"Oui, merci."

I filled both mugs and returned the pot without the waiter appearing. Returned as Mickey tore open two more packets of sugar.

"You know, Mick, if Cap's gonna try and close me out of this . . . "

"Don't worry about Cap. Give me a ring tomorrow, in the afternoon sometime. I'll tell you what I know."

"I appreciate it. Listen, thanks for meeting like this."

"We were overdue, man. Don't wait so long next time."

"I won't."

We talked a bit more about Doris and her mother. About the Knicks. About Thurman Munson. Finished our coffees and walked together to the cash register, electing not to wait for the bill. I paid while Mickey went back to the booth for the tip. We were out the door and walking back toward our cars when Mickey spoke again.

"I'm too generous," he said.

We were all of the way in front of the Giant Egg Roll before I realized Mickey had been referring to the tip. The place was still totally dark, still obviously closed.

We turned the corner and together walked over to Mickey's station wagon. He opened the back and removed the spare tire cover. A shoulder holster and service revolver lay tucked inside of the wheel. Mickey pulled it free and wrapped it inside an oily cloth before straightening and handing it to me.

"Careful with this, it's loaded. There's a box more in there, too."

"You sure . . . ?"

"Take it. And wear it."

"I'll talk to you tomorrow. Thanks again, Mick."

"Sure thing."

"Listen . . . about before . . . "

"Forget it, fella."

We shook hands and parted.

I set the bundle on the front seat and drove back up to the office. Carried it with me under my arm as I rode up and traversed the hallway to my door.

The manila envelope from Morgan was there inside on the floor. After a wary glance over into the corner behind the file cabinet, I grabbed it up without opening it and slammed the door shut.

The office was entirely dark. I stepped forward and switched on the lamp and sitting on the desk, in much the same position I had been the night before when calling the lab, I flipped through the city directory and found a listing for the Marathon. Just off of Broadway, down from Chinatown.

I jotted the address in the red notebook and managed to close and pocket the thing without any further blood loss. I unwrapped the .38 and the holster and after adjusting the strap a few times had it on reasonably well, although it still didn't fit right. Put the box of bullets and cloth in the top desk drawer. I tried a couple of times to close my suit jacket down over the apparatus but the resulting bulkiness was way too conspicuous. I decided I should head home anyway to change before driving down to the Marathon.

I remember as I left the office having this empty feeling. As though something else, something besides the holster, didn't quite fit.

# CHAPTER FOURTEEN

# ROLE-PLAYING

It was about eight or so when I finally pulled into the sizable black-top parking lot of the Marathon. I directed the Valiant on past the crowded lines of cars toward a gravel extension back behind the dumpsters and against the long row of evergreens which surrounded the lot's far corner. The Knicks were on, so I sat there listening for a moment before finally turning off Marv Albert with a fuzzy click.

Place was ostensibly just another Greek dive, though as I'd soon learn, the Marathon functioned more as a club than an eatery. This mainly because of its location. It was too far off of the beaten path for a cuisine-only outfit to survive, but the privacy had made it an attractive nightspot. Even though the piece of land on which the large, recently-erected structure sat was only a couple of miles from the much-trafficked area between the theaters and Chinatown, its only direct access was a service road running down from and then parallel to the Manhattan Bridge. A road no one other than the people who lived in the semi-circle of five houses situated in the cul-de-sac at the road's end would have any reason for frequenting.

That is, until the Marathon had opened its doors about a year before. This was my first visit to the establishment. There were a lot of cars there for a Thursday, so word-of-mouth had obviously said the right thing.

As I walked I did what I could to position the shoulder holster more comfortably underneath my left armpit. I had ended up having to cut an extra hole in the strap to make the fit more snug. The handle of the gun nevertheless rubbed against my ribcage as I walked. The .38, the standard service revolver, is a significant piece of metal to be carrying around. You get used to it walking a beat, but for me it had been a while. I finally stopped squirming and tried on what I hoped was a fairly normal-looking gait.

What kind of figure I cut, I can't say. As I do think I've mentioned, it's hard for a guy my size to be inconspicuous. So I took it in the other direction. Blue and gold floral-print shirt. Huge collar, no tie. Light-gray vest over top of the holster. All covered by a bulky brown leather jacket with the zipper attached at the bottom. Relatively nondescript gray slacks, brown and white wingtips.

Mouth open a little. A dull stare beginning to form. Nothing happening behind those eyes. A face that says "whatever."

The contents of the manila envelope left by Morgan I had transferred to the jacket pockets. There was the photograph, as requested. And fifteen crisp twenty-dollar bills, unasked for, though not unappreciated.

I made a big show of ducking my head as I stepped through the entrance. Inside I noticed the high ceilings, but kept right on bobbing up and down while I stood there a moment waiting in the foyer. Finally ambled over to the host's podium, kind of a checkpoint before you entered the bar area.

"Good evening, sir."

Said the serious-looking gentleman whose heavily-etched face still appeared engaged in the dermatological warfare of youth. What looked like genuine curiosity as he gazed up in the direction of the tall, flustered-looking man craning his neck downward to speak.

"Ah . . . I don't have a reservation or nothin'. Okay if I just sit at the bar?"

"Yes, of course . . . ."

He turned to direct me and stopped, still behind the podium.

"Are you here to meet Mr. Constantinius?"

"You mean Constantine?"

"Yes . . . Mr. Constantinius." A little taken aback at the familiarity with his employer. I decided to chance it.

"Yes I am. I'm here to meet with ah . . . with Mr. Constantinee-yus. That's right."

"He's not here tonight. Did you have an appointment to meet with Mr. Constantinius?"

"Ah . . . Appointment?" Nervousness a bit less act, a bit more real.

"For the position?"

"Ah, no. No, I surely didn't."

The host took the situation in stride, swiveling out from behind the podium and escorting his uncertain visitor over toward the bar entrance, hand on elbow.

"Why don't you go and talk to Victor behind the bar." He pointed. "He'll set you up with Mr. Constantinius? Okay?" Handsome, professional smile.

"Sure, thanks!"

"Watch your head, now."

"Thanks a lot."

I took a couple of steps toward the bar and turned back to look at the host, as if for further encouragement. The smile had begun to dissolve from the young man's ravaged face. He again waved me toward the bar.

I turned back around. There was music playing through a sound system, though the crowd noise nearly matched its volume. I took my time, deciding it best to give the smoke-filled cauldron a looksee before chancing to wade through it.

In the far right corner, only partially obscuring a swinging half-door which led into the kitchen, was a waiter's station, protected from the main floor by a tall, wooden-framed pane of frosted glass. There was an elevated little alcove on the right just beside where I stood, in which was sitting dormant a dimly-lit, black, baby grand piano. The wall to my left was lined with wine bottles and if you followed it took you toward a narrow hallway and eventually back into the main dining rooms. The bar itself ran along the opposite wall, farthest from where I stood.

This all surrounding I'd say at least a dozen tables, all full. Plus a lot of space for freelancers such as myself to wander about. Together conspiring to provide exactly the right jungle-type atmosphere required for the swinging-single's survival. That's what the bird's-eye view was yielding, anyway. Lots of gold chains and designer jeans. Chest hair and cleavage. People falling over themselves to find out one another's sign. Glass in one hand, cigarette in the other. And, of course, the retina-burning, chlorine-flake-shooting-up-your-nostril combination of sweet and sour scents employed by the beasts in the hope of attracting a mate.

Not what you'd call my cup of tea. Nor Slim's, for that matter, though every now and again his head-bobbing did happen to coincide with the beat.

Once I'd haphazardly negotiated my way through this melee and over to the bar, I saw all of the stools to be taken as well. I awkwardly lingered for a moment until at last a space opened up on the right end.

I sat down on the stool and started tapping with a knuckle at the brass rail as I continued looking around, dodging invisible bullets.

The bartender, Victor, appeared before me. Had to duck for real in order to see him clearly beneath the row of glasses suspended from above.

"What'll it be, big guy?"

"Ah . . . I am supposed to . . . I am to speak to you about possibly meeting up with ah Mr. Constantinius?"

Victor looked at me with new eyes.

"O-kay. For the position?"

"That's it. Ah . . . I need an appointment, I guess."

"Tell you what. When I get a break here I'll go back and see if I can get you that appointment? O-kay? Can I set you up here?"

"Pabst?"

"PBR." He opened the bottle as he spoke and effortlessly placed it before me with a glass and napkin. "You're fine, then? O-kay, sit tight." He moved back along the busy bar. Two minutes later he was back.

"Doing o-kay there?"

"Fine. Is there music tonight?"

"What was that?"

"Music tonight?" I pointed up front.

"Just Saturdays and Sundays. Listen, what was your name again?"

"Davies."

"Davies. O-kay. First name?"

"Slim."

"Slim Davies, o-kay. Nice to meet you, Slim, I'm Vic."

We shook hands

"Sit tight." Little wink. He walked away.

I turned up the bottle once before emptying it into the glass.

I turned on the stool and sat with my back against the bar, hoping to catch a glimpse of the maker of "3. Fireplace" and other, controversy-causing works. I waited in this fashion for something like fifteen minutes, draining the beer as I did.

Victor tapped my shoulder. I wheeled around.

"O-kay, Slim. We got you all set up here. Tomorrow work?"

"Ah . . . what? Work tomorrow?"

"No, does tomorrow work for you? Five-thirty okay?"

Victor leaned forward to try and stop me from ducking.

"Five-thirty. Sure. Ah . . . I come here?"

"Yes, here is fine. Five-thirty."

"Ah . . . I appreciate, Victor. Vic."

I held out my hand, which the bartender quickly took and released.

"O-kay. You need anything? Another Pabst?"

"Yeah, sure. Great."

He took up the glass and bottle in one hand and wiped the area clean with the other, the round circles of moisture from his bar rag giving the red chestnut a bright sheen. He produced a fresh bottle and glass. I was still grinning Vic away when I looked up from the bar and into the eyes of Joey Tettleton.

Tettleton's attention appeared divided between the loud group that encircled him and the tall stranger looking back at him from the end of the bar. Wild, hard eyes. The kind of eyes that normally might be difficult to look into for very long. I was tired, though, and coupled with the affected daze I was trying to put on I was less inclined to look away than I might have been.

He approximately fit Cheerwine's inspired description. Was fat, all right. Forty, maybe forty-five, though the unavoidable spectacle of his hair perhaps made him look a little younger. If it weren't for the length, which was considerable, the big, puffy gray-streaked oval carefully balanced atop his head might have resembled a large, round lint brush.

Or a possum, possibly.

After a few moments he turned his head to answer something said by the woman on his right arm, fully revealing the large bush of a ponytail that spilled over his jacket collar, provisionally tamed with a dirty, knot-filled rubberband. His cheeks were full and smooth. The man was obviously well-fed. Though those bulging, unsubtle eyes gave him the quality of one incapable of being satiated, no matter how much he'd filled his plate.

Just so you understand, I'd prepared to introduce myself to Tettleton as this Davies character. Tell him I'd gotten his name from a Steve somebody or other who told me he might be able to help me get to know the dark-haired girl in the fireplace loop. Needless to say, I hadn't really expected to have rehearsed the role once before meeting Tettleton.

But then again, things were feeling a lot like the night before, when I was being tailed. Like I can see I'm being followed, so how come it feels more like I'm being led?

So, in a way, it was something like fulfilling expectations when, having grabbed up the bottle and slid off the stool, I ducked my head away from the bar to see Tettleton moving swiftly toward me, the thin, auburn-haired girl still on his right arm. I decided to wait for him.

"So, my friend. You think you're gonna work here?" Tettleton's hoarse voice was twice as loud as necessary.

"Ah . . . hope so."

I ducked forward and held out a hand. Tettleton took it.

"Name's Davies. Slim Davies."

"Weh-hell, Slim. It's good to meet you. Joe Tettleton, call me Joey."

"Joey."

"Slim, meet Adrienne."

I turned and bent toward Adrienne, not failing to notice the dark, flame-like colors of her hair shifting as she moved. How do they say it? Easy on the eyes. A knockout of a dress. Wine-colored, medium length, strapless. Made up but not overly. The real deal.

Smiled a lot, too, which didn't hurt. Seemed anxious to say something. But Tettleton kept talking.

"You talk to Constantine?"

"Mr. Constantinius?"

"Yeah."

"Not yet. I meet him tomorrow."

"You'll hate him. Everybody hates him. You'll like him, though. You'll see."

Tettleton blinkingly drained his highball and pivoted toward the bar, seemingly oblivious of any confusion his words might have caused. Adrienne elbowed Tettleton's side as he turned.

"Hey Joey, another Slim." Violet eyes rolling.

"Yeah, yeah, noticed that, honey. Vic . . . "

"We know another Slim, Slim," she laughed.

"Ah . . . really?"

"He really is slim. You aren't, though."

As she spoke Adrienne was dragging her thin, bony fingers down from my shoulder and along my right arm. I tightened up, the butt of the revolver touching my side. Tettleton turned back, either not noticing or not caring about Adrienne's friendliness. I ducked forward.

"So . . . what do you do there, Mr. Tettleton?"

"Joey, please." Loud, wet throat-clearing. "What do you mean what do I do there?'

"Ah . . . sorry I . . . "

"What do I do there. What do I do here? What?"

"Ah . . . "

Tettleton moved a step closer, wincing. Staring up at me, I thought for a second I saw him cross his eyes.

"Wha-a-a-at?!"

His head shaking back and forth, the little folds under his chin rippling up and down. Suddenly his face relaxed into a big goof of a grin.

"Just jerkin' your chain, big man," he howled.

I managed an appreciative chuckle as he turned and shot a steely-look back in the direction of Victor, who had yet to produce for him another drink.

"Yo . . . Vic! I'm dyin' here." The hoarseness of his voice seemed to increase dramatically as he cried out.

"Joe hang on. Out of soda. Just a sec. O-kay?"

"Yeah yeah . . . ."

Tettleton turned back toward us and without looking lifted Adrienne's hand up and off of my arm.

"Honey, why don't you go talk with the girls while I make a new friend here? Could you do that for me, honey? Good . . . "

"So long, Slim."

"Nice meeting you Miss . . . "

"Fisher."

"Let's go honey."

Tettleton turned her around by the arms. We both watched her hair bounce behind her as she walked back across to the other side of the room. Tettleton clapped his hands together.

"Let's sit, Slim."

I watched as Tettleton secured an unused chair from a nearby table and slid it over beside the stool where I'd been sitting.

"My good man," he said.

I sat in the chair as Tettleton slid the stool away from the bar, the differing heights of our seats forcing me to look up slightly to address him. The barlights revealed a thin film of sweat collecting on Tettleton's forehead, which he presently removed with a backhand swipe.

"So, Slim. You've worked clubs before I take it."

"Ah . . . yeah. A couple."

"That's an easy one. Big guy like you."

"Yeah."

I relaxed into the chair. A bouncer.

"Where?"

"Where what?"

"Where'd you work?"

"Ah . . . 'round Chicago. Couple of places."

"You from Chicago?"

"Sure am. Thereabouts."

"I spent some time there. About a thousand years ago, though. How long you been in the City?"

"Ah . . . a while now . . . ."

"I could tell you was from somewheres. Something wrong with that accent there."

"What's that?"

"Still caught in between or something."

"Ah . . . guess you're right."

I sipped at the beer.

"You know, Constantine said something earlier about getting a guy in here. I had an idea when I saw you sitting over here that might be what it was. They don't need nobody, if you ask me, little joint like this. But hey, do I own the place?"

Maybe he didn't, but he acted like he did.

He turned around at last to find a highball waiting for him on the bar. He scooped it up delightedly and looked back at me.

"You'd be great, though. Who'd want to mess with that?"

He began to sip at the drink, almost daintily so.

"So, Joey . . . what is it that you do? If you don't mind my asking, of course." Voice cracking a little.

Tettleton smiled and suddenly knocked back the rest of what was in the glass. He sat there a moment vacantly luxuriating in the alcohol, the heat of which gathered behind those bulging eyes. Glass still in hand, he pointed a hairy pinky finger in the direction of Adrienne.

"See her. The starlet you just met. And the others . . . "

"Uh-huh . . . "

"I make them movie stars." Spoken proudly.

"Ah," I answered. "What do you mean?"

Tettleton wiggled his eyebrows as a reply.

"Did you say . . . she's a movie star?"

Tettleton looked at me sideways.

"Oh, yeah . . . sure . . . ."

He reached back, balancing himself against the bar with his elbow, and lifted out a whisky bottle backhandedly, the rubber spout sticking up between his middle and ring fingers. Helped himself to another, this time neat. I watched wide-eyed as he studiously refilled his glass. When he was done he held the bottle upright, and for a moment might have resembled that We-Will-Sell-No-Wine-Before-Its-Time guy from the commercial. He casually balanced the bottle on his knee, obviously enjoying the work of introducing his new companion to the "real world."

"No, no. Slim. Not those kind of movies."

"Ah . . . I see."

I took a moment and looked over toward Adrienne. No longer so approachable. Then back at Tettleton. Shook my head with exaggerated disbelief.

"Wow," I said. A humbled mumble.

"Hey, that's what the pervs say!" He punched my shoulder lightly, and instinctively I clamped my arm against the holster.

"So you mean those movies like they got over at Show Place."

"Yeah, exactly. You go to Show Place?"

"Some."

"Yeah, I've given them some things before."

"You shoot the movies?"

"You could say that. I'm what you call the overseer of production, if you know what I mean."

"You run the camera and everything?'

"No, not exactly." Tettleton looked around distractedly.

"You're the director, then?"

"You could say that."

"Wow."

"Oh sure. It's a wow." Tettleton finally reached back behind the bar and slipped the whisky bottle back into its holder. Victor, walking over, smirked at him.

"Listen, Slim." He bent forward on the stool, a bead of sweat dripping down the side of his face and cheek. "You get the job you'll do okay by me, right?"

"Ah . . . what do you mean, Joe?"

"You know, sometimes we like to party a little late. Constantine, he don't mind it, of course, but sometimes he gets a little edgy. I just mean if you get the job you'll keep an eye out for us, won't you?"

"I suppose I could do that, Joe."

Tettleton, still bent forward, nodded his head up and down.

"Ah . . . what's in it for me?"

Tettleton straightened up in the stool and rubbed the side of his head, unsuccessfully trying not to look surprised. Small grin.

"We'll work something out, Slim. You can count on it."

I scooted forward in the chair and dipping my head stuck out a hand.

"You got it, Joe."

He grabbed my hand and gave it a rapid shake, laughing as he did.

"I'm gonna put in a word for you, Slim. You're gonna be working here. Hey, Vic! Set my man up here agin . . . what you got there, big man?" I held up the bottle. "'Nother Pabst. You wanna drink or something?"

"Beer's fine."

"You name it."

"Thanks, Joe."

"Not a thing. Listen, you said you'd be back here tomorrow?"

"Ah . . . right, to meet Mr. Constantinius. Five-thirty."

"Yeah, to meet Mr. Constantinius. Stick around. We'll probably be in later on and you can let me know how it went. With Mr. Constantinius." Tettleton showed his teeth and stretched his mouth into an unpleasant grimace each time he pronounced the owner's last name.

"Sounds good."

"Okay, fella. You take care now."

Tettleton let himself fall from the stool with a heavy thud and with a wipe of his forehead walked back over to the group waiting for him on the other side of the bar.

Victor brought over my beer, and when I tried to settle up he held up a hand and said not to worry about it. I thanked him and drank standing at the bar. The crowd had increased during the last hour, and I had some difficulty keeping an eye on Tettleton and his little harem standing before the wines on the other side of the room.

I set the half-finished bottle on the bar and managed to get Victor's attention long enough to thank him. I made as if to leave, altering my path slightly so as to walk past the group. I could hear Adrienne's voice as I passed.

"Ask him. Damn it, Joe."

I waved to the group, slowing my pace. Tettleton waved back, signaling me to come over.

"Slim! Takin' off already?"

"Ah . . . I guess so."

"Listen, Slim. We've been talking over here and Adrienne has this idea that maybe you'd like to help us out on something."

"How . . . how's that, Joe?"

Tettleton grinned hungrily at the others and looked back up at me.

"Slim, this is your big break. Think of it as a little advance on what we were talking about."

"Yeah?"

"How would you like to come be in the movie we're making tomorrow?"

I ducked my head blushingly. A small, nervous laugh escaped from the back of my throat.

"Ah . . . I'm not sure that I'm ah . . . "

The group began to laugh. Tettleton was winking and showing his jawteeth to everyone.

"No, no," he chuckled. "Don't worry, big guy. Just a bit part. Not a starring role, if you get the picture."

"Ah."

"No lines to bone up on, heh heh."

"Ah . . . "

"It'll be easy. We'll shoot your stuff first. Thirty minutes tops. Pay you, too, even. Not a lot, but something . . . . It'll be a blast, tho'. C'mon, Adrienne's your agent on this one."

"Yeah, c'mon, Slim," said Adrienne.

"She'll make sure the arrangement is . . . satisfying," he laughed. Adrienne punched Tettleton's shoulder.

"I dunno."

"Listen, Slim. You're free, right?"

"Huh?"

"You're not busy tomorrow, right?"

"I guess not, no. Except for Mr. Constant . . . "

"Right, right. Then why the hell not? I'd be jumping at it, if I were in your place. At the very worst you'll be getting yourself a story to tell for the rest of your life."

"Ah . . . all right, I guess I could do it. What time, 'cause I got this meeting ya know . . . "

"Yeah, yeah, I know, I know. Don't worry about your damn . . . . Just don't worry. Eleven o'clock. Place called the Motor Inn up on the West Side. You know it?"

"West Side . . . Motor Inn?"

"Yeah, it's easy. Go to Riverside . . . "

"Ah . . . I can find it, I think. Yeah, okay."

"You sure?" Tettleton wasn't.

"Yeah, I got it. Eleven?"

"Eleven. Be early, actually, 'cause we'll have to get out before two."

Tettleton choked off the last syllable, the phlegm having clogged his larynx. He cleared his throat loudly and spoke again, his voice still sounding too old for a man his age.

"You won't be there that long, though."

"Okey-dokey."

"Good." Adrienne led the others in a light cheer. I smiled.

"Ah . . . I'll see you guys, then."

I shook Tettleton's hand once more and nodded to Adrienne and the others. I held the leather jacket collar between my fingers and thumbs as I turned and walked past the long row of wines and out of the bar. Bobbed toward the host as I walked timorously through the front room and out of the Marathon.

The night had turned cold. The wind had picked up, and I zipped up the jacket for the long walk over to where I had parked. I got in the car and drove home without bothering to check on how the Knicks were making out. Too busy thinking about Slim Davies's suddenly-full appointment book for the following day.

Got to my street and found a spot right in front. Walked up the stairs ploddingly. It was still early, but I was beat. By the time I'd climbed out of the holster and removed the floral shirt it was pushing eleven.

I emptied my pockets onto the coffee table. Bills, coins, keys, the crumpled yellow flyer, the red notebook, the photograph. I walked into the bedroom, gently probing the now fully-formed scab on the back of my head. The swelling had completely gone down.

I got into bed and slept soundly. No pipe dreams.

# CHAPTER FIFTEEN

# WHO IS WATCHING?

Could be you are thinking it a little weird for me to be offered that interview for the bouncer position like that. Never mind my accepting it.

Of course, one way of explaining it would be to say that it does happen that certain physical types will find themselves in certain situations over and again. You walk into a place and everybody's looking up at you and automatically they're trying to come up with a reason why you're there. It had happened me before, folks coming to the conclusion that I'd been sent to them expressly because of my size. On a few occasions I'd heard some interesting, unexpected confessions from people who thought I'd been hired to collect on an overdue loan. Or to remind them about an impending appointment. Or to influence them in a certain direction on some future decision.

As it worked out, I was more than fine with taking the interview. It parlayed well with my alleged business there. Made me interesting to Tettleton, too, saving me from finding a reason to be interested in him. Not saying I'd gone in with the idea of getting in on one of Tettleton's shoots, but if you think about it, that would seem to be a more inviting course toward finding the girl than coming on as some panting, lust-filled schmuck desirous to jump the bones of some broad he'd seen in a movie. Agreed?

Besides, that sort of approach probably would have been too much of a stretch for Slim Davies to pull off, anyway. The guy was just too damn quick to embarrass. Better to take the supporting role he'd been offered.

After a breakfast consisting of two pieces of bread and a cup of instant, I showered and shaved and dressed quickly, scooping up everything from the coffee table and into my pants pockets. Scraping my palm on the damn notebook, as had become my habit to do.

Climbed back into the shoulder holster, covering it with my black suit jacket and the topcoat over that. Stopped by the super's to talk about changing the lock. Name's Li, an okay fellow. Lives in the basement. Was nice about it, said he'd talk to the landlord and all. The gist, though, was I would be taking care of it myself.

On my way in, then, I stopped by a locksmith's a couple of blocks up from the office and scheduled to have the lock replaced on the apartment sometime the following Tuesday. I was to pick up the new keys there at the end of the day. That'd be Election Day. Shouldn't be too hard to remember.

By nine-twenty, I was behind my desk skimming through the morning editions for mention of Lanny. The *Daily* had nothing. The *Times* had a short paragraph amid other city news on page twenty-three. Nothing on the weapon other than a short, cryptic description that the victim had been "fatally assaulted with an unidentified, blunt instrument." I sensed McGhee's hand in the phrasing, and felt oddly thankful for his apparent prudence.

I took out the new photograph and looked it over closely, something I'd done in only a cursory way the night before. The edges of her face looked less sharp, like the print had been damaged somehow by my carrying it around with me.

I was put in mind of my grandfather, my father's father. The one who'd given me the miniature Swiss army knife, now lost. He'd also once given me some pictures he'd done using one of those contraptions which allows you take a picture of a picture. Funny stuff, things where he'd overlayed pictures of himself and my grandmother as kids together, of himself at different ages, that sort of thing. The hard part was getting the light right, and the resulting photos always came out a little dark. Sort of a weird, maroon-molasses color. I remember thinking that's how this one looked, like what I was holding wasn't necessarily printed from the original negative, but might have been some sort of copy or picture of a picture.

I took a moment and tried to look at the photo as the girl's parents must have once upon a time. That is, I tried to forget having seen the film and instead just see what the face told me.

The gap-toothed smile was still the center of attention, that much was the same. A kind of added gaiety there, though. At the very least, a seeming comfort, like she was at ease with herself, her family, her life.

Then she'd gone and, as the doctor had phrased it, gotten involved with the wrong sort of people. Morgan had said she'd just turned nineteen. Same age Henrietta Peters had been.

The picture changes. Sweet and studious turned raucous and rebellious. Now I'm looking at someone who even if I found her might view being taken back home as the opposite of being rescued.

I remembered nineteen. Hard to look back on nineteen with much pride. I'd been nineteen when I unceremoniously invited Coach Robinson to have relations with himself, turning my back on Westbrook and whatever possibilities I might have had playing ball. Was nineteen when I'd moved across the Hudson and to the City. Was nineteen when I'd entered the academy, another decision lacking the sort of consideration one might recommend.

Of course, to be fair to the kid, it was either that or chance a ticket to southeast Asia, so make what you will out of his decision.

It can be a scary damn time. And I'd say most of us who made it through to twenty and beyond had some kind of luck along the way.

Some, like Henrietta Peters, make one too many wrong decisions and never do make it to the point of looking back and laughing. Still others enter intact and come out shattered, that one last drunken ride permanently changing their lives. It's difficult sometimes to keep these crashes from happening. Hard enough for a parent, never mind someone who's completely out of the loop.

I flipped it over and saw where Morgan had thoughtfully taken the time to uncap that fake-wood pen of his and rerecord his two numbers and the office address. I dialed the office number and got him.

We spoke very briefly, as he explained he was in between patients. I thanked him for the money, told him I'd met the man who had supplied the print of the film to Show Place and that I was in the process of gathering information regarding the circumstance of its having been made. I asked him when we could meet. Morgan said he had a couple of patients scheduled for Saturday in the morning and that he thought he might be tied up the rest of the day.

We made a plan to make a plan. I was to call him when I had something new to share. I hung up and slid the photo into my shirt pocket.

While still in the office, I removed the shoulder holster and gun. I carried it down to the car under my coat and slid it underneath the driver's seat. By ten-fifteen I was headed north toward Riverside and the Motor Inn.

I knew all about the Motor Inn. Well-secluded, frequent vacancies. The guest register a regular graffiti board, a place where guests would write just about anything. Except their names, of course.

I'd been exactly four times. All for the same purpose. And unlike my Holiday Inn non-adventure, each trip had been successful. In the past, a lot of dealers would take rooms there as well, though I couldn't tell you if that was still the case. Now I was learning a third reason to rent there.

It was just after ten-forty when I pulled into the nearly-deserted, angled drive that wound around the motel, circling the entire structure before parking next to the large, black Oldsmobile sitting in front of room number nine. The motel was situated on sort of a raised mound, so parking at your room meant leaving the car on a severe incline. I engaged the emergency brake, stepped from the car, and made a few tentative steps up the slope.

All of the curtains on that side of the motel were drawn. I didn't want to check by the office, seeing as how the old couple who worked the desk might remember me.

Had to be number nine. I lifted the brass-plated knocker and tapped it three times. Heard voices within. The door quickly opened four inches wide, revealing the blue eyes, thin nose, and stiff upper lip of a man I did not recognize. He said nothing.

"Ah . . . I'm . . . Davies?"

The man looked back quickly toward the sound of voices, then silently opened the door to admit me. On the other side of the room, Tettleton was busily engaged in conversation with a short man wearing a backwards Yankees cap and holding an unlit cigarette in his mouth. Tettleton had wrapped his massive hair in a red and black bandana, lending him the air of authority of one who "oversaw production." The two men were bent over a small camera fitted with a large lens that sat atop a tripod, the cap-wearing man's left hand poised carefully alongside the camera's base.

The slight man who had opened the door took a seat at the large round table beside the king-sized bed, not finding it necessary to introduce himself. Had a light tan to match his sandy hair. Mid-to-late twenties. Wore a long, untucked plaid shirt, buttons open halfway down his hairless chest. Fit the look of some of the players I'd seen in the booths and Look Boxes the day before. You'd be surprised, I think. Lot of the guys in these things aren't super-specimens at all. More nerdy-looking types, like this one. He returned to shuffling a deck of cards, the noise drowning out the whispering of Tettleton and the cameraman.

The room felt small with the four of us in it, the cramped quarters making it easy for me to duck into character. After a couple of minutes, Tettleton finally looked up from his conversation, appearing for the first time to notice my arrival.

"Slim! Dressed up, too, tie and all. Perfect. Glad you made it. That's Slim, too," he said, referring to the man who had let me in.

"Slim, too. Slim one, I should say. You, you're Slim two."

"Ah . . . ?"

"Slim Davies, Slim Jim McCall."

McCall disinterestedly gazed up from his cards. He nodded as if noting an imperfection in the wallpaper on the opposite side of the room.

"Slim there, he's going to be playing the role of Slim, today."

Tettleton croaked a laugh that sounded like ripping paper. McCall did not look up from the table.

"This is Roger, our cameraman."

I stepped past the bed and held out a hand.

"Ah . . . I'm glad to meet you, Roger. Slim Davies."

The cameraman seemed displeased at being interrupted. He awkwardly moved out from behind the lens and took my hand.

"Roger Levin."

He hastily let go and retook his position.

"Tell you what, Slim," said Tettleton, referring to me. "While we're all just waiting around here with our thumbs up our arses, why don't you go ahead and take off that coat there and . . . ."

I removed my topcoat as he spoke, draping it over the unused chair opposite McCall. Tettleton stood with his arms folded, a finger raised to his lips.

"Good. Okay . . . I tell you what. Get rid of the jacket."

I took off the suitjacket and laid it over the coat.

"Good, good. Lemme think here . . . . I tell you what. Why don't you go ahead and take it all off now so we can get ourselves an idea of what we're dealing with here . . . ?"

I froze, my head unnaturally bent forward in mid-bob. Tettleton had himself a new audience for his prank, I thought, so I tried to play along. I let my mouth drop open a little more than it already was. Levin rose up from the camera with a big grin on his face. McCall stopped his shuffling and turned with a dull look in Tettleton's direction.

"Go on now, get those pants off. Roger here's gonna have to adjust the focus and . . . ."

"Ah-ha."

"Slim, let's go. Move it. We've only got the room until . . . ."

"Ah . . . I don't think so. Not today, Joe," I managed. Tettleton grinned satisfactorily.

"Aw, poor Adrienne," he said in a mock-wimper. "She'll be crushed."

Highly pleased with himself, Tettleton continued to smile as he described to the three of us how the scene would be shot. They decided to move the bed to one side and fashion a kind of makeshift office desk out of the table in the front of the room. Tettleton explained, somewhat confusingly, that the scene they were about to shoot would be taking place in a motel.

"We are in a motel, Joe," said McCall in a kind of pissed-off tenor. Can't say I was impressed by the actor's first words.

"Shaddup, you moron. Get up. Okay. Look, what I'm saying is this. We shoot an opener, just a half-minute. Big fella here, he's the manager or whatever. Sit him behind the desk . . . like that . . . ."

He shifted me around and into the seat formerly occupied by McCall. Tettleton gathered up the cards left on the table and set them on the bed. The brass-plated knocker rapped against the outside of the door.

"That's her . . . let her in." McCall opened the door and Adrienne stepped through wearing a long, orange-brown fur coat and heels.

"You guys start without me?" She giggled.

"Very funny, honey. Take a seat on the bed over there. We have got to hustle." She stepped quietly over to the bed, waving at me and mouthing a silent "hi" as she walked.

"Okay, okay. Set it up over here, Rog." Levin stuck the cigarette behind his ear and carefully lifted the tripod, setting it down near the far wall and pointed toward where I was sitting behind the table.

"Okay, listen people. We've got a scenario going here and I need you all to get it the first time." Tettleton straightened his bandana and quickly rubbed his eyes. He dropped his hands and held them out flat as if for balance.

"Our young couple comes to get a room. Slim, you and Adrienne'll approach and come into the frame from the left here. You ask for a room and hand big fella some cash. You got any cash on you, Slim?"

"Nuh-uh," said McCall.

"How you expect to pay for the room, then?"

Tettleton again found himself laughing alone.

"Anybody?"

I turned out one of my pants pockets onto the table, picking out two tens from the pile, which included several other bills, some change, and the crumpled yellow flyer. McCall quickly straightened up from his reclined position on the bed, the most energy he'd shown since I'd had gotten there. The sight of what I had placed on the table was clearly stimulating to the scrawny stud. Tettleton turned his head, noting McCall's reaction. I picked the yellow paper from the pile and threw it into the trashcan on the other side of Levin, banking it off the far wall.

"Nice shot, big man. Okay, we've got rent. Gimme that key."

McCall reached over, handing to Tettleton a metal ring with a key and a large, rectangular piece of white plastic attached to it. He tossed it on the table while I was busy returning the rest of the money to my pocket. The rectangle bore a gold-sticker, a "9."

"Okay, big man. You mind loaning our star those bills? I know he appreciates it, seeing as how he's already fallen in love with them."

Tettleton sighed exaggeratedly as I handed McCall the cash.

"Child actors," he said impatiently.

"Fuck you, Joe." McCall folded and unfolded the bills. As they spoke, I reached up with my right hand began idly swatting at the curtain in the front window.

"Okay we're almost set here," Tettleton continued, ignoring McCall. "Now, as I was saying, Slim Jim and Adrienne come up from the left and hand Slim the money. Move your jaws like you're asking for a room. Slim, you take it and slide them the key and . . . why don't you point to the right . . . no, your left . . . right . . . no, damn it . . . "

Tettleton stepped over and grabbed my left arm, holding it extended. Wide bands of sweat collected underneath his bandana.

"That way. Good. Then we'll cut and fade and move the bed back over and get on to the main show. Okay?"

Tettleton released my arm, eyeing me as he stepped backwards.

"We're set, then. Good, good . . . by the way, that's a fine-looking tie, there, big man . . . . What the hell's that sticking . . . ?"

Tettleton pointed at my shirt pocket.

"Ah . . . "

I reached up and tried to tuck the photo deeper inside my shirt pocket.

"Don't matter. Fuck it. Leave it. It's fine." Tettleton turned toward the cameraman. "Rog, good to go?"

"Not quite, Joe. Take a look."

Tettleton bent forward and peered through the lens. He sat up, hand on chin, considering what he had seen.

"Leave it. Let's roll."

"Leave it?"

"You heard me. Let's go."

"Joe, his head . . . "

"What about it?"

"His head is out of the shot."

"I saw, what am I blind? It's better this way, trust me." Tettleton hunched forward and peered into the lens once more.

"More real," he added.

"More real?" Slipped out without my even realizing it.

Tettleton looked up from the camera as if surprised I had a head at all. Still behind the camera, he leaned forward, supporting himself with a hand on his knee.

"Yeah. See this ain't no feature pic, Slim. What we're making here is documentaries."

I noticed McCall looking up from the bills and rolling his eyes. McCall leaned over past Adrienne, her crossed arms holding closed the fur, and asked Levin how long this was going to take. For reasons I wasn't completely aware of, Tettleton seemed to feel the need to explain himself.

"Let's think about this a moment. Let's talk about who is watching our epic, here. What are they thinking? The ones who watch this, what gets them off . . . ?"

McCall cracked his knuckles.

"It's the reality of it, right? Whether what they're looking at is really happening. Whether they do it or it's all a charade or something."

He jerked a thumb toward the bed. Adrienne seemed busy studying her long, flame red-polished fingernails. He rose from his crouch and began adding hand-movements to help illustrate his point.

"Know what I'm talkin' about? Now I know some don't care whether they do it or not. Thing is, though, nowadays those of us in the documentary business we've got some genuine competition. Folks with the . . . with the facilities and the where-with-all and other what-not to fake it even better than we can show it for real. You follow?"

I nodded. The others said nothing.

"Now what I'm saying is this. We cut off the giant's head here in the opening, and it's clear we're in the land of amateurs. No post-prod. No dubs.

Just point and shoot. Works without them knowing it. It's like before we ever get into the hotel room over there, they've bought into the fact that these two are truly, unquestionably . . . ."

Tettleton held his eyes shut for a moment before blinking them mockingly.

"In lu-u-uv."

Levin snickered. McCall moaned and fell backwards on the bed. I was starting to understand Cheerwine's impatience with Tettleton.

"Ah like ah . . . subliminal cut?"

I winced, recognizing too late that I had made a pun. Didn't matter though. Tettleton was the only one listening.

"Yeah, whatever."

Tettleton moved back away from the camera, allowing Levin to retake his position.

"Yeah, just like that." Still unsure. Clapped his hands.

"Okay, let's do it."

We had a couple of false starts. First had to do with the focus or something. Then I screwed up the second take when I got the room key tangled up with my tie as I tried to hand it to McCall. Don't ask me why Tettleton didn't appreciate my amateurish ad-lib.

Finally, we managed to shoot the scene as it had been prescribed. The pair entered from the left, McCall dropped the bills on the table and I flawlessly slid him the key. They noddingly passed to the right and out of frame. I kept my left hand held aloft for several seconds before Tettleton stepped in front of the camera lens and called "cut," dramatically drawing a hand across his flabby neck. The reactions of the others seemed to indicate that Tettleton's directorial gesturing was primarily for my benefit.

Tettleton thanked me and he and Levin began to slide the desk back away from him. I sensed I was about to be invited to leave. Waiting for a pause in the murmuring conversation between Tettleton and Levin, I cleared my throat.

"Why don't you have 'em come back out and go in again. For the loop."

"What?"

Tettleton had become visibly intrigued by his newest cast member, responding to my words with an odd, fascinated grin.

"Wait a minute, folks. What are you saying there, big guy?"

"Ah . . . all right, they pay and get the key. Right? They get the room, go in and ah . . . do their business. Have them come back out and return the key. Then they start to leave, but decide for another go. That's where it loops back to the beginning. Back to 'We'd like a room, please.'"

By now everyone was looking at me, each registering different degrees of attentiveness. From McCall, total disregard. Levin showed a kind of poorly-tempered impatience. Adrienne, an uncommitted amiability.

Tettleton, meanwhile, eyes bulging, was positively spellbound.

"I get it. I get it. That's good, good."

Tettleton seemed anxious to let everyone know he followed.

"I thought you said you seen these before? Nobody gives a shinola, of course, but let's do it. For a laugh. Slide that table back. Slim Jim, Adrienne, back over here."

Tettleton snapped his fingers. McCall was less than pleased, and I could sense him continuing to stare in my direction.

"You guys are gonna make this hotel a fortune!" Tettleton let out a breathy half-laugh, half-scream. Again, no one seemed to appreciate his observation. "Screwing into infinity, twenty bucks a pop!"

"We get it, Joe," exhaled Roger, speaking for everyone.

We set up the desk again and quickly shot the pair leaving, this time in one take. The only possible glitch came when McCall's toss of the key came in a little high and tight, heading right for my adam's apple. I put up a hand, however, deftly stopping it. The couple walked offscreen. Then they turned around and came back, and we reenacted the renting of the room. Tettleton once again stepped before the camera and announced "cut."

"You know we'll have to edit this, Joe." Levin looked up at Tettleton with a tired expression. I noticed the unlit cigarette had reappeared between his lips.

"No problem. Thanks again, Slim."

Tettleton extended a hand toward me. I rose from the chair and took it firmly.

"Ah . . . sure Joe, sure. Listen, can I talk to you a minute, I . . . "

"No time, big guy. I'll see you tonight, though. Right?" He winked.

"Yeah, sure. Joe, about the . . . "

"Oh, right. I'll have some money for you tonight, that okay?"

"Yeah, yeah. Fine." I followed Levin with my eyes as he pushed the camera forward and started to step out of the room.

"Right back, Joe," he called.

Tettleton turned as Levin walked out, closing the door behind him.

"Yeah, okay," Tettleton said warily. McCall had taken up the cards again. Adrienne lay next to him on the bed with her eyes closed, an idle hand on his thigh.

"Wake up you two, let's get set up in here."

I quickly slipped on my suitjacket and coat and nodding to the pair on the bed I followed Levin outside.

"Bye bye, Big Slim."

Called Adrienne, a split-second before the door had closed.

# CHAPTER SIXTEEN

# THE SIDELINE

A slow drizzle had started. The motel offered no cover other than a narrow gutter that only slightly protruded from the roof's edge. I saw Levin standing by himself close to the building, his cap turned frontways. He held a raised, cupped hand against the bill, furthering the effort to keep his cigarette dry.

I buttoned up my coat and walked over, letting the rain hit me.

"Big man," the cameraman said lazily through the side of his mouth.

"Was ah . . . I all right?" Asked unevenly, sidling over against the wall.

"Sure, sure."

Levin didn't exactly hide his lack of enthusiasm. With that cap he had kind of a Billy Martin thing going there in his straight-ahead stare, like he was trying to pick up the opposing team's third base coach's signals. I stood beside him and did what I could to help. The motel's sloping parking lot remained completely barren apart from the cars parked side-by-side before the room. A white, two-door Chrysler, obviously driven to the motel by Adrienne, sat on the other side of the black Olds.

I jammed my hands into my pockets.

"How often you guys do this?"

"What?"

I repeated the question.

"Oh, now and again. We'll get a place, we'll shoot. Depends."

"Does Joe always use the same people? I mean is it always Slim and Adrienne or . . . ah . . . does he get other people to ah . . . ?"

Levin turned to face me, leaning his left shoulder against the pale brick.

"I knew there was something."

Levin punctuated his sentence with a little satisfactory flare of the nostrils. He again drew on his cigarette and turned back toward the lot.

"What?"

"You really are looking for some work, aren't you?" He pushed the Yankees cap higher on his forehead.

"Me?" I allowed my voice to rise comically.

"Tell me," he took out the cigarette. "What was that bullstuff about the loop and everything? What was that all about?"

"Well ah . . . I just thought . . . "

"Thought you'd get Joe to keep changing it around? Find something bigger for you to do?"

"No, no . . . "

"Something more your size? Big man, big role?"

"No, it wasn't that, it . . . "

"Hey, listen. Don't fret it. I could give a rat's ass one way or the other."

I leaned back against the wall as Levin continued.

"You know the best part is hearing Joe go on like he does. The man talks like he's got some big idea about something, but the more he runs that trap the more likely it is he's gonna catch himself in it . . . ."

"How's that?"

"Well . . . crap, where do I start? Okay, for one, you heard him going on about the land of amateurs? I've heard that one before, all that 'more real' garbage. But then you come in and make your little contribution and damned if he doesn't go for something that he knows has to be recut later. He *knows* it."

"Huh. That would ah . . . kind ah destroy the effect, then? I guess?"

"That's exactly what I'm saying. The guy who buys into whatever it was Joe thinks he's selling when he cuts your head off, if indeed such a guy exists, what the hell does he care about the loop making sense like that? What's the 'more real' there?"

Levin shook his head, exhaling smoke. Retucked the cigarette in his mouth's corner.

"Ah . . . I didn't think of that. Roger."

"He talks about the audience like he's actually got one."

"Well I didn't mean . . . "

"What do you care, right? You're just aiming to get some screen time. Maybe make a little dough. Am I right?"

"Ah . . . I dunno . . . I might." I squinted and grinned. "You think?" I pointed a thumb back toward the door of the room.

"Joe? Oh, he'd do it. He'll do anything."

"What d'ye mean?"

"Big horse like you, though. That'd be verging on freak show territory. No offense, of course." Again the nostrils flared. He repositioned his hand out in front of the cap. "Joe'd do it, though. He likes you. He'd do it or he'd get you something. Just ask him."

"Ah . . . I dunno."

I looked down at my feet and a bead of water fell from my scalp, tracing a line down my forehead. I swallowed and contemplated whether the conversation was worth pursuing.

"Look." Levin inhaled heavily and spat the butt, twisting a foot over it. "If you want I'll put it to Joe, maybe even try to set something up . . . late next week."

I bit.

"Yeah, sure. Okay."

I bent forward and paused while Levin unwrapped the cellophane from a fresh pack of Marlboros.

"Joe'll do anything, you say?"

"Oh man, the guy's a regular . . . he's a deviant is what he is. A real regular deviant." Levin began slapping the pack against his palm.

"Yeah?"

"Oh man. The stranger the better, really. Any and everything. Been known to join in a time or two as well."

I laughed genuinely, imagining the spectacle.

"He said something last night about Chicago. Having been . . . ?"

"Yeah, I think that's right. Apparently ran into some trouble there sometime back. Might be why he's here, actually."

I waited, pretending to think.

"What sort of trouble was that?"

Levin continued hitting the pack against his palm as though he didn't hear me. I sighed forcefully and leaned over.

"Child actors?" Spoken hoarsely, attempting to mimic the way Tettleton had pronounced the two words earlier.

Levin abruptly stopped and looked up at me. For a moment I feared I'd made a wrong move. The rain beat a steady rhythm. The cameraman closed his eyes and frowned, then resumed.

"I wouldn't put it past that guy. I don't know about that stuff, though. Dunno what the story was . . . ." He trailed off, cautiously looking up into the cloud-covered sky. He snorted and tore out another cigarette.

"Smoke?"

"Nah . . . thanks. How long is it you been working for Joe?"

"Well just so you know I don't really work for Joe. We both work for the company. Somebody's gotta pay for this stuff, right? Actually this is only the second time I've been involved with Joe on a shoot. Directly, that is."

"You've known him a while, though?"

"Yeah, couple of years, I guess. How come?"

"Just wonderin'. Trying to get an idea of what ah . . . I might be getting into."

"Sure." He sniffed. "Look, I'll mention it to him, okay? You say you'll be down at the Marathon tonight?"

"Yeah, I have to . . . "

"Come around late, after ten." He held the cigarette before his mouth thoughtfully. "After ten sometime. I'll talk to Joe. He'll be there."

I weighed my response.

"That'll work. Ah . . . I was going for to talk to Mr. Constantinee-yus anyhow. For the position and all."

Levin briefly bore a quizzical look before it dissolved in a smoke-cloud of apathy. I held out my hand.

"Ah . . . 'preciate it, Roger."

"Don't fret it."

We shook hands. I raised my eyebrows and widened my eyes, trying on my most sincere thanks-for-giving-a-guy-a-break look. Grabbed the collar of my coat and stepped past Levin and onto the blacktop.

I withdrew my keys and hurriedly squeezed myself into the Valiant. I had backed out and was almost turned completely around before I realized that the parking brake was still engaged, recognizing after the fact the soft whine of metal against wet rubber.

I turned and looked up to see the cameraman watching me. I grinned up at him sheepishly, released the brake, and with an unanswered wave drove down the row of rooms and turned left and out onto the street.

I had gone about a quarter mile or so when I pulled off onto a muddy shoulder. Checked the rear view. Nothing. Waited for about three or four minutes, fogging up the inside of the glass with my breathing. One or two cars passed, not more.

Finally I pulled it around and drove back up the quiet road, parking just short of the motel entrance. Got out and hiked up the drive and around the front side of the motel. Hands in pockets, head down. All of the rooms' curtains remained drawn except for the window marking the manager's vestibule. I moved over closer to the building and crept up beside the office window.

I could see that the old woman was there, minding the front desk. I stood back against the wall for a moment and waited. Inside, the phone rang. I heard her answer. Her voice was muffled, and I remembered the double-glass in the rooms, something no doubt appreciated by the Motor Inn's more circumspect tenants. The conversation went on at least five minutes. She finally hung up and I heard some movement. Stealing another look, I saw that she'd disappeared into a back room.

I slipped past the window and jogged down the row of remaining rooms. The rain was coming down harder, big round drops jabbing like wet thumbs at the tender spot on top of my head.

I passed the last room, twenty-four, and turned left, splashing through puddles as I trod around the motel's back end. Stopped and titled around the corner and frankly was surprised to see the smoking Levin in the same position as I'd left him. Making the most of the break. The cameraman had another unlit cigarette between his lips and had just fished his lighter from his jacket pocket when McCall's head popped out, calling him back inside. Levin took the cigarette from his mouth and stuck it behind his ear, and while saying something followed him through the open door and closed it behind him.

I sauntered past rooms twelve, eleven, and, leaning against the door to number ten, attempted to peer into the window of number nine.

Do I need to explain myself, here?

First of all, you should know, there was a method to this. Idea was to get back there in time to listen in while Levin asked Tettleton about me. Maybe pick up something I could use later on when reuniting with Tettleton. And I was prepared with an excuse, should someone see me hanging around out there.

I know what it looks like, though. Looks like I'm that guy stumbling over the curb outside the Show Place. Too scared to go in but desperate to know what it's all about.

Depends on what kind of story you want. Maybe you're the type who's more into particulars than plot. And so here is where you'd want things fleshed out more, so to speak. An anatomy of porn. Full-fledged exposé, demonstrating the glamour-lacking, spirit-taxing, desperation-filled nature of the industry. Probably would need to do some more footwork for that, maybe request a seat in the corner at the Live Sex Shows.

To present it properly, of course. In all of its diverting, degrading detail.

Fact is, it wouldn't be that long before I'd get my chance to see what was going on in room nine at the Motor Inn that rainy Friday noon. What I mean to say is, I could tell you plainly enough right here, but that wouldn't be the way it happened.

My suggestion, though, is to put all that aside. For now, at least. We'll leave the documentary business to professionals like Tettleton. That's not what this is. If it were, I wouldn't be creeping around trying to pass myself off as an eager, semi-educated, bouncer-type looking for some kind of sideline as a stunt cock.

Nor would I be standing in the rain, trying to peep through this little sliver of an opening I'd created before, the place where I'd pulled the curtain back away from the window. An opening through which, truth be told, I could only partially see the mirror on the opposite wall. Perfectly angled onto the back part of the room, the coat rack and sink.

That is to say, the only place in the room unoccupied by anyone.

I stood and listened for a little while. Recognized Tettleton's hyperactive cadence, though couldn't really make out any words. McCall's tinny voice, sounding a bit riled. Tettleton answering back authoritatively. No surreptitious dialogues regarding the recently departed Davies or his request. None that I could make out, anyway. Finally, things settled down. Several minutes passed without anyone saying anything. Occasional creaks and scrapes of furniture the only evidence that the room was rented at all.

Here I am, I thought. Eavesdropping on a silent film.

I turned tail and walked back in the direction I'd come. Retraced my steps back to the manager's office. Seeing the woman still away from the desk, I walked on past and quickly jogged back down to the car.

My feet were beginning to turn cold what with my socks having absorbed all that water sloshing around behind the motel. I started the Valiant and drove slowly back up the motel parking lot and around to the back side, parking parallel to the motel in the far corner beside room number one.

From where I sat, I could see the row of doors out the passenger-side window, while only the front part of the Valiant could be seen by anyone standing before rooms one through twelve.

For the next thirty-five minutes I sat, leaving the power on and listening to the radio. Fun Sandwich theme only played twice. Eventually they announced the time as four to one.

"Feeling good . . . feeling good . . . about Amer-ica . . . ."

Amidst the jubilant chorus of male and female voices, there was Ford suggesting "Let's keep going" when I noticed the door of room number nine finally spring open. I started the motor and crept slowly around the corner of the building, speeding up when I saw Levin and McCall loading equipment into the back of the Olds. I skidded to a halt and climbed out, leaving the motor running.

"Hey fellas." I jogged over, hand extended and holding the room key.

"Big man," Levin said before ducking back into the car's trunk, a wisp of smoke following him. McCall stood with his arms folded, still cultivating the listless punk look. A little Peter Fondaish, though that would probably better match McCall's self-image than what others saw of him. His performance indoors seemed neither to have fatigued nor invigorated him.

"Ah . . . I got down the road before I saw I still had this. Good thing I noticed it."

McCall nodded slowly. Levin stood upright.

"Good thing," echoed McCall, tilting his head slightly as if sizing up this unwanted challenger to the kingdom of Slim. He unfolded his arms and put his hands together, cupping them against his chest.

"Right here," he called.

I stopped about six feet from McCall and with a backhand flip struck his plaid shirt front with the key ring, which dropped harmlessly into his waiting hands. A broad grin spread across McCall's face.

"Bank shot."

"Ah . . . yeah."

"Gotta call that."

McCall held the plastic rectangle up, underneath his chin. Looked like he winked, though it could be that I'm imagining that.

I turned and quickly got back in the car, forgoing more formal good-byes. In the rear-view, I watched as McCall watched me drive all of the way out of the lot and turn left.

Once on the street, I turned on the wiper blades and searched for a relatively secluded place to park. About two-thirds of a mile up from the motel was a church lot. I pulled in and waited for either the white Chrysler or the black Oldsmobile to show.

Odds were even, I thought. Fifty-fifty the group would pass this way. My hunch was they'd be heading south, toward the Marathon. Can't say I knew exactly what it was I'd get out of tailing them, other than maybe finding where Tettleton lived. I wanted to keep busy though, keep moving. Figuring that following Tettleton might make things harder for whoever might or might not be following me. Or waiting for me, like they did before, anticipating where it was I was heading.

I mean how could a person keep a step ahead if I didn't myself know what the next step would be?

That was my reasoning.

I gripped the wheel and waited.

# CHAPTER SEVENTEEN

# SLIM JIM LEAVES A CALLING CARD

"Waiting there in the church parking lot, waiting to follow the others, you're saying you hadn't yet recognized McCall from before?"

Nosy questions. Try to tell a story, and you're always getting interrupted. Folks thinking they're seeing things you don't. Wanting to finish it for you.

I can't entirely blame you, though. If I take the time to describe what a person looks like, I've got to choose what traits I'm going to tell about and what it is I'm going to have to leave to your imagination. Meaning you're only getting a few key things, like a guy's hair, for instance, to go on. And if you see something more than once you're naturally going to start making conclusions about it. That little difference coming back again, resonating in your mind like a refrain or something. A little jingle.

Hell, if you're asking questions about Slim Jim, then it might be you've got a nose for this sort of thing after all.

Of course, up to this point a lot had happened I'd yet to recognize for what it was. Only a couple of things, though, that I feel like I should've seen. McCall being one. The other having to do with the door at the office. I mean I'd like to say I knew who McCall was, but the only thing about him I'd recognized up to now was that he was a first-class creep. That and he might have been a little anxious about making sure I caught the negative vibe he was sending my way.

The point is, I can't be worrying now over what I missed then. Soon I'd sound like I was one of the Giants, crying how maybe this and maybe that and maybe it all would have been different.

Was ten minutes or so before both cars whizzed past the church, and with both still in view I let the Valiant roll forward and eased out of the church lot. Driving conditions were less than pleasurable. A steady rain, not to mention the roads were packed. Lunch-hour traffic, people getting back to work. I was able to track them both for a little while, keeping a few cars back as they crossed over to Columbus and continued south toward the theater district.

They stayed together until the Forty-second street intersection, at which point the white Chrysler moved over into the left-hand turn lane while the black Olds remained in the center lane. Once they'd split, I had little time to choose. In fact, thanks to this fool trucking a U-Haul alongside of me, the choice was basically made for me to stay left and follow the white car. I watched from behind as the Olds proceeded on through and down Ninth. The U-Haul, meanwhile, waited right there beside us straddling the two lanes, obviously hopeful of getting over and making that left.

Waiting at the light, I counted three cars between me and the Chrysler. At the time, my guess was Adrienne was driving and that Tettleton was with her. But I couldn't really see anything from where I was sitting.

Light goes green. Couple of cars go and then the white car follows them through. Then another car, a yellow cab I think, speeds along behind her. Then the next one.

Now the Chrysler's disappearing down Forty-second when I see that the guy ahead of me in a VW bug, he's not moving. He's decided to let Mr. U-Haul come on over and make that left he'd been worrying us all about. End result being he gets through on yellow, the beetle on red, and either I floor it or I'm stuck waiting through another cycle.

I floored it. As I'm turning, the Valiant started hydroplaning over the slick pavement, careening sideways toward the curb. I quickly turned the wheel toward the curb and tapped lightly on the brake, managing to right both the car and that pounding in my chest. Alongside the curb, I coasted forward and stopped behind a parked car. By now the light had changed again, and I sat there waiting while I let the traffic pass through.

All the same, I'm thinking. This a waste of time, not to mention a needless risk. I'm meeting up with these jokers later anyhow. If it happens that they see me following them, chances are good the whole Davies ruse is blown and I'm back to square one as far as finding the girl in the picture goes.

I ought to be calling Mickey is what I ought to be doing.

Wiped the windshield clear of the condensation that had collected. Finally found a opening and pulled back out into the Forty-second street traffic. Thinking about grabbing a bite, making a couple of phone calls, and readying to meet Mr. Constantinius. Slow-moving through the strip. Stopping altogether a couple of times.

I'm moving along, slowly but surely. Pinned behind this truck until we're just about out of the theater district. Trying to decide whether to turn down Lexington or Second when damned if it isn't the Chrysler darting out from in front of the truck and pulling into the entrance of one of those grindhouses. One of the last ones, off the Square. The Express, it was.

Instinctively, I followed the truck into the neighboring parking lot. Into that other Fun Sandwich, about two or three hundred yards up from The Express. Not the one down by the Port Authority, but the other one. Took a spot at the front end from which to watch.

Slim Jim McCall jumped out of the driver's side and ran through the rain to the ticket window. He had no shoes on and continued to wear the plaid button-up untucked. His ratty, blond hair became darker, a regular deluge having begun during his conversation at the ticket window. Less sandy-looking, all right? He stood before the window for five or six minutes, occasionally waving his hands in an animated fashion.

I continued watching as McCall dashed back to the idling Chrysler and sped off down Forty-second. As he drove away, I noticed no one else was in the car.

I got out and jogged through the downpour and into Fun Sandwich. Emerged five minutes later with a ham and melted swiss and a Coke. Ate in the car and listened to the radio for the next ten minutes or so. Ehrlichman to enter prison voluntarily. Something about Beame wanting to rent the Manhattan Plaza out to theater people, has the locals all in a frenzy. CBS giving up on the Giants, gonna show Dallas-Washington instead this Sunday. Knicks lose, big. More rain ahead, turning to sleet.

I shook the ice in the bottom of the cup and idly stared out at the shape in the ticket window at the Express. Above the window burned the marquee, a large, emblazoned X bursting from the cursive title: "The eXpress Delivers." What the Express delivered was posted underneath, in small capitals:

*NAUGHTY NURSES II*
*NAKED BRUNCH*
*ALL SHOWS 1.00 BEFOR 7*

Can't say I had any specific idea what McCall's business was there, although I knew it must have something to do with his career. Which as it turned out it did, though not the one I was thinking of.

I stepped from the car and hurriedly crossed over into The Express's parking lot. I lingered for a moment, staring up through the rain at the marquee. I approached the window, bending at the waist.

"Afternoon. Listen, you might be able to help me out here . . . ."

I set my hands on the counter, twisting awkwardly to speak through the little voice-holes cut into the plexiglass. The boy-faced man turned sideways on the stool to get a better look.

"What is it?"

Had a little circular button there on his shirt with too much writing on it to be his name. I leaned a little closer to read what it said.

Said "Don't You Feel Stupid Wasting Your Time Reading Buttons?"

I leaned back.

"Well, you see I . . . listen, you mind if I come inside, there?" Answered with a suspicious look. Guy probably gets all manner of requests sitting in there.

"You buying a ticket or what?"

"Well, you see . . . "

"Gotta buy a ticket to get inside, mister." Head back and forth, disapprovingly.

"No, see, I . . . all right." Hands back in pockets as I stepped back to look at the marquee again.

"Let's see . . . well, I just ate, so how 'bout one for *Naughty Nurses?*"

"*Naughty Nurses?*"

"Right. Part two."

"Did you say you just ate?"

"Yes, I . . . ." I half-heartedly pointed upwards before deciding not to explain.

"Yeah, well, sorry mister. You'll have to come back later. *Nurses* not 'til seven-fifty."

"Huh."

I stepped back from the window, standing straight as I watched as the man inside twist around, turning his back to the scratched-up window. I again leaned forward and rapped a knuckle, rattling the plexiglass. The man inside turned around.

"Yeah?" I noticed the paleness of his skin.

"Listen, I was just looking for a friend of mine. Maybe you've seen him? He's about five-ten?" I stood up straight and held a level hand against my collarbone, having to leave the voice-holes momentarily to do so. I bent back down.

"Oh, yeah. I've seen him. Five-ten, you say? Oh, yeah, he comes in every day . . . "

Had to smile. The man inside toothily grinned back, cutting short his sarcastic oration.

"That's good," I answered. "Here, let me be more specific."

The lanky figure turned sideways and waved a hand.

"Come on around."

He directed with his finger a path through the entrance and toward the doorway in back of the ticket booth. I stepped inside and shook my head, water spraying like a dog stepping from a bath. I soon appeared where I had been directed, my large frame more than filling the small doorway in the back of the booth. I raised and bent my right arm against the top edge of the entrance, leaning my forehead against it as I resumed.

"Thanks, fella. I'm looking for a guy . . . "

"Your friend."

"Yeah, my friend."

"Five-ten."

"Five-ten, dirty-blond hair, blue eyes . . . "

No response.

"Thin nose, sort of a stiff upper lip . . . "

Still nothing.

"Stupid-looking plaid button-up he wears untucked . . . "

"You mean . . . oh what the hell did he . . . Slim!"

"That's right." I pretended to look surprised. "Yes, the name is Slim."

"Slim Davies. He was just here."

"Yes . . . ." I stopped, surprised for real.

"What did you mean by you just ate?"

"Slim Davies?"

"Yeah, that's what he said. Left right before you came."

"You sure he told you he was Slim Davies?"

"Yeah, what the hell? Like just before you came up here. Five-ten, plaid shirt. Dumbfuck didn't have the sense to wear shoes in the rain."

"Well, you're right there. He ain't exactly the brightest bulb."

"So why'd you say you just ate?"

"What? Oh." I shook my still-dripping head. "Because the other one, the *Naked Brunch* . . . ."

The man closed his eyes, laughing.

"Man, I don't know which is worse, that title or your joke."

I continued standing there with my head resting against my arm. McCall must've seen me, I thought. Left my name there as a calling card or something.

The detective rubs his chin thoughtfully.

I looked over the man sitting before me, still shaking his head and grinning with his eyes closed. A strange confidence there in his face. The kind of confidence adolescent boys possess before they have been made to discover they don't know half what they think they do. Guy was severely thin, the curve of his cheekbones giving his pale look an almost feminine quality. Sort of Faye Dunaway meets Dennis the Menace. The only thing that prevented me from thinking he was indeed a minor was the wrinkled skin on the back of the hand he presently lifted between us, a cigarette clutched between his fingers.

Enough chin-rubbing. Fist on hip, getting down to business.

"All right," I said. "My name is Dick Owen. I'm a private detective. I followed Mr. Davies here and watched his little meeting with you a few moments ago."

Boyish face transfixed. Hand still poised before it.

"You mind me asking what it was you and Mr. Davies were talking about?"

"This have to do with the van Brooks?"

I squinted. "Could be."

He sniffed and dextrously folded over a pack of matches with his free hand.

"Never saw the guy before in my life. Comes by with this message from the van Brooks, all urgent-like. Kind of rude, really. Explaining everything like I don't know what the hell he's talking about."

He bent forward and lit the cigarette, sliding from the stool as he did. I stepped back from the doorway.

"I knew something was up. You see, these are for tonight." He awkwardly pointed a wrinkled finger back through the booth's ceiling in the direction of the marquee. He took a long drag on the cigarette and pulled it from his lips.

He turned his wrist to read his watch.

"Listen," he said. "I have to go change the reel, here."

He put the cigarette back in his mouth, the smoke causing one eye to twitch rapidly.

"We can talk upstairs. Name's Billy Paul."

"Me and Mrs. Jones."

"Yeah, yeah . . . what'd you say . . . Owens?"

"Owen. Dick Owen."

I took the man's thin, shrivelled hand in mine. He quickly pulled his hand free, turning and coughing into it.

"Okay, then."

I backstepped as he walked through the door and past where I stood.

"Follow me, Owen Dick Owen."

# CHAPTER EIGHTEEN

# REEL CHANGE

As we moved through the empty lobby, Paul waved at an older man leaning against a popcorn machine, jerking his thumb back toward the ticket booth as he did. I followed him to the other side of the lobby and through an unmarked door on the right. At the top of the narrow staircase, he stopped and turned around.

"Dick. Dick, the dick?"

"Yeah, yeah."

"Never heard that one before, I'll bet."

I nodded appreciatively and followed him onto the landing above.

Together we entered the cramped and noisy projector room. I had to lower my head considerably in order to move about. The room was about three times as long as it was wide, with three square windows on the right side. A large projector was positioned at the middle window, a huge reel turning sideways underneath the platform on which it sat. An odd-looking, tall, metal stool with a plastic back sat near the projector. Looked like a baby's high chair.

Paul quickly walked to the far end of the room, almost disappearing in shadow before reemerging holding a folded metal chair which he opened and let fall near the stool.

We sat down in silence, Paul peering over the top of the projector through the middle window, a thin crevice of light reflected across his brow. He shifted in the stool, removing the cigarette before spitting toward the floor underneath the projector.

"So you interested in the van Brooks?"

"*The* van Brooks or just van Brooks?"

"What? Oh, I see. Both, I guess. There's the guy, van Brooks. Oscar van Brooks. And there's the company, Van Brooks Enterprises."

"The production company."

"Right. At least I assume there's a guy. A real van Brooks, I mean. I know I've seen that name around."

"Never met?"

"Naw."

Paul scooted off of the stool and landed on the floor with a soft thud. He again disappeared into the far shadows, this time carrying back a large reel under his arm. He stopped beside the projector, removed the cigarette from between his lips, dashed it on the rubber heel of one of his black Chuck Taylors, then stuck it back in his mouth. His knees popped as he bent into a crouch beside the projector.

As he fit the new reel beneath the slowly turning wheel, my eyes began to adjust to the room's dimness. Besides a small, low wattage bulb attached to the side of the projector, the room's only light source was the blue, hazy glare that poured from the theater screen through the windows along the wall to the right.

I shifted forward in the chair and noticed a large metal canister propped against the wall, behind Paul's thin, scrawny back. He began cursing as tried to fit the heavy reel into place. Finally rose up and from his knees looked out again toward the screen, this time peering underneath the projector. He watched for twenty seconds or so, then quickly turned back to the machine, using both hands to lock the replacement reel into place and set it into motion.

I waited patiently on the other side of the projector as Paul stood up and mopped his brow, the combination of the heat from the projector and the physical exertion of changing the reels having caused him to perspire. He resumed his seat on the stool and relit his cigarette.

"So who the hell is this Davies, anyway?"

"Kind of depends who you're asking, I guess," I answered obliquely.

"Okay, let's just say I'm asking you."

"Ha, ha."

"Davies works for the van Brooks, I take it."

"Right. He's an actor. One way of putting it," I said.

"Well of course he's an actor." Spoken curtly. "Well, I guess not of course. I did work for them once and I'm not an actor. What do you mean one way of putting it?"

"Well, I mean if you wanna call what he does acting . . . "

"I get it, I get it. Say no more." Paul held up a wrinkled palm. "They all do it, I guess."

"Yes, I guess they do." I felt a knot forming behind my eyes. Paul's next words began to loosen it.

"The van Brooks are no different than every other outfit. The blue keeps 'em in business, keeps the company up and running. They strike me as kind of an out-of-control bunch, really. I doubt they operate too far in the black, if at all. Like I said, I did some stuff for them. Once. Some cutting, editing work. Facilities a wreck. Equipment falling apart. Old Steenbecks. Fed us cold ravioli. Chef Boyardee."

He sniffed, turned his head and spat.

"That was the real horrorshow."

"What do you mean 'horrorshow'?"

"What do you mean what do I mean?"

"They make horror movies. Not just the blue?" Pitch rising harmoniously with the last, questioning syllable.

"Well, yeah. Horror. More horrible than horrifying."

He smirked and fanned back his short, oily blonde hair. His cigarette had run down to the filter. He dashed it out, tossing the butt in the canister behind him. He jammed another between his lips and blinkingly lit it. I noticed Billy Paul's eyelashes, which seemed abnormally long, perhaps even false.

"They pick up six or eight titles a year. From New Zealand, mostly, I think. And they'll produce two or three themselves. Weird, riddle-in-a-mystery-in-an-enigma type shit. Lots of flashbacks and flashforwards, heavy-handed symbolism. Pretty much your standard roughie in the end, though. Would have some camp-value if they didn't take it so seriously."

He drew long and hard, causing the cigarette to point upward.

"Sometimes they'll cut up something and mix in new stuff and try to deal it with a new title. We'll let 'em know about it. Let 'em know we know. But we'll show it anyway. These popeyes, they don't give a fuck. They'll watch anything. In fact, a lot of them, the nerds and all, they love the recycled stuff. Take it as a challenge, try to guess which *Mondo*-whatever they're seeing again. Kind of justifies the whole enterprise, the lists and what not. They'll complain, sometimes, but it's just showboating."

He coughed again and spat, a huge, wet globule whizzing past the canister and against the concrete wall.

"They love it."

"So Davies. He was . . . "

"They all do it, though. They have to, you know."

Paul looked down at his sneakers. I thought I finally saw some color rising in the man's otherwise bloodless cheeks.

"We do, too. Starts tonight and runs all weekend. The skin marathons. It's what keeps the place open during the week, to be honest. We couldn't show this . . . this . . . ."

He stuck out an elbow toward the windows and titled his head.

"We couldn't get by just showing that."

"So *The Naughty Nurses*?"

"Part two. Twice as naughty, twice as nice."

"Ha. What did Davies want?"

"Oh, right. The prick. Just to let us know that they're sending some stuff over next week."

"Van Brooks?"

"We'll screen things for them during the week, sometimes. During the day. Preview stuff they've put together and report back how it played. Generally, I don't even bother to find out what the freaks think about it. I'll write up a review myself and send it back."

"Did he say what it was they were sending next week?"

"He did not."

"And he said his name was Davies, did he?"

"Yeah." Billy Paul again turned his head and coughed.

"That's funny."

"Why's that?"

"I happen to know that's not his name. Why do you think he'd give you a fake name?"

"I've no idea, pal. Why'd he give me a name at all? That's a better question."

We sat and listened for a moment as the projector hiccuped and wheezed along beside us. I could hear the sound of high-pitched chimes coming from speakers underneath the floor, followed by what sounded like the cries of a wild animal. Paul turned his head and idly looked through the left window.

"This is classic." He turned away from the window. "Got this from a guy down at The Deuce. *Savage World?* Know it?"

"No."

"No?"

The sarcastic smile returned. He closed his eyes knowingly. Suddenly his eyes popped open as he grabbed the cigarette from his mouth and waved it before him like he was writing a sentence in the air.

"You've Seen *Jaws!* Now See A Man Eaten Alive By An Actual Crocodile! See Sacred Tribal Customs Never Before Witnessed! See! See The *Savage World* In Which We Live! How could you not have . . . ?"

"What?"

"I love the beginning of this thing. The disclaimer they open this with. This is like one of those nature films. This white guy goes down into the jungle in South America or wherever and comes back with all of this allegedly true, allegedly horrific shit. Lot of animal attack footage and what not. Some sacrifices, mostly faked. Really most of it's pretty obviously fabricated. That's beside the point, though."

Paul's description was putting me in mind of my own filmmaking adventure that morning.

"There *is* some real brain surgery in there somewhere . . . from a hospital or something, I don't know where the hell they got that. Some other stuff. This old farmer supposed to be humping a llama or something. Completely out of hand. Here wait . . . listen . . . "

We sat quietly for about a minute. I heard a rhythmic thumping which I supposed were tribal drums. Then sharp, staccato tones which resolved into a discernible melody. Then what sounded like real strings, bouncing up and down, providing a simple accompaniment.

"What the hell . . . ?"

"Dance shit. Hilarious. Like KC and the Sunshine Band, that groove."

Paul laughed out loud and began rocking back and forth on the stool.

"Really gets you going, eh? This stuff is everywhere."

"Not for long."

"No, man, I'm tellin' you. You can't escape! They keep saying it'll die but . . . "

"It'll die."

"Hey, like the man in the movie says, it's a jungle. A savage world. Survival of the fittest . . . "

"Whatever." Suddenly anxious to leave.

"Anyway, I was telling you about the disclaimer. Before the thing starts, they throw up this sentence, something like 'Everything . . . .' No, wait. 'All scenes . . . '"

"I appreciate it, Billy, but . . . . " I shifted to the front of the chair and began tapping my knees.

"No, wait a minute. I got it. Before it starts it says 'All of the scenes you are about to witness, whether true or simulated, represent actual truth.' What a line. What does that mean?"

"Say it again."

Billy Paul repeated the sentence, putting a special emphasis on the words "simulated" and "actual."

"Sounds like they're saying it's all based on fact, even if the footage is faked. Right?"

"Yeah, but what does 'represent' mean? What does it mean to say that any scene, true or simulated, *represents* actual truth? And what the hell is *actual* truth, anyway? Not *simulated* truth?"

"You're reading too much into it. I think all they're saying is that it doesn't matter if it's faked . . . if it's a reenactment . . . whatever it is you see up there, they're claiming it really happened. It's all the same . . . "

"Yeah, but throwing that line out there . . . ."

He shook his head and arms as if to shake off the whole question.

"Well, that's what it's all about anyway. Trying to catch 'em in a goof. Sometimes I think that is what makes all of this work, they throw out stuff like that and we sit back and say hey, wait a minute, and feel all superior and shit and then next thing you know we're telling our friends about how you've got to see this and they're selling more tickets."

I recalled Tettleton's little speech and decided to respond with it. I leaned back in the chair and crossed my legs.

"Kind of like the boom mike in the frame?"

"Yes, exactly! That's what I keep saying."

To whom, I wondered.

"People love that stuff, the goofs. Every movie has got 'em. Even *Wizard of Oz*, for Chrissake."

"Huh."

"Yeah, you got people going nuts over how when Dorothy is chasing the Tin Man she loses his oil can, but when she catches up to him it's back in her basket. Or how the triangle theorem the Scarecrow recites after he gets his brain is all wrong. Or . . . "

"Not you, though."

"What? Oh, ha. Yeah, well. I'm intrigued, I guess. But these goofs . . . that's the whole idea behind these *Mondo* things and all the rest of it. The biggest part of it, anyway. Half of these geeks, the popeyes and all, they're just here to be stimulated. Doesn't matter how. They're all nerves. Nerve endings. But a lot of 'em are just waiting for what you said, for the mike to appear in the shot, or something else that tells 'em it's just a movie."

"Tell me something. The van Brooks movies. They like this, like this 'real-life' crap?" I pointed through the nearest blue square.

"To a point, yeah. I mean there's always some reality angle going on. Like that *Snuff* stuff . . . ."

I had actually heard of this. Big furor the previous winter over a movie actually titled *Snuff* opening in the City, playing at a couple of the grindhouses. All over the papers, editorials, everything. Nearly as rabid as the bone-business was four years before.

"Really unbelievable, the way they missed the boat on that one." Paul spat.

"The way who missed the boat?"

"All the protesters. The N.O.W. ladies. I mean, come on. A real snuff film? With that title? With fucking posters for it up there in front of The National?"

"I remember seeing the pickets up there."

"The whole thing was pure genius, I think. In fact, if you want my honest opinion, I think that's what guys like van Brooks sort of measure themselves against nowadays. Of course, what Shackleton did and said and all, that will not be topped."

"Shackleton?"

"'Pickets sell tickets.' That's what he said."

I nodded, vaguely recalling what it was Paul was referring to. The producer or director or whoever, having to deny that the film really was a snuff film in the papers.

Not at first, though. Thing went on a good while before all of these voices of reason battled with one another over who could deny the hoax the loudest. Even Severin had stepped in, pulling together a news conference where he calmly explained to reporters how what they had been reporting as a real, actual murder occurring on-screen was simple camera trickery. If I'm remembering it correctly, Severin even went so far as to track down the actress herself, to prove once and for all that she was alive and okay. Just like before, it was Severin who'd taken on the task of introducing some realism into things.

I pulled the photograph from my shirt pocket.

"You see, no one could appreciate that. No one could see past that poster. They had this dog of a movie, different title, everything. Another South American export. Something like four years later this creep Shackleton has filmed the ending, the new ending . . . "

"Yeah, appreciate it. Right. Listen, Billy. You mind taking a look at this?"

I handed him the picture. He took it and kept right on talking.

" . . . that new ending, right, where the director comes in and calls cut and then supposedly they off the actress. Disembowel her, for Chrissake. Now, never mind that you can't just cut somebody up like that and have it come out so . . . "

"Is that so? Listen, Billy . . . ?"

"No, see it's the cuts that give it away. The camera cuts. That thing was shaped and sculpted . . . "

"Yeah, yeah . . . you mind taking a . . . "

" . . . is what makes the movie. Being able to tell it's faked is what makes it work. That's an attribute, not a flaw. Even the ones who saw it missed that. See that's what I'm getting at in this screenplay I've been . . . "

"Billy!"

I stood up from the chair. Paul stopped speaking and noticed the tube of cigarette ash between his fingers. He looked over at the photograph in his hand.

"Who is this?"

"Name's Donna Morgan. An actress. Might've worked in a van Brooks production. Recognize her?"

I stepped over to the window and looked down onto the theater below.

"She looks like someone . . . "

Several men seemed to be changing their seats. The theater was maybe a third full. I pressed my forehead against the glass to get a better angle.

"That face is . . . something there. That smile. I feel like I've seen this person. The name, though. Never heard of a Donna Morgan." He handed the picture back.

"Can't remember where?" I said, nodding toward the photo.

"No, can't say I do."

"In a film, though. Not in person."

"Right. Probably in a film."

"You're sure you've seen her somewhere, though?"

"I wouldn't say definitely but she does ring a bell."

Chimes sounded. We both chuckled.

"That's to tell you something's about to happen. A warning sound," he explained.

"Let me leave you my number, in case you remember anything later." I slid the notebook out and wrote both of my numbers on a sheet. I tore it out and handed it to Paul.

"Those little chimes, that's like a public service, right? Prevents coronaries." Paul was again starting to laugh.

I looked back down through the window, still smiling. I noticed one of the men I had been watching from before suddenly stand up and move to a seat two rows closer to the screen.

His plaid shirt was untucked and flapping behind him.

# CHAPTER FIFTEEN

# IN THE GRINDHOUSE

"Listen, Billy, I do thank you for talking to me. I need to head on out."

Billy Paul slipped down off of the high stool and abruptly held out a wrinkled hand which this time I grabbed and released quickly, turning toward the door in the same motion. I hopped over the thick cord, calling back.

"Out the way I came in?"

"Yeah, sure."

I skipped down the steps two at a time and out through the door that opened onto the lobby. There was a big-shouldered man in a raincoat standing just inside the theater, looking out the glass doors onto the rain which continued to beat down outside, his dark, brown hair either wet or greasy. The old man had moved from behind the counter over into the ticket booth. I hastily concluded no one would mind my entering without a ticket, and so turned quickly and quietly toward the right-hand side theater into which I had been looking before.

My first impression on walking in was that the place seemed strangely busy for a weekday. Then I looked up at the screen and saw the tribesmen running around in a circle and remembered where I was. Probably a usual-sized grindhouse crowd for a rainy Friday afternoon. This home for some of these guys. Maybe most of them.

I slowed my pace, moving over to the side and standing against the back wall.

To my left, along the back row, I saw a scruffy-faced man wearing a lint-covered toboggan and huge overcoat sitting cross-legged and staring at the screen. He held in his lap a large, Sam Goody's plastic bag, the handle wrapped in knots about his fingers. Took a full minute before I realized he was narrating the film, right along with the guy onscreen. Had it down, too. Not just the words, he had the guy's pitch, the rhythm of his speech, everything.

As I surveyed the theater I noticed several other similarly-dressed men, many of whom seemed also to be carrying bags. Additionally scattered throughout were a number of well-built men, most wearing tanktops or tight-fitting short sleeve shirts, several sporting severe buzz cuts. One square-headed man about a dozen rows up and to the right caught my attention by continually putting his hands up behind his head and bringing them back down. I couldn't decide if it was the pulsing soundtrack or the sight of villagers appearing to stone one another up on the screen that had inspired this spontaneous, upper torso workout.

The outdoor scene kept the theater relatively well-lit for a couple of minutes. From my position in the back I had been able to pick out McCall moving a couple of rows closer to the front along the right side of the center aisle. I walked cautiously down toward the screen, slumping a bit so as to try not to draw any special attention to my having entered the theater. Finally, about twelve rows from the front and four or five rows from McCall, I chose a place on the right side, a few seats in from the aisle.

The sticky floor pulled against the soles of my shoes as I sidestepped down the row. I sat down and slid forward in the seat, putting my feet up against the plastic-covered seat back in front of me and lifting my knees up into my chest area. I craned my neck, letting my chin rest on my right knee, and from this position kept track of McCall's movements.

Once I had stopped moving myself, I began to recognize all of the movement going on around me. There was a steady stream of visitors to the restroom located below the lower right corner of the screen, the door swinging open once every minute or so, throwing a large, parallelogram of light out onto the floor. Once or twice the doors in the back of the room had swung open as patrons came and went. There were also several others who, like McCall, seemed to be shifting their locations every few minutes.

The chimes rang again. The scene abruptly changed from the outdoors to a hospital room.

The narrator offered a few further words to prepare us for the trepanation Billy Paul had mentioned before. The theater grew relatively less active as attentions became engrossed by what was happening on the screen. I slid my right knee higher against my cheek and looked down from the screen at the back of McCall's head.

McCall was presently in the right-most seat of row seven. Another, dark-haired, olive-skinned man was in the left-most seat of the same row. I watched as the raincoated gentleman from the lobby eased into a seat a couple of rows back. He sat with his arms extended along the backs of the neighboring seats. The surgery quietly continued up above.

Something was starting to click in my head. It began with the guy in the raincoat, the one with the shoulders. Body shaped like a gorilla's.

The parade of overcoat-wearing men to and from the restroom seemed to have stopped completely. The theater settled down, becoming eerily quiet as the narrator solemnly described the action above. Even the guy in the back shut up as the patient's scalp was tonsured and the skin peeled back. A small rotary blade was curving its way around the bone cap.

After about a half-minute more of non-activity in the theater, McCall turned to the right in his seat, toward the aisle. He stood up and sort of propped himself on the armrest, still looking up at the screen.

Then he dropped his head down and turned and looked straight into my eyes.

He'd known I was there. Knew it all along. Suddenly I felt more exposed than that fellow's cranium up on the screen, the meninges all pushed back, the blood vessels and various bundles of nerves glowing underneath the surgeon's rubber-gloved fingers. I futilely tried to crouch even further behind my knee.

McCall's face was in shadow, so I couldn't read his expression. I did, however, plainly see him wave a hand. He pushed himself off the arm of the chair and continued waving and pointing toward the restroom door as he walked. He leaned with his back against the door, pausing for a moment before entering.

The restroom door closed and the theater was once more dark.

I was frozen in my seat, unsure of what to do. I might have waltzed on in there and broken that little twig in two, if that's indeed what he was inviting me to do, had it not been for the raincoated man whom I suspected could be McCall's buddy. I was also wincingly aware of having left the .38 underneath the driver's seat of the Valiant. I waited.

Suddenly a short, pudgy man noisily stood up from his seat over on the left-hand side of the theater and walked across the room, his head appearing in silhouette just below the bottom of the screen. He looked to be wearing two or three overcoats, all tied closed with a black shiny belt and what looked like a large, silver buckle. As he moved across, I could see the olive-skinned man and the raincoated man both appear to react, both sitting upright in their seats as the restroom door swung shut behind him.

That's when the olive-skinned man abruptly stood up, a plastic bag softly crinkling between his fingers. Looked like he turned his head to the right before edging out into the left-hand aisle. He walked down the aisle and across the bottom of the screen, and entered the restroom. A moment or two later, the gorilla followed, exiting to the left and circling around. He walked slowly, his head down, his long arms dangling at his sides.

I brought my knees down and slid back in the seat.

As I stood, I noticed the theater to be perfectly silent other than the soft hum coming from the film's soundtrack. Everyone seemed completely absorbed in finding out whether the surgery would be successful. As I moved down to the front row and took a seat near the restroom door, I remember having the strange sense of being invisible, of suddenly being able to move about the theater without anyone noticing me at all. Something a guy my size almost never feels otherwise. I sat down and leaned forward in my seat.

Shouts came from behind the door, shattering the silence.

"Hold it! Hold it!"

I stumbled out of my seat and rushed toward the restroom door.

"Hold 'em up, man!"

The door wouldn't push open, being blocked or locked from the inside. I stepped back and started to kick at the door. It wouldn't budge.

"Fuckin' . . . . Hand me that. Give it!"

All kinds of shuffling and moving around inside the restroom. People were beginning to crowd on either side of me as well, adding to the confusion. Suddenly others were kicking and striking at the door and at the carpeted walls beside it and yelling at one another.

Soon it became difficult to tell from which side of the door noises were coming.

Loud thumps. More knocking about and cursing.

A loud, crunching sound.

Coughing noises. Gagging. Jumping up and down.

Some stumbling. Breaking glass.

More voices.

The door finally sprang open. Several men rushed past me and into the room. I pushed through an opening in the quickly-forming crowd and stepped lightly over the slick linoleum.

The room seemed unusually cold. I noticed the smell of body odor and urine, mixed with a kind of dank, sweet fragrance I could not readily identify. Unintelligble murmurs rose up from the semi-circle of overcoats and musclemen. Over their heads, I could see broken glass on the floor near the radiator against the far wall. Above it, the wooden-framed window stood wide open, letting in wind and rain, several of its lower panes either broken or missing.

I pried apart a couple of overcoats and saw that someone lay on the floor in front of them.

At first it didn't look like a person at all, just a heap of clothes. Then I saw how he was laying on his back with his legs bizarrely tucked up under his body and his arms extended. His several coats were all open and splayed about him, revealing a dark blue shirt and baggy gray pants with holes in the knees. To the right, next to his outstretched arm, I could see the silver belt buckle, the familiar "76" logo turned backwards and showing where the belt attached and ran back toward the body, disappearing amidst the many folds of material bunched underneath.

I heard the voice of Billy Paul.

"Jesus, look at how it . . . all the way . . . "

I moved closer, finally seeing what it was Billy Paul was feverishly trying to describe.

Although the body lay on its back, the man's head was turned completely around. Face downwards. Ratty black and gray hair matted to the back of his head. A dark, red pool had collected beneath the top half of the body and was swelling toward the opposite wall. I watched as it slowly coursed through the cracks and indentations in the linoleum floor, the thin curves and lines growing larger, spilling over and crossing one another.

A sinking feeling spread through my body. My knees buckled slightly.

I stepped back from the group for a moment, regaining my composure. I pushed around the group and stepping over the dead man's left arm moved toward the window on the other side. Paul interrupted his narration.

"Hey, Dick. Give us your take, here."

I turned back and looked down at where Paul was squatting. I pointed vaguely toward the open window, then let my hand drop. I swallowed.

"They killed him," I muttered, my voice shaking a little.

"They killed him," Paul repeated. "No shit, Sherlock."

A few timid chuckles. Paul continued his enthusiastic account of how he believed the death wound had been administered.

I folded my arms tightly and leaned out of the window, adopting a somewhat precarious position below a number of jagged shards of glass still attached and dangling from the wooden frame.

The window let out onto an alley that ran along the entire length of The Express, emptying to the right directly onto Forty-second and to the near left onto the service road running along the backsides of the neighboring buildings. Had they gone left to the service road, they could have taken any number of routes which exit out onto the next avenue over. Or back into one of the other theaters. I leaned back inside the room.

"Has anybody called an ambulance?" I asked, wiping my brow.

"Ye-ah, ri-i-ight."

Billy Paul's rejoinder caused a kind of manic chuckling to fill the room. It persisted for several seconds, soon growing into an uncontrolled laughter amongst the group, whose number had increased considerably. I saw Paul shaking his head back and forth and muttering. Sounded like he was saying "freaks."

A loud voice from the back began to quell the crowd.

"Okay, that's good, let's move it, let's go, okay . . . ."

I recognized the frost-colored crewcut of Larry Bowers as he poked it through the crowd. His attention was diverted for a moment while he paused to undo his nightstick from its leather thong. Evidently someone had called after all. He finally looked up.

I watched the confidence drain from Bowers's face upon seeing the body, and for a second I was sure he would faint. He righted himself, however, and knelt beside the man and started to check his numerous pockets. I stepped closer and into a crouch.

"Bowers, right?"

The policeman looked up, the surprise in his face taking the place of words.

"Where's Huff?" I asked.

"He's . . . in the lobby." He pointed abstractly up at me, his head turned to the side.

"Owen," I said plainly.

"Right, Owen. Huff's in the lobby. What the hell happened?"

"Listen, it's none of my business, but you probably ought to wait and let somebody else see this before you check him over. At least wait for Huff. See what he says."

"Yeah, right. Okay."

"Ambulance coming?"

"Yeah, it should be out front by now."

"Good. I'm going to go talk to Huff."

"Okay. Hey, what the . . . ?"

I had pushed back through the crowd and out of the door before Bowers could finish his question. Whatever it was, I knew I didn't want to answer it.

I remember as I walked back through the theater looking over my shoulder at the screen, which had gone completely white. A few men remained in theater, the harsh light from the screen casting an odd, metallic glow on their faces.

The lobby, meanwhile, was surprisingly quiet. The cold from outside had come in through doors propped open by the ambulance drivers. A pair of white-suited men jogged through, each holding either end of an empty stretcher. Two uniformed policemen followed. I saw Huffington speaking to the old man in front of the counter. A couple of overcoats lingered along the back wall. I walked over and touched Huff's elbow.

"Dick? What're you doing here?"

Huffington took off his hat, the shock of his orange hair helping further the caricature of amazement.

"You need me?" the old man squeaked.

"Huh? Yeah, give me a minute old-timer. Stick around." Huffington waved him aside.

"Old guy fill you in?" I leaned toward the spot the old man had just vacated.

"Larry . . . ." Huff held his radio up toward me before sliding it into his belt. "Body in the john? A popeye. Theater two, right?"

"Yeah, that's it. Listen, Huff. I was there, you need to get a statement from me."

"What?"

"I know one of the guys who did this."

"You know one of them?"

"I know who he is."

"You see anything?"

"Not exactly. Heard it happening, though."

"You're a witness, then?"

I nodded.

"Dick, what the hell you doing here?" Huffington asked again. I turned to the side and coughed.

"I'm here 'cause I'm trying to track down a girl. A runaway, missing person. For a client of mine. Ended up following this guy, this guy Jim McCall, whom I thought could know something or have something to do with it. Followed him into the theater, okay?"

"Okay." Huffington nodded as he placed his hat back onto his head. He took out his notepad and began writing.

"Okay. McCall goes into the john, then the short guy . . . the victim . . . then two other guys, buddies to my guy . . . "

"Your guy?"

"Yeah, the guy I'm following. Jim McCall."

"Right. Go on."

"Once they're all inside, I hear them shouting and scuffling. Me and the rest of the theater all run over to the door, which is locked or something. Lot of yelling, noises. Then the window."

"The window?"

"You'll see it. They made themselves a new exit down there."

"So who is this McCall?" Huffington looked up from the pad.

"I just came across him today. Porn star, believe it or not. The name I got on him is Jim McCall. Slim Jim McCall. I don't know if that's a stage name or what . . . "

I described in detail McCall's physical appearance to Huffington, who wrote down everything I said. I then described as well as I could the other two men. I waited inside while Huffington went out to call in the descriptions. The clock over the counter read five 'til four.

The white-coated medics awkwardly emerged from the entrance and carried the covered body through the lobby and out the glass doors, taking it around to the back of the ambulance and out of my view. They seemed to be taking their time, and a crowd had begun to gather around the sides of the ambulance during the delay. Two more policemen entered as the ambulance finally sped away. Without hesitating, they walked through the lobby and straight through the open doors.

Huffington finally returned, hat and notepad pressed against his chest, his usually sanguine face having turned significantly pale.

"Christ a-mighty. I'm not getting paid enough for this. You see that?"

"Yes. I saw it, Fred."

"Christ a-mighty," he repeated, dramatically turning his head back and forth.

"Fred . . . "

"Dick, I have a feeling McGhee's gonna want to talk to you about this."

"Yeah, I know. Look, Fred, I have to get out of here. Tell Cap I'll call."

"Okay, well . . . okay." I started to walk away and stopped.

"Might wanna go look in on your partner down there."

"Yeah. Okay. Thanks, Dick."

Huffington walked across the lobby, scratching his forehead with the brim of his cap as he continued to shake his head.

I left the Express and unhurriedly walked the couple of hundred yards in the still-driving rain back to where my car was parked. I stood beside the car for a moment letting the rain beat down on me, the large drops loudly smacking the shoulders of my raincoat.

# CHAPTER TWENTY

# IN THE DOGHOUSE

"Maggie, it's Dick. Dick Owen."

"Hiya, Dick. Twice in one week. What's news?"

"Mickey around?"

"He was. He might have already left, though. Hang on a second."

I stooped uncomfortably inside of the stuffy telephone booth. Looked at the reflection of my chin in the strip of stainless steel across the top of the pay phone. A short, dark stubble there.

Let me point something out here before it's pointed out for me. Yes, I'd left out part of what had happened in what I told Huff. The interruption in my tail of McCall, that blank time during which I was speaking to Billy Paul all about movies and van Brooks and catching goofs and so forth. The time during which McCall was able to hook up with his partners, and during which I was made to realize I wasn't just snooping around after McCall, but that this was in fact a game of fetch and I was the dog.

They'd put it together later, I knew. They'd question Paul and learn how I'd spent a half-hour or so up in the projection booth with him. Paul was a talker, would probably tell them all about our conversation and the Slim Davies character I'd asked him about. And if Huff was worth his salt, he'd see how both Paul and I were describing the same guy. The hair, the stiff upper lip, the plaid shirt. He'd have to see it.

I couldn't be sticking around to see to it that he made the connection, though. I had to get down to the Marathon, to the meeting with Constantinius. Before McCall did.

About ten minutes had passed between the time I had left the theater and my dialing up Maggie at her desk. I had taken off with the idea of going back to my apartment and getting a change of clothes. Only took a couple of lights, though, for me to realize that might not be such a good idea. Pretty soon I'm slipping into a not-so-small fit of paranoia. Driving slower, checking the rearview, cursing the rain. Thinking I could have been followed out of there.

Finally calmed down. No one was after me. No white Trans Ams about. Or Chryslers. Decided to put my anxiety to having left a crime scene so hastily and so enigmatically. As if Huff would send a car after me or something. That's when I stopped along Second at a phone box and decided to make some calls, starting with Mick. Tell him what happened, get whatever he had for me, and get on with things.

I took in a deep breath, filling my lungs with air and holding it for a moment before exhaling. Fogging up my reflection, temporarily.

Maggie's second became a minute. The minute three.

I began to have second thoughts.

Probably should've ridden in with Huff after all. Gotten it over with. Being roundly chastised by McGhee. Again. The accompanying life-lesson. Always I'm in the doghouse with that guy.

"Dick, where are you?"

"What? Maggie . . . ?"

"That a phone booth? I hear an echo."

"Yeah it is."

"Read me the number there, big fella."

I gave her the number.

"Got it. Listen, dear. Mickey's just left but I can put a call to him in his car and have him call you back. Okay? Can you wait?"

"I can. For a few minutes. Thanks, Maggie."

I replaced the receiver and continued thinking. Thinking about how poor it looked to have tagged someone, then to sit back and let him not only commit murder right in front of you but escape the scene as well.

I worried that this was starting to become habit with me. This wait-and-see, let-it-play-out-in-front-of-me approach. Borne from having snuck around after one too many infidels.

Because, generally speaking, that's exactly how it worked. There I'd be, following from afar, then sitting back, usually slouched in a car a half-block away, and waiting for the damn thing to play out. Better for me if it did, right? Then I've got something to take back. Some proof. What I'd been hired for.

Sometimes I got nothing. Not like what happened at the Holiday Inn a couple of days before. Not that kind of nothing, where no one shows, nothing happens, where the whole thing's a fiction designed to keep you occupied. I mean a real nothing, where I'm reporting back that nothing especially unusual is going on. I'd say upwards to about a third of the time, that's what happened. Nothing to show. Which'd always sit fine with me, but not so well with the client, for whom the story doesn't have an ending.

It was pushing four-thirty by now. I continued to wait.

Finally the phone rang in the loud, confusing way public phones always ring.

"Mick?"

"That you, Owen?"

"McGhee?"

"What the hell's going on, Dick? Lookit, I just talked to Huff. Can you please tell me why the hell it is I'm talking to you on a phone right now? Why aren't you down here . . . ?"

"Cap, listen . . . "

"No, you listen, Dick. And cut the Cap crap. Where are you?"

"I'm in a phone booth. All right? On the corner of . . . "

"Lookit, Dick. I can't believe I'm saying this. I *specifically* asked . . . "

"McGhee, listen. Slow down a minute. I'm up here working a case, okay? This thing was completely apart from Lanny and what happened at the lab. Or so I thought. Now I'm not so sure. You gotta believe me. That's not why I was there."

Silence.

"I'm listening," he exhaled. "Tell your story."

"Okay." I swallowed. "I'm working here, right? Working a case. Meet up with this guy, McCall, who maybe has something to do with my client's business. So I track him up to the Express and watch him talk to the kid working the window. Then watch as he leaves."

I paused.

"The kid?"

"The guy working . . . Billy Paul's his name."

"Okay . . . I'm still listening."

"I let McCall go so I can talk to Paul, right? Find out what McCall's up to. Meanwhile here he comes back, into the Express again. That's when I follow him and his buddies down into the theater. Three of them . . . "

"Lookit, Dick. Irregardless. You have got to come down here and see if this McCall turns up in the scrapbook. Slim Jim McCall? Is that the name he gave you?"

"That's the one. Could be a stage name or something, I don't know."

"Stage name?"

"That's what I said . . . "

"Well, like I said . . . . Come down, look at the books, see if you can help us get a make on any of these guys."

The phone booth was starting to feel smaller. Smelled like some animal had pissed in there.

"What? Get a make?"

"Lookit . . . "

"What say we make getting a make a couple of hours from now? You've got the kid, right? He saw McCall . . . "

"Goddamnit . . . "

"Listen, Cap, I've got a meeting to go to. Someone who might know about where McCall is. But it's gotta be . . . "

"No, Dick. No. I am not going to sit here and listen to you talk to me about you're working a case and how this is your client's business and meanwhile two people . . . "

"Cap, you got it wrong you . . . "

I kept trying to explain, continuing to talk right on through McGhee's successive spasms. Went on like that for a couple of minutes, both of us talking, neither listening to what the other was saying. After a while, I couldn't even hear myself. Just tones. Vowels and consonants. Bass notes flying out, either left open to waft up above the short, athletic bursts coming over the line, or stopped short, playing off the second voice's high-pitched dissonances.

My solo ended a few beats short of the end of the measure. Which McGhee completed.

" . . . or are you gonna make us come pick you up?"

"What's that?"

"Again."

"Aw, Christ . . . ."

"You don't have a choice here, Dick."

"What time is it?"

"What the hell difference . . . ?"

"Okay, I'm coming, Cap. Gimme fifteen minutes. Don't send yer dogs after me."

"Make it ten. Lookit, I ain't gonna be here when you come. Some damn rally or something, you'll see it when you come. I'll be outside, but you know where to go, right?"

"Yeah, yeah, all right . . . ."

The line disconnected. No, not all right, I thought.

I pushed against the far wall of the booth and managed to produce a handful of change and the red notebook. Found the number to the Marathon, picked out a dime, and dialed.

"Marathon." It was the young host.

"Ah . . . yeah, ah . . . I'm calling for ah Mr. Constantine . . . "

"Mr. Constantinius?"

"Ah . . . right. I had an appointment with Mr. Constantinee-yus and I'm gonna be late and I wondered if . . . "

"Who, sir, is calling?" he interrupted. "Please?"

"Davies. Slim Davies, sir."

"Davies . . . oh yes. You were in yesterday, were you not?"

"Um, yes? No?"

"Mr. Davies. Please hold."

I sorted through the change as I waited, picking out two nickels and shaking them in my left fist. Tucked the phone against my shoulder while I pulled the photo from my shirt pocket. The host returned.

"Mr. Davies?"

"Yes?"

"Mr. Constantinius is very anxious to meet you, Mr. Davies. He has asked me to inquire when might be a convenient time for you to come in this evening."

"Ah . . . yes." I straightened up slightly in the booth. "Ah . . . I think I can make it later. Eight o'clock? It's hard for me to say, really. Something came up and I'm . . . "

"After eight, then?"

"Is that okay? Because I . . . "

"No, Mr. Davies, that is fine. Mr. Constantinius has plans to be here all evening and so has said that any time to meet would be fine. We will begin looking for you at eight, Mr. Davies?"

"Thanks ah . . . I do appreciate it."

"Certainly, sir. Good-bye, sir."

"Good-bye, sir."

I quickly pressed and released the lever and inserted the nickels. Dialed Dr. Morgan's office number from the back of the picture. Let it ring seven or eight times before I hung up and tried the home number.

"Hello?"

"Doc, is that you?"

"Yes?"

"Dick Owen calling."

"Who?"

"Dick Owen."

"How are you doing?" The doctor's greeting.

"Okay, okay. We need to talk. I've got another meeting tonight. We should probably talk after that. You free?"

"Tonight?"

"Yes."

"How late?"

"Say ten?"

"Ten . . . . Actually, Dick, my wife has taken ill and . . . "

"She okay?"

"Oh, she's fine, she's fine. Just has a bug or something. I'd kind of prefer just to sit with her tonight, if that's okay. Do you need more money?"

"What? Oh, yes."

"Is it enough? Do you need more?"

"It's fine, thanks. I'll let you know."

"Because I can . . . "

"How about tomorrow morning?"

"Tomorrow?"

"Yeah, I can come by the office, like around . . . ?"

I waited to let Morgan finish my sentence.

"I suppose that would be fine. Yes. Do you still have the address?"

"Right here . . . Morningside?"

"That's right."

"All right, then. Anytime best?"

"Let's see, I don't have the book here so I don't know what to tell you. I'd hate for you to come up and have to wait. Can you call before you come?"

"Okay, I'll call first."

"Thanks a lot."

"Yep."

I hung up the phone and turned the picture over. The picture of a picture. Kind of like the way Morgan and I always seemed to be talking to each other. Like we were talking about talking.

It's hard for me to explain it, but there was this deep, unquestionable sincerity to Morgan that was hard to ignore. Had kind of a revelatory quality to it. You know how when you go to the doctor and tell your problem and you've got this hidden feeling like he's not going to take you seriously? That the way you've diagnosed your symptoms is way off base? Then there's that moment when suddenly the doctor convinces you that his concern is genuine, that he wants nothing more than to help, whatever the problem is? That's how it was with Morgan, all the time. Always asking what more can I do. Total sympathy.

But like what also sometimes happens with doctors, with Morgan there was also this detachment. That sense of professionalism which forbids the physician from getting too close. Which in this situation was frankly worrisome. I mean, if you really wanted to, I suppose you could come up with some possible explanations for this type of behavior . . . .

Not one question, though. About Donna. The whole call.

The money was probably worth thinking over as well.

Could have been just his way of feeling like he was doing something, of lending encouragement to the search.

You should always take the time to consider everything, though, whenever money unexpectedly comes sliding under your door.

# CHAPTER TWENTY-ONE

# SQUEEZE PLAY

I quickly scooped the remaining change back into my pocket, bumping my elbow hard against the phone box as I did. Pushed out and walked back to the car I'd left in the gas station lot about forty yards away. Along the way I pulled out the red notebook and wedged the photograph down into its front pocket. The rain had all but ceased, though the skies remained overcast. Gray turning grayer as night began to fall.

Ended up about five-thirty before I made it down to the precinct. As McGhee had warned, there was some sort of production going on there on the concrete steps leading up to the station. I could see the podium and the small platform on which it was placed. A lot of posters and banners and whatnot. Some photographers about. Didn't seem as though too many people had bothered to stop and see what was going on, no more than a hundred, I'd guess. The lousy weather probably didn't help.

I spotted McGhee and Walton sitting side by side to the right of the stage. Sol Severin there, too. Looked as though things were starting to break up.

I edged up along the left-hand side, looking across as I climbed. I caught Walton's eye, who immediately leaned over and said something to McGhee. I lowered my head and kept climbing. Saw out of the corner of my eye McGhee angling toward me, hustling up the steps as well as he could. We met a few steps shy of the top, on my side. I held up my hands.

"Sorry, sorry, I'm late. I know . . . "

McGhee had this weird, beaming look on his face, accentuated by the fatigue caused by his running over.

"Lookit, Dick. Peters is here. He wants to talk to you."

"What?"

"Henry Peters." Pronounced the name softly, even reverently. McGhee turned his head back over his left shoulder.

I folowed McGee's gaze to see the much-televised, well-composed, stern but responsive face of the state senator. An unflinching smile. Delivering handshakes and kisses.

I'd never met the man whose daughter's body I'd helped locate nearly five years before.

"To me? What about?"

"Didn't say. I have an idea."

"Does he know?"

McGhee nodded yes.

"What do I do?"

"Go on in and upstairs. You know Judy, just as you go in?"

"Right."

"She'll put you somewhere. Just wait where she tells you. You can look at the books after. Get a sketch done, as well."

"Okay, I will."

McGhee appreciatively slapped my shoulder and walked back down. I turned and went inside. Climbed upstairs as ordered. The precinct was again busy as usual, its operation seemingly unaffected by the rally out front. The woman, Judy, was there as promised.

She found a place for me, all right.

Not five minutes after I'd arrived at the station and there I was, sitting alone in the interrogation room. Brooding.

The confessional, some called it. Also known as the vise, the cramped space being designed to squeeze out admissions of guilt. Fifteen feet wide, no more than eight across. With the table just enough room for two men to sit, one to stand. Much too small for modifiers like "alleged" and "presumed" to remain attached for long to those whom they described before entering. No, you went in there you came out stripped of such ambiguities. You were the perpetrator. The malefactor. The charged.

Several minutes passed. Plenty of time to do a little interrogating of my own. To ask myself about Morgan. To convince myself whether or not McCall was part of the Marathon crowd. To recount to myself what Billy Paul had said about V.B.E.

To try and decide why someone would want to fix it so I didn't ask any more questions.

A knock at the already-open door.

"Come in?"

The man who first leaned his head in and then strode into the small room was taller than I had imagined he would be.

"Sorry to keep you, Mr. Owen. Hank Peters."

He held out both long-fingered hands, wrapping my right hand inside of them. The papers had said that the state senator was forty-nine years old. Harvard law. Practiced as a real estate lawyer before entering into public service. Having some experience then, one would think, with interrogative techniques. With finessing situations by asking the right questions, or by producing the right answers.

Significant gray around the temples. A heavily-made-up but nevertheless well-creased face. Light-gray eyes. Nose upturned just slightly, though all of his agreeable nodding made this potentially off-putting attribute seem less obvious. Could be that *I, Spy* guy, I guess, plus a few years. Not Cosby, of course, I mean the other one. Culp.

He wore a smart-looking, dark gray raincoat fastened closed with these several little square buckles. He didn't bother to unfasten them, which I took as a sign that our meeting would be brief.

He pushed the door to where it was open just a sliver. We took seats on opposite sides of the table.

"Call me Dick."

"Dick, I truly appreciate your taking the time to talk."

"Not a problem."

"Bill tells me you're working privately?"

"That's right. Since I left the force."

"How long ago was that?"

You should know, I thought. From the witness stand.

"Going on five years." He read my expression.

"That's right, that's right. Of course." Peters held one of those long fingers up to his lips in thought. "You know, Dick . . . I never had a chance to thank you, for . . . well, you know. For doing what you could for Henrietta."

"Wish it could've been different."

"As do I."

I slid my chair back an inch or two and leaned against the brick wall.

"You know about the bone, about what happened?" I asked.

"Yes, yes. I was just talking with Bill and Sol about it. Do you know Sol?"

"Not personally, no."

Peters shook his head.

"It just seems so incredible, Dick. The young man, Mr. Williams. He was young, wasn't he?"

"Thirty-five, thereabouts?"

"He was a friend, yes?"

"Yes, he was."

"Just terrible. This is exactly the sort of thing that my constituents bring to me and ask me how on earth can this happen. In a country two hundred years old, the greatest country in the world, how can this sort of thing go on?"

Shaking gradually turning into nodding. The no's to yes's.

"Tell me, Dick. You have probably had at least some time to think about this. I know that in many respects there can never be an explanation for this sort of crime. I mean how does one explain to Mr. Williams's parents that their son's life ended like this? One cannot . . . "

"But how do I explain it?"

"What do you think? You know why I ask, of course."

"Do I think Lanny's murder has something to do with your daughter's?"

"Yes."

"Well, yes I do. That much is obvious, I'd say."

"You think so? Yes, yes. Dick, you had said, when Henrietta was found, you had said something then about a bone, about how . . . "

"That's right. How your daughter had been killed in something like the fashion Lanny was killed."

"Right. But Henrietta . . . "

"Mr. Peters, let me say something."

"Yes? And please, Hank."

"Hank. First of all, I am really very glad to have the chance to talk like this. There is something I have wanted to tell you for a long time. Those stories, about me and the bone and all that, they were wrong. What I mean to say is, that was never my story to begin with, even if that is how it was reported. I'm not saying that I can completely deny responsibility for what got reported. But I do want you and your family to know that I never meant to imply anything different from what was found in the coroner's report."

"I understand."

"I do sincerely apologize for having added to the pain you must have been experiencing at that time."

Peters continued to nod.

"Yes, yes. Well, allow me to say, Dick, that I sincerely appreciate your telling me this. What you say is sensitive and observant and shows me that you are a person who cares about others' feelings. Yes, it is true. I cannot deny that when the stories you mention appeared it was troubling for us."

I continued listening, head lowered.

"But I am also well aware, Dick, of how these things can happen. Every time I give a speech, I am misquoted. What I said out there today, that will be misreported, edited beyond recognition in tomorrow's paper."

Peters put both elbows on the table and held his hands open.

"You see, during the years I've spent in office as a servant to the public, I've learned something. I have learned to have greater and greater respect for clear and honest communication. Such a thing has become increasingly rare, in our time."

"I'd have to agree with that."

"And Dick, I'm not simply talking about the papers and the news. The sort of miscommunication I am talking about I have seen occurring at all levels. Public, private, what have you. Especially in cases where intentions are in conflict, where the two parties might have different goals or different agendas or different interests regarding a common issue."

Peters slid his chair forward, his knee bumping mine.

"That, to me, is the most insidious form of miscommunication. Wherein one party purposefully misconstrues the other's intended meaning in order to further its own interests. We see this all the time with the press, who will often misplace the message in favor of supporting their own campaign, a campaign to report the most salacious and prurient version of a story or an event so as to sell more papers. But this kind of dishonesty occurs elsewhere, too, Dick. This is partly what I spoke about today, about the need for us to elect officials who are honest in their dealings with the people, with each other. Those who don't break the promises they have made or withhold information when dealing with others. Those for whom the exchange of ideas is open and unfettered and conducted in daylight and not in backrooms, behind closed doors, in secret."

Peters stopped and wiped his mouth. That last line must play better outdoors, I thought. I wondered if I should clap now or hold my applause to the end.

"You see, Dick, there is a reason why drug dealers do their business in the dark and government officials do not. The dealer, he wants to hurt you, not help you. He will lie to you and cheat you and do all he can to make his life better and your life worse. He is the antithesis of the public servant, whose only goal should be to better the lives of those whom he serves. That is why I feel so strongly about the need for open, honest communication, Dick."

"I see."

"So, tell me, Dick. As honestly as you can. Do you think the people who killed Lanford Williams are the same who killed my daughter?"

I now fully understood why such a meeting place had been chosen. I sat upright in the chair and tried to talk directly into Peters's widening eyes.

"That would be very hard for me to say, Mister . . . Hank. A lot of time has passed."

"Yes. That's true."

"I will tell you this, though. I do think that what happened to Lanny was somehow meant for me."

"Do you mean to say that you think they meant to kill you?" Long finger pointing my way.

"No, not necessarily. I mean it was meant for me, as in it was intended for me to take special note of what happened. I know this sounds strange, but I think these people have an idea that I know something, something to do with your daughter's murder. Something special, that only I know."

"Yes, yes. I see. And do you?"

"Do I?"

"Do you know something? Something special about Henrietta's murder?"

Little pause. Lungs filling fast.

"No, sir, I do not. Not that I am aware of."

Peters exhaled.

"What I mean to say is, if you look at the way Lanny was murdered, that seems almost as though someone were trying to prove that what I had said happened to Henrietta was possible. Not what I actually said, mind you, but as far as anyone knows . . . "

"Yes, yes. I understand you. So you do think it could have been the same people? The crowd with whom my daughter was involved?"

"Yes. It could have been. What?"

"The people who killed Mr. Williams, they were the same . . . "

"The crowd with which your daughter was involved?"

"Yes." Peters grimaced as if locating something in a mouthful of food, like a fishbone or something. "The junkie crowd, the ones who supplied her with drugs. I have always said that I believe they had something to do with my child's death." He swallowed.

"I see. Well, it might be that these people are part of the same crowd, as you put it. At the very least, they seem to be showing some sort of interest in what happened five years ago."

"Yes. Yes it does seem that way. That's good detective work, Dick."

"That's really all I can say, Hank. Honestly."

"Well I appreciate your sincerity."

"Did Captain McGhee say anything about the bone? They are examining it, apparently."

"No, nothing. I wonder what they might find?"

"Might tell them something. Help them in their investigation."

"Yes, yes."

Peters had slid his chair back and appeared to be preparing to leave. I watched and waited.

"Tell me, Dick. You say help *them* in *their* investigation. Is this not also your investigation? Are you not also looking into this?"

"No, Hank. I'm not. It is best for the department to handle it."

"Bill McGhee's a good man. He knows what he's doing."

We both nodded feverishly. I wondered which of us was less sincere.

"I'll let you get back to your work, Dick."

"And I'll let you get back to yours."

We both started to rise, then recognized that the room made it necessary to do so one at a time. I sat back down as Peters stood and started to move for the door.

"What are you working on these days, if you don't mind me asking?"

"No, no. Not at all." As I spoke I pushed the table forward and stood. "In fact, it has to do with a runaway. I'm trying to help someone locate his daughter."

Peters stopped and leaned on the open door.

"Is that so?"

"That's right. I'll be honest, Hank. This case has more than once put me in mind of your Henrietta."

We both stepped outside of the room and into the considerably cooler hallway. Two men in black suits and ties stood along the wall on either side of the door. We began to walk down the hall and toward the front staircase. There were people passing into and out of offices on either side of us. The two men followed behind.

"Tell me this, Dick. Are drugs involved?"

"Excuse me?"

"Are drugs involved? In the case you are working on, the missing girl?"

"I don't know of any drug use, no."

"Could be, though? Let me guess, she went to City?"

"That's right. She was a student up at City College."

"Yes."

Peters was obviously aware of City's reputation. We neared the third floor entrance.

"She's dropped out now, though," I added.

We turned to face one another. Peters held out his hand and I took it. Again, he covered the back of my hand with his free hand.

"Well I say to you with the utmost conviction that I hope you are successful in finding this girl. Have you any possibilities? Have you talked with anyone who has seen her?".

"I have, I have. I've spoken to someone who might have known her in the past. A film . . . "

"A filmmaker?"

We awkwardly continued our hand-holding as people passed around us and through the doorway.

"Yes, the girl she has appeared in a film," I said distractedly.

"What kind of film? You mean a pornographic film, don't you?"

"Yes, that's right."

Peters finally dropped my hand and stopped nodding, seeming to lower his head.

"You know, my Henrietta. She also was once involved in something like that."

"She was?"

"You find that girl, Dick. You find a way to bring that girl home, where she belongs."

"I'll do what I can."

"It was very nice meeting you, Dick."

"Same here." He turned to leave.

"Hey, good luck on Tuesday." I tried to chuckle.

"Yes, yes. Thank you very much."

I could sense Peters to be shifting gears. One of the suited men held open the door while the other stood over to the side.

"Don't forget to vote," he said.

I nodded.

"You are registered aren't you?" he called, stepping backwards. Face fixed in that I'm-counting-on-your-support look as he moved through the doorway, his bodyguards following.

"Yes, yes," I nodded.

Hey, it's not like I was under oath or something.

# CHAPTER TWENTY-TWO

# GETTING A MAKE

I walked down to the second floor and back through to the Squad Room, from which I was escorted into an office where I was made to sign four separate documents, in triplicate, including an affidavit which basically signified my undying promise never under any circumstances to reveal to anyone any incidental information I might happen upon when referencing official City documents, files, photographs, criminal dossiers, and/or anything else I might accidentally see, smell, hear, taste, or touch when on or around the premises or risk prosecution including a penalty of not less than one year in the state's correctional facility and a fine of not less than two thousand American dollars.

You'll just have to forgive me here, then, if I happen to leave out a detail or two.

By the time I was all signed in and taken down to the windowless Records Room -- where, need I say it, I signed in -- it was ten past six. Began thumbing through the several big, black notebooks of mug shots in search of the dopey-eyed visage of our virile, virulent stallion.

I ended up taking my time down there, the desire to get in and out having been all but snuffed out by the sit-down with Peters and these other hassles. Besides, if McCall had any sense at all, he'd know that most of the City's Finest would have had his description read out to them during the last couple of hours. McCall'd keep himself scarce tonight. I imagined the chances of him going down to the Marathon and partying it up to be, well, slim.

The detective gives his chin a rest and rubs his eyes. Cracks his knuckles.

The Records Room is an odd place. Real easy to lose your perspective down there. To go in with a specific purpose and come out with a head full of everything else.

Even though it had been several years since my last visit, the present organization had just enough familiar elements to trigger a host of memories as I searched. Of course, recollecting old patterns was no good in that it all it accomplished was my misusing the new ones. Meaning I would've been better off having had no experience whatsoever with Records, since my outdated memory of the place kept causing me to anticipate incorrectly, to forget where I'd been, to retrace steps over and again in order to make sure my search of the files would at least seem comprehensive.

The system of cataloguing mug shots had always been a source of conflict in the department. Everybody had an opinion about it, and sometimes it felt as though they intended to give each of these ideas a try, the way the system was constantly being updated and revised. One of those permanently-temporary type deals. Obviously, there were a ton of variables to consider. And even more ways to rank them. Things like race, gender, age, height, weight, eye color, hair color, when the crime was committed, where the crime was committed, what kind of crime was committed, the severity of the offense, and so forth. The criminals themselves would also impose their own network of liaisons and partnerships, and there had to be some avenue of cross-checking available that would accurately reflect those connections as well.

One thing about how they handled it, though, always stumped me. About every other month or so they'd come around and say they were introducing more of what they called these "systemic improvements." Usually by way of neatly-typed memoranda which we'd find tacked to pegboards and file cabinets and doorways and inside of restroom stalls and everywhere else so as to get our attention. A lot like all those political posters you see all over the City just before an election.

Now, of all these variables I mentioned, it would seem like the most important ones had to do with what the person looked like. Right? Physical appearance. In fact, most times that'd be all the searcher had to go on. But it seemed like whenever they'd monkey with the system, they'd inevitably make it harder to do a simple search based on what a guy looked like. Problem was, or so the argument went, all of these physical things could be altered, and so their value as indicators seemed to shift within the department depending on who it was making all of these filing decisions.

How things got arranged thus became a political thing. The old guard, usually they'd insist on these things and fight like hell to keep them. Saying look, there's gotta be a way to come in and look up five-foot-ten guys with blond-hair and blue eyes and never mind your hair-dyes or contact lenses or elevator shoes or whatever. Whereas the younger administrators were always wanting to entertain more complicated, less cut-and-dry procedures of distinguishing. Such as starting with a person's facial structure or body type or skull shape and from that coming up with ways to anticipate all of the possible guises available to the suspect. Ways to look not just for what you saw, but also to recognize what it might have become since you saw it.

What you'd end up with, though, would be some compromise that neither side liked and no one ever bothered to learn. Maybe there's something interesting about that on a theoretical level, but trying to deal with it meant risking a real pain in the ass.

Risking a penalty of not less than a pain in the ass, I should say.

Of course, the biggest problem was that despite all the effort no one ever read the damn memos, anyway.  Guys'd pull a folder out of one system and file it back according to another.  Maybe if they threatened fines or extra duties for the guy who misfiles something that'd get them at least to respect the order in which they found things.

This is what happens in the Records Room, then.  What I mean is, even if I didn't find anything useful in the Records Room during my visit, I did come out of there with a whole hell of a lot of what they call incidental information.

After nearly two-and-a-half hours, I gave up my searching for McCall, along with all of these other reflections, and carefully stacked the books back along the shelves they usually inhabited.  I stopped at the desk outside and signed out.  Then filled out a form describing the futility of my search, a copy of which eventually would be appended to my earlier statement to Huffington.

I went back up to the Squad Room and after fifteen minutes of getting sent from one desk to another finally found someone to set me up with a sketch artist.  This whiz kid, twenty-one or something.  Turned out a right accurate portrait, sort of thing he could charge five bucks for down on Coney.  Completely overcoming the so-so quality of the information I was supplying him.

I might as well point out also that it was only then that I finally placed McCall in the white Trans Am.  Wasn't until I looked over the drawing and saw how the sketch guy'd made McCall's hair long and ratty-looking that I was able to see him there in the passenger's seat, turning his head the other way.  That artist knew his stuff.

Of course, the thing was I had an idea of where I might be able to find an even more genuine portrait of the guy.  In his birthday suit, even.

I left the precinct seeing a lot of people but no one I knew.  McGhee and Walton had both left.  Maggie was gone for the day.  Someone else was sitting at Judy's desk at the front of the floor.  And Mickey was gone as well.

I'd completely forgotten about Mickey.  Never did call me back at the booth, though he might've tried during my sparring with McGhee.  I mentally pictured McGhee badgering Maggie for the number at the phone booth.

The steps outside had been cleared of chairs, the podium, and the dais.  A few banners and backers lingered behind.  I hustled down and walked over toward the visitor's lot where I'd put the Valiant.  Removed my still-damp topcoat as I walked, bracing against the cold.  Sky had suddenly become cloudless, the winds having blown the front away.  Looking like that sleet warning was a misfire.

The lot guard looked up from his magazine as I passed, and I suddenly felt conspicuous with the coat under my arm.  He seemed unconcerned, though.  Actually tipped his cap to me.  I walked quickly over and got into the car and started it and idled there for a minute while, in the shadow of darkness, I retrieved the holster from underneath the seat. Deciding the guard wasn't interested, I removed my suit jacket and once again semi-successfully rigged the thing up and over my shoulder. Put the jacket and coat back on and with a wave I was driving out of the lot.

Stopped at the Esso station on the other side of the Manhattan Bridge and went inside and called Mickey. He had heard the basics of what had happened up at the Express. After I filled out the story a bit, he agreed with me that going back to my apartment might not be wise. I also told him all about the talk with Peters. And the meeting down at the Marathon and the likelihood of meeting Tettleton and Levin there later.

Here's what we decided. I'd go on and make my meeting with Constantinius. Make it brief, begging off, if necessary. Sorry but I've other prospects, whatever. Then find out what I could from the other patrons of the Marathon regarding McCall and his buddies and leave. Either call or show up at Mickey's by midnight, where I'd stay the night. If Mickey didn't hear from me by twelve-thirty, he'd arrange for a squad car to come down and check after me.

Mickey had offered to go with me, but I ended up convincing him otherwise. I was starting to feel some guilt about dragging Mickey out from behind his desk and into this mess. Back into this mess. I knew if Doris had been around there'd be no way Mickey would be offering himself up to go out like that.

The drive down had been busy, and so was the lot at the Marathon. Busier than the night before. Probably around nine-thirty or so when I again pulled the Valiant around and into the far corner behind the dumpsters. Got out and made the long walk toward the restaurant's entrance. The sky was clear, but it was not a pleasant evening, what with the wind mercilessly beating against the faces of myself and several others headed toward the front entrance. Even so, there were a lot of them who had ventured out, their minds set on enjoying each other's company at the out-of-the-way place.

I filed into the foyer and stood for a minute or two amid the gathering crowd before my head-bobbing finally caught the eye of the young, pock-marked host. He waved a finger to me over the others' heads, calling me over to the podium.

"Mr. Davies. Would you prefer to wait here or at the bar while I let Mr. Constantinius know you have arrived?"

"Ah . . . here, no wait . . . I'll be at the bar."

"That's fine, Mr. Davies."

I followed the man into the bar area and watched him as he speed-walked through the crowd, disappearing through the swinging kitchen door behind the wait station. The piano was playing behind me, and I turned to see the professorial-looking face of its player, the stage bathed in the light coming from the numerous tiny spots positioned above. I could see behind the thick windows of his glasses the twin beads of his eyes seemingly fixed in deep concentration upon the upcoming key change. This was hardly Greek music, I remember thinking. More like Hoagy Carmichael.

"Slim! Big man!"

I turned toward the voice to see the fat, moist jowls of Joey Tettleton appearing to wave me over to the group positioned at a table in the center of the room. He looked mighty comfortable, like he'd been there a couple of hours, at least. I made as if to squint and stood leaning against the wine cabinet for a moment, letting my arms dangle while I quickly surveyed Tettleton's current company.

There was Levin. A tall-looking woman with long, black hair done up with a silver bow who appeared to be Levin's date. Two more young, heavily made-up women sitting on either side of Tettleton. No Adrienne. And no McCall.

I ambled over.

"Ah . . . hey there Joe."

"Slim, you gotta help me out here . . . "

Tettleton still wore the red and black bandana from earlier in the day. The bar's irregular lighting made him look like an enormous pirate.

"Slim, take a seat and explain to these nice ladies what it was we did today. With the loop. What we did with the loop today. Explain how we made the . . . what's so funny?"

Everyone at the table, including Levin, was laughing at Tettleton's struggle. Apparently this had been going on for some time. Tettleton, obviously drunk, looked as though he wanted to get angry but lacked the energy to do so.

"Jesus how many . . . h-how many times have I tried to explain this, Rog?"

Levin lifted his eyebrows and looking down into his drink said something which caused the tall woman to laugh. The others followed suit.

"No, really, how many . . . now what are you laughing about?"

He smilingly wrapped an arm around the brunette to his right and squeezed.

"H-help me out, big man," he sputtered.

"Well . . . ah . . . ."

"You 'splain it to 'em. You see, ladies, it was big Slim here had the idea that we . . . "

"Listen, Joe. You seen McCall around? Since the motel?"

"Wha?" The syllable briefly interrupted Tettleton's grin. Levin continued to whisper well-received witticisms to his friend. I repeated my question. The fat man scratched his fat head.

"Nope, nada. What do you . . . ?" Tettleton's eyes rolled back into his head and fell back down, signifying the completion of a thought. "Did he not give you back those bills? Is that it?"

"Ah . . . well, in fact . . . "

"Little shit. Hey, I'm sorry as hell about that, Slim. We should-a kept an eye out for that."

"Forget about it, Joe."

I noticed how Levin, at the mention of money, had broken off his private monologue and was looking my way.

"Ah . . . Roger . . . "

Levin held up his glass to stop me.

"Sorry, Slim, I was just getting to that." He downed the last of his drink and leaned forward onto his elbows, resting his chin on his fists.

"To what?" Tettleton heaved.

"Well, Joe, it turns out that Slim here wants . . . "

"No, wait. Fuck that right now. Sit down here, Slim, and explain . . . where's a goddamned chair . . . ?"

Tettleton was helplessly looking about the table when the host returned.

"Mr. Davies?"

"Ah."

"Follow me?"

I stepped around the table.

"I havta meet Mr. Constantine, fellas. I'll be back."

As I moved away from the group, I sent Levin a meaningful look. The cameraman nodded in response.

I followed the host as he ably coasted through the bar area. We stepped through the swinging door and into the kitchen, heated considerably by the open grills and the furor of surrounding activity. Snappily dressed waiters and waitresses skillfully avoided us, pirhouetting about with trays full of food and drinks as we made our way through the kitchen and into the large office located at the back of the building.

"Mr. Constantinius?" gently called the young host, an odd note of hope in his voice, as if the short man with the straight white hair who sat bent over the desk might not be Mr. Constantinius at all.

The man looked up from the papers on his desk and turned toward us, the consternation in his face caused by whatever puzzle was spread out on the desk seeming to dissolve as he smiled and spoke.

"Mr. Tavies," he said, a kind of quiet relief evident in his voice.

"For you I have been waiting."

# CHAPTER TWENTY-THREE

# A KING IN NEW YORK

The young host dismissed himself without saying another word, closing the large, maple office door behind him as he left.

Constantinius's well-lit office was enormous. More than twice mine, I'd guess. A large, glass-covered desk occupied most of the wall farthest from where I stood. Several wooden file cabinets were stacked directly behind the oversized, brown leather recliner where my host was seated. Between us and to the right was an impressively-constructed oaken cabinet, possibly containing a stereo or television. On the left, turned away from me and facing the desk, a matching recliner was pushed against the wall.

I edged forward, leaning my head in concert with the large rubbertree plant near the office entrance, awaiting further instructions from the diminutive, hoary-haired owner.

"Please, please. Sit down."

I rotated the recliner around and sat. Friction between the seat and my topcoat caused a series of chirps and squeaks to emit from the chair, each of which was sympathetically registered by a tiny, pained grimace on the owner's face.

"I'm sorry . . . your coat . . . ."

"Ah . . . I'm okay thanks."

I partially turned the chair back to its original position. Thus we sat at an oblique angle, not quite facing one another.

"Ah . . . I do surely appreciate you waiting up for me like this, I . . . "

"No, no, Mr. Tavies. To me there is no problem. Friday I stay. I am just glad we finally get chance to talk."

"About the position . . . is it . . . ?"

"Wait first. Tell me a dr-rink you woot like? Wine?"

"Ah . . . a beer all right?"

"But certainly. Are you hungry?"

"No, thanks."

"A salat?"

"Huh? No."

Constantinius picked up the black phone and punched one of the clear, square buttons along its base. Had a businessman's demeanor, a man seemingly with experience directing others and handling the difficulties sometimes associated with that kind of responsibility. Although obviously on the other side of middle-aged, his face seemed reasonably free of any evidence of the stress of management. Was fair-complected, more so than any Greek I'd ever met. His clear cheeks were wrinkle-free, shining like porcelain under the overhead light as he softly spoke into the receiver.

You might say Constantinius looked a lot like the old Charlie Chaplin. Not the tramp. I mean the old one, you know, the *King in New York* one. Had this mad little gleam in his eye like Chaplin. Sat with his shoulders pushed forward, even when talking on the phone. Was always holding his head up and away from you, like he was trying to keep his nose from bleeding. And every now and then as he spoke he'd smile that crazy smile, unembarrassedly revealing dingy gums and crooked teeth.

He appeared utterly comfortable there on his throne. The only detectable sign of vanity was that his chair had been elevated nearly a foot higher than his guest's.

"Mr. Tavies," he said, replacing the receiver. The mister like "missed stare."

He placed his palms on his knees and with his head up leaned forward in his chair.

"I was very interested hearing them tell me . . . about film you made today?" Glassy eyes enlarging.

"Ah . . . oh that. Who told you?"

"Mr. Tettleton, but certainly. Your first? Your debut?"

"Ah."

"Exciting?"

"Oh, yes, yes. Exciting."

"You have story to tell now?"

"What?"

"But certainly, about your film debut you will be telling story now . . . ?"

For the most part, I understood the owner just fine. The words I mean. Every now and then the accent would poke up through the surface of his speech. Nothing too distracting, though. Still, I was genuinely unsure how to respond to this last question. Was I being asked to tell a story, or merely to reflect amiably on the likelihood of telling the story at some future date?

"Yes . . . that was ah . . . that was something, all right."

"I know, I know . . . r-real movies these are not. Tell me anyway. How tid you like acting?"

"It wasn't really acting," I shrugged. "More like just standing there."

"You not like?"

"Not like?"

"Standing there?"

"Do I not like standing?"

"Dah, yes?"

"Oh . . . ah . . . I don't mind standing none, I guess. You mean for the position? This bouncer job?" I noisily shifted in the seat.

"Mr. Tavies, if standing you do not like, a chair you could have."

"What?"

"I am saying a chair . . . a chair you could have . . . "

The owner was interrupted by a knock at the door. A waitress gracefully deposited a tall, pint mug of dark beer and a small shotglass on two coasters in between us. Constantinius thanked her, I nodded, and she left. He resumed.

"There. Where were we?"

"My story?"

"Yes, as we were talking." He lifted his glass. "They were talking to me about your film, about how they were making your film like circle." He gestured with his free hand.

"You mean like a loop?"

"Loop?" Constantinius looked concerned.

"Yes?"

"To me there is fascination. How same can be beginning and end."

He began to sip at his drink. I was starting to be fascinated myself.

"That's right, that's it. They made the loop into a little story."

"To me there is fascination," he repeated.

"Right, well, it's ah . . . it's fascinating all right."

"Tell me how."

"How we made the loop?"

"Yes."

The talk of the town, it seemed.

"Well, there was ah . . . there was nothing to it. Did Tettleton tell you how it went?"

"Mr. Tettleton did. I want you to."

"Sure, sure." I cleared my throat. "Well, what we did, see, we started out having the couple come in. That was ah . . . Adrienne and Jim. Slim Jim. Do you know them?"

"Do I?"

"Yes?"

"Nyea . . . no, no. I do not."

"Well, they come in and they ah . . . they pay for their room and all. Rent the room, I mean. And then they go to the bedroom and all and then come back and decide to rent the room again."

My mouth was suddenly bone dry. I took a large, noisy swallow.

"So there you have the loop, right? It starts over."

"Fascinating," he said, shaking his head and holding the shotglass just before his lips. "But incor-rect."

Constantinius leaned back his head and smiled down over his chin. "Incorrect?"

"Two times they are r-renting? I am r-right?"

"Yeah, well . . . yeah. They go in again."

"To me there is a problem. Here . . . movie starts and couple r-rents room. Cor-rect?"

"Yeah." I took another loud gulp and wiped my upper lip.

"They go into room and they have a little fun. Cor-rect? Then they leave."

"Ah . . . yep. Then they leave."

"And then, in movie, they decide to go back in."

"Yep."

"And then they rent room again. Second time."

"That's right."

"*That* is where movie will end."

"No, see . . . it loops back . . . "

Suddenly I realized what the little man was getting at. The film's narrative was flawed, as they had shot it. There was no need to film the pair rerenting the room, it should have ended with their decision to return. As a loop, it made no sense. Constantinius smiled as he sipped at his vodka.

"To me there is a pr-roblem. Do you see?" Dark marble-eyes beaming.

"Ah . . . I think I do."

"Before they are paying second time, that is where movie should stop."

"Mr. Constantinee-yus, ah . . . I think you are right there."

"But that they can change. Nyo?" Big, triumphant smile.

"Ah suppose so, yes."

"But as we were talking. About your film debut you will be telling story. But certainly. The question must be this. How will you be telling story?"

"Ah . . . afraid I don't follow you there, Mr. Constant . . . "

"Will story you will be telling like it happened, or will story you will be telling like it was supposed to happen?"

"When I tell it? Later on, you mean?"

"When you tell it, dah. Your story you will be changing to make it right? To make it cor-rect?"

Whether intended or not, I began to sense in the owner's questions a test of the Slim Davies character. I mean, while I was tempted to get into it with Constantinius about the loop and so forth, I wasn't sure how much interest Slim should reveal. Woot Slim really give a damn?

"That's something, there. Ah . . . I guess probably I'll be telling the whole story. The whole real story, I mean. It's more interesting that way, I think. If I remember it all, that is." Chuckled nervously into the glass.

"But does it matter? But they will never know?"

"I guess they won't, no."

I had reached the end of my beer. The owner showed his teeth.

"So we are go back now. To me this is fascinating. To you there is fascination also, nyo? Mr. Tavies? Were you not asking scene to do again? Second scene?"

"You mean asking Joe?"

"Yes."

"Yes, ah . . . I did asking . . . I did ask Joe to do the second scene."

"So to you there is fascination. Am I cor-rect?"

"Ah . . . that's right. Sure I did."

"You woot like to see it? Woot you like that?"

I turned the chair so that I faced him directly.

"See the film?"

"Yes, woot you like? Since you are so fascinating." Sipping and smiling.

"Fascinated. I am fascinated."

"Da."

"Sure, ah . . . I'd like to see it. Only my head . . . "

"Tomor-r-row, movies we will be showing. You come and I will take you there."

"Take me? Where?"

"You come here. Nine tomor-r-row. I take you."

"You can do that? You can show it . . . ?"

He nodded, or at least moved his head up and down in a stiff approximation of nodding.

"Listen ah . . . I have a buddy who'd love to come, too. He'd get a big kick out of it, out of seeing me."

Constantinius set down the glass on the coaster before him and wiped his mouth before answering.

"Da, yes yes. Fine."

"Kind of short notice, though. He might not be able . . . "

"Either or. If he can come, then please do bring your friend. Nine o'clock? Both of you I take."

"Right here?"

"Here."

Constantinius leaned forward.

"I am just glad we are finally getting chance to talk."

"About the position? The bouncer position?"

"Da. Yes. For our security."

"This is ah . . . happening joint."

"Easvy neat, yeah?"

"Easy eat?" It was Greek to me, as they say.

"Happening joint?"

"The Marathon . . . you're doing right well out here?" Slugged back what remained in the glass.

"Very well, very well. But certainly, for our security someone we need."

"To work the door? The bar?"

"Da, yes. The bah. To me there is no problem for you."

"I got the job?"

"Tomorrow about it we can talk more."

"When would I start?"

"Tomorrow, Mr. Tavies. I assure to you about it we can talk tomorrow."

I sensed Constantinius hadn't any plans to order us another round. I reached forward and set down the empty pint glass. The owner shifted in his chair like he might stand up, but didn't.

"Well ah . . . I guess I better be heading out, then."

"You are welcome." To leave, that is.

He held out his hand. I took it as I stood, the chair loudly releasing its grip.

"Ah thank you, Mr. Constantinee-yus."

"You are welcome," he repeated.

"Nine o'clock."

"Nine."

"It's okay that I . . . ah bring my friend?" Backing away.

"Da, yes."

"Da," I repeated, ducking past the rubbertree plant and through the doorway.

The door quickly shut behind me.

# CHAPTER TWENTY-FOUR

# A TURNING POINT

I turned and walked back through the warm, steam-filled kitchen and out the swinging door. I stood behind the wait station for a moment thinking and breathing in the bar smoke, the relatively cool air causing my face to flush. I did what I could to recheck the bar for signs of McCall. Tettleton was still holding court. I shuffled out from behind the little counter and over to an open stool at the bar. The bartender, Victor, recognized me and moved my way.

"Back again, eh? Mister . . . ?"

"Davies."

"Right. Slim, right? What're you having . . . Pabst?" Finger pointed toward me, pulling the trigger.

"That's it. Thanks."

I kept my back to the tables until the beer arrived. Still wanting to talk to Tettleton, although unless he'd sobered up during the last twenty minutes I was less than hopeful I'd get anything useful out of him. I wanted to take a minute to regroup, these last couple of meetings having disordered my thoughts somewhat.

Both Peters and Constantinius had taken unexpected interest in my recent activities. I could see pretty easily why Peters was curious. In fact it would've been stranger if he wasn't. About Constantinius, though, I was less sure. I'd have to see if Tettleton could clue me into where the little king was coming from with his impromptu critique and surprise invitation to the screening. Constantinius had spoken like he was a fan or something. Though I seemed to remember Tettleton wasn't such a fan of the Marathon's owner.

Now and then someone would wedge in between where I was sitting and those on the neighboring stools and flag down Victor with orders for drinks. I hunched over my bottle, carving for myself a space in which to think.

I was trying to plan for what exactly I'd be saying to Tettleton, but my mind stubbornly kept going back to the loop and its flaw. It bothered me for a couple of reasons. Least important was the sort of irrational pride you always invest in your own ideas, that sort of selfish belief that you're immune to mistakes such as the one I had made.

But the thing was, the idea wasn't mine. It was Slim Davies who'd come up with that one. Screwing that up gave me the uncomfortable feeling I didn't have complete control over the part he was playing. It's one thing to bumble knowingly through my intercourse with others, but unplanned blunders could be dangerous.

Something you can appreciate, I'm sure. I mean, why does a writer go to the trouble of researching a character? So you can keep him under control, right? Keep everything reasonably probable as far as go his decisions, motivations, behaviors and so on. This Davies, though, it seemed like he just went with the flow. Stood around checking out the landscape and then just blurted out whatever came to him. Hard to plan for a guy whose whole world was improvised.

There I was, then, sitting at the bar, telling the story of my film debut, just as Constantinius had predicted I would. Only I was telling it to myself. And as he had also suggested, the version I was telling was a doctored one. The flaw in the loop better fits Davies's character, I decided. Fits it better than if it had been pulled off correctly, given what sort of person Davies was.

Yes, I thought, convinced. It's better flawed. More real.

After what seemed a lengthy ragtime tangent, the piano player suddenly segued into a sluggish-but-weirdly-moving Somewhere Over the Rainbow, with the crowd seeming to calm down as well. I finished off the bottle and was about to move when I felt a hand suddenly pinch my left shoulder, just below the strap underneath.

"Surprise!"

I turned and seeing Adrienne's energetic smile jumped involuntarily.

"Hey . . . do I look that bad?" she said laughingly, batting her eyelashes while giving my forearm a squeeze.

"Ah . . . Adrienne, hi. No, no. You look great, really . . . ." Which she did. Really. Auburn forelocks bouncing as she spoke.

"Well that's nice of you to . . . "

"Adrienne, ah . . . you seen Slim around? The other one?"

"You mean Little Slim?" Adrienne covered her mouth in exaggerated laughter.

"Yea-heh. He around?"

"Honey, I haven't the slightest."

"You didn't come together?"

"What? No, of course not. You see, me and Slim, our relationship is strictly professional." Said with a wink, also strictly professional.

I smiled back and raised my bottle. Was just opening my lips when an approaching Tettleton appeared in the corner of my eye. I set the bottle down.

"You gonna sit wif us or what, big guy?" His bandana was crazily pushed back, revealing a massive, shiny pink forehead.

"Just cooling my jets, Joe. Ah . . . had my meetin'."

"Oh, right, right . . . ." Tettleton was communicating gesturally with Victor.

"What meeting?" asked Adrienne.

"With Constantinius, the owner . . . you know him?"

"The little guy? White hair . . . ?"

"That's the one."

"He's the owner? I thought that's who that was."

We both nodded meaninglessly. I attempted to engage Tettleton.

"Listen, Joe. Did ah . . . did Roger talk to you?"

"Huh?" Still facing the bar.

"Did Roger . . . ?"

"Oh yes, yes, yes, yes. As a fact . . . as a matter of fact he did."

Even in profile, I could see the broad smile which had spread across Tettleton's face. He completed his transaction with Victor, another of the put-it-on-my-tab variety, and with glass securely in hand turned back toward us.

"Let us go sit somewhere and talk," he said.

"Where we going?" asked Adrienne.

"Honey, me and Slim got somethin' we gotta go talk about, honey."

"You guys going to talk about me?"

"Of course. What else?" Chuckles all around.

"Just so I know."

The three of us moved away from the bar and toward the table in the center of the room. I stood back while Adrienne found a chair and Tettleton spoke animatedly to Levin. I then followed the plundering pirate as he sailed through the tables, along the wine rack, and through the short hallway opening up onto the dining area. Tettleton abruptly stopped and wheeled around, comically looking on either side of me. Finally he looked up.

"Oh . . . heh. There you went. This-a way."

As we passed before the open entryway to the kitchen on the right, the piano faded, replaced by the piped-in sound of a particularly rambunctuous bouzouki solo. Around the top of the walls were carefully calligraphied Greek letters, with dozens of decathletes running around and throwing things underneath. We found an empty booth and slid in across from one another. A waiter appeared and glasses of water, napkins, and utensils quickly materialized before us. We reordered drinks and Tettleton asked for an order of spanikopita, all the while continuing to wear the conspiratorial smile.

"Shit that reminds me . . . your money . . . "

"Don't worry 'bout it, Joe. We'll take care of it later."

I couldn't imagine my stipend for the day's work was worth sniffing around for. Nor was Joe in any condition to handle it were I to explain that indeed McCall had returned my twenty dollars to me.

Tettleton looked around dramatically before leaning over the table.

"So, heh, heh. Rog tells me you're thinging . . . you're thinking of moving for real into a . . . into a starring role?" A little slurred. Adding to the already harsh grogginess of his voice. I cleared my throat, as if that would help.

"Ah . . . yeah, well, I was sort of thinking."

Tettleton leaned back and started to cough. The spanikopita arrived. He scooped up the napkin roll and seemed to be having trouble freeing the fork.

"Like I was saying I was thinking if maybe . . . "

"Oh we can get you somethin'. Don't you worry 'bout it."

"Really?"

"Oh hell yes . . . always a part fer someone as willin' as yerself."

Prongs finally emerged from one end of the napkin and Tettleton yanked it through, sending the spoon and knife twirling across the table.

"So ah . . . tell me, Joe. You see a lot of turnover? I mean do you always work with the same people or do . . . "

"Turnover? Oh yes, yes, yes. Well, no."

"No?"

"Well it depends, see. A lot of folks'll try it and not like it and they'll get out . . . but then you got those who do and they keep coming back. Ya know what I'm sayin'?"

He cut the pastry with the side of his fork and gouged a large piece, holding it aloft as he spoke.

"So the answer is yes and the answer is no . . . what th'hell were we talkin' about?" He hungrily thrust the fork into his mouth.

"Turnover."

"Right, right, right. Yes and no."

"For example, today. With Slim and Adrienne."

"Exactly what I'm talkin' 'bout. Adrienne, she ain't goin' nowhere. She's how do you say it . . . she's found her callin'. Heh, heh. Get it? Slim Jim, though, I dunno 'bout that guy."

"He did seem kind of out of it."

"What you mean?"

"Ah . . . you know, Joe. Had that look like . . . you know, like he was coked up or somethin'."

"Well . . . that could be, I s'pose. Would explain a lot, really. No, I'm guessin' Slim Jim probably ain't too long for this bidness. Unprofessional as hell. Like you say probably a damned cokehead. And you can't trust a cokehead much farther'n you can throw him . . . "

"How old a guy you think Slim Jim is?"

"Wha? Mid-twenties, I'd say . . . ?"

"He from around here?"

"I think so. I dunno."

"You know was he ever at City College?"

"What? Heh, heh, heh . . . . No, no. Slim Jim does not strike me as exactly collegiate material, if you follow me there . . . heh, heh.  Besides, as I was sayin', on top of everythin' else, the guy's one lousy performer.  No more'n average as far as looks . . . well you saw him, you know what I'm talkin' 'bout."

"Sure, sure."

"You saw.  The guy's no head-turner."

I watched carefully as Tettleton shovelled home another mouthful.  I was utterly convinced the man meant nothing more than to comment on McCall's looks.

"Right, right."

"So he's a goner, I'd say."

"A lot of these people you work with, they come and go pretty ah . . . pretty regular then?"

"You smart . . . .  *You* ever at City College?"  Pointing his fork and laughing.  I smiled, trying to cover my impatience.  Had a little start when Tettleton suddenly dropped his fork and looked up.

"What the hell are we talking 'bout?"

"Ah . . . ."

"Spit it out, man."  Spitted out, in fact.  Bits of flaky crust hanging on his lower lip.

"Ah . . . I'm sorry, Joe.  I just had this question and ah . . . I was just shy about asking is all.  See I was wondering maybe if you might know about this one girl, maybe see if you worked with her, this one girl I seen over at the Show Place once."

"What're sayin', Slim?"

"I told you how I'd seen the loops over at the Show Place before, right?"

"Yeah . . . I guess you did, yeah."

"Well there was this one they had there I seen with ah guy and two girls and ah . . . I was wondering if maybe you'd ever . . . "

"Whoa, big man!"

Tettleton lifted his left palm to his forehead with a wet smack.

"I really think maybe one's enough for starters."  Laughing and chewing.

"No, no, no."  I held out my hands and laughed as well.  "Not that.  No.  Shit."

"Shit is right, heh heh . . . "

"No what I meant was I'm talking about one girl in particular.  She was in this one with another girl and a guy.  In front of a fireplace."

Tettleton continued chewing as he set his fork down.  He looked up into the stained glass shade that hung over the table as if in thought.  He took a big gulp of water, spilling ice cubes as he did.  His face suddenly cringed.

"Where the hell's our drinks?"

I held my glass up for Tettleton to see.  Tettleton made an aw-shucks face as he recognized he'd already downed his highball.

"Lemme know when the . . . when the boy comes 'round agin." He lifted the side of his plate and scraped the last forkful of spinach and cheese from it and into his gaping mouth.

"So anyway, Joe, there was this one girl in the loop. Dark-haired. On the right."

"The right? Wait you're talkin' about dis girl. You sayin' you want to make a movie with her?" Tettleton seemed more than a little confused.

"Well, ah . . . I was just wondering, Joe. If she was around and all."

"Tell me which one is dis agin?"

"There was this fireplace in the back. Two girls. One was blonde, the other had dark hair."

Tettleton tapped the area just above his left eye with his finger. The waiter cleared his plate and utensils and quietly asked if we needed anything else. Tettleton continued tapping. I shook my head no, fearful of breaking the spell. The waiter left.

"I made one like that. I remember. The fireplace. Last winter."

"Was it last winter? It wasn't more recent?"

"No, no, I remember it. The guy I don't know. Never saw him again. The girls . . . ."

Tettleton seemed to stop his slurring as he tried to recollect their names. I lifted my glass to my mouth and noticed my hand shaking slightly. Would be easier just to show Tettleton the photo, but I decided not to risk it. Tettleton was pretty far gone, but he'd remember that. I put the glass back on the table and my hands in my lap.

"Well hell, Slim. One of them was Laura, I think. Or Linda. Linda Victors. Vickers. Her name was Linda Vickers. Something like that . . . "

"What about the other one . . . the dark-haired one?"

"Yeah . . . that was her name." Spoken with satisfaction.

"What about the other one?"

"The other one . . . ? Dammit, Slim, I'm gonna git a headache trying to think of this."

"Think."

"I am thinking, goddamnit." The sweat dripping down the sides of his face seemed proof enough that he was.

"Brenda?"

"What?"

"Jennifer? Deborah? Ah . . . Alice?"

"What the hell are you sayin'?"

"Just throwing out names, Joe. Donna?"

"Naw, naw. That never works. I don't remember the other one's name. What do you care for anyway?"

"I told you. I wondered if maybe . . . "

"Yeah, but I already told you . . . ."

Tettleton reached out and grabbed the apron of a waiter passing by, who graciously responded by promising him that he would send out his waiter as soon as Tettleton let go of him. He exhaled and folded his hands on the table in front of him.

"Slim. Big guy. Listen to what I say. Both those girls are long gone. History. Put 'em out of yer mind. I got a better idea for you, as yer a beginner an' all. We'll set you up with Adrienne. She'll be tickled when I tell her. You watch . . . "

"Oh jeez ah . . . I don't know ah . . . "

"No, no you just wait and see. Hell, I'm gettin' a boner just thinkin' 'bout it."

Tettleton stopped short and looked up sheepishly.

"Heh, heh. You know what I mean."

"Ah . . . well, I tell you what let me ah . . . let me scram before you say anything to her? Okay?"

"Okay, okay."

Our waiter appeared and Tettleton ordered another highball. He tried to buy his buddy Slim another beer, but I managed to refuse the offer.

"Listen, Joe. Constantine invited me to this thing tomorrow to see the movie we made today. You know anything about it?"

"What? The one I made?"

"Yeah. Like ah private screening or something?"

"Huh."

"Does he do this sort of thing often?"

"Who, Constantine? Yeah, well, he is a dirty old man. He's in with the company somehow, he must get . . . "

"Van Brooks, you mean?"

"Yeah, yeah." Tettleton looked up at me, seemingly puzzled. Then continued. "He must have gotten it today or hell I don't know. Well damn. That little . . . he ain't Greek at all, you know."

"Ah . . . kinda doubted it."

Tettleton sat stewing, running a finger around the rim of his glass. Yet another highball appeared, and the length of the delay required for Tettleton to react to it dissuaded me from lingering any further.

"Well, listen, Joe, I need to head out."

"Head out? Huh . . . ?"

"Gotta go."

"Gotta go, gotta go . . . . Slim, wait. We'll set something up next week. I promise, Slim." Tettleton laid a brotherly hand on mine.

"Thanks a lot, Joe."

I slid out and held out a hand which Tettleton took and, using my weight for balance, awkwardly pulled himself up and out of the booth.

"Okay, big Slim."

Tettleton clapped my shoulder and stumbled past me, his bandana sliding even further back on his puffed bed of hair as he went. He moved uncertainly toward the back of the restaurant, presumably toward the restrooms. I stood for a moment in the hallway, watching him bump into a couple of table corners.

I turned to leave.

I was able to shuffle on through the bar area and out the door with only a nod and a wave toward the table where Levin, Adrienne, and the others were sitting.

The night wind had stilled. Cars continued to file to and from the Marathon's lot. I made kind of a vague search, looking for white Chryslers and Trans Ams. Seeing none I moved quickly back toward the Valiant.

Turned the car around and switched on the radio as I left the Marathon. Made it up to Twenty-third and instead of keeping straight hung a left and headed toward Mickey's. I was listening for the time. They were playing that trivia thing which went on for a while before finally the announcer said it was twenty to twelve. You might have heard it before, has a funny name like "Says Who?" or something. They read out a quote and people call in and say what it is and win something. I think this particular night it might have been Giants tickets. Which would've made sense, since giving them away was the only way they were going to get anybody to come and watch that sorry squad.

I had just gotten over to Eighth when they threw out this one, "It is a riddle wrapped in a mystery inside an enigma." Had to come up with who had said it and what the it was.

I remember thinking as I drove how I'd heard that one over and again but never knew where it had come from or what it was about. To be honest, I'd always thought it to be one of those gag lines. You know, one of those pretend Shakespeare quotes that sounds like it could be real but isn't. Ended up thinking it had to be from some movie.

Then, finally, just as I moved over onto Seventy-second and made the turn back down Columbus toward Mickey's high-rise, some guy calls in with the answer. Winston Churchill, he said. The it?

Russia.

# CHAPTER TWENTY-NINE

# THE POWER OF SUGGESTION

Mickey and Doris live in a roomy one-bedroom unit located in that huge high-rise just off Columbus on Seventy-first. I'd been there only once, right after they'd first moved in a couple of years before. A real comfy set-up. Pool and laundry. Huge damn lobby, from which you had to call up to your party. Mickey buzzed me in and I rode on up to the twenty-fifth floor where they lived. Mick met me in the deserted hallway.

"O-wen . . . . You're just in time. I was about to call it in."

We walked side-by-side.

"What a night." I yawned and scratched at my scab.

"After you," he said.

I crossed in front of Mick and into the spacious apartment. Walked over to the sliding glass doors which faced out onto the Hudson. A nice, long view, including the Trade Center and extending all the way out to Jersey. I turned around, still stretching.

"Hey, nice. You guys have really done the place up."

"Picked up your bed there last month." Mickey gestured toward the large white-cushioned couch in the center of the living room.

"Great . . . hey, Mick thanks a bunch for . . . "

"Come over here for a minute."

We walked into the kitchen where I took off my coat and jacket and began to undo the holster. Mickey took a yellow sheet of paper off the table.

"Remember this?"

"Sure, sure."

"Remember how you got one of these, too?"

"Yeah."

"Look at this thing."

I read the flyer again as Mickey continued speaking.

"I was curious and did some checking this afternoon. This has the Egg Roll opening at six. Remember how we were early? I went by the place today about four o'clock and they were open, just like always. I went in and asked some questions and come to find they're open everyday, eleven to eleven."

"Except yesterday?"

"Except yesterday. Closed all day. The cook said there'd been a fire or something in the kitchen."

"What're you saying? This thing's a fake?"

"Seems that way. I'd be willing to bet only two of these got made."

I draped the holster over a chair as we sat down. I remembered McCall's reaction when I'd pulled the flyer out of my pocket at the hotel.

"We were invited there, then? At six?"

"Two for one special."

"Seems like a hell of a gamble."

"Not really. What's to risk?"

"Nothing, I guess. Who owns the . . . ?"

"Whoever's after you, they know you. Pretty damn well, I'd say. Know your car, your office, everything."

"Hell, now, if they really wanted to they could drive my car, live in my apartment . . . "

"Right. And with those old newspapers they'd know we were partners, that we were both there that night. My car's a cinch, too. My name's right there on the spot where I park it."

"Hey, hey . . . not bad," I cracked.

"After what happened Wednesday night, they'd also know you'd been into the station. And that you'd probably be getting in touch with me."

"You know I hadn't even seen this thing when you called me."

"Well, it almost worked. They almost got us there, together, after six."

I continued to read the flyer. Mickey rose and walked over to the range. "Coffee?"

"Well goddamn, Mickey," I blurted. "If you thought all this why'd you invite me over here? I mean if someone wants to get us together . . . ?"

"Hold on, hold on. We're fine here. Nobody's getting up here without our knowing it, and even if they did we'd be waiting for them."

"I get it."

"You can grab a nap if you want to . . . I'll stay up."

"No . . . suddenly I ain't so tired."

Mickey got out two matching black mugs and set them on the counter.

"I talked to Cap a little while ago and he said the lab will have something by morning."

"The bone?"

"Yep. I told him you'd be staying here. They're gonna call us."

"Nothing yet?"

"No. Somebody said something about there being good samples, that it was a good specimen to work with. Although I think part of what's holding things up is you've got pieces of Lanny mixed up in there as well."

"Christ. McGhee didn't say anything about me being here? For when news comes?"

"I don't know what McGhee's thinking. I get the feeling he's a little dumbstruck by all of this."

"Has he said anything at all to you?"

"He's keeping tight-lipped. I think he's scared shitless somebody's gonna find out about the bone and the whole mess is going to get out again. That he's going to wake up one of these mornings and find himself back in the papers talking about how Peters's daughter is going to be just fine."

Mickey brought the filled, steaming mugs over to the table.

"You hungry?"

I remembered I hadn't eaten since lunch.

"Yeah, I could use something."

"Eggs? Toast?"

"Yes. Yes."

Mickey nodded and walked back over to the other side of the kitchen.

"So Mick, tell me what do I do with this Morgan character?"

"Morgan?"

"The doctor whose daughter I'm supposedly looking for."

"Right, right. Another Henrietta Peters, right?"

"Yeah . . . right . . . ." I trailed off, Mickey's words having triggered something.

"Well?"

"Mick, lemme use your phone."

"Sure? Who . . . ?"

"Morgan. I got something to ask him."

Mickey directed me over to the phone next to the couch. I hurriedly removed the red notebook from my pocket, this time scraping my palm. Dug out the photo and dialed up Morgan's home number. Rang maybe twice before being answered.

"Hello?"

"Dr. Morgan?"

"Yes. Wh-who is calling, please?"

"Dick Owen."

"Oh, excuse me, Mr. Owen. I didn't recognize you."

"Listen, Dr. Morgan . . . sorry to be calling so late, but . . . "

"Um, Donna . . . ? You've found . . . ?" Morgan's voice was a little shaky. I had the impression, though, that I hadn't woken him up.

"No, no. I'm afraid I haven't. As a matter of fact, I was calling to say that I can no longer in good faith continue this case."

"What? Why?"

"I'll refund you the money you advanced."

"No, listen. Mr. Owen. Dick. You have to keep looking . . . "

"Dr. Morgan, I . . . "

"Harry."

"Harry, listen to me. I have done all I can reasonably do. I think it's time you took this to someone more qualified to help you."

"D-did you talk to the man. The man you said who . . . ?"

"I did that. Joe Tettleton is his name. According to him, the film was made last winter."

"Yes?"

"That would've been Donna's freshman year, then. Before she disappeared."

"That's right. I guess that would have."

"This fellow Tettleton, he has an imperfect memory of the shoot, and no knowledge of where Donna might be today."

"No idea?"

"None."

"Dick, you have to keep looking. You have to."

Mickey had walked over and stood beside the couch, listening.

"Harry, like I said, I can't. To be perfectly honest, I was surprised when you came to me. I don't know what your friend or patient or whoever it was told you about me when you were referred, but I think it's time you went down and talked to someone in the investigative unit of the . . . "

"But we can't go to the police. I told you . . . "

"Yes, I know that, Harry. But still, you need to talk to someone else. If not the police, which would be the course of action I'd recommend most to you now, then a private investigator with more direct experience with missing person cases. Someone who can . . . "

"No, no. Dick, I want you. You've got to stay with . . . "

"Listen, Harry, I can't . . . "

"I'll pay you more, if . . . "

"No, no. You don't understand. You're not hearing me, Harry. You should be paying me less, is what I'm saying to you. Take it to someone else."

"But, Dick. Wait . . . "

"Trust me on this, Harry."

"Dick, wait. Stay on it for a few more days, at least. Mrs. Morgan thinks you're the greatest thing that's ever happened to us. I can't go back to her and tell her it's all been for nothing. All I am saying, Dick, is that I am willing . . . no, not just willing. I'm wanting to stay with you as far as you can go."

The line went silent. Morgan again spoke.

"I do trust you, Dick. I know you've got Donna's interests in mind."

I waited for a moment, looking up at Mick who was holding out an oven mitt upturned in a what-the-hell-is-this-all-about kind of gesture.

"Well, Harry. Like I said, I'm at kind of a dead end here."

Waited a moment. At last I asked my question.

"What do *you* suggest I do?"

"What do I suggest?"

"Yes?"

"I don't really know, Dick."

"Well, I'm out of . . . "

"You could go back to the Show Place?"

"Okay."

"What about this trash Tettleton? Do you think you've gotten all you can out of him?"

"I think so."

"He didn't remember Donna at all?"

"Nope."

"He remembered the filming, though?"

"Yes. Last winter."

"Did he recall the names of any of the other actors?"

"As a matter of fact, he did."

"That person might know her. Th-that would be something good to try, wouldn't it?"

"Yes, I could do that."

"What about the distributor? You had said there were several prints floating about. Maybe they know something about her?"

"They might."

"Maybe she signed a contract or something?"

"Maybe. Probably not."

"Just stay on it, Dick."

"Okay."

"Okay?"

"You've convinced me, Harry. A couple more days."

"That's great, Dick. Really."

"Tell me something, though. Is there anything at all that I should know that you haven't told me? Something you might've forgotten to mention before? That you've remembered since you first came to me?"

I smelled something burning. I looked up at Mickey and nodded toward the kitchen.

"Oh shit," he whispered, dashing toward the source of the smoke.

"No, Dick. Not that I can think of."

"You're sure about that?"

"Yes."

"Okay, then. I'll try these things. Should we meet tomorrow as planned or wait . . . ?"

"Maybe Monday? Monday morning?"

"I'll just come by the office like we'd said before?"

"That'll be fine. Like we said before, call first. Thanks a lot, Dick. I can't tell you how much I . . . how much we appreciate . . . "

"I understand, Harry. I'll be calling Monday."

"Talk to you then."

I hung up quickly and walked into the kitchen.

"What're you trying to reenact what happened at the Egg Roll?"

"These aren't quite ruined . . . what was that all about?"

Mickey pointed toward the table where I again sat down.

"This Morgan knows more than he's telling me. A lot more. He's involved somehow. With the bone, with everything. I wanted to see how committed he was to keeping me on."

"Very much so, it sounds like."

"Which is damned curious, seeing as how in my mind the doctor already knows what's going on. This second opinion stuff, this is some kind of formality . . . "

"You think he knows where his daughter is?" Ears wiggling.

"Well, I talked to him this afternoon. Brief chat, just checking in, setting up to meet later. Doesn't ask about Donna."

"The daughter."

"Right. Gets me thinking maybe he doesn't have to ask . . . "

"Like maybe he knows who's got her? Like they're using her as bait and having the doc try and draw you in . . . ?"

I raised my eyebrows and gulped the coffee.

"Did he ask about her just now?"

"First thing, once he'd recovered from the shock of my calling. There's another, better reason, though, to doubt the doc. When I was jumped at the office Wednesday, I had a picture of the girl on me which got lifted along with everything else. So yesterday I call Morgan for another copy and we arrange for him to leave it at the office. Which he does, in an envelope with some cash to boot."

"How much?"

"Three hundred. Which I should have wondered about a little more than I did. There's something else, though, something even more shady."

"What? What?" Mickey set a plate down on the table and took up the mug.

"Morgan claims he slid the envelope under my door. But there's no space between the door and the floor to slide anything through. No way that envelope gets inside my office without someone opening the door to deliver it."

"Huh."

Mickey set a refilled mug in front of me and sat down at the table. I began wolfing the makeshift breakfast he'd prepared. Slightly burnt eggs, a couple of slices of ham, toast and coffee.

"You think the guys who clocked you are the ones who left the bread, then."

"Yeah. Could've been a couple of them twenties were mine to start with."

"How'd they get in the first time, though?"

"No idea."

Mickey sat forward, chin in palm, as I made quick work of the meal.

"I met Henry Peters today," I said, swallowing.

"Yeah?"

"In the vise."

"What the hell?"

"Tell me. State senators generally have bodyguards?"

"I don't know. Peters?"

"Two suits. He mentioned something to me about Henrietta having gotten involved with shooting porn. Ever hear anything about that?"

"She was one wild child. Can't say I'd heard that, though . . . "

Mick and I continued our conversation through the rest of the night, testing theories and scenarios in kind of a replay of the last time we had worked together, that cold December five years before.

We talked in greater detail about what Henry Peters had said to me. I told him all about the meeting with the diminutive owner of the Marathon and how I'd been invited to the screening Saturday night. We talked about Winston Churchill. We talked about Slim Davies and his sudden prospects for success in two separate careers. We talked about Joey Tettleton. We talked about the still-at-large porn star and popeye killer, Slim Jim McCall.

We talked about Cap, as well, taking the opportunity to revisit the source of our argument from the previous spring.

It was plain to me that our opinions regarding McGhee had diverged considerably since the stake-out. You could, if you wanted, describe the original incident as inciting a break or rupture between us and the captain, though because one of us had stayed and the other had left, the healing since then had taken different courses. Whereas my fracture had been left alone and had more or less repaired itself, Mickey's had worsened, constant aggravation having caused a kind of irreversible atrophy to the surrounding tissue. Meaning as far as Mickey and I were concerned, the best we could do was agree to disagree about the man and his motives.

We were still talking when the phone rang about five-thirty that morning.

# CHAPTER TWENTY-SIX

# WHY WE HIDE OUR SKELETONS

While Mickey's on the phone, the detective gets up and stretches his arms and takes a walk down the hall. Sees a crib set up in the corner of one of the rooms along the way, distracting him for just a moment. He steps across the hall and into the bathroom and looks at himself in the mirror. Long face seems even longer, the droop of his eyes exaggerated by bags underneath. Skin looking all stretched, cheekbones jutting out. The lower part of his face a dark gray, a rougher grade of sandpaper having developed since yesterday afternoon.

Decidedly Lurch-like.

Have him collect handfuls of water and splash himself into a more presentable state.

Don't feel as though you're missing something when I don't describe every little thing Mick and I said to one another that night. There were a lot of pieces to deal with and even more ways to assemble them. Basically we spent most of the evening ruling out possible combinations. Besides, you know everything I knew at this juncture and so if you wanted to try and reconstruct our overnight dialogue well no one's stopping you.

I will say this much, though. A lot of the time we spent comparing the stories of the two runaways, Henrietta Peters and Donna Morgan. How they were both at City College. How Henrietta might've been in the movies. How Donna might've been into drugs. How their fathers were both successful, caring daddies and so on. Trying to see what one case might say about the other.

We also made plans for the Saturday night screening with Constantinius.

Big Slim had fixed things so that he could bring a friend if he wanted. And the way Mickey talked it seemed as though he thought coming along might be a good idea. Telling me how the moment McCall appears on screen he could start cuffing folks to bring them in for questioning and confiscating the film and so forth. Which all sounded peachy except for two things.

First was the welfare of this person whose photo I'd been carrying around for the past three days. The doctor's evasiveness didn't exactly make me less anxious about that.

In fact, it made me more so.

And Mickey's crashing the party, as far as I could tell, would only decrease the likelihood of my ever seeing the gap-toothed girl in the photograph. In the flesh, I mean.

What would it accomplish? Might get us closer to McCall. Then again, it might not. Might get Constantinius a slap on the wrist for showing dirty movies without the City getting their cut. About which, to use Roger Levin's phrase, I could give a rat's ass. Not to mention the fact that the episode would necessarily expose Slim Davies, figuratively speaking. Which might mean forget about ever going back to Tettleton and finding once and for all the girl in "3. Fireplace."

Damn lot of might, there, for one to consider.

The other thing keeping me from endorsing Mickey's idea to come along was the guilt I'd mentioned before. Already two people had died for what seemed no other cause than their accidental assocation with me. I could see that Mickey had a real life going here with Doris. And I couldn't see putting all that at risk.

We ended up reaching a kind of compromise.

The plan was to split up during the day, each of us pursuing different lines of inquiry brought up during the night. We'd then meet back in the lobby of his high-rise at seven and I'd take him over to the city pound to pick up some anonymous set of wheels in which he could follow me down to the Marathon and then to Constantinius's home or wherever it was he planned to take me. Once we arrived, Mick could keep an eye on things. Any funny business, and he could radio in the location and have uniforms there within a few minutes.

We'd be starting our day together, though. I walked back down the hall to find Mickey strapping on a holster and indicating for me to do the same. It had been McGhee on the phone. He and Sol Severin wanted to meet with the two of us in Severin's office. At seven sharp.

Sounded like they'd gotten some interesting news back from the lab.

Something about getting a make.

We rode down together in Mickey's wagon, the police radio buzzing along as we spoke. On the way we did some more comparing, this time between Severin and his predecessor, Mack McClellan.

Solomon Severin had been an assistant D.A. for less than a year when McClellan died in June 1973. While I'd had some limited interaction with Mack, I'd never once met Severin. Knew next-to-nothing about him. So I let Mick fill me in.

Apparently there had been a fairly lengthy adjustment period when Severin had first come in. As assistant, Severin occasionally was made to play the role of devil's advocate to an optimistic McClellan. And now and then some of Severin's criticisms regarding how realistic Mack was being regarding a particular grievance would filter down the chain and into the cabs of patrolling officers, which didn't do much for Severin's popularity prior to his ascension.

Then, if things weren't chilly enough for Severin, about six months into his tenure he started in with a campaign to beef up Internal Affairs, which under McClellan had been a paltry division, nearly impotent in its capacity to regulate. Of course, graft was something that never went away. Way too many Huffingtons in the department who'd come to expect the steady stream of fringe benefits as their just due. Which after having experienced it myself I can't rightly pretend to have a problem with. But, according to Mick, Severin had at least succeeded in making it a less open affair. Eventually guys got used to his approach, and now there existed among the department a kind of grudging respect for the man.

The only thing I did know about Severin was he was a hell of an orator. What McGhee had himself eloquently described before as the ability to use big words.

It was more than that, though. Anytime I'd read or hear him, there'd always be this mix of idealism and practicality sort of setting the tone for whatever cause he was pleading. You never once forgot the man was a lawyer, but he could be damned persuasive. And in the end, the whole package had been convincing enough for him to have been reelected to the post on his own.

Mickey parked behind the building in a guest spot and together we climbed up the back steps of City Hall. The building was quiet, although a few smartly-dressed persons could be seen criss-crossing the great open hallway on the ground floor. Doing what was necessary that Saturday morning to keep the City functioning. Mick and I rode up to the top floor and I followed him over to the slightly-open large black door marking the D.A.'s suite.

I waited and watched while Mickey rapped the back of his hand against the door and leaned inside. A voice called and Mickey led me past the secretary's vacant desk and into Severin's inner office. The two men inside simultaneously rose from their chairs. Through a forced smile, a tired-looking McGhee spoke first.

"Mickey, Dick . . . thanks a whole hell of lot for coming. Dick Owen, I want you to meet Solomon Severin."

The district attorney energetically stepped forward to greet me.

"Please, Sol."

I leaned over and shook the blond-haired, hazel-eyed man's hand for the first time. Severin had one of those meaningfully firm handshakes. A hard squeeze, brought slowly upwards and then back down quickly, like your playing paper-scissors-rock or something. Choosing rock, of course. An unmistakably professional greeting, no doubt practiced hundreds of times during his climb up the City's politically-complicated ladder.

There was a noticeable hurriedness in his movements, verging on pushiness. He wore a navy suit with matching bow tie. Was of medium build, and judging by his having to look squarely into my adam's apple perhaps not quite six feet tall. Could be as young as thirty-five, I thought. Ruddy cheeks, a little dimple in his chin. No Kirk Douglas, but all in all a clean, sincere-looking face which together with the early hour helped to communicate his eagerness to get on with things.

Severin took both of our coats and hung them carefully on the rack along the far wall. He resumed his seat in the leather chair, his smooth hands upturned. His three guests followed the invitation, each taking a side at the long, walnut desk. The uniformed McGhee sat to Severin's left, Mickey across, and I to the right. Severin looked at me when he spoke.

"Let me echo Bill's thanks to the two of you for coming in so early on a Saturday. We won't take up too much of your time. Can I get either of you some coffee?"

Mickey and I both nodded our heads and Severin quickly got up again and poured us each a cup from the maker in the corner by the window. Didn't bother asking whether we took cream or sugar, which I didn't though Mick did. Severin continued talking as he served us.

"Dick, Bill here was telling me how you were with him on upper east for . . . four years was it, Bill?"

"Little over four . . . Dick?" McGhee cringed.

"That's it, I think."

"Dick, I must apologize . . . "

Severin retook his seat.

"If circumstances were different, we could certainly be more leisurely with our introductions. But, unfortunately, that is not the case, and so I think it in everyone's interests if we just move on to what the lab has found out for us and are all clear on what we know to this point. Fine?"

"Fine."

"Fine, then."

Severin sat forward in his chair with his elbows atop the several folders positioned neatly on the blotter in front of him. Touched the fingertips of each hand together, rocking the little knuckled web back and forth as he spoke.

"First, Dick, Mickey, you should know that our departmental facilities have a great deal of experience analyzing this sort of material evidence. Additionally, and I myself was unaware of this until recently, we now have the means to refer out specific data to external laboratories whose interpretive capabilites far exceed our own and then to incorporate these expert readings into our own findings."

We all nodded appreciatively.

"Now, given the special nature of this case we had performed among other tests what is called a 'directed search.' A 'directed search' means, well, it means just what it sounds like. It's a search with a particular directive in mind, looking for a particular match . . . "

"With Barbara Rocca," I said evenly.

"That's right, Dick. That's exactly right. Now before we get into what we've got here let me just ask you just a couple of things and do pardon me as I am aware you have discussed all of this previously with Bill."

"All right."

"When you first received the item in your office, the bone . . . "

Severin paused briefly, demonstrating a kind of distaste at having had to prounounce the word. Let it pour out of his mouth, bending it so that it almost rhymed with the last name of his primary addressee.

" . . . was delivered inside of a large, brown cardboard box?"

"That's right. Yellowish brown."

"And this package was then taken from you in a theft later Wednesday evening, correct?"

"Yes. Also at the office." I sipped at the hot coffee and looked over at McGhee fidgeting in his chair.

"Now . . . and by the way, we are not here today, Dick, to consider the wisdom of your decision to take the item to Mr. Williams's lab rather than to bring it in to us. On the face of it, it would be a simple thing to pass judgment and conclude that you made the wrong choice. And not at all because of what happened at the lab as I am sure none of us could have ever anticipated such an awful, inhumane crime as occurred there."

I nodded, waiting for the "but."

"But it was the wrong decision. Because you knew, Dick, especially with your past experience, how valuable that box and everything it contained could have been in terms of our being able to identify its handlers."

Severin was right. I again nodded. McGhee shrugged. Mickey studied the ceiling.

"Tell me, Dick. You mentioned Miss Rocca."

"Yes?"

"When you delivered the item to Mr. Williams, what exactly did you think he would find?"

I tried to ignore feeling as though I was once again on a witness stand.

"Well . . . Mr. Severin. I wasn't sure what he would find."

"But you must have had some idea?"

"Yes, I suppose. Like I told Captain McGhee before, I had wanted to be sure of a couple of things before I brought it in. Mainly that it wasn't a fake. That it was real. Also, Lanny had said to me that he might've been able to determine other things . . . things I assume the department's lab has found . . . ?"

An attempt to put the conversation back on course. Answered by a stern smile.

"Yes, well, as you say, we do have some news, here, Dick."

"Yes?"

"Yes."

"What the hell is going on here?" Mickey suddenly interjected.

"What?" said McGhee, startled.

"No, no, Bill. Mickey is right to ask."

Severin let his hands fall and began to pick at the edge of one of the folders.

"I apologize for the theatrics, Dick. And Mickey. I simply felt it necessary to establish that we are now in a situation where we *must* work together. We cannot afford any mistakes similar to the one involving the package. I am depending on all of you. This case is uniquely complicated, especially so for me since I came into it relatively late. You three each share an involvement here which is both historically longer and more personal than my own."

Glances exchanged across the desk.

"And so I just wanted to make it clear as we proceed just how much I value your openness and your honesty when I ask for your complete commitment here. As well as to assure you that you have mine as well."

"You got it, Sol," said McGhee, to whom we all turned at once. "You got it," he repeated.

"Okay, okay . . . we're all on the same page. Tell us what they found," said Mickey, appearing to demonstrate a greater freedom with Severin than McGhee enjoyed. Severin coughed into a fist, then began.

"The laboratory has reported to this office that they have discovered a genetic match between much-decayed samples obtained from the marrow inside of the piece and some previously-preserved blood samples. This discovery has led them to opine that the chances are high that the fragment found at the scene of Mr. Williams's death can be linked to the crime scene involving Miss Peters and Miss Rocca . . . from December 1971. Now this match they are describing as occurring on what they call a primary level, and from what I gather they are reserving judgment until they are able to make their case even stronger. That is, until they are able to make an even more comprehensive match between the samples. What we have now, however, is the estimation of a seventy-five percent chance that the bone . . . "

Again the pause. The bend.

" . . . indeed came from Miss Barbara Rocca, with a five percent margin of error. They still await reports back on tests being performed by forensics facilities down at Hopkins where they have sent frozen samples."

"You were right, Dick," said McGhee, impatiently shrugging.

The warmth of the coffee in my chest was compounded by a feeling of good fortune, as if I was being unexpectedly, undeservedly rewarded for something.

The feeling soon passed.

"Yes, well . . . ." The young D.A. held up a cautionary hand. "First, this report is not at all conclusive. These are still preliminary findings. Secondly, there is still no reason to suggest that this in any way alters previously determined findings regarding the cause of Miss Peters's death."

"Of course," I said, declining to repeat earlier denials.

"Right, I mean . . . that's not what I meant," added McGhee.

"Tell me . . . does the report say anything else? Anything about how the bone might have been preserved?"

"Yes, it does. There was a preservative used, and they have here broken down the solution according to its chemical composition." Severin opened one of the folders and nimbly thumbed through it.

"It seemed like it had a finish to it, like a shellac or . . . "

"Yes . . . yes, they do I recall describe some sort of alcoholic mixture here . . . "

"That was part of what had made me unsure about it. I mean it looked like a bone but it felt like a table leg or something."

"Yes. That is understandable."

Severin abruptly let the folder fall closed and leaned back in his chair, folding his hands underneath his smooth, clean-shaven chin.

"Tell me, Dick. What happened yesterday afternoon?"

"Yesterday?"

"At the . . . . At the moviehouse," chimed McGhee uncertainly. Obviously uncomfortable. With Severin. With me. The whole situation.

"You've seen the report, I take it?" I asked.

"Yes, Dick. I have read the report."

Severin's dry eyes were utterly expressionless.

"I was wondering, though, Dick. Do you have anything further to add to what you told Officer Huffington?" Again, the effortless smile.

I set my cup on the desk and looked from Severin over to McGhee who began busily studying the corner of his end of the desk. I wiped my mouth and looked back at the district attorney.

"I take it they haven't found McCall?"

"Not yet, no."

"They identify the victim?"

"They have."

Severin again opened another of the folders. I exchanged a quick look with Mickey, who had the expression of someone who normally took sugar being forced to go without.

"The deceased was a man by the name of Thomas Deutsch Krass. A fellow patron of the Express was able to provide the information which led to his identification. Apparently the deceased had no next of kin. You mentioned in the report how Mr. McCall seemed to be waving to you?"

"That's right."

"Yes. You wrote here that 'he appeared to signal in my direction'? To follow him into the restroom? Is that correct?"

"Yes."

"And so is it safe to assume that, in your opinion at least, what happened to Mr. Krass was simply a case of his being in the wrong place at the wrong time."

"I'd say so, yes."

"I see. And have you anything else . . . ?"

"I wish I could say that I did, but I . . . "

"You were following Mr. McCall, correct?"

"That's right."

"You followed him to the theater and then spoke for a time with a . . . Mr. Paul, correct?"

"That's right. Is that not clear in the report?"

"No, Dick, it ain't," said McGhee, scooting forward. He stopped and looked over toward Severin. "It's not clear in the report." Scooting back.

"What happened was McCall left the theater and then returned. When he left that's when I ended the tail and decided to speak with Paul. It was later, a half-hour? While I was in the projection booth, that's when I saw McCall enter the theater. It was then I resumed following him."

"And from whence did you begin the pursuit of Mr. McCall?"

"I began following Mr. McCall from a motel called the Motor Inn over in Riverside."

"And what is the connection between Mr. McCall and your client, Dick?"

I realized I had yet to see Severin blink since we had entered the office fifteen minutes before.

"My client?"

I heard McGhee exhale. I again looked over at Mickey looking back at me. Shaking his head. Slightly.

"Yes, your client. I understand that you were following Mr. McCall because he has something to do with a case you are presently working on, correct?"

"Yes, that is correct. And in fact the connection between Mr. McCall and my client is something I am also curious about. This was why I was following him . . . "

"Dick." McGhee stopped himself.

" . . . to try and determine how he might figure into my client's situation. As a lawyer, Mr. Severin, I am sure that you can appreciate my reluctance to divulge anything specific regarding my client and the reasons for his having hired me."

"Christ Almighty." McGhee scowlingly crossed his arms.

"Of course, of course. We cannot enjoin you from fulfilling duties prescribed to you by your client, Dick. This office fully respects the rights and privileges of such an agreement."

I nodded. Mickey leaned back in his chair.

"However, that being said, neither can we sanction the withholding of any evidence that may potentially be of value to our own investigations. You do understand our position? Yes?"

"I do, I do."

"This is what I meant before by working together. We have to know, Dick, if you have any further ideas about Mr. McCall's role . . . in the Williams murder, in the delivery of the package, or in any previous criminal activity."

"I understand that. Believe me. It is just that I am not prepared to risk the agreement of confidentiality I have made with my client so as to speculate about . . . "

McGhee had reached his limit.

"Lookit!"

Severin quickly rose from his chair and walked with his head down over to the oak cabinet in the near corner. As if to give McGhee adequate space in which to speak.

"Dick, you've gotta come clean here. You've gotta meet us halfway. I *know* that you know something more than what you're telling us about this McCall. About the whole goddamned lot of it. And I'll be damned if I'm going to sit here and listen while you dick around with us about client confidentiality like some . . . like some half-cocked paperback detective stalling for time. That ain't what this is, Dick? You see?"

"What are you saying, Cap?"

"I'm saying this ain't like some goddamned Random Chandler story where we're all gonna sit around and wait until you're good and ready to tell us what the deal is."

Severin looked up from his leaning position. Mickey covered his mouth. I couldn't suppress a smile.

"Hey, that's pretty good. I gotta remember that one."

"Lookit. All I mean is that we ain't working for you, here. See? We aren't yer goddamned clients. Whether I like it or not, we're working together on this one. And you have *got* to be straight with us, Dick."

McGhee swallowed hard and looked at Severin confusedly, obviously unsure as to whether he had overstepped any boundaries. Severin had adjusted his gaze downward. Cap shook his head, gesturally communicating a determination to continue.

"And just because I can't run yer ass out of here again don't make it any different."

I saw the grin dissolving from Mickey's face.

"But there is a difference, Cap," I said.

McGhee made himself shrug.

"Now you're the one asking me to be straight. Seems I remember a time when you were less than straight with Mick and me."

McGhee loudly slapped his palm on the edge of the desk. Severin lifted himself away from the oak cabinet with his elbows, retaking the floor.

"Yes, well . . . ."

Severin looked down, holding his chin with his thumb and forefinger, his other hand on his right hip.

"Bill is right. Dick, Mickey. If either of you have anything to share with us here . . . ?"

"Can I just say something?"

The suddenness of Mickey's voice again altered the dynamic of the room. He looked around and hearing no objection proceeded.

"First off, Sol, you're right. All of this is maybe a little more personal for Dick and me. And Cap. We could sit here, I suppose, and let Dick and Cap try and see who can piss the other off the most. Or we could get on with trying to track down this McCall and whomever else might be involved. But before we do, I just want to point out something here. As far as these questions you guys are putting to Dick . . . if I could just say one thing . . . "

"Mickey, please do," said Severin.

"Other than some misjudgment regarding when he first got the package, Dick here has been as straight as they come. With me and with you. From the beginning, Dick has remained in touch and has conscientiously reported everything that has happened. Additionally he has spent many, many hours, on two separate occasions, in the precinct providing whatever information was asked of him. Last night, the two of us spent several hours discussing what has happened and considering all kinds of possible explanations for it. I can assure you both that as much as we wish there was something more to share at this point, there is not. Your guess is as good as ours as far as McCall or anyone or anything else goes here."

The four of us sat silently for a moment. I watched as Mickey stared impassionately at Severin. Sunlight was beginning to fill the room. As Severin stepped back over behind his chair, I could sense the mood beginning to relax.

"Thank you, Mickey, for your candor."

"Of course."

"And as far as I am concerned this office is satisfied with what you have said."

"Thank you."

"Bill, do you have anything to add here?"

McGhee shook his head.

"Now . . . just so everyone understands. Chief of Detectives Walton is overseeing both of these cases. That includes whatever evidence he deems relevant to either homicide. Now, Dick. This office has a couple of pieces of advice for you. First of all, be extremely wary. Any phone calls, visits, anything, I want you to examine as closely as possible. I suggest for you to remain in close communication with Mickey and with this office and should you learn of anything that might bear some relation to our investigation to inform us immediately. We can forward whatever information you happen upon to Marty Walton and Homicide and allow them to deal with it accordingly."

"Okay. I will."

"Is there anything either of you wish to say?"

"Dick is going to be staying with me for a while," said Mickey.

"That sounds like a good idea. Bill, if you would remain for a moment?"

Severin stood and extended his hand toward me.

"It was good to meet you, Dick."

Again that handshake. Sealing a deal.

"Good to meet you, Mr. Severin. And let *me* apologize for the theatrics."

Severin chuckled.

"Not a problem. Like I said, do keep in touch."

"You do the same."

The three of us walked over to where the coats had been hung. Severin made an attempt at helping me on with my coat, although the difference in our heights made the maneuver nearly impossible. As Mickey and I turned to leave, McGhee jumped from his seat.

"Lookit, Dick. You call if anything turns up." A hand on my back.

"I will, Cap."

"That ain't just a suggestion."

"Got it."

"Just watch yourself . . . " Turning away.

"Will do."

# CHAPTER TWENTY-SEVEN

# RED FACES & GREENBACKS

I have to say Mickey had surprised me. Stepping in the way he did. Not to mention lying his ass off about there being nothing more to tell. I asked him about it as we walked back down to his car.

"Well, it was pretty plain that you weren't of a mind to tell them anything."

"About tonight, you mean."

"Yeah. Then you mentioned that about Cap not being straight with us once and I thought maybe I'd see what you were thinking before saying anything more."

We got into the car and began heading north toward the Park. I rolled down the passenger's side window.

"Well, I appreciate it."

"No problem."

"I'd have told them, though."

"What?"

"Why shouldn't I have?"

"But what you said . . . about Cap? And that malarkey about client privilege?

"I know, I know. I thought I'd see what *you* were thinking. I thought you were signaling to me in there."

"Signaling?"

"Yeah . . . not to say anything."

"Yeah, well. Maybe I was," Mickey interrupted. More than a little flustered.

"Better this way, though," I offered. "Gives us a chance to see what we dig up today first."

Mickey silently nodded.

"Before we let Cap in on it."

Mickey continued his nodding. We remained silent while Mickey turned right and began up Eighth. At Columbus Circle we might've gone Broadway, but I let Mickey do the driving. He took the slower route, up Central

Park West.

"It's definitely Rocca, then?" Mick finally asked, eyes on the road.

"Seventy-five percent," I quipped.

"With the five percent margin of error," he answered.

"I'd put it closer to ninety-nine and forty-four one-hundredths . . . no way that thing isn't from the girl."

"You know, Dick, I'm less surprised that you were right . . . I mean with what you said then about Rocca getting chopped up at the scene . . . "

"Yeah?"

"Yeah. I mean like you were saying at the time there was a hell of a lot of blood, plus those deposits or whatever they were . . . . I mean it was obvious some grievous harm had been done to the girl inside of that house."

I continued nodding, remembering how such clarity had been less readily appreciated at the time.

"To me that's less surprising than the fact that they saved that thing all this time. Preserved, even. Why do that? For what purpose do you hang onto something like that?"

"I dunno. Blackmail?"

"Blackmail you?"

"Or somebody . . . . Look at that . . . "

I pointed out the driver's side at a huge display up in front of the Museum of Natural History. Flightless Birds. A Prehistoric Retrospective. A flock of skeletons standing around like they were waiting on a bus. Or a plane.

"I think Cap's finally starting to lose it," Mickey said.

"What he say? Random Chan . . . ?"

"You see his face . . . ?"

"He don't care for Severin too much, does he?"

"The guy drives him absolute nuts. Stuff like setting up this meeting. You see, Mack would've allowed Cap to handle something like this himself. Whereas Severin wants his fingers in everything. Nothing McGhee hates more than sitting there letting a roomful of men twenty years younger than he is dictate his business to him."

"But Cap knows his place. The order of things."

"Exactly. McGhee's all about following orders. Protocol, respect for authority."

I fiddled with the rear-view on my side to get a better angle.

"Cap'd never set us up, though," I said.

"Did once." His cheeks reddened.

"No, Mick. He didn't. He didn't know what he was doing. Like you say, he was just following orders."

"From whom, though? Tell me that."

"Here it is," I said, ending the conversation before either of us could get too worked up over it.

Mickey turned left on Cathedral and circled around and onto Morningside. He pulled up to the curb and idled.

"Well, we'll see what the doctor has to say. Meet back at your place?"

"Seven. The lobby."

I got out and watched as Mickey turned the station wagon around in the neighboring drive and headed back downtown. It was breezy, but nothing like the day before. Sky a uniform gray. I buttoned my raincoat and readied myself for a day of walking.

I stepped across the sidewalk and up to the address Morgan had given me. I had a couple of reasons for wanting to check it out. One was simply to ensure it was legit, that he in fact had an office at all. I also wanted to surprise him, maybe catch him off his guard and see if he'd come clean about the copied picture, the envelope under the door, the money. And whatever else a little friendly arm-twisting might inspire him to talk about.

There was indeed a neatly-stenciled little plate there across the middle of the windowless door: "Harold D. Morgan, M.D., Adult Gastroenterologist. Appointment Only." As had been described to me, the office was a converted residence, and alongside the door was a small grid of six round buttons for buzzing into the different apartments. One of the buttons had been colored red. The Panic Button. I pressed it and waited. After a few seconds the door opened automatically and I let myself in.

The door opened into a long, narrow hallway. Took the first left and found myself inside what looked like a waiting area. A tired-looking, bald-headed gentleman in a double-breasted suit and his legs crossed acknowledged my entrance by nodding his round, pink head at me over a well-thumbed copy of *Field & Stream*. I looked around for a moment and decided to take a seat in one of the several different-colored folding chairs arranged in a semi-circle around the square glass table in the center of the room.

A few minutes passed.

There were several vestiges of the room's former existence, such as the unused fireplace and waterpipes visible along the top of the left wall. The room was painted solid magenta with white trim. For some reason, the bulb in the overhead light seemed an inordinately low wattage, and I noticed the bald man straining to read his magazine. Beside and over the fireplace were hung watercolor prints of various garden scenes, each functionally framed with pastel-colored plastic borders.

After a while I noticed that the man had taken the room's only reclining chair, a Chippendale covered in a deep red corduroy with huge cushion-rolls at the end of each armrest. The hard-as-hell chair I was sitting in, meanwhile, I had picked because it directly faced the room's only other door, which I presumed to be the entrance to Morgan's examining room.

I leaned forward. Elbows on knees. Rubbing my chin.

The door through which I had entered suddenly swung open. We both looked up to see a middle-aged woman in a blue print dress and white handbag under her arm standing in the open doorway giving us the once-over. Gave a little huff and left, footfalls sounding as though she was walking further down the hall. A minute later I heard those heels coming back up the hall and out the front door. I stood up.

"Is this Dr. Morgan's office?" I asked. The man seemed to crouch as I spoke.

"That it is."

"Are you seeing him today?"

"Nine o'clock." The man continued to leaf through his magazine. In no hurry to leave that chair, I thought. I left and walked further down the hall. The building was inordinately quiet. At the end was an open door. I stepped through to find a smiling woman waving me over from underneath an impressively-styled brunette bouffant.

"Good morning, sir." The woman I'd spoken to over the phone. Pert as always.

"Good morning . . . is Dr. Morgan here?"

"I'm sorry but the doctor is not in today. Did you have an appointment?"

"No, actually. I'm a friend . . . Richard Owen?"

"Oh . . . you are the one who . . . *Richard* Owen?"

"That's right. We've spoken before." I watched as the memory slowly revived in her face.

"I remember . . . "

"Is the doctor all right?"

"What? Oh, yes . . . well . . . he phoned earlier and cancelled today's schedule. He said there was a family emergency and he wouldn't be able to . . . "

"A family emergency? Is it serious? Is his wife . . . ?"

"I don't know. He didn't say, Mr. Owen. Do you want to leave a message for him?"

I noticed that the bald-headed man had managed to escape the Chippendale and had followed me in and was now quietly studying the pamphlets along the front wall.

"No. I will try to get him at home. Thanks very much."

The man and I changed places and I stood for a moment while he and the receptionist negotiated when to reschedule his appointment.

I was tired and disappointed, finding it difficult to think clearly. Found myself just sort of standing there, lingering over the titles of some of the patient handouts. Things like *Your Colon and You. Breaking it Down: Your Digestive System. Common Irregularities.* Morgan's irregularity was becoming increasingly common. I had just grabbed up a pamphlet on *The Perfect Stool* for Mick when I heard the receptionist explaining:

" . . . I'm sorry but Wednesday's the only day during the week the doctor does not schedule . . . "

I wheeled around.

"Say that again?"

The receptionist looked startled. I reapproached the counter, noting the receptionist's nametag.

"Excuse me . . . ?"

"Say that again . . . Gwen. Say that about how Wednesday's the only day during the week. Only this time say that Wednesday's the only day during the week your sister doesn't have classes."

Gwen blushed. I realized that my overly haggard appearance probably didn't lessen her discomfort. The man quickly sidestepped, deferring his position before the desk.

"I . . . uh . . . " she stammered. I turned toward baldy.

"Listen, pal. Can you give us a few minutes, here? You know where the waiting room is, right . . . ?" He backed out of the office without a word, closing the door as he left.

"Okay," I said. "Let's have it. Why'd you do it?"

"I knew I shouldn't have . . . I knew it was a mistake to . . . "

"What did Morgan tell you to say when you called me last week?"

"I . . . I . . . "

"Listen to me, Gwen. I haven't got the time or the patience to stand around and wait for you to decide whether or not to talk. Two people are dead, and your boss may or may not be involved. May or may not be in danger himself . . . "

"Harry . . . ?"

"That's right. If you want to help Harry out here, I suggest you spill it."

She swallowed and held a hand against the counter as if to balance herself, her other hand employed needlessly brushing back that well-disciplined, well-colored do.

"He told me it was a practical joke. A friend of his from medical school was in town for a convention that they're having over at the Holiday Inn. Harry said that his friend had done something like it to him before. A few years ago, he said. He asked me to call you and act like I was his friend's wife, to hire you to spy on him while he was at the convention."

"He gave you the whole story, then?"

"Yes, sir. I honestly had no idea that . . . "

"Tell me something, Gwen. Where might Harry've gotten the idea? For the story, about the man cheating on his wife?"

The color in Gwen's face raced toward an even darker purple. It'd be too obvious to say she was red as a beet, because with that hair she really was starting to resemble one.

I let her off the hook.

"Anything else unusual this week, Gwen? Any other stories?"

"No, sir. Not until this morning."

"The family emergency story, that on the level?"

"Yes, yes it is. That's exactly what he told me. To reschedule all appointments because there was an emergency in the family."

"Do you know Morgan's family? His wife, his . . . "

"No, not at all. He . . . he doesn't talk about them."

"And you prefer it that way."

Gwen said nothing. Head bowed. Hair, too.

Like McGhee, Gwen just followed orders. A pawn.

After convincing her she'd be absolved should dear Harry be found culpable of any misdoing, Gwen agreed to report it should Morgan try to contact her again. I instructed her to call the station and ask for Mickey Rowe, explaining how they would then have him phone her back.

I left quickly and walked back down the hall. Stuck my head in the waiting room door and gave baldy the all-clear. He stammered his thanks, and I remember thinking how that head was starting to blend a little too closely with the Chippendale's covering.

One of Morgan's stress cases, I supposed.

My stomach rumbled.

I found a phone box on Amsterdam and climbed inside. Tried Morgan's home and there was no answer. Continued north to the station on 125th into which I descended. After a moment's wait, I was on the One, heading south.

I don't take the subway that often. No more than a couple or three times a month, when driving or parking is too much of a hassle. But I think even those with a more intimate knowledge of the City's public transport would likely agree with me when I say the subway at times can be a damn desperate place.

When I think of the subway I think of cars full of zombies all silently meditating upon the misery of the present. The occasional panhandler coming around just in case you start to feel at all comfortable. An unavoidably unhealthy mix of fear and smoke, urine and distrust, sweat and anticipation. A situation epitomizing the mundane. At least a contender for the lowest of all of the lowest common denominators.

What's funny though is let's say you have some guy riding along in this slow train to hell and suddenly something grand occurs to him, some idea about the universe and where he fits in, the whole damn epiphany fueled by the misguided notion that he and he alone has thought this thing. You know, crazy, passage-of-life stuff. Stop-and-go philosophy. Enter the station one person and come out another. And that's not even getting into what the train and the tunnel really represent. My point is it's easy to fool yourself in such a setting into thinking you're the only one with a brain that functions.

You need a for instance? Say you're sitting there and you see somebody has doctored the little sign above the door that used to read "Obstructing the doors can be dangerous" so now it says "Obstruct~~ing~~ the doors ~~can~~ be dangerous." That's interesting, you think. Guy had to obstruct the door to do that. Practiced what he preached. A couple of stops on and you're still thinking about it. About the dangers of posting your message publicly like that. How what you say will be changed, will itself become the medium through which others speak to one another.

Since everyone else is hypnotized by their own thoughts, no one comes forward to save you from yourself. Hey, you're starting to forget about the bathing habits of that guy next to you. You indulge even further, becoming more abstract. Start thinking about how easily suggestions become imperatives. About the doors of communication, and strategies for obstructing them. About possibility and inevitability. About margins of error. About differing agendas, differing interests. Openness and secrecy. Light and dark.

On and on like that.

All of which resolves into this feeling that you're somehow special for having noticed all of this. When the truth is you're about the millionth person so far who has.

This is why I'm always suspicious of any remotely interesting thought that occurs to me when riding the subway. I get on and try to forget where I am. Try not to let this train interrupt whatever train of thought I was riding before.

Which in this case had to do with the extent to which Morgan had set me up. Of course, it was hard to conceive of his motives. Or to where he might've disappeared. I could say a couple of things, though. He'd undoubtedly had an interest in having me out of the office when the package had been delivered. And, it followed, he also must have some connection with the goons who'd broken in and clubbed me . . .

"Wheeee-e-e-e-e-enk! Wheeee-e-e-e-e-enk!"

All was lost inside the high-pitched, reedless squeal of a saxophone. I looked up with the rest of the car to locate the source of the racket.

Which let me tell you was a memorable sight to behold. Postcard-worthy. Big, bearded black guy wearing x-ray glasses and a headband with star-topped antennae that bounced back and forth as he juked. Striped t-shirt, multicolored suspenders, stained baggy jeans. Obviously some crude kind of Sun Ra tribute going on there, but with a consciously added, much unwanted nausea effect. Making the performance special. Kept up that shrilling wail for a minute at least, not even bothering to finger any notes.

At last he stopped to breathe. And to explain the method behind this madness.

"Money makes me go awa-a-a-ay! Money makes me go awa-a-a-ay!"

Which after a while it finally did.

Only to be replaced by more obsessive-type thinking from the one whose life journey you've joined.

Money had made me go a certain way with things. I found myself thinking about who it was had the money amongst our cast of characters. Morgan seemed to be doing all right, what with his new offices and all. Constantinius, too.

What did Billy Paul say about Oscar van Brooks? Barely in the black, if at all. Tettleton acted like a big shot, but then he's also stealing slugs of liquor and making friendly with folks who might try and stop him from doing so. Got the feeling that despite all the partying the guy was hand-to-mouth.

Of course, it was Henry Peters who had the most cash to throw around. Probably had tens of thousands in the campaign coffers at his disposal.

But to whom might he throw it? And for what reason?

I had to get out of there.

# CHAPTER TWENTY-EIGHT

# DOUBLE-TEAM

The Twenty-third street stop mercifully arrived.

I climbed up out of the station and back onto the sidewalk. The sun was starting to break through, which didn't sit too well with me as I was still wearing that heavy topcoat over top of my suit jacket. And Mick's .38.

Here you might have me plodding along, thinking about what it was Mick was up to at that moment. We'd already essentially agreed on how we'd handle the evening meeting, the only question being when and whether Mick would phone in for back-up.

I was having second thoughts, though. Again. Third thoughts. About Mick coming at all, serving as my back-up. Was starting to figure on ways I might talk him out of it.

As I walked through the YMCA parking lot, I could already hear the familiar screeching sounds of tennis shoes against hardwood. Trotted on over to the graffitti-spattered side entrance and pushed my way inside, the heat from the gymnasium instantly enveloping me like I'd suddenly slipped on a cocoon.

It was pushing ten o'clock. There were still several half-court games going, and one full-court on the far side. I wiped at my forehead and walked along in front of the folded bleachers along the floor's perimeter.

"Lurch!"

I jerked my head back and saw Moses raising his eyebrows at me, sweat pouring off of his gleaming, freshly-shaved head. I waved and continued walking, looking for the ratty green Philadelphia Eagles t-shirt Russ always wore. I stopped and peered into the tangle of men involved in the full-court contest. The five shirts were all varying shades of black, gray, or white. There was a loose ball, and a skin broke out of the pack to retrieve it.

It was Russ, ably converting the turnover into an easy hoop. He laid the ball in delicately over the front rim, and as he turned I caught his eye.

"Lurch! Where you been, dude?" he called, back-pedalling.

I held out my hands and titled my head, pleading no-contest. The group moved to the far end. I recognized the herky-jerky ball-handling of Phil, the only other person of the regular crowd besides myself whom I knew had played some college ball. I watched as he darted over to the right side, long afro closely following. He abruptly stopped about three feet short of the baseline and launched a high-arcing shot which kissed off the wooden backboard before rattling home.

"Gotta call that shit," someone yelled.

At which I involuntarily ducked, quickly scanning the court for the speaker. McCall couldn't be here, I thought.

He wasn't.

I relaxed and watched Phil grinning mischeviously as he jogged back downcourt. The guy could bank it from anywhere, no matter how wide the angle, and noviciates often mistook his accuracy for good fortune.

Someone called a score, but I missed it. I pulled out the bottom row of bleachers and took a seat, enjoying the respite of watching until the game's completion some fifteen minutes later. As the players left the court for the water fountain on the other side, I slapped hands with several of them. Some I knew by name, others only by sight. Russ sat down hard next to me and leaned back against the wooden slats, wiping his face and arms with the green shirt balled up in his hand.

"How you doing, Dick?" Russ's breathing was starting to slow down.

"Good, good."

"You sure?" I kept forgetting how rough I looked.

"I'm fine. Little tired is all. Listen, thanks for the other night."

"Oh, dude, forget it. Weird stuff. This guy, this . . . who was it . . . Williams?"

"Walton."

"Walton! Yeah, he's all like . . . ." Russ cleared his throat and uncannily mimicking Walton's labored cadence said, "'Is it true, Mister Davenport, that you telephoned a Richard Owen at his residence at approximately eight o'clock p.m. . . . ?'"

"Yeah, Marty's a riot," I said.

"I didn't even know your last name when he said it to me. I can't believe it about Lanny."

"You know, I'd seen Lanny earlier that night. That's why they called you."

"I can't believe it. He hadn't come out for a couple of months. Some of the guys were talking about the funeral being tomorrow . . . ."

Collective head-shaking. Lanny had had nothing but friends. Sort of thing puts you in mind of your own end. Gets you thinking about what you want to get done before it comes.

"So you saw him? The night he was . . . ?"

"Yeah, I did. In fact, that's why I'm here, Russ."

"Yeah?"

"You're at City and Regional, right?"

"Uh-huh."

"Can you get into the office today?"

"Sure, of course. But . . . "

"I might have an idea about what happened, but I need to check some things. I need to look at some records of ownership, mortgages, stuff like that. Might tell me something, might not. Worth looking at, though."

"I could, but . . . "

"Listen, any trouble comes of it, my former partner can handle it. He and I are kind of working together on this."

"Serious?"

"You got my word."

"Well, yeah. What am I saying? Of course, it's fine. No problem, dude."

Russ's head disappeared as he pulled the Eagles t-shirt on.

"You wanting to head over now?" Eyes poking out the neckhole.

"If it's okay, but if it's not good . . . ?"

"No, no. In fact now's good. Nobody'll be over there. Come on."

I followed Russ over to his duffel bag sitting against the wall and waited while he pulled on a second t-shirt and a pair of sweats. We walked side by side out of the gymnasium, waving and calling good-byes to several others as we left. I silently resolved to start coming out again the following week.

As Russ drove, I tried to answer all of the questions he was putting to me about the night Lanny was killed. What I'd told him about Mickey taking care of any hassles over at C & R, that was completely on the level. Some of Russ's questions, though, I probably answered with a bit more creativity than Russ deserved. Managed to tell all about going to Lanny's lab, being followed, knocked out, and robbed, and the later discovery of the body without mentioning the main reason for my having visited Lanny in the first place. Nor what the blunt instrument was Russ had read about in the paper. Was even more vague when it came to why it was I needed to know who owned a couple of downtown restaurants, but Russ kept right on nodding throughout. Like I mentioned before, Russ really wasn't much of a shooter. More of a rebounder, what they call a team player.

Russ pulled his convertible into the empty parking lot, right across from the Municipal City and Regional sign. He grabbed the duffel bag and bounded out of the car and up the steps of the well-landscaped facility. I followed and waited as he retrieved a set of keys from his bag, unlocked the doors, and led me inside.

We walked part of the way down the first floor hallway before turning right into a large room with a desk in front and several rows of metal shelves extending behind it. I went over to the desk and leaned forward, noticing still more shelves extending to the right, beyond my view.

I watched Russ drop his bag and circle around behind the desk. He squatted for a moment and retrieved from underneath a long, well-creased tube of paper which he expertly unrolled and let fall over the desk. It was a huge, massively-detailed map of the borough's lower third. Russ spent the next few minutes explaining to me the arcane system of quadrants and locator codes which I would need to know if I hoped to make any use of the thing. Satisfied of my understanding, he left me alone with the map while he went down to visit the vending machines in the building's basement.

I knew approximately where the Giant Egg Roll was on Lexington and so it was only a few minutes before I'd found the little red square representing it. Took considerably longer to spot the Marathon. To spot the spot, I should say. No building was marked on the service road that ran down beside the Manhattan Bridge. In fact, the road itself didn't seem to have a name, other than the cryptic abbreviation "Ext." I slowly brought two fingers together on either side of the shaded area where the Marathon should have been and waited until Russ returned with two Cokes.

"Got something?"

"Got the one . . . here." I stretched with my pinky finger over to the Egg Roll and Russ noted verbally its quadrant and code.

"What's that?"

"A restaurant. The Giant Egg Roll."

"Ha."

"You need the address?" I asked.

"Nah . . . that's how come the codes. Street numbers change. What's that?" He tilted a can toward the little wrinkle that I'd made between my fingers.

"There's a building here, not marked though. Another restaurant, called the Marathon. Can we . . . ?"

Russ studied the spot. He set the Cokes down and frowned.

"Nothing? No mile markers or anything?"

"Down at the end here should be some houses, but they're not marked either."

He bent over the desk.

"Yeah, okay. See this where it says 'Extension'? That's what they call the roads which pass through state-owned land. Okay here's four . . . and twenty-nine . . . ."

I slid back in the chair and opened one of the Cokes while Russ calculated out loud. He quickly rose up from the map.

"Okay . . . be right back . . . ."

Russ grabbed the other can and opened it as he disappeared into the shadowed stacks. About ten minutes later he was still searching and so I pushed the ill-fitting red notebook up out of my back pocket and readied it there on the table. Had begun pulling off pieces of the peeling plastic binding when Russ finally reemerged into the room's florescent light, a large stack of folders in his hands with the Coke can balanced on top.

"I grabbed 'em all, just in case."

"What do you mean?"

"Well, this one here . . . ." He tossed the empty can into a cardboard box by the door and handed me the top folder. "This is for the one on Lexington. The rest are all the SE-17's, up and down that extension. Your restaurant . . . the Marathon? . . . could be any one of these."

I raised my eyebrows at the two-and-a-half-foot high stack Russ was cradling.

"Tell you what . . . take a look at that and I can start weeding. Some of these will be for those houses."

"Russ, I appreciate it."

"Forget it. Dude, I ain't doing nothing else."

I looked over the thick sepia-colored folder Russ had handed me. Covered in clear plastic tape with several names and numbers scribbled and crossed out in different colors of ink. Sorted through all of the deeds, titles, grants, and other whatnot inside, and within the hour had eventually pieced together a crude history of the little red square there on the corner.

After housing a savings and loan for twenty-odd years, the building was the site of a series of failed eateries until '67 when it was bought by a man named Chen under whose wise ownership the Giant Egg Roll was finally hatched. In early '72 the business began changing hands several times, apparently keeping the moniker throughout the transferrals. Last purchased in late 1973 by a fellow unexpectedly named Yakov Konstantin.

Da, I thought.

Meanwhile, Russ had sorted out eight or ten possibles from the formidable stack with which he'd begun, and together we worked through them until locating a piece of land whose physical description seemed most closely to match my memory of the Marathon's location. I let Russ read to me who owned it.

"Yakov Konstantin?" he asked.

"That's the one. Same here," I held up the crinkling carbon.

"Are you kidding? Yakov?"

"I think I've met this guy," I replied. "Goes by a different name these days."

"Well I'd change it, too. If my name was Jack-off Constantly . . . !"

The researchers momentarily in stitches. Bordering on tears.

"Listen . . . is there any way to find out if Mr. Jack-off has his name on anything else in the City. Other restaurants or properties . . . ?"

"Can do."

Russ disappeared again into the shadows while I read through the rest of the folder. Land purchased in early 1975. Notarized copies of building permits and so forth seeming to indicate the structure was erected in the summer and fall of the same year. Interestingly, appended to the original documents of purchase was a hard-to-decipher, nearly illegible orange-tinted carbon describing the Guarantor of Assignee. No name. A P.O. box in the City. No signature but there was a little stamped box with a company name scribbled inside of it.

"V.B.E."

Hey, I'd have been the last guy to have guessed anything called the Guarantor of Assignee could be so interesting.

"Russ!" I yelled.

No answer.

Called again. Nothing.

I stood up and walked back into the shadows in the direction Russ had gone before. The stacks were long and tall and there wasn't a lot of space between them so there really wasn't much choice but to walk all of the way through them and out the far end.

As I walked I called a couple of more times, and still receiving no answer turned sideways between the shelves.

I undid my topcoat, holding a hand underneath my suit jacket as I passed along. At last I made it to the opposite wall and into a semi-lit workspace in which sat a small desk covered with boxes of papers, some replacement bulbs, and dozens of cellophane-wrapped bundles of manila folders.

I pulled Mickey's revolver out from the holster and held it under the light. Pushed up the lever and flipped the cylinder out so as to ensure it was loaded. It was. Snapped it shut and held it down beside me as I walked over to a doorway which led back out onto the hallway.

I opened the door partially and peered out into the hall. The building was completely silent. I tiptoed out, guiding the door closed with one hand so it wouldn't slam.

I walked further down the hall and looked through a few office windows before walking back up to where Russ and I had initially entered.

I was wiping my forehead with the back of my hand when the door suddenly sprung open behind me.

I pivoted quickly, raising the gun as I turned.

"Du-hu-ude!"

"Shit, sorry Russ." I held up a palm as I quickly returned the .38 to its holster.

"Looks like you mean business, there." Said as we stepped back inside.

"Been a weird week."

"You don't shoot that thing as quick as you shoot 'em on the court, do you?"

I smiled.

"Whatcha find?"

Russ read from the spiral-bound notebook he held open in one hand.

"A few things came up on the register. Looks like besides the two restaurants, Mr. Yakov or whatever he goes by these days has ownership of at least three other properties. I say at least because this office has nothing beyond July 1 of this year. Anything since then is still in processing."

"Okay."

"All three are different. One is definitely a private residence located at the other end of that service road. We should have the folder for that one right here. Other one's up in East Tremont off of the Sheridan Expressway. What looks like an office building or possibly an apartment complex."

"And the third?"

"A storage facility down on Staten Island. Pretty diverse portfolio, if you ask me. Spread out, too. If it's all the same guy, that is. We can check this stuff out, too, if you want to."

I wanted to.

Ended up staying there until the middle of the afternoon tracking down all of the official transacting done by the enterprising Mr. Konstantin. At one point, Russ ran out and got us a couple of Cubanos and some fries. Found several things of note, but I'll spare you a complete rundown of everything that went into the little red notebook.

Here are the highlights, though.

A straightforward, generic homeowner's dossier ably described the private residence down the road from the Marathon. Bought in '65. Built a deck out back in '72. End of story.

The building in East Tremont was purchased in the spring of '73 and apparently continued to host a variety of businesses until March 1974, when Konstantin managed to buy out all of the individual units. Nothing was available on the businesses themselves, and apparently the structure had remained unoccupied for the last two-and-a-half years, which would seem to indicate the owner had plans to sell it in the near future.

The storage place, located off Hylan Boulevard, near the Great Kills Harbor, was according to Russ a standard thirty-two unit facility. Land bought in late 1970. Building erected two years later. All the required permits for leasing spaces suitably in place. Like with the Marathon, though, this one had the V.B.E. listed as a guarantor as well. I asked Russ what that meant, and he said it had to do with the fact that in both cases the land was purchased before the buildings were put up on it. The guarantor was usually a business, he said, and performed the same sort of function that collateral does for a loan. A kind of insurance with regard to any future construction occurring on the site.

Taking a closer look, he found a couple of other things both properties had in common. Both stood on what formerly had been state-owned land. And both changed hands for what Russ considered a low purchase price.

Of the latter, Russ had a couple of possible explanations. One was that the listed amount represented a rate and not a final sum. Like a monthly or quarterly payment or whatever. The other was that since both had been state-owned, the prices could have been set in such a way so as to reflect certain tax-exemptions. As if these were in fact municipal buildings, like the C & R was.

But that seemed unlikely.

We took another forty minutes or so to put everything back where it belonged, making it well after four when we finally got out of there.

Russ offered to drive me back up to Mickey's high-rise. We rode in silence for a while. Finally Russ spoke up.

"You gotta start comin' out."

"I'm going to. Next week."

"There's a couple of big guys who've started showing up. We need somebody who can guard 'em."

I nodded, thinking about how often my presence tended to wreck whatever balance these pick-up games struggled to achieve. Generally I'd have at least a half-foot on whoever I'd be matched with, and so a lot of times I would end up trying to even things out a bit by passing a little more. Which probably partially explained why I wasn't going out so much.

"You should see some of these young studs we got comin' out. A couple of 'em still in high school, I think. Good athletes, but . . . "

"Don't know how to play."

"Yeah, they show up with all this energy and then just stand around, clogging up the lane. Don't know a thing about moving without the ball."

"You hear that one today, the 'call that shit' guy?" I asked.

Russ laughed.

"You know Phil loves that," he said.

"He's a helluva a player."

"Drives 'em crazy, that bank. Makes you feel like you've done everything, pushed him to the side, to the baseline, and still . . . "

"Counts the same, bank or swish."

"Maybe pointwise, but it's pretty demoralizing to see that stuff go in."

"I'd agree there."

"Guy doesn't know what to do the next time. Pushing him to the side is the right thing to do. Takes two to make him go middle. That's really the only way, put two guys on him and take your chances."

"You know . . . you're right."

"Phil's got more game than one guy can handle. One normal-sized guy, that is."

Russ slapped the seat.

"Hell, I can't handle Phil alone. Takes too long to get my big butt in gear."

We drove the rest of the way in silence, other than my directions.

Pointed out Mick's building and Russ glided to a stop in front of it.

"Thanks a ton, Russ. Above and beyond."

"No trouble, dude. Let me know if you need anything else."

"I will."

"Next week, right?"

"I'll be there." I nodded and shut the door.

I was a good two hours early. Walked around to the parking lot and saw my car was still where I'd left it. Another yellow piece of paper under the wiper. I went over to see what it was.

A ticket. To my relief.

Tried buzzing but Mick wasn't in. Hung outside of the lobby studying my shoes until I was able to slide one of them between the door and frame after someone left. Went inside and took a seat in one of the highly comfortable loungers turned away from the television set incessantly playing in the far corner.

I sat there for several minutes in that tired state between waking and sleeping. Might have been fatigue, but I was starting to feel just this side of putting it all together. One thing I was fairly certain about, whatever it was I'd been invited to that night, it probably wasn't just some stag party.

Started to slip off, but the high treble of the set kept me from doing so. I let myself close my eyes.

Found my mind going back, repicturing things like I'd done before with the photograph. This time, though, I was thinking of another picture. One of Slim Davies. Doing a double-take, picturing him as if his alter ego didn't exist.

As if there was no Richard Owen behind him. Pulling on his strings. Putting him up to things.

I heard a woman's voice.

Big Slim. Available for security work, but with higher aspirations. Or lower. Currently in demand following his much-acclaimed performance as the Tall Hotel Guy. Finally, on his own. A character released from the limitations of his creator.

What would it be like?

Improbably, I found myself picturing a plump, middle-aged woman in an apron look pleadingly into the camera.

"I work my fingers to the bone scraping and scrubbing, and still I can't do a thing with this baked-on grease!"

A thunder-voiced announcer begs to differ.

The woman responds sarcastically.

The announcer explains himself.

The woman communicates surprise.

I was able to disengage from the kitchen drama long enough to consider leaving Mickey a message and heading over to the apartment for a quick nap.

Just get in the Valiant and go.

# CHAPTER TWENTY-NINE

# THE BENEFIT OF THE DOUBT

Big yawn.

I fumblingly unlocked the deadbolt. The key jammed in the spring lock and I had to jostle it some before it would turn. For a second I thought I was hearing some jostling within, echoing my own. But my tiredness and the lock's stubbornness double-teamed to chase the idea from my mind.

Finally releasing the catch, I leaned in shoulder-first. Moving in slow motion, I closed the door with my right hand and stepped inside, dropping the key on the burgundy coffee table. I quickly loosened my tie, sliding it off through my shirt collar and dropping it next to the key. I took off the topcoat and the suit jacket, slinging both over the chair, and undoing the holster walked back into the bedroom.

I stood before the mirror opposite the bed. Had just set the holster on the bureau and was digging through my pockets when I thought I noticed a shadow moving across the opposite wall.

I quickly looked up into the mirror, instantly recognizing the dark, auburn hair of my guest. Change fell loudly from my hand onto the table.

"Surprise," she called. Mischevious smile.

I pivoted to face her. She held the striped-print spread up under her chin. Her dark, violet eyes gleamed with a slow intensity, forcing me to swallow rather than reply.

She sat up in the bed, very purposefully allowing the covers to fall down to her midriff. I glanced downward involuntarily. She continued to smile demurely. I thought I heard her giggling. I ventured a step forward.

"How'd you get in here?" I managed, shaking my head. An important question, I knew. For some reason anyway.

She wasn't answering it, though. She was crawling toward me across the bed.

Her body had worked its way entirely out from under the spread. I stood frozen, hands at my sides, mesmerized by the milky whiteness of her skin. She quickly moved to the edge of the bed, holding her arms outward in an inviting gesture. I again moved forward.

"Ah . . . "

Her touch stifled my capacity for speech. She ran her hands over my chest and deftly began to unbutton my shirt. Her mouth was slightly open, her lips moist. She slid the shirt down off of my shoulders, drawing me closer as she did.

She bent forward and began touching my stomach with light kisses, playfully running her lips back and forth. She brought her hands down and began running them up and down the sides of my legs, pausing now and then to grasp them tightly. Still caressing my stomach, she undid my belt and began slowly to unfasten my pants. They fell to the floor, revealing a hard-to-hide enthusiasm. I carefully shuffled the pants away, kicking off my shoes as well. She helped remove my socks and returned to kissing the area just above the brim of my boxers.

This can't be happening, I thought. This shouldn't be happening.

Still sitting on the edge of the bed, she drew me still closer. I now stood mere inches away from her. She slowly wrapped herself around the backs of my legs, rubbing my calves with the tops of her feet.

"Ah . . . Adrienne," I uttered, the final syllable trailing away.

She tugged at the sides of my shorts, still quietly mouthing the lower part of my stomach. She simultaneously pulled downward while moving her head in the same direction, now lightly nuzzling the area below my navel.

"Ah . . . don't think . . . "

The boxers were swiftly removed. As were any further doubts about what would happen next.

I let myself fall forward, extending my hands on either side of her torso to catch myself. She communicated her intentions via a slight tug with her feet at my calves, and with my knees against the corner of the bed, I positioned myself above her.

Suddenly she uttered a soft exhalation. Then she sat up, forcefully wrapping both legs around mine.

I think I like this girl, I thought.

With each thrust, we began moving across the bed, a few inches at a time. A slight moisture began to appear between her breasts. We rhythmically continued toward the wall, our breathing becoming more audible.

As we slid across the bed, I found myself mentally trying out different perspectives, different angles.

First came the bird's eye view. This the most abstract. Legs, arms, muscles, bones. All melded together. Like an animated sculpture, moving in steady syncopation. Arty, even.

Reaching the headboard, she began to lift herself up against it, still holding fast with her lower legs as the frequency of our movements began to increase.

In profile, now. The figures decidedly less angelic-looking. One's attention becomes fragmented. A elbow points outward. Her smooth stomach. His bicep. A sudden, dark flash down below confirms the logic of the composition. To tease, to titillate. The traditionally chosen perspective of the voyeur.

Her back was now against the headboard, the back of her head against the patterned wallpaper. She began letting loose short, inarticulate cries, turning her head upwards. Eyes closed, mouth open. Sweat poured off us both. Curves of light illuminating our skin in intermittent waves.

A quick cut reveals the action from behind, the camera positioned on the edge of the bed. The mechanics of the act now fully articulated. The actors reduced to their constituent parts. The viewer's emotions revolving on a wheel, making intermittent stops. Captivation. Shame. Disgust. Arousal. Disbelief.

The grind continued.

The sounds escaping from her began to form into lithe little "oh's," each slightly louder than the one before. She began letting loose more articulate cries, signaling the onset of climax.

"Oh yes," she said. She said it again.

I lifted my head upwards, continuing the series of thrusts below, each accompanied by her two-word exhalation.

I looked up to see her closing her teeth together.

Little gap there in front. Maybe it was the light, but her hair looked darker than before.

The words began to overlap one another, the second sounding as though it began somewhere inside of the first.

It was her . . .

"Oh-yes!"

The girl I'd been looking for . . .

"O-yes!"

Since Wednesday, anyway.

Suddenly a word formed of itself, jolting me into bitter consciousness: "Oh-when."

Huh?

"O-wen! Owen! Hey-hey! Sunshine . . . !"

I recognized the sarcastic lilt of Mickey Rowe's voice and quickly bolted upright, taking a couple of seconds to register a sheepish look in response.

"Man, you were out," he said.

"Ah . . . uh . . . I must've drifted off. I guess."

"Big man sleeps big sleep."

I rubbed my eyes and filled my cheeks, exhaling uncertainly. I thought myself a little crazy as I silently marveled at the vividness of the daydream.

"How long you been here?" Mickey didn't wait for a response. "C'mon, let's go."

I stumbled a little as I followed Mickey through the lobby and into the elevator.

"Dead on yer feet?" asked Mickey.

"Literally." The automatic reply. An old McGheeism.

I blew out a slow whistle.

"I think my brain's turning to mush," I said as we stepped from the elevator and started down the hall toward Mick's apartment.

"You know this Gwen Michaels?"

"Who?"

"Gwen Michaels . . . knows yer doctor?"

"She call?"

"Just now." Mickey unlocked the door and led me inside.

"She talk to Morgan?"

"No. She'd been trying to get in touch with him and couldn't find him and now she's all upset something might've happened to him."

"If I get ahold of him, that's when she should start worrying."

While Mickey fixed up a couple of sandwiches and coffees, I tried Billy Paul at the Express to see if he'd gotten anywhere with his remembering where it was he'd seen Donna Morgan. He wasn't around and I ended up leaving a complicated message saying how he could get me through Mickey.

We ate. I explained to Mick everything Gwen had told me that morning. I also relayed all that I'd discovered at City & Regional, and we spent some time speculating about the connection between V.B.E. and Constantinius/Konstantin.

Mick had also tracked down a couple of other van Brooks-related items.

On two occasions his name had been given as a reference by arrestees, which was lucky, because whenever that happens the referent gets put in a separate index. Kind of a double-or-nothing type deal. First was a Linda Vickers for a simple solicitation charge. Paid her moneys and was back at work in an hour. Second, an Antonio Meachem, a less-simple charge for possession of a class II narcotic. Ended up with a suspended sentence.

Nothing more on the company or the man, though.

Mick's other primary task that day was to see if he could find anyone who remembered Henrietta Peters's acting career. He'd made a quick round of the adult film & bookstores, including the Show Place, without turning up anything.

His mentioning Cheerwine reminded me of the pamphlet I'd picked up from Morgan's office, over which we had a brief chuckle. Lightened the mood a bit, which was good, since I was beginning to notice Mick's patience with his former partner's theories starting to wane. Just a little.

Mick also had some contacts through Vice and was able to follow a few avenues that would've been unavailable to me. A couple of different guys had said they recognized Peters from the papers, but no one had ever seen her up on the silver screen. Or in a Look Box or any other similar setting.

By the time we finished it was already nearing seven-thirty. We would have to leave soon. I decided to give Mick one more chance to beg off.

"Mick, listen. I have to say this. I've been having all kinds of doubts about your coming tonight."

"What're you talking about?"

"I'm just saying . . . I mean, if Doris weren't at her mom's, what would you . . . ?"

"Come off it."

"No, seriously. If . . . "

"Dick. Listen to me. I'm coming and that's that. Doris didn't put me behind a desk. A punk with his daddy's pistol did. Things worked out and I felt like I could do as much or more in-house than out on the street. So I stayed. But this is different. Somebody, McCall and whoever else, is after you. And me. And there's no chance I'm sittin' at home while you try and deal with it by yourself."

"What do you think about calling Marty in?"

"I'll be honest with you. About that . . . I've got some doubts of my own."

"What are you saying?"

"I'm saying I don't like the idea."

"No?"

"Not one bit. I spent some time in Records today. Also went down to Archives and checked out some of the old microfiches. Picture book stuff, special events, ceremonies. I looked at a lot of pictures of Cap today. Cap and McClellan. Cap and Henry Peters. I thought a lot about us waiting outside that shack. About Cap and his fucking stories."

"And . . . ?"

"We didn't know any better then. We do now. I don't know about you, but I feel I've got good reason to doubt Cap this time around."

Mickey's words caused me to think of my father. Of how long it took me before I began doubting the stories first told to me after his death.

"All right. I follow your word, brother."

"Okay."

"Let's go, then."

Mick grabbed his radio and together we went out and down to the Valiant.

I'd been ticketed a second time. I pulled out the first one and handed them both to Mickey. Probably made some comment to him about the City facing default and how I'd be putting them back in business, twenty-five bucks at a time. Mick must've pocketed them both, because that was the last I saw of them.

On the way over to the pound we finalized our strategy for the evening.

I told Mickey that I suspected the party would probably happen down the street at Yakov's. I'd drive up and try and put the Valiant somewhere near the well-lit entrance while Mick would take my usual spot around and behind the dumpsters in the far corner. From there he could wait and watch. If we turned right out of the restaurant, we could only be heading down the service road and to the house, and Mick could take his time before joining us. If we turned left, our destination would be less easy to predict, and so Mick would have to tail us.

I left it to Mick's discretion whether or not to call in.

Mickey had a somewhat pristine-looking but otherwise inconspicuous silver-gray Triumph picked out and ready for him at the yard. We shook hands and that's where I left him. Mick was to wait fifteen minutes or so before heading down to the Marathon. Would've sort of defeated the purpose of his getting the Triumph for us to have shown up there together. I had Mick's hand-held, in case for any reason I'd need to contact him on the way down.

About a mile or so from the Marathon I heard them announce the time as eight-thirty, so we were running early. I stopped and pulled into the Esso station down from the Bridge, the same one I'd called Mickey from the night before. I picked up Mickey's radio and studied it a moment, refamiliarizing myself with its operation.

Then I called for him. Took a moment before his voice crackled back in response.

"Rowe here. Over."

"Mick, listen. Just arrived. Turns out the party's been pushed back. Eleven o'clock. Over."

"Eleven, you say? Over."

"That's right, partner. That's a . . . twenty-three hundred over."

"How do we play it? Over."

"Go home and sit tight. Come down, ten-thirty . . . uh . . . ten-three . . . no I mean that's uh twenty-two and . . . ." I gave up.

"Twenty-two-thirty," he laughed. "Got it. You've turned civ, my brother over."

"That I have over."

"Ten-thirty it is. I'll be right behind you. Over and out."

"Got it. Over. I mean over and out over. Whatover."

Mick transmitted a few more chuckles before clearing the channel. I put the radio under the seat and went inside the station to use the facilities and to make a phone call. I'd say it was about ten before nine when I turned off the service road and into the busy parking lot of the Marathon. For the last time.

I pulled over to the side and idled for a few minutes, letting the traffic clear before finding a spot just off the right corner of the building. Twenty yards or so from the entrance, I'd say.

I waited for about twenty minutes, watching the lot entrance through my rearview, making certain that Mickey hadn't followed anyway. I climbed out and stepped up onto the sidewalk that ran along the building's front.

A group of women were approaching the entrance from the opposite direction, and I skipped ahead and gallantly held the door open for them. I started to follow the last of them when my path was abruptly obstructed by an oafish-looking brute who was heading out.

Or was he?

He stood motionless in the open doorway. Arms crossed. Had a severe underbite, causing his already jutting chin to jut even further. Made his face look as though it ended in a heel.

I had about six inches on him heightwise, a deficit he more than made up with his significant girth. His shoulders nearly touched the sides of the wide doorframe.

From which he seemed in no hurry to leave.

I knew this guy.

He looked up at me, a raised eyebrow slowly curling up over his cranial ridge. A sickly glower in his eyes.

"Davies?" he asked, as if just remembering it.

"Ah . . . that's right, ah . . . "

Before I could continue he took a step in my direction, and out from behind him appeared rabbit-like the little white-haired owner of the Marathon. In a white suit, even. A royal blue handkerchief peeking out from his suit pocket.

"Mister Tavies." Spoken reverently, with a bow. His accent challenging his appearance in a close competition for Most Precious.

"Mister Constantinee-yus," I replied.

"You are ready?" Still bowing.

"Ah . . . sure am."

"To me there is anticipation," he said.

"To me, too . . . . Ah mean, me too."

"Let me to introduce you to Ronald."

He held open a white-gloved hand toward the large man already turning to walk down the sidewalk. As he turned, I realized he was still stooped over, his curved spine causing an already short man appear even shorter.

He let the hand drop. We fell in behind Ronald.

"Your friend . . . where?" he asked. In a manner anything but nonchalant. Non-nonchalant.

"Ah . . . he couldn't make it." I tried to see over Ronald's massive shoulder where we were heading.

"Too bad. You are sure?"

"I am sure?"

"You are sure."

"Well, sure I'm sure. He couldn't make it all right." I unbuttoned the top two buttons of my topcoat. We approached the corner of the building.

"Tell me . . . where is it we goin'?  To see the ah . . . the movie?"

"We will go there now.  We will take you, Mister Tavies."

We turned right, around the corner and toward a long, black Caddy parked alongside the restaurant.  I noticed Ronald's long arms dangling beside him as he walked.  I unbuttoned a third button.

I watched as Ronald quickly opened up the driver's door and squeezed in.  I was led over to the other side of the car.

"Allow me," he said, opening the door.

Chin-rubbing time.  An innocent glance around the lot.  No Triumph.  I got in.

The little man ambled around the front of the vehicle and to the back and cautiously slid himself onto the red-velvet plush back seat.

"We are ready, Ronald," he called forward, pulling his gloves off a finger at a time.

As Ronald started the motor, sound blared from the stereo speakers behind our heads.

"You say tom-AY-to . . . I say tom-AH-to . . . "

Ronald quickly turned the volume down to a more comfortable level.

"Pot-AY-to, Pot-AH-to . . . Tom-AY-to, Tom-AH-to . . . "

He pulled the Caddy around in front of the restaurant and toward the exit.

"Let's call the whole thing off."

Ronald ejected the eight-track.  We turned left.  The little man shifted toward me in his seat.

"Dat dare . . . dat's what ya call a disagreeable sediment."

"Ah . . . what is that?"

"Dat song dare.  'Let's call the whole thing off.'  Wouldn't it be better ta try and work tings out?  Reach some sorta camp . . . pro . . . mise?"

Last word pronounced very deliberately.  Damn lot of camp in that compromise.

"Ah . . . suppose?"

Ronald circled the Caddy around and up onto the Manhattan Bridge, toward Brooklyn.

"It's all about understanding one 'nother, am I right?  Is the way a poyson pronounces a word dat important?  Is the way a person speaks at ya, his accent, his intonation . . . should dese be da tings by which he's ta be judged?"

I scratched my ribcage, making as if to admire Lady Liberty all lit up against the night sky.

"I am innerested ta hear ya 'pinion.  Especially so.  You tell me, Mr. Owen, by what means is it dat you estimate a poyson's character?"

I quickly unsnapped the holster and pulled the .38 out from under my coat, training the muzzle on the forehead of the man whose accent and intonation had suddenly shifted from eastern European to full-fledged Flatbush.

"Where's Morgan?" I blared.

He blinked slowly. Tiredly. I'll admit to being a little astonished at the calm being demonstrated by the person to whom I'd asked the question. And of Ronald, who seemed totally ignorant of what was happening behind him.

"You'll see him. Soon enough."

"You've got the doctor?" I asked.

"Yes, yes we do. Oh, I see. Where's Morgan, you asked. You meant the doctor's daughter."

He leaned his head back and smiled as he had in his office the night before. Accent still present, though less exaggeratedly so.

"You will see the girl as well, Mr. Owen. Or should I say Richard? Is that what people call you? Normally, I mean?"

"Should I call you Yakov?"

"Ha ha"

"Or Oscar?" I titled the barrel downwards, pointing it at his chin.

He stopped smiling.

"A detective after all."

He titled his head to the side as if he were trying to see inside of the muzzle.

"Yes, well . . . ." He resumed his usual nose-in-the-air posture. "Before we go any further, let me explain something to you. It's now approximately nine-ten. Our destination is about forty-five minutes away. The doctor has an appointment to meet us there. I said you will see him and that is what I meant. Only understand something. It is absolutely essential that we reach our destination before ten-thirty. If we fail to do so, our mutual friend the doctor unfortunately will no longer be able to greet us when, eventually, we do."

"And the girl?"

"Oh, yes. You will see the girl as well. Now let me suggest you put that nasty thing away. Or perhaps I should hold onto it, for safekeeping?"

He again showed his dun-colored teeth.

"Do you doubt the reality of what I am saying, Mr. Owen?"

I looked over at the folds in the back of Ronald's thick neck. He seemed relaxed as he piloted the Caddy from the Elevated Expressway and onto Hamilton.

Then I looked back at that ghastly, crooked smile. Those glassy eyes.

I lowered the revolver.

He reached up, covering his mouth.

Big yawn.

# CHAPTER THIRTY

# HONEST LIVING

We sat in silence for a minute or so while Ronald continued southward in the direction of Bay Ridge. Big Ron might've looked aggressive, but drove cautiously, keeping it around forty.

To be honest, I wasn't so sure at that point if I'd done the right thing misdirecting Mickey the way I had. Even though it had felt right when I was doing it. And never mind whether or not I wanted to do it. I had to.

Despite all the sneaking around my chosen line of work requires of me, it's a rare situation when I'm compelled to lie like that. Because, generally speaking, I'm working alone. And I think I mentioned before how it wasn't my usual policy to hide things from clients. But here I had a partner again. And me and my partner, we'd reached a sort of impasse as far as our negotiations had gone. So I lied.

Still, the farther we drove, the more coffin-like felt that red velvet interior in back of the Caddy. Maybe I'd made another bad decision, here. Maybe it'd been better to have taken our chances, to have gone ahead with the double-team.

I continued to hold the revolver in my lap.

"So, Oscar . . . "

"Please," interrupted my backseat companion, shaking the gloves and then neatly refolding them on the pantleg of his white slacks. "Call me Os."

Was that ah's? Oz?

"As in the great and powerful?"

"Oz, Os. Either is fine."

"So, Os," I said. "Tell me about Yakov Konstantin."

"A pathetic creature, really. One should never attempt to base an entire character around a few verbal vagaries."

Again, he preened.

I kept my mouth shut.

"If this were a fiction, of course, such a strategy might indeed work. Unfortunately for you, Mr. Owen, this is not a fiction. It was a game effort, however."

I hesitated for a moment, calculating my response.

"Your Yakov," I said. "Your expatriate. More than verbiage, no?"

"That is correct. Mr. Konstantin has left his footprints elsewhere."

"Point being?"

"Must I explain?"

"I can see how Constantinius might be a convenient enough moniker for someone running a Greek joint. But why . . . ?"

"Why Konstantin?"

"Yes?"

"A simple tax dodge, Mr. Owen. Nothing more. One employs the other."

"I see."

"Haven't you ever lied on your tax return, Mr. Owen?"

"Not that I know of."

"A safe answer. Have you ever considered running for office?"

Van Brooks unnecessarily shook his head, withdrawing the question as rhetorical. He resumed the work of folding his gloves, and having at last settled on a satisfactory arrangement, he delicately slid them into his coat pocket as he continued.

"Indeed, perhaps I am too critical of dear Yakov. You are correct to suggest there is more to him than words. He is a character in whom a certain amount of thought has been placed. Whether or not your Slim Davies was composed with the same care is something I will not venture to speculate upon. In the end, it makes no difference. The handicap with which you operate is just too large."

"That right?"

"Yes. Your size limits you greatly as a performer, I would suggest."

"You would?"

"Yes, yes . . . . Tell me, being a man of such great height, how did you ever expect to keep a low profile?"

This guy was becoming more Chaplinesque every minute. Though I'd have preferred the younger, silent version. Kept rocking back and forth in his seat while he spoke, as he had done at the Marathon. Like he was nodding his whole body.

"It's a riddle, all right . . . "

"Indeed. The answer to which I am especially curious to know. What could it have been that inspired you, Mr. Owen, to presume to play detective? Wherever did such an idea come to you . . . ?"

" . . . wrapped in a mystery . . . "

"Was it from mysteries? From the movies? This reminds me of something I had meant to share with you. From one of the Bogie and Bacall films. One of those detective thrillers, of which, incidentally, I have never been particularly fond. In any case, Bogart plays the detective, of course, and in the very first scene he walks . . . "

" . . . inside an enigma."

" . . . into a house, his client's. He speaks briefly with the butler who then leaves him to wait in the front room. A very standard *mise en scène*, correct? A young girl then enters stage right and begins looking Bogart over. Not Bacall. The other girl. And do you know what she says? The very first thing she says to him when she sees him standing there?"

"That's a pretty standard *mise en scène* you've got on?"

"Ha, ha. No, no." Van Brooks's bird-like cackle caused Ronald to check the rearview. He recovered himself and cleared his throat and then batting his eyelashes in what appeared to be some sort of mimicry of femininity, answered his own question.

"'You're not very tall, are you?'"

"So Bogart's a short guy."

"As the part required."

"I thought this wasn't a fiction."

"Indeed. I am only trying to make a point, Mr. Owen. I am only suggesting that perhaps you have been miscast. That perhaps you have chosen a role you are ill-qualified to play."

"I see," I said, rubbing my right temple. The detective is tired. He's edgy. And van Brooks and his criticisms are causing his head to ache.

"Understand, I am not commenting on your abilities as a performer. It is just that your size dooms you to only a few possible roles. All of which would have to be supporting."

"Supporting."

"Yes, you know. Another face in the locker room. The gentle giant cop walking a beat. The bouncer down at the club."

He leaned forward and winked.

"No, no . . . you could only be a bit player." Sitting back up, folding his arms. Rocking.

"Is that what I am?"

"Unless, of course, you were the heavy," he continued, as if in conversation with the back of Ronald's greasy head. "In fact, that was my idea. That's how I had wanted to cast you from the beginning."

"You know, Os, the words, they're nice and clear and all. Problem is they ain't meaning much. You wanna start talking plain?"

"That's it, that's good. Big man, tough talk."

Head throbbing. Blood starting to boil.

"Well here's some more, Os. You can start explaining right now what the hell kind of game it is you're playing. With me and Morgan. And the girl. Or . . . "

"Or . . . or . . . ?"

"Or maybe I'll decide it doesn't matter one way or the other what condition the doctor is in when we finally meet up with him."

"Absolutely fantastic. Please, go on."

"I don't think you're hearing me, Os."

I raised the revolver once more, this time getting Ronald's attention up front. We were on the Shore Parkway, still a few hundred yards from Fort Hamilton and the intersection to the Verrazano-Narrows Bridge. He cradled an arm around the passenger's headrest, keeping one eye on the road and the other on the activity in the backseat.

"It's fine, Ronald. It's fine. Everything's under control."

Van Brooks patted the air in front of him.

"And the girl, Mr. Owen? What about the girl?"

"What about the girl?" I responded.

He exhaled.

"Mr. Owen. You do need to try to understand the reality of the situation. You may think you have been acting according to your own free will. Indeed, you were allowed to improvise certain things and if I do say so your decisions on the whole improved upon the script. As originally planned, that is."

I again lowered the gun.

He turned to face the front of the car.

"Aren't you curious how it ends?"

"I know how it ends."

He grinned.

"To me there is anticipation." Spoken like a regular Cold War vet.

I sat silently, the gun in my lap, going over everything that had happened that week, starting with the package's arrival Wednesday afternoon. Tried to envision what van Brooks might've meant by an original script, and how exactly I had deviated from it.

We crossed over onto the Island.

We made a sequence of turns on roads I didn't know before I finally recognized the long bank of greenery to our left signalling our passing by the Great Kills Park area. Soon, though, we were leaving Hylan, and again I had difficulty following as Ronald maneuvered the Caddy through a neighborhood unfamiliar to me. The residences disappeared, the pines reappeared, and eventually we were turning left off a quiet two-laner down a steep gravel slope, easing through a small opening in the woods and onto a large clearing below.

The moon was nearly full, and the white gravel drive gleamed like sugar crystals crunching underneath the Caddy's wheels. As we followed the drive's leftward curve, I noticed that beams burned through the back windshield. I turned to look, recognizing the squarish lights. The white Trans Am, the one that had followed me the night Lanny had been killed. Both cars slowed to a stop.

Ronald got out and walked ahead to unlock the gate of a chain-link fence, on the other side of which could be seen one side of the large, concrete structure.

"The storage facility," I said, still clutching the revolver against my left leg.

"Indeed." Slightly unsteady.

"Bought the property in '70. Building went up in . . . 1972, right?"

"Good work, shamus." The sarcasm a little defensive.

"This is the place, all right."

"What's that?"

"Where they're meeting us."

Ronald returned and we coasted through the opening and up beside the facility, the other car following suit. He shut off the motor, its hum soon being replaced by the sound of crickets chirping and scraping all about us.

"They?"

"The other gentle giants."

"Oh, of course. You mean the City's Finest." Furrowed brow, almost pouting.

"The City's Finest," I repeated.

The ape shifted to watch. The lower half of van Brooks's face quickly opened up, revealing a large, toothy grin.

"I see what you are trying to achieve, Mr. Owen. It is of course what a person in your position would be most likely to do. These bluffs, I mean. Entirely probable. We'll make you into a realistic character yet."

Car doors slammed behind us.

"I've seen it before. It's your only chance, really. So you take it."

I could hear voices.

"How do they say it . . . ?"

Feet shuffling through the gravel.

"You roll the bones."

The sentence was punctuated by the sudden, shattering sound of a rifle being cocked. Ronald rested the sawed-off barrel over the front seat, his chosen aim appearing to indicate his intention of making literal what was by now a splitting headache. I became aware of people standing next to the automobile, on my side.

"We're calling your bluff, Mr. Owen."

Van Brooks rotated his marble-eyes downward as he peered out over my shoulder, inviting me to look. I turned and saw two men holding Dr. Morgan up by the armpits like some record catch they'd just pulled out of the Great Kills Harbor. His head lolled forward heavily. Looked as though while I was giving Mickey the slip, the doctor had been slipped a mickey.

The man standing on the right with a cigarette in his mouth fit my memory of the olive-skinned man from the Express. On the left was my thin-nosed, stiff-lipped, sandy-haired nemesis. And namesake.

"It's showtime," said van Brooks, taking the .38 from between my fingers.

With not-so-gentle, prompting nudges from Ronald's rifle against my shoulder blade, we moved from the car and over toward the building, the two men dragging Morgan ahead of us. Van Brooks moved very deliberately, bent over as if contemplating the quality of the footing. We walked in silence, the crickets' loud chorus all but obliterating any sounds of traffic from the road above.

For a storage place, the building was massive. The slightly elevated crest in the center of the roof was at least two stories high, possibly nearer to three, with the base of the building's shorter side being around forty feet wide. We turned the corner and began to walk down the right side of the structure. A three-foot wide paved sidewalk surrounded the building's base, and there were several short driveways leading up to the side of the building extending all of the way down to its far end.

I noticed the even numbers above the doors counting upwards as we passed them. One of the doors toward the far end was open, casting a semi-circle of yellowish light onto the narrow walk. At about door six or eight, van Brooks began to speak. To our shoes.

"Let explain what is going to happen. I find it best if the performers have some indication beforehand what is to transpire. Our goal is to achieve a certain realism, here, an admittedly difficult standard, but one well worth striving for . . . "

The lecture trailed off as our pace slowed. Up ahead, a second door was being opened, the metal chain loudly clanging against the aluminum as the door rolled back. I watched as a light came on, creating a second yellow halo on the sidewalk. The two men dragged Morgan inside. The door crashed down. Another push from Big Ron, and we continued.

"Performers?"

"That's right."

"The doctor and myself?"

"Yes."

"And the girl?"

"Yes, yes . . . . Here, after you."

We were standing in the light shining from the open door number thirty. I walked inside and was surprised to be immediately accosted by McCall and the other man. Ronald followed, keeping the rifle trained on me as the two men each took an arm. I tried to orient myself to the remarkably large room.

It looked as though the walls that would normally separate the final eight units on that end of the building had been knocked out. Or it could be it had been constructed this way. In any case, the eight doors remained, four on each side. Instead of walking into a relatively small, single unit of, say, twelve feet by twenty feet, then, the room we had entered was exactly eight times that.

There was a single, albeit powerful, lightbulb suspended from the ceiling, under which sat a wooden chair. As they removed my topcoat and began undoing the holster, I could see how the space functioned as a screening room, with the wall painted white on the far side serving as a suitably large screen. Van Brooks shuffled in and again began to speak, his voice reverberating in the large, nearly empty room.

"Didn't I promise you a chair?"

"Right," I muttered.

"Now I have invited you to a screening and that is what we will have. You see, Mr. Owen, I don't bluff as readily as some people do. I am the sort of person who makes good on his promises."

"Or threats?"

"Indeed. I am a man who deals openly and honestly and whose word is true."

"Have you ever considered running for office?"

"Ha, ha."

"A man of such obvious integrity would be invaluable to the community," I continued while my pockets were being emptied. "Don't tell me you haven't observed some flaws amongst our present group of elected officials?"

I watched as his grin hardened.

"Yes, well . . . . Indeed. Who hasn't?"

After a little struggle, McCall managed to dislodge the red notebook from my back pocket. I watched as he flipped through it.

"Hey, Os," he called over his shoulder in that tinny voice. "Read this." He handed the open notebook to van Brooks.

"Yes, yes . . . the detective's jottings. Fascinating. Is this typical? These questions you've written here? Is this how you normally . . . ?"

I said nothing.

"'Connection between Rocca and . . . ' what does this say? 'Lenny'?"

"Lanny."

"Lanny. Oh, well. And what was the answer?"

"That would be me."

"Indeed, indeed. Don't worry, Mr. Owen. I will allow you one more chance to prove my theory incorrect. To show how it can be that a man such as yourself can indeed play the detective. As for now, I've something to show you."

I was pushed down into the chair. Big Ron had moved over and now stood between me and the screen, rifle still drawn. My arms were being tied behind me with some sort of rubberized rope, like a clothesline. Van Brooks walked behind us, his footfalls echoing against the concrete floor. He pulled open a door on the left side of the room and stepped outside, rolling the door closed behind him.

McCall began wrapping the rope tightly around my right shin, fastening it hard to the chairleg.

"Little Slim," I said, shaking my head.

He looked up as he yanked closed another knot.

"I'm disappointed. The movies . . . well, I can't say I approve, but at least it's an honest living. But kidnapping? Murder?"

McCall stared up at me with the same dull look he always sported. He finished tying down the left shin and lifted himself up. He wordlessly held his hands out and leaned forward against my shoulders while two hands busily circled the rope around my chest from behind. I stared into his blue eyes.

"All right, McCall. What the fuck is this about?" I asked. "Tell me. What does van Brooks want? With Morgan? The girl? Tell me you little . . . "

McCall suddenly spat into my face, the spray causing me to shut my eyes. I opened them to see his grinning face not four inches from my own.

I thought my response was realistic.

I brought my head down fast and hard, butting him squarely between the eyes. Heard a tiny little crunch which sounded like his thin nose breaking. He stumbled back with his hand over his face and tripped over strands of rope onto his backside, causing Ronald to sidestep out of the way.

I began to rock back and forth in the chair while the two hands struggled to hold my shoulders from behind. The bonds were too tight, and as McCall crabwalked away, Ronald moved forward and pushed the rifle barrel hard against my sternum.

"Why'd you go and do that?" he asked through his underbite.

Again I rocked, trying to loosen the pressure of the ropes. The hands fell away from my shoulders. Ronald removed the barrel and I watched as he rotated the gun in his hands.

Seemed like he might've been shaking his head.

Just before the wooden handle eclipsed my view of him, that is.

# CHAPTER THIRTY-ONE

# ACTION!

No more daydreams. No flashbacks. Just a solid plane of black, which after a time resolved into an only slightly less ominous gray.

During the first moments of my coming to, I had a sensation there was something on my face where I had been struck. I thought my vision had been impaired, reduced down to two little tunnels. Which didn't seem to be working together as they should.

After a lot of head-shaking I eventually became cognizant that I was wearing a mask or hood or something.

And that Ronald, whom I'd disappointed so, was still in the room. Leaning against the wall to the left of where I sat facing the screen. An orange dot of light hung in the air to his right, around which the silhouette of the cigarette-smoking, olive-skinned man eventually traced itself.

Apparently my actions had gotten the pair's attention, because the little orange dot was bouncing out of my view, leaving a laser trail behind as it passed. A shrill cranking noise, followed by a cool draft on my left side. My jaw felt inordinately rigid, my mouth bone-dry. I began blinking hard several times in a futile attempt to trick the pain away.

Suddenly a projector whirred to life somewhere behind my head, throwing a large rectangle of light on the far wall. Huge black numbers appeared against a gray background onscreen, a line rotating in a clockwise direction counting them down to two before disappearing.

The hotel room at the Motor Inn sprang into view, my own headless body ludicrously filling the frame. Not your standard *mise en scène*, I'd venture. The film stock was color, but extremely washed-out-looking, with imperfections bubbling by as the film clicked along. I could make out my large hands fumbling on the table, then disappearing behind the table, then reappearing with the white rectangle key ring in hand. Miss Fisher and Mr. McCall appeared arm in arm, their backs to the camera. McCall dropped two crumpled tens on the table, and I slid the key across. The couple then walked across the screen, exiting to the right. The headless proprietor remained on screen for several seconds, left hand outstretched. The scene faded to black.

The screen then reilluminated, revealing the part of the day's filming to which I had not previously been witness. McCall and Adrienne were both unclothed and atop the motel bedspread. As I watched, three separate things came to my mind.

My first thought was prompted by the extreme lankiness of McCall's body. I could practically count the actor's ribs. It again occurred to me how easy it would be to snap the slimmer Slim in two, were the opportunity to arise.

I then thought about Tettleton's little speech about the importance of giving the impression that what was being portrayed was really happening. What was it Billy Paul had said? All of the scenes, whether true or simulated, represent actual truth. Well, Tettleton should be satisfied, I thought. Maybe McCall was a lousy performer, I hadn't the critical acumen to say one way or the other. But as far as I could tell, nothing appeared simulated here.

The third thing I thought was how much more actual the simulation I had dreamed up that afternoon had seemed.

The screen again faded to black. Again, the headless proprietor appeared, the room key zinging up toward his neck. A large hand rose, closing around it. The couple exited to the left.

The pair then reappeared onscreen for a moment, and I noticed for the first time the look on Adrienne's face. Whereas Slim Jim continued to stare vacantly about, Adrienne had titled her head upwards, a small wrinkle appearing between her dark eyebrows. She was acting it out, miming a kind of contemplation over whether to rerent the room. The screen abruptly went black, and the projector fell silent.

Van Brooks had had the film fixed. The loop had been repaired.

The door to my left again clanged up and down and I thought I heard two sets of footfalls moving behind the chair. Reel change. Moisture was beginning to collect on my lip. As well as around the area on my forehead where I'd been struck. Sweat. Or blood.

A humming from behind and the broad white rectangle of light returned. Again the numbers, counting down to our second feature.

A large, mostly empty room appeared. Probably a living room, but with only a mattress and a single table in the back. A young, dark-haired woman walked out from behind and stood for several seconds with her back to the camera. Like the loops at the Show Place, the black-and-white film was hopelessly overexposed, suppressing the contours of the actress's bone-white skin as she turned to the side, extending a hand leftward.

An arm appeared within the frame, soon followed by the muscular, tanned body of the actor to which it belonged. Dark, curly hair. Wide cut sideburns. I found myself too distracted to make out the loop's putative scenario. There was a ritualistic quality to the actors' gestures as they half-walked, half-danced toward the large, grayish mattress positioned on the floor behind them.

The pair quickly commenced their performance, with the fair-skinned woman still facing away from the camera as she straddled her companion. Within a half-minute or so, a second young gentleman performer, light-haired though physically the twin of the first, appeared from the right, and after awkwardly advancing upon his knees toward the pair, artfully insinuated himself into the proceedings.

The single, hand-held camera tremblingly edged closer to the trysting triumvirate. The second man reached forward with his hands and began massaging the woman's temples, holding back her longish black hair as he did. The camera swung around to the left, the woman's face rhythmically rotating to face it. I swallowed hard and tried unsuccessfully to look about the room. I could feel the others' presence behind me, but only Ronald remained in view to the left. I looked back at the screen.

To see another inspired performance by the girl whose photograph I'd been carrying around all week. The girl of my dreams, I guess you could say. Who, despite the apparent glee communicated during the brief close-up, was again engaged in actions one would think her parents would be reluctant to endorse.

I began to fidget in the chair, prompting one of the others to press the cold steel of what felt like it could be my own revolver against the back of my neck.

The reel eventually played out. The door opened once more and I noticed Ronald moving along the wall. The gun was pulled off of my neck and there was more shuffling behind me.

"As promised. Cor-rect, Mr. Owen?"

I leaned my head in the direction of van Brooks's voice and tried to produce enough saliva to speak.

"The girl . . . "

"Wha . . . ?" My voice was muffled underneath the tight-fitting mask, my lips scratching against the plastic as I spoke.

"Yes, yes. What it is, Mr. Owen?"

" . . . is dis about . . . ah . . . "

"Yes . . . ?"

"Os."

"Mr. Owen." Pronounced disapprovingly. "You are failing me, here. You're more like a lost little girl than a detective. One more piece, Mr. Owen. Then we will see which role better suits you."

I lunged, managing to slide the chair a whole quarter of an inch. Van Brooks was cackling.

"You . . . ya sit tight, now."

He walked quickly from the room, cranking the door shut behind him.

Again, the by-now familiar sound of a projector turning its wheels behind me. Once more I tried to move in the chair, though the more I struggled the tighter the ropes felt.

As the film started, I found myself stopping to watch. I tried to wiggle the fingers of my right hand.

This time there were no numbers. The film jumped up and down nervously, eventually settling enough to reveal an extremely poor, black-and-white stock, its jerkiness seeming to indicate an abundance of splices. A young, light-haired woman dressed in simple underclothes nervously danced for the camera, a forced smile on her attractive face. She uncertainly began to disrobe, appearing to look up and over my shoulder as she did. I clenched my teeth.

It was Henrietta Peters.

I suddenly felt nauseous. I began to rock back and forth in the chair. The light from the screen flickered. A sequence of noisy clicks and the film was over. The door again sprung open. The bulb overhead came on, filling the room with harshly bright light.

Van Brooks strolled back into the room, his hands behind him, and positioned himself very deliberately between the chair and the far wall.

"That last was some rare footage, indeed, Mr. Owen."

"Indee . . . " I tried to echo. The wind blew through the open doorway, curling around the legs of the chair.

"You recognized . . . ?"

"Peters," I said.

"Dear Henrietta," he answered. "I do apologize for the quality of the print. Although it does add a certain . . . vitality, I would suggest."

"You shoo' be carefuh wi' . . . " I attempted.

"What was that?"

"Take dis ting off."

Van Brooks stepped forward cautiously. He reached out with one hand and slid the mask up over my chin and mouth, obscuring my vision completely, though making it easier to speak.

"You were saying?"

I licked my lips and tried to swallow. What felt like hair resting on my sweat-covered neck.

"You should be careful with that film. Considering its value."

"Yes, yes . . . you are correct to say so. This is one of a kind."

There was movement behind and in front of me, though I could see nothing.

"You'll want to protect your investment."

"Yes, indeed. This is good, Mr. Owen. But I want to see the detective in action. This is your chance to prove me wrong."

I thought I heard the sound of a chair scraping against the concrete.

"Those cuts," I began. "And splices. Pieces for Peters?"

"Pieces for Peters," he echoed, as if admiring the sound of the sentence.

"To ensure the senator's backing, so to speak. Right? He funded a couple of properties, at least.  Including this one.  Among other Van Brooks Enterprises.  Am I right?"

"Go on."

"Began with someone, probably pretty boy Slim right here, seducing dear Henrietta into your vicious circle."  I heard footsteps advancing toward me from the right.

"Leave him alone," van Brooks admonished.

"With the film you had the senator over a barrel, and that night up in east Harlem, I'm guessing he had hoped that would be the end of it."

"Good.  Very good.  But are you suggesting that Henry Peters, a pillar of the community, wanted his daughter dead?  Mr. Owen, really . . . ?"

"I didn't say that.  What I said was that Peters had hoped the blackmailing would end, not his daughter's life.  Although I'll bet that in his heart of hearts, Henry Peters might have at least pondered the possibility of how Henrietta could be more useful to his career in memorium.  Alive, she was killing him.  I can't imagine you had wanted her dead.  Not according to the original script, anyhow.  So, if we were to count the number of people in this world who might've derived some benefit from Henrietta Peters's death, we'd really have to stop at one."

"Logically deduced, Mr. Owen.  Do continue."

"Once Homicide found out about the meeting at the shack with the Rocca girl, that's when Peters used whatever influence he had in-house.  Somehow he helped arrange things so that Mr. Rowe and myself would be there.  And that you and your . . . the actors in your little production, that you would know about our coming so you could get out before we arrived.  Is that right?"

"This was so long ago . . . I can't say I remember everything as well as you seem to."

"Anyway, a couple of things happened.  When you were calling my bluff back in the car, you said you'd seen it before."

"That's right.  I did.  The bluffing . . . "

"The Rocca girl?"

"Astounding, Mr. Owen.  If only you weren't so tall."

"It was Rocca . . . doing what a person in my position would be most likely to do.  She told you she had a friend who knew all about where she and Henrietta were going that night.  Frightening Slim Jim and company into acts of mayhem . . . "

"But *she* wasn't bluffing, Mr. Owen."

"That's right.  In case you'd forgotten, the friend's name was Christina Salvadori, and whatever else she might've known became inconsequential the following spring."

"Poor girl.  Really should have worn a helmet."

"In any case, there were a couple of consequences to Rocca's claim.  Henrietta died because of it."

"Yes?"

"And Rocca lived. For a while anyway."

"Again, quite logical, Mr. Owen."

"Otherwise, she'd have been left behind with Henrietta. Now there is still the matter of the bone . . . and the surgery required to remove it."

"Go on."

"Rocca must have bought herself some time with her story, enough for you to want to keep her alive. Long enough to find out about Salvadori, at least. Enter the doctor."

"Yes, indeed. Quite a scene, I do remember that."

"Morgan helped you out then, and you, or I suppose I should say, Henry Peters, in return helped him out later, setting him up with those nice, new offices on the upper west side. Got him out of that cramped location up in East Tremont. Which is now another of Yakov's properites, no?"

"Yes, yes . . . . Meanwhile, we are all reading crazy stories about bones. Or should I say, tall tales . . . ?"

I became aware of heavy, labored breathing to my right. Panting.

"You knew nothing, of course. More bluffing, correct?"

"That's what it amounted to, I suppose."

I began to speak more deliberately, pausing for greater periods of time between each sentence.

"You didn't know what I knew, nor did Peters . . . . You had to assume I knew something . . . . At least that's what you led Peters to believe."

I could hear van Brooks pacing slowly back and forth. There were sounds of metal scraping against the concrete floor toward the front of the room.

"Peters is running unopposed this year. Little chance of him losing, I suppose? Unless, of course, it managed to get out about how he'd helped cover up the murder of his daughter. Practically arranged for its occurrence, in fact. Not the sort of thing that helps strengthens one's constituency, would you say? So you go back to him. You remind him about me. About Morgan. About that fossil you'd kept all these years. Talk about skeletons in the closet . . . "

The confident cackle now a challenged chuckle.

"You go to Peters and you've got a new script that you've written and you'd like his support . . . "

"And how was that new script to have played out, Mr. Owen? I invite you to . . . "

"Well, first of all, I'd say that what happened with Lanny was some version of what was supposed to have happened in my office Wednesday. You said something about casting me as the heavy. Now what could you mean? The way things worked out, I'm guessing I was supposed to have killed Lanny, right? But your boys botched that when they couldn't find their way out of the building and had to bust out. The attempt to pin it on the drunk, that was just sloppiness. An afterthought."

Again I paused. Swallowed. Would've rubbed my chin, but . . . .

"So going back to the original script, I suppose I was to have killed the doctor, right? Using the bone . . . "

"That's close, Mr. Owen, though you are missing a few pieces. Try to think, though. Have we met before?"

"Before the Marathon?"

"Yes?"

I thought back to Wednesday. I walk into the office. The box on the desk. I hang the jacket on the doorknob. I walk around the desk and pick up the box. I shake it a little. I look out the window.

"King Weiner?"

"Brilliant."

"Your highness . . . "

"Ha, ha."

"And Ronald here . . . he was there, too."

"That's correct."

"And . . . Antonio?"

"Good, good."

"Shouldn't they be at the Wescott right now? Cleaning up? Art really needs to check references a little more closely before hiring . . . "

"Indeed."

"So what happens? I kill Morgan . . . and he kills me?"

"That's correct. Only . . . "

"Only we got out too quick . . . . Before the custodial staff could come and make a mess of us."

"Did you not see the articles, Mr. Owen?"

"Right. No, not until later. I see, those were to keep me there. Reading, waiting . . . "

"Of course."

"Of course. But we left. And you had to get the box back, so your boys tracked me down, followed me back to the office later on that night. Took me outside to make it look like a mugging. The guard downstairs might be slow, but he probably would have noticed a body big as mine being dragged out of there. I suppose your workers had a key to the service elevator."

"That's right."

"And the back entrance? And the offices, as well?"

"Of course . . . "

"That's how the package got in there to begin with, then. But I'd thought Art had the only . . . ? Oh, I see. Don't tell me. A skeleton key."

"Ha, ha."

I could sense van Brooks stepping toward me. He made a few noises as if he were gesturing to the others. I again began tugging and shifting. I

**249**

continued to hear heavy, labored breathing to my right. Suddenly a hand came down from behind, palming my skull.

"You've done well, Mr. Owen. More than proved yourself. Have you any other questions?"

"Yeah. Mickey."

"That was your doing, Mr. Owen. Mr. Rowe had no place in the original script. It was your improvisations that brought him in."

"Well . . . he's out now . . . ."

"Yes . . . well . . . not entirely. We may be able to find him a part yet."

The palm moved forward, pushing the mask back down over my face. Too far forward, actually. All I could discern through the little holes were van Brooks's white wingtips stepping backwards.

"If that's everything, then . . . let us take care of these loose ends."

Hurried shuffling on either side.

"Everyone ready?"

Muffled affirmations.

"Action!"

# CHAPTER THIRTY-TWO

# RIGHT UNDER YOUR NOSE

Well, you can guess what happened next.

Van Brooks had obviously heard all he wanted to hear. I'd done everything I could to keep the conversation going, but he'd reached a limit. And, really, I don't blame him. Once we'd gotten to the point in the story where his boys had retrieved the box of newspapers, beyond that, his control over things had become somewhat less precise.

The Great Giant Egg Roll Caper hadn't worked out.

Then came the business with McCall at the Express, which I now believe van Brooks's hadn't planned for in the least. Sort of like Nixon trying to control the plumbers, there. McCall had got himself an idea, and really, it almost worked. Like Tettleton said, though, there's a limit to how far you can trust a cokehead.

I'd known that much about McCall from the first moment I laid eyes on him. I guess you could say it was right under his nose. That upper lip, frozen-stiff. Which was one reason why later on I had guessed Slim Jim to have been the one to draw Henrietta Peters into van Brooks's circle to start with.

Of course, even if McCall and the others had been able to corner me in the Express, it would have only partially pleased van Brooks, seeing as how there still would have been more loose ends to tie up.

Then again, maybe it was in Os's interest to keep himself a loose end or two . . . .

All right. I know. I've some loose ends of my own.

Let's start by attempting to look at things from van Brooks's perspective. And I'm not talking his moral perspective, which would be some trick to try to understand. It's enough that you understand his value system was more than a little whacked. If you want to go further with it and psychoanalyze him or blame it on his being a Taurus or a Cancer or whatever, well go right ahead. Like Cap would say, life's too short and the shadows too long . . . .

No, what I'm saying is, let's look at it practically. In terms of the script he'd planned and how he'd been forced to alter it. He dreams up a scheme to take out both Morgan and myself and is given the go-ahead from his benefactor, Henry Peters. Like Peters had a choice in the matter.

They have to alter Plan A. Then they botch Plan B.

They recover their box of goodies and beat a retreat. Deliver their flyers and sit around heating up the wok, waiting for Mick and I to waltz on in for that two-for-one special, which probably entailed a ride down to Staten Island. With plans to pick up Morgan along the way, possibly.

Meanwhile, I wake up and it's back to the office, business as usual. Back to routine, right? A reasonable fascimile, anyway. I'm on a case, determined to begin the search for Morgan's daughter. I'm not saying I expected to find her. But I knew better than to ignore the coincidence of the doctor showing up when he did. With that story, anyway. And weren't we saying something earlier about the detective being a person who distrusted first impressions?

Following it up was the only thing to do.

I wonder now how van Brooks interpreted this behavior. How did you? That I was stubborn beyond help, I'd imagine. Or just dumb. Or maybe I'm just looking for an excuse to visit the Show Place . . . ?

Well, whatever you thought, my guess is that van Brooks decided that if I was going to remain fool enough to follow up Morgan's story, he wouldn't rush in to stop me. In fact, for him this was a good way to keep an eye on me. Just like the business over at the Holiday Inn, it kept me occupied. Gave van Brooks a chance to rewrite his script.

He knew I'd end up seeking out the reel over at the Show Place on Thursday. It was the only tangible lead Morgan had given me. And he also knew that, eventually, I'd get down to the Marathon to find Joey Tettleton.

Cheerwine had said someone had called him about the very reel I was interested in that morning. In fact, though I couldn't have known it at the time, that had been van Brooks's black Fleetwood whose spot I'd waited for that very morning. Triple-checking the reel was still there, still in the booth for me to see.

Later on, when I'd pushed Cheerwine, it turned out this was just another reel to him. An investment. Which in his opinion had turned out to be a pretty poor one. On top of that, he was a stool. And overly enthusiastic at that, as Mickey had explained. All of which satisfied me that Cheerwine had told me everything he possibly could about the reel and its production.

So Thursday night, I'm at the Marathon. As invited, essentially. I walk in, give a fake name, and suddenly I'm being offered an interview for some unnamed position. Of course, I'm expected. Or, I should say, a guy my size is expected.

My thinking is, if this Constantinius or whoever he is wants to see me, I damn well want to see him.

I hook up with Tettleton. I'm not going to spend too much energy apologizing for him. The epitome of a slimeball. Figurative and literal. He knows the little Greek is a con, but hadn't the first clue about the extent of it. Tettleton was clueless about a lot of things. Knew nothing about the screening. Certainly didn't know for whom he was making his little masterpieces.

But most importantly, to my mind, he didn't know me. He might've been the only one who never suspected Big Slim of anything. I believe he really did think of me as his new, big buddy. All his questions that first night about where I was from, where I'd worked before, and so forth, all that basically acquitted the guy in my mind.

Still a slimeball, of course.

Hardly of the Oscar van Brooks variety, though.

If I were to classify these guys, I'd have to perch old Os at the top of the tree. Then, on the branch just below sits our dishonorable state senator, who now and then would have to dodge whatever rained down from above. Then, getting down and dirty, there's Slim Jim, Big Ronald Jeffries, and Antonio Meachem. Family, Genus, Species. The others, and I mean Tettleton, Levin, Adrienne, even Cheerwine . . . they don't register, as far as I'm concerned. Not to condone any of it, mind you. But what they do doesn't exactly represent the bone I am choosing to pick here.

I apologize for yet another pun. Like I said before, once something like that is out there, no one is safe.

Anyhow, after the adventure at the Express with McCall and company during the day, I'm back at the Marathon Friday night. And I'll admit it, I came out of the meeting a little perplexed. I mean I understand the lower east side is America's Melting Pot, but this guy had himself quite a little stew simmering there all on his own. Still, a little Russian man pretending to be a little Greek man, though suspect, was incidental. His interest in the day's filming, that's what began to clarify things a bit. And by the time I'd made it back to Mickey's apartment, I was already starting to think about how Constantinius might have something to do with V.B.E. Which suspicion the C & R visit would help confirm.

Before all that, though, I'm privileged to witness the magic and artistry of a highly inebriated Joey Tettleton attempting to eat a spanikopita and carry on a conversation simultaneously. Definitely a high degree of difficulty there. I push him for details about the film. He says he shot it the previous winter, confirming the date on Cheerwine's invoice for it.

And confirming what I had already suspected. Namely, Donna Morgan couldn't have appeared in "3. Fireplace." Nor in any other film.

That's right.

There is no Donna Morgan.

Just like there's no postman ringing twice. Or Maltese falcon.

Linda Vickers was the girl's name. Tettleton had remembered it, after all. Worked for van Brooks, as the file on her solicitation arrest had indicated.

Remember how I said the doctor's story sounded rehearsed? That's because he hadn't written it. Van Brooks had. Even supplied him with the photograph. This explained why the second photograph, the one Morgan gave me to replace the stolen one, looked the way it did. They'd taken a picture of the picture because they couldn't get another one. They couldn't very well give me back the one that had been taken from me, seeing as how I had written on it. Would've been obvious if they had.

Everytime I called Morgan back, he sounded more surprised to be hearing from me. Probably had been told our first meeting would be our last. But there I was. Inexplicably, still on the hunt for his daughter. His phantom daughter.

And incidentally, Mrs. Morgan was a phantom as well. Gwen's guilt was unfounded. She wasn't an adulterer, after all.

Van Brooks had gotten Morgan to get his secretary to call me. Then, once Morgan had hired me and I kept calling and reporting back, van Brooks instructed Morgan to keep me on, regardless of what I had to say to him. And to avoid meeting me again. I could have told him I'd fallen off of a building. Was paralyzed from the neck down, and wasn't too sure about the neck up. He'd have still begged me to keep up the search for dear Donna.

See, Henry Peters wasn't the only one van Brooks was capable of blackmailing. Morgan knew about what had happened to Henrietta Peters. And as I'm sure van Brooks kept reminding him, as long as Morgan withheld that information he remained an accessory to her murder. Chances are van Brooks had given Morgan the impression that I could be trouble for him. That I knew something about the bone and what he had done and that if he just played along the Richard Owen problem eventually would be taken care of.

The mystery referral had come from Os, then. Hell, maybe van Brooks really was Morgan's patient. A guy that twisted probably would need a specialist to help straighten him out now and again.

Bringing us to the storage facility. Where van Brooks can hardly contain himself, making this big play with regards to my bluffing.

This, to me, was doubly interesting.

Because, for one thing, he had been bluffing all along. To Morgan, of course. And to Henry Peters, whom he was able to convince after all of these years that my knowledge of what had happened to his daughter could eventually threaten not just his political career, but land him in prison to boot. Peters going on with me like he did about fair dealing and open, honest communication had planted the idea in my mind that perhaps someone wasn't dealing with him fairly.

More specifically, though, was the way Peters had angled his questions toward finding out if I indeed knew anything about his involvement with his daughter's death. Which, of course, I did not. Not at the time, anyway. Once convinced of that, he then began offering his own ideas about how both Lanny and Henrietta might have been done in by the same "crowd." It was like he wanted to tell me about van Brooks and what he was doing, but had to keep things just vague enough so as not to implicate himself. When I responded by asking him what he meant by the same crowd, he backed off, reverting to his stump speech on junkies and drugs.

See, during the course of his interrogation of me there in the vise, Peters saw once and for all that van Brooks's claims about what I had known had been a lot of smoke. Peters had had a hell of a lot to hide, though, and calling van Brooks's bluff was something he couldn't rightly afford to do. So he'd cut a deal, telling van Brooks that if he and his boys took care of Morgan and myself, he'd continue to take care of them.

But talking to me, he realized he'd been mistaken to allow van Brooks to keep on extorting from him. Of all people, Henry Peters should've understood how the addictive properties of blackmail rival those of any drug. Give them a taste and they're hooked. No amount of land or money would ever make it all go away.

Then came the less innocent-sounding questions about what I was currently working on. Which if he didn't know before, he quickly figured out van Brooks to be on the other end of. As we chatted our way down the third floor hallway, Peters seemed to know as much about the story as I did. That the missing girl had been at City. That she'd met up with a filmmaker. That it was porn. Peters knew this script better than most.

Because the Donna Morgan fiction had been based on a true story, Henrietta's. Together creating one of those patterns or routines like I was trying to explain about Wednesday morning at the Chock Full 'o Nuts.

Still, despite all the signals and the earnest encouragement for me to keep on the case and bring the girl home, Peters had almost remained ambiguous enough to keep himself in the clear. Like the successful politician he is. The one who knows it's better not to say I am not a crook.

Almost.

That's when he let it drop that Henrietta had also made movies. That turned out to be a regular red flag. That was Henry Peters telling me to go get Oscar van Brooks off of his back for good. Once he'd convinced himself I didn't know anything about the bone or what he had done to protect his daughter's killers, he had no reason to fear van Brooks. After her death, the film of Henrietta certainly no longer held any blackmail value. And now neither did Richard Owen and his crazy theories.

Telling me about the film, though. Something no one else had ever heard about.

Might as well have said "Sic him, boy!"

It was interesting, then, for van Brooks to look down his nose like that at the idea of bluffing. Seeing as how he was himself such a master.

There was another reason it was interesting, though.

Because what I'd said before, about the City's Finest. That was no bluff.

All of this is documented, by the way. Which is a good thing, too, because this definitely falls under the heading of it-must-be-seen-to-be-believed.

The camera was rolling when the first two officers entered the facility. High quality, color stock, too. Sound and everything. In the end, only two shots were fired. One from Slim Jim, using the .38 Mickey had given me. Through the roof. Kind of like the whole week had been. Answered by a single report from an Officer Askenasy, instantly shattering McCall's shinbone and discouraging any further fire.

Two more officers enter. Then two more. That would be stage right, through the open door van Brooks and the others had been coming in and out of all along. Apprehended all four of them without further incident.

Just after midnight when all of this finally took place, by the way. Halloween. And, accordingly, some of the actors wore masks.

You can see them taking the lion mask off of McCall as he's being placed on the stretcher and carried out to the right.

Antonio instinctively handed over the rifle to the approaching uniform, who cuffed him first, then removed from his head the straw-colored mask and felt hat he was wearing.

Big Ron had this weird-looking, silvery mask with a long nose sticking out of the middle. A brief moment of drama when it appeared he might resist handing over the long, wooden-handled ax. He did though. Might've been heartless, all right, but the sight of all those revolvers trained on him brought him to his senses.

And, of course, the wonderful wizard. Led out from behind, hands cuffed. Head forward, just a puff of white hair visible above that hump. Had to drag him practically. The spots they'd set up in each corner shining brilliantly against the back of that white suit jacket.

Meanwhile, the other two players, seated next to one another onstage, were being unbound. Their belongings returned. Somehow I ended up with an extra set of keys in the bargain. There was the doctor on the left, or my right. A crude, hairy dog-face fitted over his head.

And then there's me.

So that's what van Brooks meant. Calling me a lost little girl.

I'd rather not get into speculating about what exactly van Brooks had in mind. Like I said before, if you're interested in exploring that minefield, be my guest. I suppose I will be curious to learn what those folks, Billy Paul among them, currently digging through the V.B.E.'s back catalog finally end up uncovering.

But as for the little playlet in the haunted forest, I'm glad to say we never quite got to the point of performing that one. As planned, anyway.

It was McGhee who I'd called, as he'd asked me to do. From the Esso. Told him about the meeting. Gave him details regarding the locations of what I thought to be the three possible sites for it: the private residence at the end of the service road, the empty office building up in East Tremont, and the storage facility.

Mickey had talked about not knowing better before. I realized that this was probably exactly what McGhee had felt. That he had been set up before, and that this time he wasn't going to take any chances. I knew if I called Cap, he'd have uniforms at all three locations as quickly as he could dispatch them. Took them longer than I'd have liked for them to find the storage place, whose location could only be identified approximately. But they made it.

Like I said before, I didn't like going behind Mickey's back that way. But I felt I had to. He knew Severin and Walton better than I, and so I had to defer to his judgment about whether or not they could be trusted.

The one person I knew he wouldn't be calling, though, was McGhee.

And when it came down to it, Cap was the only person about whom I hadn't any doubts.

What happened next? Well, there were the elections. The peanut farmer won. Seems to be a good enough guy, like his heart's in the right place. Even if a little lust pumps through it now and again. I guess folks decided that made him more human, I guess. More real.

Peters won back his state senate seat, of course, but replaced the acceptance speech with a teary resignation. Then came the trials. Cap was as surprised as everyone else when it came out that Mack McClellan had been the one who'd helped engineer the misdirection back at the shack in '71. Turned out Henry Peters had good old Mack under his thumb all along. Peters didn't enjoy the same leverage with Severin, though. Which had worked to strengthen van Brooks's bargaining position with the state senator, I'd say.

A lot of the credit for the collars, by the way, ended up going to Cap, which ultimately went a long way toward restoring the good graces between himself and the higher higher-ups. Not to mention improving things between Cap and myself, which I have to confess at the end of the day made for a right fine reward.

The markings on Henrietta Peters's back? It took some creative questioning from the prosecuting attorney even to get the court to address it, but they did finally determine it highly likely Peters's wounds had been inflicted with one of those metal tripods. Such as a camera sits atop. By either McCall, Meachem, or Jeffries, each of whom happily implicated the other two when given the opportunity.

And yes, there were more bones. The rest of Rocca, on the Staten

Island site.

That's about it, I guess. Oh, I'd end up forgetting all about the locksmith's coming on Election Day and found myself locked out of my apartment that night.

It was all right. I used the skeleton key and it worked just fine.

Maybe you were surprised I looked you up, after being so antagonistic during that first meeting. Not to mention all of the nose jokes. But I have to say I feel better for having told all of this. Been sitting in my brain tormenting me for a while now. Kind of like that damned Fun Sandwich jingle, though not exactly.

I've had to tell it several times, of course, but it's always been in bits and pieces. Parts of other stories. The ones they tell to juries, I mean. When the last of the trials ended and I was free again to talk about all of this, that's when I got the idea of calling you back.

Not that others haven't asked. But I believe I've already made clear my reasons for refusing them.

By now a lot of people have said a lot of things about what happened. I couldn't help noticing, though, how often their stories seemed to feature what you might call strategic omissions. Even somebody like Sol Severin, who will call another news conference and who will carefully couch all of his words inside claims for its "realism," he'll leave out what seems to me to be one of the more important details of the story.

Now maybe he's right to try and suppress certain things. Maybe he's just trying to protect the species from learning how low it is capable of going. I can appreciate that, I suppose.

But what he's saying ain't everything.

So here's me making it whole.

Now maybe this sort of "whole truth" attitude puts me on a level with those press dogs. I don't know. That's why I'm leaving it up to you to choose how you are going to want to share this thing with others. Maybe you'll change it around some. You know, the order of things. Which is only fair, seeing as how you're the one who paid for it. Fill in or take away here or there. Change the names to protect the innocent. That sort of thing. Hell, even change my name if you want to. Like a hundred years from now that's going to matter.

All that's for you to decide. You're the one trying to build a story out of it.

Maybe you won't touch it, though. Maybe you'll leave it all like it is.

Doesn't matter, really.